LIVES OF GIRLS AND WOMEN

Alice Munro was born in 1931 and is the author of thirteen collections of stories, most recently *Dear Life*, and a novel, *Lives of Girls and Women*. She has received many awards and prizes, including three of Canada's Governor General's Literary Awards and two Giller Prizes, the REA Award for the Short Story, the Lannan Literary Award, the WH Smith Book Award in the UK and the National Book Critics Circle Award in the US. She was shortlisted for the Booker Prize for *The Beggar Maid*, was awarded the Man Booker International Prize 2009 for her overall contribution to fiction on the world stage and in 2013 won the Nobel Prize in Literature. Her stories have appeared in the *New Yorker*, *Atlantic Monthly*, *Paris Review* and other publications, and her collections have been translated into thirteen languages.

She lives with her husband in Clinton, Ontario, near Lake Huron in Canada.

ALSO BY ALICE MUNRO

Lying Under the Apple Tree
Dear Life
Too Much Happiness
The View from Castle Rock
Runaway
Hateship, Friendship, Courtship, Loveship, Marriage
The Love of a Good Woman
Selected Stories
Open Secrets
Friend of My Youth
The Progress of Love
The Moons of Jupiter
The Beggar Maid
Something I've Been Meaning to Tell You
Dance of the Happy Shades

ALICE MUNRO

Lives of Girls and Women

VINTAGE BOOKS
London

Published by Vintage 2015

4 6 8 10 9 7 5 3

Copyright © McGraw-Hill Ryerson Limited 1971

Alice Munro has asserted her right under the Copyright, Designs
and Patents Act 1988 to be identified as the author of this work

First published in the USA in 1971 by the
McGraw-Hill Book Company

First published in Great Britain in 1973 by Allen Lane

Vintage
20 Vauxhall Bridge Road,
London SW1V 2SA

www.vintage-books.co.uk

A Penguin Random House Company

Penguin
Random House
UK

global.penguinrandomhouse.com

A CIP catalogue record for this book
is available from the British Library

ISBN 9781784700881

MIX
Paper from
responsible sources
FSC® C018179

Penguin Random House is committed to a sustainable future for our business,
our readers and our planet. This book is made from Forest Stewardship Council®
certified paper.

Printed and bound by CPI Group (UK) Ltd, Croydon, CR0 4YY

*This novel is autobiographical in form but not in fact. My family, neighbors
and friends did not serve as models – A. M.*

FOR JIM

CONTENTS

THE FLATS ROAD

We spent days along the Wawanash River, helping Uncle Benny fish. We caught the frogs for him. We chased them, stalked them, crept up on them, along the muddy riverbank under the willow trees and in marshy hollows full of rattails and sword grass that left the most delicate, at first invisible, cuts on our bare legs. Old frogs knew enough to stay out of our way, but we did not want them; it was the slim young green ones, the juicy adolescents, that we were after, cool and slimy; we squished them tenderly in our hands, then plopped them in a honey pail and put the lid on. There they stayed until Uncle Benny was ready to put them on the hook.

He was not our uncle, or anybody's.

He stood a little way out in the shallow brown water, where the muddy bottom gives way to pebbles and sand.

He wore the same clothes every day of his life, everywhere you saw him – rubber boots, overalls, no shirt, a suit jacket, rusty black and buttoned, showing a V of tough red skin with a tender edge of white. A felt hat on his head had kept its narrow ribbon and two little feathers, which were entirely darkened with sweat.

Though he never turned around he knew if we put a foot in the water.

'You kids want to splash in the mud and scare off the fish you go and do it someplace else, get off of my riverbank.'

It was not his. Right here, where he usually fished, it was ours. But we never thought of that. To his way of thinking the river and the bush and the whole of Grenoch Swamp more or less belonged to him, because he knew them, better than anybody else did. He claimed he was the only person who had been right through the swamp, not just made little trips in around the edges. He said there was a quicksand hole in there that would take down a two-ton truck like a bite of breakfast. (In my mind I saw it shining, with a dry-liquid roll – I had it mixed up with quicksilver.) He said there were holes in the Wawanash River that were twenty feet deep in the middle of summer. He said he could take us to them, but he never did.

He was prepared to take offense at a glimmer of doubt.

'You fall into one of them, then you'll believe me.'

He had a heavy black moustache, fierce eyes, a delicate predatory face. He was not so old as his clothes, his moustache, his habits, would lead you to believe; he was the sort of man who becomes a steadfast eccentric almost before he is out of his teens. In all his statements, predictions, judgments there was a concentrated passion.

In our yard, once, looking up at a rainbow, he cried, 'You know what that is? That's the Lord's promise that there isn't ever going to be another flood!' He quivered with the momentousness of this promise as if it had just been made, and he himself was the bearer of it.

When he had caught what fish he wanted (he threw back the black bass, kept the chub and redfin, saying that redfin was a tasty fish, though full of bones as a pincushion is of needles), we would all climb out of the shady river trough and head across the fields toward his house. Owen and I, barefoot, walked easily on stubble. Sometimes our unsociable dog, Major, followed at a distance. Away at the edge of the bush – the bush that turned into the swamp, a mile further in – was Uncle Benny's house, tall and silvery, old unpainted boards, bleached dry in the summer, and dark green blinds, cracked and torn, pulled down over all the windows. The bush behind it was black, hot, thick with thorny bushes, and dense with insects whirling in galaxies.

Between the house and the bush were several pens in which he had always some captive animals – a half-tame golden ferret, a couple of wild minks, a red fox whose leg had been torn in a trap. She limped, and howled at night, and was called Duchess. The coons he did not need pens for. They lived around the yard and in the trees, tamer than cats, and came to the door to be fed. They were fond of chewing gum. Squirrels came too and sat boldly on the window sills and foraged in the piles of newspapers on the porch.

There was also a shallow sort of pen, or excavation, in the dirt beside the wall of the house, with boards nailed up around it on the other three sides, to the height of about two feet. This was where Uncle Benny had kept the turtles. One summer he had abandoned everything to catch turtles. He said he was going to sell them to an American from Detroit, who would pay him thirty-five cents a pound.

'Make them into soup,' said Uncle Benny, hanging over his turtle pen. Much as he enjoyed taming and feeding animals, he enjoyed also their unpleasant destinies.

'Turtle soup!'

'For Americans,' said Uncle Benny, as if that explained it. 'I wouldn' touch it myself.'

Either the American did not show up, or he would not pay what Uncle Benny wanted or he had been no more than a rumor in the first place; the scheme came to nothing. A few weeks later Uncle Benny would look blank if you mentioned turtles; he would say, 'Aw, I'm not botherin' my head about that business no more,' as if he felt sorry for you, for being so far behind the times.

Sitting in his favorite chair just inside our kitchen door – he would sit there as if he hardly had time to sit down, did not want to trouble anybody, would be off in a minute – Uncle Benny was always full of news about some business venture, always an extraordinary one, by which people not very far away, down in the south of the county or as near by as Grantly Township, were making preposterous sums of money. They raised chinchilla rabbits. They bred budgie birds. They made ten thousand dollars a year and barely had to work for it. Probably the reason he kept on working for my father, though he had never worked steadily at any other job, was that my father raised silver foxes, and there was in such a business something precarious and unusual, some glamorous and ghostly, never realized, hope of fortune.

He cleaned the fish on his porch and, if he felt like eating, fried some immediately in a pan which kept its ancient, smoky grease. He ate from the pan. No matter how hot and bright it was outside he had a light on, one single bulb hanging from the ceiling. The deep, deep, layered clutter and dirt of the place swallowed light.

Owen and I, going home, would sometimes try to name off the things he had in his house, or just in his kitchen.

'Two toasters, one with doors, one you lay the toast on.'

'Seat out of a car.'

'Rolled-up mattress. An accordion.'

But we weren't getting half, we knew it. The things we remembered could have been taken out of the house and never missed; they were just a few things revealed and identifiable on top of such a wealth of wreckage, a whole rich, dark, rotting mess of carpets, linoleum, parts of furniture, insides of machinery, nails, wire, tools, utensils. This was the house Uncle Benny's parents had lived in, all their married life. (I could just remember them, old and heavy and half-blind, sitting on the porch in the sunlight, wearing many dark layers of disintegrating clothes.) So part of the accumulation was that of fifty years or so of family life. But it was also made up of other people's throwaways, things Uncle Benny would ask for and bring home, or even lug from the Jubilee dump. He hoped to patch things up and make them usable and sell them, he said. If he had lived in a city he would have run an enormous junk shop; he would have spent his life among heaps of soiled furniture and worn-out appliances and chipped dishes and grimy pictures of other people's relatives. He valued debris for its own sake and only pretended, to himself as well as to others, that he meant to get some practical use out of it.

But what I liked best around his place, and would never tire of, were the newspapers piled on the porch. He did not take either the Jubilee *Herald-Advance* or the city newspaper which arrived in our mailbox a day late. He did not subscribe to the *Family Herald* or the *Saturday Evening Post*. His paper came once a week and was printed badly on rough paper, with headlines three inches high. It was his only source of information about the outside world, since he seldom had a radio that was working. This was a world unlike the one my parents read about in the paper, or heard about on the daily news. The headlines had nothing to do with the war, which had started by that time, or elections, or heat waves, or accidents, but were as follows:

FATHER FEEDS TWIN DAUGHTERS TO HOGS

WOMAN GIVES BIRTH TO HUMAN MONKEY

VIRGIN RAPED ON CROSS BY CRAZED MONKS

SENDS HUSBAND'S TORSO BY MAIL

I would sit and read on the edge of the sagging porch, my feet brushing Sweet William that Uncle Benny's mother must have planted. Finally Uncle Benny would say, 'You're welcome to take those papers home if you want to. I'm all done reading them.'

I knew better than to do that. I read faster and faster, all I could hold, then reeled out into the sun, onto the path that led to our place, across the fields. I was bloated and giddy with revelations of evil, of its versatility and grand invention and horrific playfulness. But the nearer I got to our house the more this vision faded. Why was it that the plain back wall of home, the pale chipped brick, the cement platform outside the kitchen door, washtubs hanging on nails, the pump, the lilac bush with brown-spotted leaves, should make it seem doubtful that a woman would really send her husband's torso, wrapped in Christmas paper, by mail to his girl friend in South Carolina?

Our house was at the end of the Flats Road, which ran west from Buckles' Store, at the edge of town. This rickety wooden store, so narrow from front to back it looked like a cardboard box stood on end, haphazardly plastered with metal and painted signs advertising flour, tea, rolled oats, soft drinks, cigarettes, was always to me the sign that town had ended. Sidewalks, street lights, lined-up shade trees, milkmen's and icemen's carts, birdbaths, flower borders, verandas with wicker chairs, from which ladies watched the street – all these civilized, desirable things had come to an end, and we walked (Owen and I coming from school, my mother and I coming from shopping on a Saturday afternoon) on the wide meandering Flats Road, with no shade from Buckles' Store to our house, between fields ragged with weeds, and yellow with dandelions, wild mustard, or goldenrod, depending on the season of the year. Houses here were set further apart and looked in general more neglected, poor, and eccentric than town houses would ever be; half a wall would be painted and the job abandoned, the ladder left up; scars of a porch torn away were left uncovered, and a front door without steps, three feet off the ground; windows could be spread with yellowed newspapers in place of blinds.

The Flats Road was not part of town but it was not part of the country either. The curve of the river, and the Grenoch Swamp, cut it off from the rest of the township, to which it nominally belonged. There were no real farms. There were Uncle Benny's and Potters' places, fifteen and twenty acres, Uncle Benny's going back to bush. The Potter boys raised sheep. We had nine acres and raised foxes. Most people had one or two acres and a bit of livestock, usually a cow and chickens and sometimes something more bizarre that would not be found on an ordinary farm. The Potter boys owned a family of goats, which they turned loose to graze along the road. Sandy Stevenson, a bachelor, kept a little gray donkey, like the illustration to a Bible story, pasturing in the stony corner of a field. My father's enterprise was not out of the way here.

Mitch Plim and the Potter boys were the bootleggers on the Flats Road. Their styles were different. The Potter boys were cheerful, though violent tempered when drunk. They gave Owen and me a ride home from school in their pickup truck; we were in the back, flung from side to side because they drove so fast and hit so many bumps; my mother had to take a deep breath when she heard about it. Mitch Plim lived in the house that had newspapers over the windows; he did not drink himself, was crippled up with rheumatism, and spoke to nobody; his wife came wandering out to the mailbox, any hour of the day, in a tattered flounced housecoat, barefoot. Their whole house seemed to embody so much that was evil and mysterious that I would never look at it directly, and walked by with my face set stiffly ahead, controlling my urge to run.

There were also two idiots on the road. One was Frankie Hall; he lived with his brother Louie Hall who operated a watch- and clock-repair business out of an unpainted, false-fronted store building beside Buckles' Store. He was fat and pale like something carved out of Ivory soap. He sat out in the sun, beside the dirty store window cats slept in. The other one was Irene Pollox, and she was not so gentle or so idiotic as Frank; she would chase children on the road and hang over her gate crowing and flapping like a drunken rooster. So her house too was a dangerous one to pass, and there was a rhyme to say, that everybody knew:

> *Irene don't come after me*
> *Or I'll hang you by your tits in a*
> *crab-apple tree.*

I said it when I went past with my mother, but knew enough to change *tits* to *heels*. Where had that rhyme come from? Even Uncle Benny said it. Irene was white-haired, not from age but because she was born that way, and her skin also was white as goosefeathers.

The Flats Road was the last place my mother wanted to live. As soon as her feet touched the town sidewalk and she raised her head, grateful for town shade after Flats Road sun, a sense of relief, a new sense of consequence flowed from her. She would send me to Buckles' Store when she ran out of something, but she did her real shopping in town. Charlie Buckle might be slicing meat in his back room when we went by; we could see him through the dark screen like a figure partly hidden in a mosaic, and bowed our heads and walked quickly and hoped he did not see us.

My mother corrected me when I said we lived on the Flats Road; she said we lived *at the end* of the Flats Road, as if that made all the difference. Later on she was to find she did not belong in Jubilee either, but at present she took hold of it hopefully and with enjoyment and made sure it would notice her, calling out greetings to ladies who turned with surprised, though pleasant, faces, going into the dark dry-goods store and seating herself on one of the little high stools and calling for somebody to please get her a glass of water after that hot dusty walk. As yet I followed her without embarrassment, enjoying the commotion.

My mother was not popular on the Flats Road. She spoke to people here in a voice not so friendly as she used in town, with severe courtesy and a somehow noticeable use of good grammar. To Mitch Plim's wife – who had once worked, though I did not know it then, in Mrs McQuade's whorehouse – she did not speak at all. She was on the side of poor people everywhere, on the side of Negroes and Jews and Chinese and women, but she could not bear drunkenness, no, and she could not bear sexual looseness, dirty language, haphazard lives, contented ignorance; and so she had to exclude the Flats Road people from the really oppressed and deprived people, the real poor whom she still loved.

My father was different. Everybody liked him. He liked the Flats Road, though he himself hardly drank, did not behave loosely with women, or use bad language, though he believed in work and worked hard all the time. He felt comfortable here, while with men from town, with any man who wore a shirt and tie to work, he could not help being wary, a little proud and apprehensive of insult, with that delicate, special readiness to scent pretension that is some country people's talent. He had been raised (like my mother, but she had cast all that behind her) on a farm deep in the country; but he did not feel at home there either, among the hard-set traditions, proud poverty, and monotony of farm life. The Flats Road would do for him; Uncle Benny would do for his friend.

Uncle Benny my mother was used to. He ate at our table every day at noon, except Sunday. He stuck his gum on the end of his fork, and at the end of the meal took it off and showed us the pattern, so nicely engraved on the pewter-colored gum it was a pity to chew it. He poured tea into his saucer and blew on it. With a piece of bread speared on a fork he wiped his plate as clean as a cat's. He brought into the kitchen a smell, which I did not dislike, of fish, furred animals, swamp. Remembering his manners in the country way, he would never help himself, or take a second helping till asked three times.

He told stories, in which there was nearly always something happening that my mother would insist could not have happened, as in the story of Sandy Stevenson's marriage.

Sandy Stevenson had married a fat woman from down east, out of the county altogether, and she had two thousand dollars in the bank and she owned a Pontiac car. She was a widow. No sooner had she come to live with Sandy, here on the Flats Road, twelve–fifteen years ago, than things began to happen. Dishes smashed themselves on the floor during the night. A stew flew off the stove by itself, splattering the kitchen walls. Sandy woke up in the night to feel something like a goat butting him through the mattress, but when he looked there was nothing under the bed. His wife's best nightgown was ripped from top to bottom and knotted in the cord of the window shade. In the evening, when they wanted to sit in peace and have a little talk, there was rapping on the wall, so loud you couldn't hear yourself think. Finally the wife told Sandy she knew who was doing it. It was her dead husband, mad at her for getting married again. She recognized his way of rapping, those were his very knuckles. They tried ignoring him but it was no use. They decided to go off in the car for a little trip and see if that would discourage him. But he came right along. He rode on the top of the car. He pounded on the roof of the car with his fists and kicked it and banged and shook it so Sandy could hardly keep it on the road. Sandy's nerves collapsed at last. He pulled off the road and told the woman to take the wheel, he was going to get out and walk or hitchhike home. He advised her to drive back to her own town and try to forget about him. She burst into crying but agreed it was the only thing to do.

'But you don't believe that, do you?' said my mother with cheerful energy. She began explaining how it was all coincidence, imagination, self-suggestion.

Uncle Benny gave her a fierce pitying look.

'You go and ask Sandy Stevenson. I seen the bruises, I seen them myself.'

'What bruises?'

'From where it was buttin' him under the bed.'

'Two thousand dollars in the bank,' mused my father, to keep this argument from going on. 'Now there's a woman.

You ought to look around for a woman like that, Benny.'

'That's just what I'm going to do,' said Uncle Benny, falling into the same joking-serious tone, 'one of these days when I get around to it.'

'A woman like that might be a handy thing to have around.'

'What I keep telling myself.'

'Question is, a fat one or a thin one? Fat ones are bound to be good cooks but they might eat a lot. But then so do some of the skinny ones, hard to tell. Sometimes you get a big one who can more or less live off her fat, actually be a saving on the pocketbook. Make sure she has good teeth, either that or all out and a good set of false ones. Best if she has her appendix and her gallbladder out too.'

'Talk as if you're buying a cow,' said my mother. But she did not really mind; she had these unpredictable moments of indulgence, lost later on, when the very outlines of her body seemed to soften and her indifferent movements, lifting of the plates, had an easy supremacy. She was a fuller, fairer woman than she later became.

'But she might fool you,' continued my father soberly. 'Tell you her gallbladder and her appendix are out and they're still in place. Better ask to see the scars.'

Uncle Benny hiccuped, went red, laughed almost silently, bending low over his plate.

'Can you write?' said Uncle Benny to me, at his place, when I was reading on the porch and he was emptying tea leaves from a tin teapot; they dripped over the railing.

'How long've you been goin' to school? What grade are you in?'

'Grade Four when it starts again.'

'Come in here.'

He brought me to the kitchen table, cleared away an iron he was fixing and a saucepan with holes in the bottom, brought a new writing pad, bottle of ink, a fountain pen. 'Do me some practice writing here.'

'What do you want me to write?'

'I don't care. I just want to see how you do it.'

I wrote his name and address in full: *Mr Benjamin Thomas Poole, The Flats Road, Jubilee, Wawanash County, Ontario, Canada, North America, The Western Hemisphere, The World, The Solar System, The Universe.* He read over my shoulder and said sharply, 'Where is that in relation to Heaven? You haven't got far enough. Isn't Heaven outside of the Universe?'

'The Universe means everything. It's all there is.'

'All right, you think you know so much, what is there when you get to the end of that? There has to be something there, else there wouldn't be an end, there has to be something else to make an end, doesn't there?'

'There isn't,' I said doubtfully.

'Oh yes there is. There's Heaven.'

'Well what is there when you get to the end of Heaven?'

'You don't ever get to the end of Heaven, because the Lord is there!' said Uncle Benny triumphantly, and took a close look at my writing, which was round, trembly, and uncertain. 'Well anybody can read that without no trouble. I want you to sit here and write a letter for me.'

He could read very well but he could not write. He said the teacher at school had beat him and beat him, trying to beat writing into him, and he respected her for it, but it never did any good. When he needed a letter written he usually got my father or mother to do it.

He hung over me seeing what I wrote at the top: *Flats Road, Jubilee, August 22, 1942.* 'That's right, that's the way! Now start it off. *Dear Lady.*'

'You start with *Dear* and then the person's name,' I said, 'unless it's a business letter and then you start with *Dear Sir,* or *Dear Madam* if it's a lady. Is it a business letter?'

'It is and it isn't. Put down *Dear Lady.*'

'What is her name?' I said troublesomely. 'I could just as easy put her name.'

'I don't know her name.' Impatiently, Uncle Benny brought me the newspaper, his newspaper, opened it at the back, in the classified ads, a section I never got to, and held it under my nose.

> *Lady with one child desires housekeeping position*
> *for man in quiet country home. Fond of farm life.*
> *Matrimony if suited.*

'There is the lady I am writing to so what can I do but call her lady?'

I gave in and wrote it down, executed a large careful comma and waited to start the letter under the *a* in *Dear* as we had been taught.

'Dear Lady,' said Uncle Benny recklessly, 'I am writing this letter –'

> *I am writing this letter in reply to what you put*
> *in the paper which I get through the mail. I am a*
> *man thirty-seven years old living alone on my own*

place which is fifteen acres out at the end of the Flats Road. There is a good house on it with stone foundation. It is right by the bush so we never run out of firewood in winter. There is a good well on it drilled sixty feet down and a cistern. In the bush is more berries than you can eat and good fish in the river and could have a good vegetable garden if you could keep off the rabbits. I have got a pet fox in a pen by the house, also a ferret and two minks and there is coons and squirrels and chipmunks around all the time. Your child will be welcome. You don't say if it is a girl or a boy. If a boy I could teach it to be a good trapper and hunter. I have a job working for a man that raises silver foxes on the next place to this. His wife is an educated woman if you like to go visiting. I hope I will have a letter from you soon. Yours truly, Benjamin Thomas Poole.

Within a week Uncle Benny had a letter back.

Dear Mr Benjamin Poole, I am writing for my sister Miss Madeleine Howey to tell you she will be glad to take up your offer and will be ready to come any time after the 1st Sept. What are the bus or train connections to Jubilee? Or it might suit better if you could come down here, I will write out our full address at the end of the letter. Our place is not hard to find. My sisters child is not a boy it is a girl 18 mos. old named Diane. Looking forward to hearing from you I remain, Yours truly, Mason Howey, 121 Chalmers Street, Kitchener, Ont.

'Well it is taking a chance,' said my father, when Uncle Benny showed us this letter at the dinner table. 'What makes you think this is the one you want?'

'I don't figure any harm in lookin' her over.'

'It looks to me as if the brother is pretty willing to get rid of her.'

'Take her to a doctor, have a medical examination,' said my mother firmly.

Uncle Benny said he sure would. Arrangements from then on went swiftly forward. He bought himself new clothes. He asked for the loan of the car, to drive to Kitchener. He left early in the morning, wearing a light green suit, a white shirt, a green, red, and orange tie, a dark green felt hat, and brown-and-white shoes. He had got his hair cut and his moustache trimmed and he had washed. He looked strange, pale, sacrificial.

'Cheer up, Benny,' said my father. 'You're not going to your own hanging. If you don't like the looks of things turn around and come home.'

My mother and I went across the fields with a mop, broom, dustpan, box of soap, Old Dutch Cleanser. But my mother had never been in that kitchen, never really inside it, before, and it defeated her. She started throwing things out on the porch, but after a while she saw that it was hopeless. 'You'd have to dig a pit to put it in,' she said, and sat down on the steps holding the handle of the broom under her chin, like a witch in a story, and laughed. 'If I didn't laugh I'd cry. Think of her coming here. She won't stay a week. She'll go back to Kitchener if she has to walk. That or throw herself in the river.'

We scrubbed the table and two chairs and a central space

of floor and rubbed the stove with bread papers and knocked down the cobwebs over the light. I picked a bouquet of goldenrod and put it in a jug in the center of the table.

'Why wash the window,' said my mother, 'and illuminate more disaster inside?'

At home she said, 'Well I think my sympathies are with the woman, now.'

After dark Uncle Benny laid the keys on the table. He looked at us with the air of one arriving home from a long journey whose adventures can never properly be told, though he knows he will have to try.

'Did you make out all right?' said my father encouragingly. 'Did the car give you any trouble?'

'Nossir. She run fine. I got off the road once but I hadn't got too far when I figured what I'd done.'

'Did you look at that map I gave you?'

'No, I seen some fellow on a tractor and I asked him and he turned me round.'

'So you got there all right?'

'Oh, ye-uh, I got there all right!'

My mother broke in. 'I thought you'd bring Miss Howey in for a cup of tea.'

'Well she's kind of tired from the trip and all and got to put the baby to bed.'

'The baby!' said my mother remorsefully. 'I forgot about the baby! Where will the baby sleep?'

'We'll rig up something. I think I got a crib over there somewheres if I can put some new slats in it.' He took off his hat, showing the red streak across his sweating forehead, and said, 'I was goin' to tell you it isn't Miss Howey anymore, it's Mrs Poole.'

'Well, Benny. Congratulations. Wish you every happiness. Made up your mind the minute you saw her, was that it?'

Uncle Benny chuckled nervously.

'Well they was all there. They was all set up for the wedding. Set it up before I got there. They had the preacher there and the ring bought and fixed up with some fellow to get the license in a hurry. I could see they was all set up. All prepared for a wedding. Yes sir. They didn't leave a thing out.'

'Well you're a married man now, Benny.'

'Oh ye-uh, married man all right!'

'Well you'll have to bring your bride to see us,' said my mother valiantly. Her use of the word *bride* was startling, evoking as it did long white veils, flowers, celebration, not thought of here. Uncle Benny said he would. He said yes he sure would. As soon as she got herself together after the trip, yes, he sure would.

But he didn't. There was no sign of Madeleine. My mother thought that now he would go home for his dinner but he came into the kitchen as usual. My mother said, 'How is your wife? How is she managing? Does she understand that kind of stove?' and he replied to everything with vague affirmatives, chuckling and shaking his head.

Late in the afternoon when he finished his work he said to me, 'You want to see something?'

'What?'

'You come along and you'll see.'

Owen and I tailed him across the fields. He turned and stopped us at the edge of his yard.

'Owen wants to see the ferret,' I said.

'He'll have to wait till another time. Don't come no closer than here.'

After some time he came out of the house carrying a small child. I was disappointed; she was what it was. He set her on the ground. She bent, tottering, and picked up a crow's feather.

'Tell your name,' said Uncle Benny coaxingly. 'What's your name? Is it Di-ane? Tell the kids your name.'

She would not say it.

'She can talk good if she wants to. She can say Momma and Benny and Di-ane and dink watah. Eh? Dink watah?'

A girl in a red jacket came out on the porch.

'You come in here!'

Was she calling Diane or Uncle Benny? Her voice was threatening. Uncle Benny picked up the little girl, and said softly to us, 'You better run on home now. You can come and see the ferret some other day,' and headed for the house.

We saw her at a distance, in the same red jacket, going down the road to Buckles' Store. Her hands were in the pockets of the jacket, her head was bent, her long legs going like scissors. My mother met her, finally, in the store. She made a point of it. She saw Uncle Benny outside, holding Diane, and she asked him what he was doing there and he said, 'We're just waitin' on her Momma.'

So my mother went in and walked up to the counter where the girl stood, while Charlie Buckle wrote up her bill.

'You must be Mrs Poole.' She introduced herself.

The girl said nothing. She looked at my mother, she

heard what was said, but she herself said nothing. Charlie Buckle gave my mother a look.

'I guess you've been busy getting settled. You'll have to walk over and visit me whenever you feel like it.'

'I don't walk nowhere on gravel roads unless I have to.'

'You could come across the field,' said my mother, merely because she did not like to walk out and give this girl the last word.

'She's a *child*,' she told my father. 'She's not any older than seventeen, not possibly. She wears glasses. She's very thin. She's not an idiot, that's not why they were getting rid of her, but she is mentally deranged, maybe, or on the borderline. Well, poor Benny. She's come to live in the right place though. She'll fit in fine on the Flats Road!'

She was already getting known there. She had chased Irene Pollox back inside her own yard and up her steps and brought her to her knees and grabbed that babyish white hair in both her hands. So people said. My mother said, 'Don't go over there, never mind about the ferret, I don't want anybody maimed.'

Nevertheless I went. I did not take Owen because he would tell. I thought I would knock on the door and ask, in a very polite way, if it was all right for me to read the newspapers on the porch. But before I got to the steps the door opened and Madeleine came out with a stove-lid lifter in her hand. She might have been lifting a stove lid when she heard me, she might not have picked it up on purpose, but I could not see it as anything but a weapon.

For a moment she looked at me. Her face was like Diane's, thin, white, at first evasive. Her rage was not immediate. She needed time to remember it, to reassemble her forces.

Not that there was any possibility, from the first moment she saw me, of anything but rage. That or silence seemed to be the only choices she had.

'What are you come spyin' around here for? What are you come spyin' around my house for? You better get out of here.' She started down the steps. I retreated before her only as quickly as was necessary, fascinated. 'You're a dirty little bugger. Dirty little spy-bugger. Dirty little spy-bugger, aren't you?' Her short hair was not combed, she was wearing a ragged print dress on her flat young body. Her violence seemed calculated, theatrical; you wanted to stay to watch it, as if it were a show, and yet there was no doubt, either, when she raised the stove lifter over her head, that she would crack it down on my skull if she felt like it – that is, if she felt the scene demanded it. She was watching herself, I thought, and any moment she might stop, fall back into blankness, or like a child brag, 'See how I scared you? You didn't know I was fooling, did you?'

I wished I could take this scene back to tell at home. Stories of Madeleine were being passed up and down the road. Something had annoyed her in the store and she had thrown a box of Kotex at Charlie Buckle. (*Lucky she wasn't holding a can of corn syrup!*) Uncle Benny lived under a hailstorm of abuse, you could hear it from the road. 'Got yourself a Tartar there, didn't you, Benny?' people would say, and he would chuckle and nod, abashed, as if receiving congratulations. After a while he started telling stories himself. She had thrown the kettle through the window because there wasn't any water in it. She had taken the scissors and cut up his green suit, which he had only worn once, at his wedding; he did not know what she had against it. She had said she would set fire to the house, because he had brought her the wrong brand of cigarettes.

'Do you think she drinks, Benny?'

'No, she don't. I never brought a bottle into the house and how is she going to get a bottle by herself and besides I would of smelt it on her.'

'You ever get near enough to her to smell it, Benny?'

Uncle Benny would lower his head, chuckling.

'You ever get that close to her, Benny? Bet she fights like a pack of wildcats. You have to tie her up sometime when she's asleep.'

When Uncle Benny came to our house to do the pelting, he brought Diane along. He and my father worked in the cellar of our house, skinning the bodies of the foxes and turning the pelts inside out and stretching them on long boards to dry. Diane went up and down the cellar steps or sat on the top step and watched. She would never talk to anyone but Uncle Benny. She was suspicious of toys, cookies, milk, anything we offered her, but she never whined or cried. Touched or cuddled, she submitted warily, her body giving off little tremors of dismay, her heart beating hard like the heart of a bird if you capture it in your hand. Yet she would lie on Uncle Benny's lap or fall asleep against his shoulder, limp as spaghetti. His hand covered the bruises on her legs.

'She's always goin' around bumpin' into things over at my place. I got so much stuff around, she's bound to bump into things and climb up places and fall.'

Early in the spring, before the snow was all gone, he came one day to say that Madeleine had left. When he went home at night, the day before, she had been gone.

He had thought she might be in Jubilee and he waited for her to come home. Then he noticed that several other things were gone too – a table lamp which he was planning to rewire, a nice little rug, some dishes and a blue teapot that had belonged to his mother, and two perfectly good folding chairs. She had taken Diane too, of course.

'It must have been a truck she went off in, she couldn't of put all that in a car.'

Then my mother remembered that she had seen a panel truck, she thought it was gray, and it was going towards town, about three o'clock in the afternoon of the previous day. But she hadn't been interested or noticed who was in it.

'Gray panel truck! I bet you that was her! She could've put the stuff in the back. Did it have a canvas over it, did you see?'

My mother had not noticed.

'I got to go after her,' said Uncle Benny excitedly. 'She can't take off like that with what don't belong to her. She's always tellin' me, get this junk out of here, clear this junk out of here! Well it doesn't look so much like junk when she wants some herself. Only trouble is, how do I know where she went to? I better get in touch with that brother.'

After seven o'clock, when the cheaper rates came on, my father put through the long distance call – on our phone, Uncle Benny didn't have one – to Madeleine's brother. Then he put Uncle Benny on the phone.

'Did she go down to your place?' Uncle Benny shouted immediately. 'She went off in a truck. She went off in a gray panel truck. Did she show up down there?' There seemed to be confusion at the other end of the line;

perhaps Uncle Benny was shouting too loudly for anybody to hear. My father had to get on and explain patiently what had happened. It turned out that Madeleine had not gone to Kitchener. Her brother did not show a great deal of concern about where she had gone. He hung up without saying good-bye.

My father started trying to persuade Uncle Benny that it was not such a bad thing to be rid of Madeleine, after all. He pointed out that she had not been a particularly good housekeeper and that she had not made Uncle Benny's life exactly comfortable and serene. He did this in a diplomatic way, not forgetting he was talking about a man's wife. He did not speak of her lack of beauty or slovenly clothes. As for the things she had taken – *stolen*, Uncle Benny said – well, that was too bad and a shame (my father knew enough not to suggest that these things were of no great value) but perhaps that was the price of getting rid of her, and in the long run Uncle Benny might consider that he had been lucky.

'It's not that,' said my mother suddenly. 'It's the little girl. Diane.'

Uncle Benny chuckled miserably.

'Her mother beats her, doesn't she?' cried my mother in a voice of sudden understanding and alarm. 'That's what it is. That's how the bruises on her legs –'

Once Uncle Benny had started chuckling he couldn't stop, it was like hiccups.

'Well ye-uh. Ye-uh she –'

'Why didn't you tell us when she was here? Why didn't you tell us away last winter? Why didn't I think of it myself? If I'd known the truth I could have reported her –'

Uncle Benny looked up startled.

'Reported her to the police! We could have brought charges. We could have had the child removed. What we have to do now, though, is put the police on her trail. They'll find her. Never fear.'

Uncle Benny did not look happy or relieved at this assurance. He said cannily, 'How would they know where to look?'

'The provincial police, they'd know. They can work on a province-wide basis, Nation-wide, if necessary. They'll find her.'

'Hold on a minute,' said my father. 'What makes you think the police would be ready to do that? They only track down criminals that way.'

'Well what is a woman who beats a child if she isn't a criminal?'

'You have to have a case. You have to have witnesses. If you're going to come out in the open like that you have to have proof.'

'Benny is the witness. He'd tell them. He'd testify against her.' She turned to Uncle Benny who started his hiccups again and said witlessly, 'What's that mean I have to do?'

'Enough talk about it for now,' my father said. 'We'll wait and see.'

My mother stood up, offended and mystified. She had to say one thing more, so she said what everybody knew.

'I don't know what the hesitation is about. It's crystal clear to me.'

But what was crystal clear to my mother was obviously hazy and terrifying to Uncle Benny. Whether he was afraid of the police, or just afraid of the public and official air of such a scheme, the words surrounding it, the alien places it would take him into, was impossible to tell. Whatever it was, he crumpled, and would not talk about Madeleine and Diane any more.

What was to be done? My mother brooded over the idea of taking action herself, but my father told her, 'You're in trouble from the start when you interfere with other people's families.'

'Just the same I know I'm right.'

'You may be right but that doesn't mean there's a thing you can do about it.'

At this time of year the foxes were having their pups. If an airplane from the Air Force Training School on the lake came over too low, if a stranger appeared near the pens, if anything too startling or disruptive occurred, they might decide to kill them. Nobody knew whether they did this out of blind irritation, or out of roused and terrified maternal feeling – could they be wanting to take their pups, who still had not opened their eyes, out of the dangerous situation they might sense they had brought them into, in these pens? They were not like domestic animals. They had lived only a very few generations in captivity.

To further persuade my mother, my father said that Madeleine might have gone to the States, where nobody could ever find her. Many bad, and crazy, as well as restless and ambitious people went there eventually.

But Madeleine had not. Later in the spring came a letter. She had the nerve to write, said Uncle Benny and brought the letter and showed it. Without salutation she said: *I left my yellow sweater and a green umbrella and dianes blanket at your place send them to me here. 1249 Ridlet St., Toronto, Ont.*

Uncle Benny had already made up his mind that he was going down there. He asked to borrow the car. He had never been to Toronto. On the kitchen table, my father spread the road map, showing how to get there, though he said he wondered if it was a good idea. Uncle Benny said he planned to get Diane and bring her back. Both my mother and father pointed out that this was illegal, and advised against it. But Uncle Benny, so terrified of taking legal and official action, was not in the least worried about undertaking what might turn out to be kidnapping. He told stories now of what Madeleine had done. She had held Diane's legs to the bars of the crib with leather straps. She had walloped her with a shingle. She had done worse than that, maybe, when he wasn't there. Marks of the poker, he thought, had been on the child's back. Telling all this, he was overcome with his apologetic half-laughter; he would have to shake his head and swallow it down.

He was gone two days. My father turned on the ten o'clock news, saying, 'Well we'll have to see if old Benny's got picked up!' On the evening of the second day he drove the car into our yard and sat there for a moment, not looking at us. Then he got out slowly and walked with dignity and weariness towards the house. He did not have Diane. Had we ever expected him to get her?

We were sitting on the cement slab outside the kitchen door. My mother was in her own sling-back canvas chair, to remind her of urban lawns and leisure, and my father sat in a straight-backed kitchen chair. There were only a few bugs so early in the season. We were looking at the sunset. Sometimes my mother would assemble everybody to look at the sunset, just as if it was something she had arranged to have put on, and that spoiled it a bit – a little later I would refuse to look at all – but just the same there was no better place in the world for watching a sunset from than the end of the Flats Road. My mother said this herself.

My father had put up the screen door that day. Owen was swinging on it, disobediently, to hear the old, remembered sound of the spring stretching, then snapping back. He would be told not to, and stop, and very cautiously behind my parents' backs begin again.

Such steadfast gloom hung around Uncle Benny that not even my mother would directly question him. My father told me in an undertone to bring a chair from the kitchen.

'Benny sit down. You worn out from your drive? How did the car run?'

'She run okay.'

He sat down. He did not take off his hat. He sat stiffly as in an unfamiliar place where he would not expect or even wish for a welcome. Finally my mother spoke to him, in tones of forced triviality and cheerfulness.

'Well. Is it a house they are living in, or an apartment?'

'I don't know,' said Uncle Benny forbiddingly. After some time he added, 'I never found it.'

'You never found where they are living?'

He shook his head.

'Then you never saw them?'

'No I didn'.'

'Did you lose the address?'

'No I didn'. I got it down on this piece of paper. I got it here.' He took his wallet out of his pocket and pulled out a piece of paper and showed us, then read it. '1249 Ridlet

Street.' He folded it and put it back. All his movements seemed slowed down, ceremonious, and regretful.

'I couldn't find it. I couldn't find the place.'

'But did you get a city map? Remember we said go to a gas station, ask for a map of the city of Toronto.'

'I did that,' said Uncle Benny with a kind of mournful triumph. 'You bet. I went to a gas station and I asked them and they said they didn't have no maps. They had maps but only of the province.'

'You already had a map of the province.'

'I told them I did. I said I wanted a map of the city of Toronto. They said they didn' have none.'

'Did you try another gas station?'

'If one place didn' have none I figured none of them would.'

'You could have bought one in a store.'

'I didn' know what kind of a store.'

'A stationery store! A department store! You could have asked at the gas station where you could buy one.'

'I figured instead of runnin' all over the place tryin' to find a map I would be better off just askin' people to direct me how to get there, seein' I already had the address.'

'It's very risky, asking *people*.'

'You're tellin' me,' said Uncle Benny.

When he got the heart to, he began his story.

'First I asked the one fellow, he directed me to go across this bridge, and I done that and I come to a red light and was supposed to turn left, he told me to, but when I got there I didn' know how it was. I couldn' figure out do you turn left on a red light ahead of you or do you turn left on a green light ahead of you.'

'You turn left on a green light,' cried my mother despairingly. 'If you turned left on a red light you'd turn across the traffic that's going across in front of you.'

'Ye-uh, I know you would, but if you turned left on a green light you gotta turn across the traffic that's comin' *at* you.'

'You wait until they give you an opening.'

'You could wait all day then, they're not going to give you no opening. So I didn' know, I didn' know which was right to do, and I sat there trying to figure it out and they all starts up honkin' behind me so I thought, well, I'll turn right, I can do that without no trouble, and then I'll get turned around and headed back the way I come. Then I ought to be going in the right direction. But I couldn' see any place to turn round so I just kept goin' and goin'. Then I turned off up a street that went crossways and kept on driving until I thought, well, I've gone and lost track completely of what the first fellow told me, so I may's well ask somebody else. So I stopped and asked this lady was walking with a dog on a leash but she said she never heard of Ridlet Street. She never *heard* of it. She said she lived in Toronto twenty-two years. She called over a boy on his bicycle then and *he* heard of it, he told me it was way the other side of town and I was headed out of town, the way I was goin'. But I figured it might be easier to go round the city than go through it, even if it took longer, and I kept on the way I was goin', sort of circling it was the way it seemed to me, and by this time I could see it was getting dark and I thought, well, I sure's hell better get a move on, I want to find where this place is before dark because I am not goin' to like driving in the dark here one bit –'

He ended up sleeping in the car, pulled off the road, outside a factory yard. He had got lost among factories, dead-end roads, warehouses, junkyards, railway tracks. He described to us each turn he had taken and each person he had asked for directions; he reported what each of them had said and what he had thought then, the alternatives he had considered, why he had in each case decided to do what he did. He remembered everything. A map of the journey was burnt into his mind. And as he talked a different landscape – cars, billboards, industrial buildings, roads and locked gates and high wire fences, railway tracks, steep cindery embankments, tin sheds, ditches with a little brown water in them, also tin cans, mashed cardboard cartons, all kinds of clogged or barely floating waste – all this seemed to grow up around us created by his monotonous, meticulously remembering voice, and we could see it, we could see how it was to be lost there, how it was just not possible to find anything, or go on looking.

Even though my mother protested, 'But that is what cities are like! That is why you have to have a map!'

'Well I woke up there this morning,' Uncle Benny said as if he hadn't heard her, 'and I knew what I better do was just get out, any way I could get.'

My father sighed; he nodded. It was true.

So lying alongside our world was Uncle Benny's world like a troubling distorted reflection, the same but never at all the same. In that world people could go down in quicksand, be vanquished by ghosts or terrible ordinary cities; luck and wickedness were gigantic and unpredictable; nothing was deserved, anything might happen; defeats were met with crazy satisfaction. It was his triumph, that he couldn't know about, to make us see.

Owen was swinging on the screen door, singing in a cautious derogatory way, as he would when there were long conversations.

> Land of Hope and Glory
> Mother of the Free
> How shall we ex-tore thee
> Who are bo-orn of thee?

I had taught him that song – that year we were singing such songs every day at school, to help save England from Hitler. My mother said it was *extol* but I would not believe that, for how would it rhyme?

My mother sat in her canvas chair and my father in a wooden one; they did not look at each other. But they were connected, and this connection was plain as a fence, it was between us and Uncle Benny, us and the Flats Road, it would stay between us and anything. It was the same as in the winter, sometimes, when they would deal out two hands of cards and sit down at the kitchen table, and play, waiting for the ten o'clock news, having sent us to bed upstairs. And upstairs seemed miles above them, dark and full of the noise of the wind. Up there you discovered what you never remembered down in the kitchen – that we were in a house as small and shut up as any boat is on the sea, in the middle of a tide of howling weather. They seemed to be talking, playing cards, a long way away in a tiny spot of light, irrelevantly; yet this thought of them, prosaic as a hiccup, familiar as breath, was what held me, what winked at me from the bottom of the well as I fell into sleep.

Uncle Benny did not hear from Madeleine again or, if he did, he never mentioned it. When asked, or teased, about her, he would seem to call her to mind unregretfully, with a little contempt for being something, or somebody, so long discarded, like the turtles.

After a while we would all just laugh, remembering Madeleine going down the road in her red jacket, with her legs like scissors, flinging abuse over her shoulder at Uncle Benny trailing after, with her child. We laughed to think of how she carried on, and what she did to Irene Pollox and Charlie Buckle. Uncle Benny could have made up the beatings, my mother said at last, and took that for comfort; how was he to be trusted? Madeleine herself was like something he might have made up. We remembered her like a story, and having nothing else to give we gave her our strange, belated, heartless applause.

'Madeleine! That madwoman!'

HEIRS OF THE LIVING BODY

The house at Jenkin's Bend had that name painted on a sign – Uncle Craig's doing – and hanging from the front veranda, between a red ensign and a Union Jack. It looked like a recruiting station or like a crossing point on the border. It had once been a post office and still seemed an official, semipublic sort of place, because Uncle Craig was the clerk of Fairmile Township, and people came to him to get marriage licenses and other kinds of permits; the Township Council met in his den, or office, which was furnished with filing cabinets, a black leather sofa, a huge roll-top desk, other flags, a picture of the Fathers of Confederation and another of the king and queen and the little princesses, all in their coronation finery. Also a framed photograph of a log house which had stood on the site of this large and handsome, ordinary brick one. That picture seemed to have been in another country, where everything was much lower, muddier, darker than here. Smudgy bush, with a great many black pointed evergreens, came up close around the buildings, and the road in the foreground was made of logs.

'What they called a corduroy road,' Uncle Craig instructed me.

Several men in shirtsleeves, with droopy moustaches and fierce but somehow helpless expressions, stood around a horse and wagon. I made the mistake of asking Uncle Craig if he was in the picture.

'I thought you knew how to read,' he said, and pointed out the date scrawled under the wagon wheels: *June 10, 1860*. 'My father wasn't even a grown man at that time. There he is behind the horse's head. He wasn't married till 1875. I was born in 1882. Does that answer your question?'

He was displeased with me not on account of any vanity about his age, but because of my inaccurate notions of time and history. 'By the time I was born,' he continued severely, 'all that bush you see in the picture would be gone. That road would be gone. There would be a gravel road.'

One of his eyes was blind, had been operated on but remained dark and clouded; that eyelid had a menacing droop. His face was square and sagging, his body stout. There was another photograph, not in this room but in the front room across the hall, which showed him stretched out on a rug in front of his seated, elderly-looking parents – a blond, plump, self-satisfied adolescent, head resting on one elbow. Auntie Grace and Aunt Elspeth, the younger sisters, in frizzed bangs and sailor dresses, sat on hassocks at his head and feet. My own grandfather, my father's father, who had died of the flu in 1918, stood up behind the parents' chairs, with Aunt Moira (slender then!), who lived in Porterfield, on one side and Aunt Helen, who had married a widower and gone round the world and lived now, rich, in British Columbia, on the other. 'Look at your Uncle Craig!' Aunt Elspeth or Auntie Grace would say, dusting this picture. 'Doesn't he look full of himself, eh, like the cat that licked up all the cream!' They spoke as if he were still that boy, stretched out there in beguiling insolence, for them to pamper and laugh at.

Uncle Craig gave out information; some that I was interested in, some that I wasn't. I wanted to hear about how Jenkin's Bend was named, after a young man killed by a falling tree just a little way up the road; he had been in this country less than a month. Uncle Craig's grandfather, my great-great-grandfather, building his house here, opening his post office, starting what he hoped and believed would someday be an important town, had given this young man's name to it, for what else would such a young man, a bachelor, have to be remembered by?

'Where was he killed?'

'Up the road, not a quarter of a mile.'

'Can I go and see where?'

'There's nothing marked. That's not the sort of thing they put up a marker for.'

Uncle Craig looked at me with disapproval; he was not moved to curiosity. He often thought me flighty and stupid and I did not care much; there was something large and impersonal about his judgment that left me free. He himself was not hurt or diminished in any way by my unsatisfactoriness, though he would point it out. This was the great difference between disappointing him and disappointing somebody like my mother, or even my aunts. Masculine self-centeredness made him restful to be with.

The other kind of information he gave me had to do with the political history of Wawanash County, allegiances of families, how people were related, what had happened in elections. He was the first person I knew who really believed in the world of public events, of politics, who did not question he was part of these things. Though my parents always listened to the news and were discouraged or relieved by what they heard (mostly discouraged, for this was early in the war), I had the feeling that, to them as to me, everything that happened in the world was out of our control, unreal yet calamitous. Uncle Craig was not so daunted. He saw a simple connection between himself, handling the affairs of the township, troublesome as they often were, and the prime minister in Ottawa handling the affairs of the country. And he took an optimistic view of the war, a huge eruption in ordinary political life which would have to burn itself out; he was really more interested in how it affected elections, in what the conscription issue would do to the Liberal Party, than in how it progressed by itself. Though he was patriotic; he hung out the flag, he sold Victory Bonds.

When not working on the township's business he was engaged on two projects – a history of Wawanash County and a family tree, going back to 1670, in Ireland. Nobody in our family had done anything remarkable. They had married other Irish Protestants and had large families.

Some did not marry. Some of the children died young. Four in one family were burned in a fire. One man lost two wives in childbirth. One married a Roman Catholic. They came to Canada and went on in the same way, often marrying Scotch Presbyterians. And to Uncle Craig it seemed necessary that the names of all these people, their connections with each other, the three large dates of birth and marriage and death, or the two of birth and death if that was all that happened to them, be discovered, often with great effort and a stupendous amount of worldwide correspondence (he did not forget the branch of the family which had gone to Australia) and written down here, in order, in his own large careful handwriting. He did not ask for anybody in the family to have done anything more interesting, or scandalous, than to marry a Roman Catholic (the woman's religion noted in red ink below her name); indeed, it would have thrown his whole record off balance if anybody had. It was not the individual names that were important, but the whole solid, intricate structure of lives supporting us from the past.

It was the same with the history of the county, which had been opened up, settled, and had grown, and entered its present slow decline, with only modest disasters – the fire at Tupperton, regular flooding of the Wawanash river, some terrible winters, a few unmysterious murders; and had produced only three notable people – a Supreme Court judge, an archaeologist who had excavated Indian villages around Georgian Bay and written a book about them, and a woman whose poems used to be published in newspapers throughout Canada and the United States. These were not what mattered; it was daily life that mattered. Uncle

Craig's files and drawers were full of newspaper clippings, letters, containing descriptions of the weather, an account of a runaway horse, lists of those present at funerals, a great accumulation of the most ordinary facts, which it was his business to get in order. Everything had to go into his history, to make it the whole history of Wawanash County. He could not leave anything out. That was why, when he died, he had only got as far as the year 1909.

When I read, years afterwards, about Natasha in *War and Peace*, and how she *ascribed immense importance, although she had no understanding of them, to her husband's abstract, intellectual pursuits,* I had to think of Aunt Elspeth and Auntie Grace. It would have made no difference if Uncle Craig had actually had 'abstract, intellectual pursuits,' or if he had spent the day sorting henfeathers; they were prepared to believe in what he did. He had an old black typewriter, with metal rims around the keys and all the long black arms exposed; when he began his slow, loud, halting but authoritative typing they dropped their voices, they made absurd scolding faces at each other for the clatter of a pan. *Craig's working!* They would not let me go out on the veranda for fear I would walk in front of his window and disturb him. They respected men's work beyond anything; they also laughed at it. This was strange; they could believe absolutely in its importance and at the same time convey their judgment that it was, from one point of view, frivolous, nonessential. And they would never, never meddle with it; between men's work and women's work was the clearest line drawn, and any stepping over this line, any suggestion of stepping over it, they would meet with such light, amazed, regretfully superior, laughter.

The veranda was where they sat in the afternoons, having completed morning marathons of floor scrubbing, cucumber hoeing, potato digging, bean and tomato picking, canning, pickling, washing, starching, sprinkling, ironing, waxing, baking. They were not idle sitting there; their laps were full of work – cherries to be stoned, peas to be shelled, apples to be cored. Their hands, their old, dark, wooden-handled paring knives, moved with marvelous, almost vindictive speed. Two or three cars an hour went by, and usually slowed and waved, being full of township people. Aunt Elspeth or Auntie Grace would call out the hospitable country formula, 'Stop in awhile off of that dusty road!' and the people in the car would call back, 'Would if we had the time! When you going to come and see *us*?'

Aunt Elspeth and Auntie Grace told stories. It did not seem as if they were telling them to me, to entertain me, but as if they would have told them anyway, for their own pleasure, even if they had been alone.

'Oh, the hired man Father had, remember, the foreigner, he had the very devil of a temper, excuse my language. What was he, Grace, now wasn't he a German?'

'He was an Austrian. He came in off the road looking for work and Father hired him. Mother never got over being afraid of him, she didn't trust foreigners.'

'Well no wonder.'

'She made him sleep in the granary.'

'He was always yelling and cursing in Austrian, remember when we jumped across his cabbages? The flood of foreign cursing, it would freeze your blood.'

'Till I made up my mind I'd show him.'

'What was he burning that time, he was down the orchard burning a lot of branches –'

'Tent caterpillars.'

'That's it, he was burning up the tent caterpillars and you got yourself into a pair of Craig's overalls and a shirt and stuffed yourself with pillows and put your hair up under a felt hat of Father's, and you blacked your hands and your face to look like a darky –'

'And I took the butcher knife, that same long wicked knife we've got still –'

'And crept down through the orchard, hid behind the trees, Craig and me watching all the time from the upstairs window –'

'Mother and Father couldn't have been here.'

'No, no, they'd gone to town! They'd gone to Jubilee in the horse and buggy!'

'I got to about five yards of him and I slipped out from behind a tree trunk and – O my saints, didn't he let out a yell! He yelled and lit for the barn. He was a coward through and through!'

'Then you were into the house and out of those clothes and scrubbed yourself clean before Father and Mother got back from town. There we were, all sitting round the supper table, waiting on him. We were hoping secretly he'd run off.'

'Not me. I wasn't. I wanted to see the effect.'

'He came in pale as a sheet and gloomy as Satan and sat down and never said a word. We expected him at least to mention there was some crazy darky loose in the county. He never did.'

'Didn't want to let on what a coward he'd been, no!'

They laughed till fruit spilled out of their laps.

'It wasn't always me, I wasn't the only one could think up tricks! You were the one thought of tying the tin cans over the front door the time I'd been out to a dance! Don't let's forget about that.'

'You were out with Maitland Kerr. (Poor Maitland, he's dead.) You were out at a dance at Jericho –'

'Jericho! It was a dance in the Stone School!'

'All right, whatever it was you were bringing him into the front hall to say good night, oh, you were sneaking him in, quiet as a pair of lambs –'

'And *down* they came –'

'It sounded just like an avalanche had hit. Father jumped out of bed and grabbed his shotgun. Remember the shotgun in their room, it was always behind the door? What a confusion! And me under the bedclothes with the pillow stuffed in my mouth so's nobody could hear me laughing!'

They had not given up playing jokes yet. Auntie Grace and I entered the bedroom where Aunt Elspeth was having her nap, flat on her back, snoring regally, and we lifted the quilt with great care and tied her ankles together with a red ribbon. On a Sunday afternoon when Uncle Craig was asleep in his office, on the leather sofa, I was sent in to wake him up and tell there was a young couple outside who had come to apply for a marriage license. He got up grumpily, went out to the back kitchen and washed in the sink, wetted and combed his hair, put on his tie and waistcoat and jacket – he could never have given out a marriage license without his proper clothes on – and went to the front door. There was an old lady in a long checked skirt, a shawl over her head, bent away over, leaning on a stick, and an old man bent likewise, wearing a shiny suit and an ancient fedora. Uncle Craig was still dazed from sleep; he said dubiously, 'Well, how do you do –' before he burst out in a jovial fury, 'Elspeth! Grace! You pair of she-devils!'

At milking time they tied kerchiefs over their hair, with the ends flopping out like little wings, and put on all sorts of ragged patchwork garments, and went wandering along the cowpaths, taking up a stick somewhere along the way. Their cows had heavy, clinking bells hung on their necks. Once Aunt Elspeth and I followed the sporadic, lazy sound of these bells to the edge of the bush and there we saw a deer, standing still, among the stumps and heavy ferns. Aunt Elspeth did not say a word, but held her stick out like a monarch ordering me to be still, and we got to look at it for a moment before it saw us, and leapt up so that its body seemed to turn a half-circle in the air, as a dancer would, and bounded away, its rump heaving, into the deep bush. It was a hot and perfectly still evening, light lying in bands on the tree trunks, gold as the skin of apricots. 'It used to be you'd see them regularly,' Aunt Elspeth said. 'When we were young, oh, you used to see them on the way to school. But not now. That's the first I've seen in I don't know how many years.'

In the stable they showed me how to milk, which is not so easy as it looks. They took turns squirting milk into the mouth of a barn cat which rose on its hind legs a few feet away. It was a dirty-looking striped tom, called Robber. Uncle Craig came down, still wearing his starched shirt, with the sleeves rolled up, his shiny-backed vest with pen and pencil clipped in the pocket. He presided at the cream separator. Aunt Elspeth and Auntie Grace liked to sing while they milked. They sang, 'Meet me in St. Louis, Louie, meet me at the Fair!' and, 'I've got sixpence, jolly jolly sixpence' and, 'She'll be comin' around the mountain when she comes –' They would sing different songs at the same time, each trying to drown the other out and complaining, 'I don't know where that woman gets the idea she can sing!' Milking time made them bold and jubilant. Auntie Grace, who was afraid to go into the storage room of the house because there might be a bat, ran through the barnyard hitting the big long-horned cows on their rumps, chasing them out the gate and back to pasture. Aunt Elspeth lifted the cream cans with a strong and easy, almost contemptuous, movement like a young man's.

Yet these were the same women who in my mother's house turned sulky, sly, elderly, eager to take offense. Out of my mother's hearing they were apt to say to me, 'Is that the hairbrush you use on your hair? Oh, we thought it was for the dog!' Or, 'Is that what you dry your dishes with?' They would bend over the pans, scraping, scraping off every last bit of black that had accumulated since the last time they visited here. They greeted what my mother had to say usually with little stunned smiles; her directness, her outrageousness, paralyzed them for the moment, and they could only blink at her rapidly and helplessly, as if faced with a cruel light.

The kindest things she said were the most wrong. Aunt Elspeth could play the piano by ear; she would sit down and play the few pieces she knew – 'My Bonny Lies over the Ocean' and 'Road to the Isles.' My mother offered to teach her to read music.

'Then you can play really good things.'

Aunt Elspeth refused, with a delicate, unnatural laugh, as if somebody had offered to teach her to play pool. She went out and found a neglected flower bed and knelt in the dirt, in the hot midday sun, pulling up weeds. 'That flower bed I just don't care about any more. I've given up on it,' called my mother airily, warningly, from the kitchen door. 'There's nothing planted in it but that old London Pride, and I'd just as soon yank that up anyway!' Aunt Elspeth went on weeding as if she never heard. My mother made an exasperated, finally dismissing face and actually sat down in her canvas chair, leaned back and closed her eyes and remained doing nothing, smiling angrily, for about ten minutes. My mother went along straight lines. Aunt Elspeth and Auntie Grace wove in and out around her, retreating and disappearing and coming back, slippery and soft-voiced and indestructible. She pushed them out of her way as if they were cobwebs; I knew better than that.

Back home at Jenkin's Bend – bearing me with them for the long summer visit – they were refreshed, plumped out as if they had been put in water. I could see the change happening. I too with some slight pangs of disloyalty exchanged my mother's world of serious skeptical questions, endless but somehow disregarded housework, lumps in the mashed potatoes, and unsettling ideas, for theirs of work and gaiety, comfort and order, intricate formality. There was a whole new language to learn in their house. Conversations there had many levels, nothing could be stated directly, every joke might be a thrust turned inside out. My mother's disapproval was open and unmistakable, like heavy weather; theirs came like tiny razor cuts, bewilderingly, in the middle of kindness. They had the Irish gift for rampaging mockery, embroidered with deference.

The daughter of the family on the next farm had married a lawyer, a city man, of whom her family was very proud. They brought him over to be introduced. Aunt Elspeth and Auntie Grace had baked, and polished silver, and got out their hand-painted plates and little pearl-handled knives, for this visit. They fed him cakes, shortbread, nut loaf, tarts. He was a greedy or perhaps desperately bewildered young man, eating out of nervousness. He picked up whole cakes and they crumbled as he was getting them into his mouth; icing was smeared on his moustache. At supper Auntie Grace without saying a word began to do an imitation of his way of eating, exaggerating gradually, making gobbling noises and grabbing imaginary things from her plate. 'Oh, the *law*-yer!' cried Aunt Elspeth elegantly, and leaning across the table inquired, 'Have you always – been interested – in *country life*?' After their marvelous courtesy to him I found this faintly chilling; it was a warning. *Didn't he think he was somebody!* That was their final condemnation, lightly said. *He thinks he's somebody. Don't they think they're somebody.* Pretensions were everywhere.

Not that they were against ability. They acknowledged it in their own family, our family. But it seemed the thing to do was to keep it more or less a secret. Ambition was what they were alarmed by, for to be ambitious was to court failure and to risk making a fool of oneself. The worst thing, I gathered, the worst thing that could happen in this life was to have people laughing at you.

'Your Uncle Craig,' said Aunt Elspeth to me, 'your Uncle Craig is one of the smartest, and the best-liked, and the most respected men in Wawanash County. He could have been elected to the legislature. He could have been in the cabinet, if he'd wanted.'

'Didn't he get elected? Uncle Craig?'

'Don't be silly, he never ran. He wouldn't let his name stand. He preferred not.'

There it was, the mysterious and to me novel suggestion that choosing not to do things showed, in the end, more wisdom and self-respect than choosing to do them. They liked people turning down things that were offered, marriage, positions, opportunities, money. My cousin Ruth McQueen, who lived in Tupperton, had won a scholarship to go to college, for she was very clever, but she thought it over and turned it down; she decided to stay home.

'She preferred not.'

Why was this such an admirable thing to have done? Like certain subtle harmonies of music or color, the beauties of the negative were beyond me. Yet I was not ready, like my mother, to deny that they were there.

'Afraid to stick her head out of her own burrow,' was what my mother had to say about Ruth McQueen.

Aunt Moira was married to Uncle Bob Oliphant. They lived in Porterfield and had one daughter, Mary Agnes, born rather far along in their married life. During the summer Aunt Moira would sometimes drive the thirteen miles from Porterfield to Jenkin's Bend, for an afternoon's visit, bringing Mary Agnes with her. Aunt Moira could drive a car. Aunt Elspeth and Auntie Grace thought this very brave of her (my mother was learning to drive our car, and they thought that reckless and unnecessary). They would watch for her old-fashioned, square-topped car to cross the bridge and come up the road from the river, and go out to greet her with encouraging, admiring, welcoming cries, as if she had just found her way across the Sahara, instead of over the hot dusty roads from Porterfield.

That nimble malice that danced under their courtesies to the rest of the world was entirely lacking in their attentions to each other, to brother and sister. For each other they had only tenderness and pride. And for Mary Agnes Oliphant. I could not help thinking they preferred her to me. I was welcomed and enjoyed, yes, but I was tainted by other influences and by half my heredity; my upbringing was riddled with heresies, that could never all be put straight. Mary Agnes, it seemed to me, was received with a more unmixed, and shining, confident, affection.

At Jenkin's Bend it would never be mentioned that there was anything the matter with Mary Agnes. And in fact there was not much the matter; she was almost like other people. Except that you could not imagine her going into a store by herself, and buying something, going anywhere by herself; she had to be with her mother. She was not an idiot, she was nothing like Irene Pollox and Frankie Hall on the Flats Road, she was certainly not idiotic enough to be allowed to ride free all day on the merry-go-round at the Kinsmen's Fair, as they were – even provided Aunt Moira would have let her make such a spectacle of herself, which she would not. Her skin was dusty looking, as if there was a thin, stained sheet of glass over it, or a light oiled paper.

'She was deprived of oxygen,' my mother said, taking some satisfaction as always in explanations. 'She was deprived of oxygen in the birth canal. Uncle Bob Oliphant held Aunt Moira's legs together on the way to the hospital because the doctor had told them she might hemorrhage.'

I did not want to hear any more. In the first place I shied away from the implication that this was something that could happen to anyone, that I myself might have been blunted, all by lack of some namable, measurable, ordinary thing, like oxygen. And the words birth canal made me think of a straight-banked river of blood. I thought of Uncle Bob Oliphant holding Aunt Moira's heavy, vein-riddled legs together while she heaved and tried to deliver; I never could see him afterwards without thinking of that. Whenever we did see him in his own house he was sitting by the radio, sucking his pipe, listening to *Boston Blackie* or *Police Patrol*, tires shrieking and guns cracking while he seriously nodded his nut-bald head. Would he have his pipe in his mouth while he held Aunt Moira's legs, would he give businesslike assent to her commotion, just as he did to Boston Blackie's?

Perhaps because of this story it seemed to me that the gloom spreading out from Aunt Moira had a gynecological odor, like that of the fuzzy, rubberized bandages on her legs. She was a woman I would recognize now as a likely sufferer from varicose veins, hemorrhoids, a dropped womb, cysted ovaries, inflammations, discharges, lumps and stones in various places, one of those heavy, cautiously moving wrecked survivors of the female life, with stories to tell. She sat on the veranda in the wicker rocker, wearing, in spite of the hot weather, some stately, layered dress, dark and trembling with beads, a large hat like a turban, earth-colored stockings which she would sometimes roll down, to let the bandages 'breathe.' Not much could be said for marriage, really, if you were to compare her with her sisters, who could still jump up so quickly, who still smelled fresh and healthy, and who would occasionally, deprecatingly, mention the measurements of their waists. Even getting up or sitting down, or moving in the rocker, Aunt Moira gave off rumbles of complaint, involuntary and eloquent as noises of digestion or wind.

She told about Porterfield. Not a dry town like Jubilee, it had two beer parlors facing each other across the main street, one in each of the hotels. Sometimes on a Saturday night or early Sunday morning there would be a terrible street fight. Aunt Moira's house was only half a block from the main street and close to the sidewalk. From behind her darkened front windows she had watched men hooting like savages, had seen a car spin sideways and crash into a telephone pole, crushing the steering wheel into the driver's heart; she had seen two men dragging a girl who was drunk and couldn't stand up, and the girl was urinating on the street, in her clothes. She had scraped drunks' vomit off her painted fence. All this was ho more than she expected. And it was not only Saturday drunks but grocers and neighbors and delivery boys who cheated, were rude, committed outrages. Aunt Moira's voice, telling things at leisure, would spread out over the day, over the yard, like black oil, and Aunt Elspeth and Auntie Grace would sympathize.

'Well, no, you couldn't be expected to take that!'

'We don't know how lucky we are, here.'

And they would run in and out with cups of tea, glasses of lemonade, fresh buttered baking-powder biscuits, Martha Washington cake, slices of pound cake with raisins, little confections of candied fruit rolled in coconut, delicious to nibble on.

Mary Agnes sat listening and smiling. She smiled at me. This was not a guileless smile but the smile of the person who arbitrarily, even rather highhandedly, extends to a child all the sociability which cannot, through fear and habit, be extended to anybody else. She wore her black hair bobbed, prickles showing on her thin olive neck; she wore glasses. Aunt Moira dressed her like the high-school girl she had never been, in plaid pleated skirts loose at the waist, too-large, long-sleeved, carefully laundered white blouses. She wore no make-up, no powder to tint the soft dark hairs at the corners of her mouth. She spoke to me in the harsh, hectoring, uncertain tones of somebody who is not just teasing but *imitating* teasing, imitating the way she had heard certain brash and jovial people, storekeepers maybe, talking to children.

'What do you do that for?' She came and caught me looking through the little panes of colored glass around the front door. She put her eye to the red one.

'Yard's on fire!' she said, but laughed at me as if I had said it.

Other times she would hide in the dark hall, and jump out and grab me from behind, closing her hands over my eyes. 'Guess who, guess who!' She would squeeze and tickle me till I shrieked. Her hands were hot and dry, her hugs fierce.

I fought back as hard as I could but could not call her names as I would somebody at school, could not spit at her and pull her hair out, because of her age – she was nominally a grownup – and her protected status. So I thought her a bully and said – but not at Jenkin's Bend – that I hated her. At the same time I was curious and not altogether displeased, discovering that I could be so important, in a way I could not even understand, to someone who was not important at all to me. She would roll me over on the hall carpet, tickling my belly ferociously, as if I were a dog, and I was as much overcome by amazement, each time, as by her unpredictable strength and unfair tricks; I was amazed as people must be who are seized and kidnapped, and who realize that in the strange world of their captors they have a value absolutely unconnected with anything they know about themselves.

I knew something, too, that had happened to Mary Agnes. My mother had told me. Years ago she had been out in the front yard of their house in Porterfield while Aunt Moira was washing clothes in the cellar, and some boys had come by, five boys. They persuaded her to go for a walk with them and they took her out to the fairgrounds and took off all her clothes and left her lying on the cold mud, and she caught bronchitis and nearly died. That was why, now, she had to wear warm underwear even in summer.

I supposed that the degradation – for my mother told me the story to warn me that some degradation was possible, if ever you were persuaded to go off with boys – lay in having all her clothes taken off, in being naked. Having to be naked myself, the thought of being naked, stabbed me with shame in the pit of my stomach. Every time I thought of the doctor pulling down my pants and jabbing the needle in my buttocks, for smallpox, I felt outraged, frantic, unbearably, almost exquisitely, humiliated. I thought of Mary Agnes's body lying exposed on the fairgrounds, her prickly cold buttocks sticking out – that did seem to me the most shameful, helpless-looking part of anybody's body – and I thought that if it had happened to me, to be seen like that, I could not live on afterwards.

'Del, you and Mary Agnes ought to go for a walk.'

'You ought to chase around the barn and see if you can find Robber.'

I rose obediently, and around the corner of the veranda beat a stick on the latticework, in savage dejection. I didn't want to go with Mary Agnes. I wanted to stay and eat things, and hear more about Porterfield, that depraved sullen town, filled with untrustworthy, gangsterish people. I heard Mary Agnes coming after me, with her heavy tripping run.

'Mary Agnes, stay out of the sun where you can. Don't go paddling in the river. You can catch cold any time of the year!'

We went down the road and along the riverbank. In the heat of dry stubble fields, cracked creek beds, white dusty roads, the Wawanash river made a cool trough. The shade was of thin willow leaves, which held the sunlight like a sieve. The mud along the banks was dry but not dried to dust; it was like cake icing, delicately crusted on top but moist and cool underneath, lovely to walk on. I took off my shoes and walked barefoot. Mary Agnes hooted, 'I'm telling on you!'

'Tell if you like.' I called her *bugger* under my breath.

Cows had been down to the river and had left their hoof prints in the mud. They left cowpats too, nicely rounded, looking, when they dried, like artifacts, like handmade lids of clay. Along the edge of the water, on both sides, were carpets of lily leaves spread out, and here and there a yellow water lily, looking so pale, tranquil, and desirable, that I had to tuck my dress into my pants and wade in among the sucking roots, in black mud that oozed up between my toes and clouded the water, silting the leaves and lily petals.

'You're going to drown, you're going to drown,' cried Mary Agnes in cross excitement, though I was hardly past my knees. Brought to shore, the flowers seemed coarse and rank and began to die immediately. I walked on forgetting about them, mashing the petals in my fist.

We came upon a dead cow, lying with its hind feet in the water. Black flies were crawling and clustering on its brown-and-white hide, sparkling where the sun caught them like beaded embroidery.

I took a stick and tapped the hide. The flies rose, circled, dropped back. I could see that the cow's hide was a map. The brown could be the ocean, the white the floating continents. With my stick I traced their strange shapes, their curving coasts, trying to keep the point of the stick exactly between the white and the brown. Then I guided the stick up the neck, following a taut rope of muscle – the cow had died with its neck stretched out, as if reaching for water, but it was lying the wrong way for that – and I tapped the face. I was shyer about touching the face. I was shy about looking at its eye.

The eye was wide open, dark, a smooth sightless bulge, with a sheen like silk and a reddish gleam in it, a reflection of light. An orange stuffed in a black silk stocking. Flies nestled in one corner, bunched together beautifully in an iridescent brooch. I had a great desire to poke the eye with my stick, to see if it would collapse, if it would quiver and break like a jelly, showing itself to be the same composition all the way through, or if the skin over the surface would break and let loose all sorts of putrid mess, to flow down the face. I traced the stick all the way round the eye, I drew it back – but I was not able, I could not poke it in.

Mary Agnes did not come close. 'Leave it alone,' she warned. 'That old dead cow. It's dirty. You get yourself dirty.'

'Day-ud cow,' I said, expanding the word lusciously. 'Day-ud cow, day-ud cow.'

'You come on,' Mary Agnes bossed me, but was afraid, I thought, to come nearer.

Being dead, it invited desecration. I wanted to poke it, trample it, pee on it, anything to punish it, to show what contempt I had for its being dead. Beat it up, break it up, spit on it, tear it, throw it away! But still it had power, lying with a gleaming strange map on its back, its straining neck, the smooth eye. I had never once looked at a cow alive and thought what I thought now: why should there be a cow? Why should the white spots be shaped just the way they were, and never again, not on any cow or creature, shaped in exactly the same way? Tracing the outline of a continent again, digging the stick in, trying to make a definite line, I paid attention to its shape as I would sometimes pay attention to the shape of real continents or islands on real maps, as if the shape itself were a revelation beyond words, and I would be able to make sense of it, if I tried hard enough, and had time.

'I dare you touch it,' I said scornfully to Mary Agnes. 'Touch a dead cow.'

Mary Agnes came up slowly, and to my astonishment she bent down, grunting, looking at the eye as if she knew I had been wondering about it, and she laid her hand – she laid *the palm of her hand* – over it, over the eye. She did this seriously, shrinkingly, yet with a tender composure that was not like her. But as soon as she had done it she stood up, and held her hand in front of her face, palm towards me, fingers spread, so that it looked like a huge hand, bigger than her whole face, and dark. She laughed right at me.

'You'd be scared to let me catch you now,' she said, and I was, but walked away from her insolently as I could manage.

It often seemed then that nobody else knew what really went on, or what a person was, but me. For instance people said 'poor Mary Agnes' or implied it, by a drop in pitch, a subdued protective tone of voice, as if she had no secrets, no place of her own, and that was not true.

'Your Uncle Craig died last night.'

My mother's voice, telling this, was almost shy.

I was eating my favorite, surreptitious breakfast – Puffed Wheat drowned in black molasses – and sitting on the cement slab outside our door, in the morning sun. It was two days since I had returned from Jenkin's Bend and when she said *Uncle Craig* I thought of him as I had seen him, standing in the doorway, in his vest and shirtsleeves, benignly, perhaps impatiently, waving me off.

The active verb confused me. He *died*. It sounded like something he willed to do, chose to do. As if he said, 'Now I'll die.' In that case it could not be so final. Yet I knew it was.

'In the Orange Hall, at Blue River. He was playing cards.'

The card table, the bright Orange Hall. (Though I knew it was really the Orange*men*'s Hall, the name had nothing to do with the color, any more than Blue River meant the river was blue.) Uncle Craig was dealing out cards, his heavy-lidded, serious way. He wore his sateen-backed vest, with pens and pencils clipped in the pocket. *Now?*

'He had a heart attack.'

Heart *attack*. It sounded like an explosion, like fireworks going off, shooting sticks of light in all directions, shooting a little ball of light – that was Uncle Craig's heart, or his soul – high into the air, where it tumbled and went out. Did he jump up, throw his arms out, yell? How long did it take, did his eyes close, did he know what was happening? My mother's usual positiveness seemed clouded over; my cold appetite for details irritated her. I followed her around the house, scowling, persistent, repeating my questions. I wanted to know. There is no protection, unless it is in knowing. I wanted death pinned down and isolated behind a wall of particular facts and circumstances, not floating around loose, ignored but powerful, waiting to get in anywhere.

But by the day of the funeral things had changed. My mother had regained confidence; I had quieted down. I did not want to hear anything more about Uncle Craig,

or about death. My mother had got my Black Watch plaid
dress out of mothballs, brushed it, aired it on the line.

'It's all right for summer, cooler than cotton, that light
wool. Anyway it's the only dark thing you own. I don't
care. If it was up to me you could wear scarlet. If they
really believed in Christianity that's what they'd all wear.
It'd be all dancing and rejoicing – after all, they spend their
whole life singing and praying about getting out of this
world and on their way to Heaven. Yes. But I know your
aunts, they'll expect dark clothes, conventional to the last
hair!'

She was not surprised to hear that I did not want to go.

'Nobody does,' she said frankly. 'Nobody ever does. You
have to, though. You have to learn to face things sometime.'

I did not like the way she said this. Her briskness and zeal
seemed false and vulgar. I did not trust her. Always when
people tell you you will have to face this sometime, when
they hurry you matter-of-factly towards whatever pain
or obscenity or unwelcome revelation is laid out for you,
there is this edge of betrayal, this cold, masked, imperfectly
hidden jubilation in their voices, something greedy for
your hurt. Yes, in parents too; in parents particularly.

'What is Death?' continued my mother with ominous
cheerfulness. 'What is being dead?

'Well, first off, what is a person? A large percent water.
Just plain water. Nothing in a person is that remarkable.
Carbon. The simplest elements. What is it they say? Ninety-
eight cents' worth? That's all. It's the way it's put together
that's remarkable. The way it's put together, we have the
heart and the lungs. We have the liver. Pancreas. Stomach.
Brain. All these things, what are they? Combinations of

elements! Combine them – combine the combinations – and you've got a person! We call it Uncle Craig, or your father, or me. But it's just these *combinations*, these parts put together and running in a certain particular way, for the time being. Then what happens is that one of the parts gives out, breaks down. In Uncle Craig's case, the heart. So we say, Uncle Craig is dead. The person is dead. But that's just our way of looking at it. That's just our human way. If we weren't thinking all the time in terms of persons, if we were thinking of Nature, all Nature going on and on, parts of it dying – well not dying, changing, *changing* is the word I want, changing into something else, all those elements that made the person changing and going back into Nature again and reappearing over and over in birds and animals and flowers – Uncle Craig doesn't have to be Uncle Craig! Uncle Craig is flowers!'

'I'll get carsick,' I said. 'I'll vomit.'

'No you won't.' My mother, in her slip, rubbed cologne on her bare arms. She pulled her navy blue crepe dress over her head. 'Come and do me up. What a dress to wear in this heat. I can smell the cleaners on it. Heat brings out that smell. Let me tell you about an article I was reading just a couple of weeks ago. It ties in perfectly with what I'm saying now.'

She went into her room and brought back her hat, which she put on in front of my little bureau mirror, hastily scraping the front hair underneath and leaving some back tails out. It was a pillbox hat of a hideous color popular during the war – air-force blue.

'People are made up of parts,' she resumed. 'Well when a person dies – as we say – only one part, or a couple of parts, may actually be worn out. Some of the other parts could run thirty, forty years more. Uncle Craig, for instance – he might have had perfectly good kidneys that a young person with sick kidneys could use. And this article was saying – someday these parts will be used! That's the way it will be. Come on downstairs.'

I followed her down to the kitchen. She started putting her rouge on, at the dark mirror over the kitchen sink. For some reason she kept her make-up there, on a sticky tin shelf above the sink, all mixed up with bottles of dark old pills, and razor blades and tooth powder and Vaseline, no tops on anything.

'Transplant them! For instance eyes. They are already able to transplant eyes, not whole eyes but the cornea, I think it is. That's only the beginning. Someday they'll be able to transplant hearts and lungs and all the organs that the body needs. Even brains – I wonder, could they transplant *brains*? So all these parts won't die at all, they'll go on living as part of somebody else. Part of another combination. Then you won't be able properly to speak of death at all. 'Heirs of the Living Body.' That's what the article was called. We would all be heirs of one another's bodies, we would all be donors too. Death as we know it now would be done away with!'

My father had come down, in his dark suit.

'Were you planning to discuss these ideas with the folks at the funeral?'

In a back-to-earth voice my mother said, 'No.'

'Because they do have a different set of notions, and they might easy be upset.'

'I never mean to upset anybody,' cried my mother. 'I

never do! I think it's a beautiful idea. It has its own kind of beauty! Isn't it better than Heaven and Hell? I can't understand people, I never can make out what they really believe. Do they think your Uncle Craig is wearing some kind of white nightshirt and floating around Eternity this very minute? Or do they think they put him in the ground and he decays?'

'They think both,' my father said, and in the middle of the kitchen he put his arms around my mother, holding her lightly and gravely, careful not to disturb her hat or her newly-pink face.

I used to wish sometimes for this very thing, to see my parents by look or embrace affirm that romance – I did not think of passion – had once caught them up and bound them together. But at this moment, seeing my mother go meek and bewildered – this was what the slump of her back showed, that her words never would – and my father touching her in such a gentle, compassionate, grieving way, his grieving having not much to do with Uncle Craig, I was alarmed, I wanted to shout at them to stop and turn back into their separate, final, unsupported selves. I was afraid that they would go on and show me something I no more wanted to see than I wanted to see Uncle Craig dead.

'*Owen* doesn't have to go,' I said bitterly, pushing my face into the loosened mesh of the screen door, seeing him sitting in the yard in his old wagon, barelegged, dirty, remote, pretending he was something else, anything – an Arab in a caravan or an Eskimo on a dog sled.

That drew them away from each other, my mother sighing.

'Owen's young.'

*

The house was like on one of those puzzles, those mazes on paper, with a black dot in one of the squares, or rooms; you are supposed to find your way in to it, or out from it. The black dot in this case was Uncle Craig's body, and my whole concern was not to find my way to it but to avoid it, not to open even the safest-looking door because of what might be stretched out behind it.

The hay coils were still there. Last week, when I was visiting, the hay was cut, right up to the veranda steps, and coiled into smooth, perfect beehives higher than anybody's head. In the evening, first casting long, pulled-out shadows, then turning gray, solid, when the sun went down, these hay coils made a village, or, if you looked around the corner of the house down the rest of the field, a whole city of secretive, exactly similar, purple-gray huts. But one had tumbled down, one was soft and wrecked, left for me to jump in. I would stand back against the steps and then run at it with my arms spread passionately, landing deep in fresh hay, still warm, still with its grassy growing smell. It was full of dried flowers – purple and white money-musk, yellow toadflax, little blue flowers nobody knew the name of. My arms and legs and face were covered with scratches, and when I roused myself from the hay these scratches stung, or glowed on me, in the rising breeze from the river.

Aunt Elspeth and Auntie Grace had come and jumped in the hay too, with their aprons flying, laughing at themselves. When the moment came they would hesitate, and jump with not quite sufficient abandon, landing in a decorous sitting position, hands spread as bouncing on a cushion, or holding their hair.

When they came back and sat on the veranda, with basins of strawberries they were hulling, to make jam, Auntie Grace spoke breathlessly, but in a calm, musing voice.

'If a car had come by, wouldn't you just have wanted to die?'

Aunt Elspeth took the pins out of her hair and let it down over the back of her chair. When her hair was pinned up it looked nearly all gray, but when it was loose it showed a great deal of dark, silky brown, mink's color. With little snorting sounds of pleasure she shook her head back and forth and drew her spread fingers through her hair, to get rid of the little bits of hay that had flown up, and were sticking in it.

'Fools we are!' she said.

Where was Uncle Craig this while? Typing undauntedly, behind his closed windows and pulled-down blinds.

The squashed hay coil was just the same. But men were walking on the hay stubble, all in dark suits like tall crows, talking. A wreath of white lilies hung on the front door, which was standing ajar. Mary Agnes came up joyfully smiling and made me stand still while she tied and retied my sash. The house and yard were full of people. Relatives from Toronto sat on the veranda, looking benevolent, but voluntarily apart. I was taken and made to speak to them, and avoided looking into the windows behind them, because of Uncle Craig's body. Ruth McQueen came out carrying a wicker basket of roses, which she set on the veranda railing.

'There are more flowers than will ever go in the house,' she said, as if this was something we might all grieve for.

'I thought I'd set them out here.' She was fair-haired, discreet, wanly solicitous – already an old maid. She knew everyone's name. She introduced my mother and me to a man and his wife from the southern part of the county. The man was wearing a suit jacket with overalls.

'He give us our marriage license,' the woman said proudly.

My mother said she must go to the kitchen and I followed her, thinking that at least they could not have put Uncle Craig there, where the smells of coffee and food were coming from. Men were in the hall, too, like tree trunks to work your way through. Both doors of the front room were closed, a basket of gladioli set in front of them.

Aunt Moira, draped in black like a massive, public pillar, was standing over the kitchen table counting teacups.

'I've counted three times and every time I come up with a different number,' she said, as if this was a special misfortune that could happen only to her. 'My brain is not able to work today. I can't stand on my feet much longer.'

Aunt Elspeth, wearing a wonderful starched and ironed apron, with frills of white lawn, kissed my mother and me. 'There now,' she said, backing up from her kiss with a sigh of accomplishment. 'Grace is upstairs, freshening her eyes. We just can't believe it, so many people! Grace said to me, I think half the county is here, and I said what do you mean, half the county, I wouldn't be surprised if it's the whole county! We miss Helen, though. She sent a *blanket* of lilies.

'There ought to be enough, goodness!' she said practically, looking at the teacups. 'All our good ones and kitchen ones and the ones we borrowed from the church!'

'Do like at the Poole funeral,' whispered a lady by the table. 'She put away her good ones, locked them up and used the ones from the church. Said she wasn't risking her china.'

Aunt Elspeth rolled her red-rimmed eyes in appreciation – her usual expression, just tempered by the occasion.

'The food will hold out anyway. I think there's enough here to feed the five thousand.'

I thought so too. Everywhere I looked I saw food. A cold roast of pork, fat roast chickens, looking varnished, crusted scalloped potatoes, tomato aspic, potato salad, cucumber and beet salad, a rosy ham, muffins, baking-powder biscuits, round bread, nut bread, banana loaf, fruitcake, light and dark layer cake, lemon meringue and apple and berry pies, bowls of preserved fruit, ten or twelve varieties of pickles and relishes. Watermelon-rind pickles, Uncle Craig's favorite. He always said he would like to make a meal out of those, with just bread and butter.

'No more than enough,' said Aunt Moira, darkly. 'They all bring their appetites to funerals.'

There was a stir in the hallway; Auntie Grace passing through, the men making way, she thanking them, subdued and grateful as if she had been a bride. The minister trailed behind her. He spoke to the women in the kitchen with restrained heartiness.

'Well, ladies! Ladies! It doesn't look as if you have let time lie heavy on your hands. Work is a good offering, work is a good offering in time of grief.'

Auntie Grace bent and kissed me. There was a faint sour smell, a warning, under her eau de cologne. 'Do you want to see your Uncle Craig?' she whispered, tender and sprightly as if she was promising a reward. 'He's in the front room, he looks so handsome, under the lilies Aunt Helen sent.'

So. Some ladies spoke to her, and I got away. I went through the hall again. The front-room doors were still closed. At the bottom of the stairway, by the front door, my father and a man I did not know were pacing, turning, measuring discreetly with their hands.

'This'll be the tricky place. Here.'

'Take the door off?'

'Too late for that. You don't want to make a commotion. It might upset the ladies, seeing us take it off. If we back around like this –'

Down the side hall two old men were talking. I ducked between them.

'Not like in the winter, remember Jimmy Poole's. The ground was like a rock. You couldn't put a dent in it with any kind of a tool.'

'Had to wait over two months for a thaw.'

'By that time must have been three–four of them waiting. Let see. There'd be Jimmy Poole –'

'Him all right. There'd be Mrs Fraleigh, Senior –'

'Hold on there, she died before the freeze, she'd be all right.'

I went through the door at the end of the side hall into the old part of the house. This part was called the storeroom; from outside, it looked like a little house of logs tacked on to the side of the big brick house. The windows were small and square and set slightly askew like the never-quite-convincing windows in a doll's house. Hardly any light got in, because of the dim towering junk piled up everywhere even in front of the windows – the churn and the old washing machine that was turned by hand, wooden bedsteads taken apart, trunks, tubs, scythes, a baby carriage clumsy as a galleon, keeling drunkenly to one side. This was the room Auntie Grace refused to go into; Aunt Elspeth always had to go, if they wanted something out of it. She would stand in the doorway and sniff boldly and say, 'What a place! The air in here's just like a tomb!'

I loved the sound of that word when I first heard her say it. I did not know exactly what it was, or had got it mixed up with womb, and I saw us inside some sort of hollow marble egg, filled with blue light, that did not need to get in from outside.

Mary Agnes was sitting on the churn, not looking surprised.

'What are you coming in here for?' she said softly. 'You're going to get yourself lost.'

I didn't answer her. Not turning my back, I wandered round the room. I had often wondered, thinking back, if there was anything in that baby carriage. Sure enough there was; a pile of old *Family Herald*s. I heard my mother's voice calling my name. She sounded slightly anxious, unwillingly deferential. I didn't make a sound and Mary Agnes didn't either. What had she been doing in here? She had found a pair of old-fashioned ladies' boots, laced up the front and trimmed with fur, and she was hanging on to them. She rubbed the fur under her chin.

'Rabbit fur.'

Now she came and stuck the boots in my face.

'Rabbit fur?'

'I don't want them.'

'Come and see Uncle Craig.'

'No.'

'You haven't seen him yet.'

'*No.*'

She waited with a boot in each hand, blocking my way, then said again in such a sly, inviting voice, 'Come see Uncle Craig.'

'I will not.'

She dropped the boots and put her hand on my arm, dug the fingers in. I tried to shake her off, and she got me with the other hand and pulled me towards the door. For someone so clumsy, someone who had nearly died three times from bronchitis, she had shocking strength. She worked her hand down to my wrist and with a clutch like a bear's she got hold of my hand. Her voice was still at leisure, mild and gloating.

'You come and – *see* – Uncle Craig.'

I dropped my head and got her arm in my opened mouth, I got her solid downy arm just below the elbow, and I bit and bit and broke the skin and in pure freedom thinking I had done the worst thing that I would ever do, I tasted Mary Agnes Oliphant's blood.

I did not have to be in the funeral. Nobody was going to make me look at Uncle Craig. I was put in his office, on the leather sofa where he had taken his naps and where couples had sat waiting for their marriage licenses. I had a blanket over my knees in spite of the hot day, and a cup of tea beside me. I had been given a slice of pound cake too but had eaten that immediately.

When I bit Mary Agnes I thought I was biting myself off from everything. I thought I was putting myself outside, where no punishment would ever be enough, where nobody would dare ask me to look at a dead man, or anything else, again. I thought they would all hate me, and hate seemed to me so much to be coveted, then, like a gift of wings.

But no; freedom is not so easily come by. Though Aunt Moira, who would always say she had to pull me off Mary Agnes's arm with blood on my mouth (a lie – I was already off and Mary Agnes, all her demon power deflated, was crouched there, amazed and weeping), did clench my shoulders and shake me, holding me so my face was hardly an inch from her armored breasts, and her body hissed and trembled above me like a monument about to explode.

'Mad dog! Mad dogs bite like that! Your parents ought to have you locked up!'

Aunt Elspeth laid a handkerchief to Mary Agnes's arm. Auntie Grace and other ladies hugged and patted her.

'I'll have to get her to the doctor. She'll have to have stitches. I'll have to get shots for her. That child could be rabid. There is such a thing as a rabid child.'

'Moira dear. Moira dear. No. She barely broke the skin. It's the pain of a moment. Just a bit of a wash and a bandage and it'll be all right.' Both Aunt Elspeth and Auntie Grace transferred their attention from Mary Agnes to their sister, and held on to her and soothed her from either side, as if they were trying to keep the pieces of her together until the danger of explosion had passed. 'No lasting harm, dear, no lasting harm.'

'My mistake, my mistake entirely,' said the clear and dangerous voice of my mother. 'I never should have brought that child here today. She's too highly strung. It's barbaric to subject a child like that to a funeral.' Unpredictable, unreliable, still at the oddest time someone to be grateful for, she offered understanding, salvation, when it was no longer, strictly speaking, of much use.

But she had an effect – though sometimes, just by using a word like *barbaric*, she could make a pool of silence, of consternation round her. This time she found sympathy, various ladies readily taking up her explanation and enlarging on it.

'She didn't know what she was doing, likely.'

'She was hysterical from the strain.'

'I passed out at a funeral myself, one time before I was married.'

Ruth McQueen put her arm around me and asked if I would like an aspirin.

So while Mary Agnes was being comforted and washed and bandaged, and Aunt Moira was being calmed down (she was the one who got the aspirin, and also some special pills – *for her heart* – out of her purse), I also was surrounded and taken care of, shepherded into this room and put on the sofa, blanketed, as if I was sick, given the cake and the tea.

My behavior had not spoiled the funeral. The door was closed, I could not see it, but I could hear the voices singing, raggedly at first and then with greater and greater effort, longing, and conviction.

A thousand ages in thy sight
Are as an evening gone
Short as the watch that ends the night
Before the rising sun.

The house was full of people pressed together, melted together like blunt old crayons, warm, acquiescent, singing. And I was in the middle of them, in spite of being shut up here by myself. As long as they lived most of them would remember that I had bitten Mary Agnes Oliphant's arm at Uncle Craig's funeral. Remembering that, they would remember that I was highly strung, erratic, or badly brought up, or a *borderline case*. But they would not put me outside. No. I would be the highly strung, erratic, badly brought up *member of the family*, which is a different thing altogether.

Being forgiven creates a peculiar shame. I felt hot, and not just from the blanket. I felt held close, stifled, as if it was not air I had to move and talk through in this world but something thick as cotton. This shame was physical, but went far beyond sexual shame, my former shame of nakedness; now it was as if not the naked body but all the organs inside it – stomach, heart, lungs, liver – were laid bare and helpless. The nearest thing to this that I had ever known before was the feeling I got when I was tickled beyond endurance – horrible, voluptuous feeling of exposure, of impotence, self-betrayal. And shame went spreading out from me all through the house, covered everybody, even Mary Agnes, even Uncle Craig in his present disposable, vacated condition. To be made of flesh was humiliation. I was caught in a vision which was, in a way, the very opposite of the mystic's incommunicable vision of order and light; a vision, also incommunicable, of confusion and obscenity – of helplessness, which was revealed as the most obscene thing there could be. But like the other kind of vision this could not be supported more than a moment or two, it collapsed of its own intensity and could never be reconstructed or even really believed in, once it was over. By the time they started the last hymn of the funeral I was myself again, only normally weak as anybody would be after biting a human arm, and the Fathers of Confederation across from me had resumed their clothes and believable dignity, and I had drunk the whole cup of tea, exploring its adult, unfamiliar, important taste.

I got up and slowly opened the door. The front-room doors were both open. People were moving, slowly, their hunched worried-looking backs moving away from me.

> *Jesus call us, o'er the tumult,*
> *Of our life's tempestuous sea –*

I entered the room unnoticed and wedged myself in line, in front of a kind, sweating lady who did not know me, and who bent and whispered encouragingly, 'You're just in time for the Last Look.'

All the blinds were down, to keep out the afternoon sun; the room was hot and gloomy, pierced with stray shafts of light, like a haymow on a blazing afternoon. It smelled of lilies, waxy, pure-white lilies, and also like a root cellar. I was moved forward with the other people till I reached the corner of the casket, which was sitting in front of the fireplace – the never-used, beautiful fireplace with its tiles waxed like emeralds. Inside the casket was all white satin, gathered and pleated like the most gorgeous dress. The bottom half of Uncle Craig was covered with a polished lid; the top half – from shoulders to waist – was hidden by lilies. Against all that white his face was copper colored, disdainful. He did not look asleep; he did not look anything like he looked when I went into the office to wake him up on a Sunday afternoon. The eyelids lay too lightly on his eyes, the grooves and creases on his face had grown too shallow. He himself was wiped out; this face was like a delicate mask of skin, varnished, and laid over the real face – or over nothing at all, ready to crack when you poked a finger into it. I did have this impulse, but at a level far, far removed from possibility, just as you might have an impulse to touch a live wire. Uncle Craig was like that under his lilies, on his satin pillow; he was the terrible, silent, indifferent conductor of forces that could flare up, in an instant, and burn through this room, all reality, leave us dark. I turned away with humming in my ears, but was relieved, glad that I had done it after all, and survived, and was making my way through the crowded, singing room to my mother, who was sitting alone by the window – my father being with the other pallbearers – not singing, biting her lips, and looking preposterously hopeful.

After this Aunt Elspeth and Auntie Grace sold the house at Jenkin's Bend, and the land and the cows, and moved to Jubilee. They said they had chosen Jubilee, rather than Blue River, where they knew more people, or Porterfield where Aunt Moira was, because they wanted to be what use they could to my father and his family. And they did sit in their house on a hill at the north end of town like amazed and injured but dutiful guardians, thoughtful for our welfare, dubious about our lives. They darned my father's socks, which he got into the habit of bringing them; they kept a garden still, and did preserving for us; they mended and knitted and baked for us. I would go to see them once or twice a week, at first willingly enough, though it was partly because of the food; when I was going to high school I visited them more and more reluctantly. Every time I came they said, 'What kept you away so long? You're quite the stranger here!' They would be sitting waiting for me as if they had waited the whole week, on their little dark screened porch if the weather was nice; they could see out but nobody going by could see in.

What could I ever say? Their house became like a tiny sealed-off country, with its own ornate customs and elegantly, ridiculously complicated language, where true news of the outside world was not exactly forbidden, but became more and more impossible to deliver.

In the bathroom, over the toilet, hung their old reproof, done in cross-stitch:

> Freshen the air before you leave
> A courtesy others will perceive

A container with fresh matches hung beneath it. I always felt ashamed, caught out, reading that, but I always lit a match.

They told their same stories, they played their same jokes, which now seemed dried out, brittle with use; in time every word, every expression of the face, every flutter of the hands came to seem something learned long ago, perfectly remembered, and each of their two selves was seen to be something constructed with terrible care; the older they got the more frail and admirable and inhuman this construction appeared. This was what became of them when they no longer had a man with them, to nourish and admire, and when they were removed from the place where their artificiality bloomed naturally. Aunt Elspeth was gradually going deaf and Auntie Grace was troubled with arthritis in her hands, so that eventually she would have to give up all but the coarser kind of sewing, but they were not radically exposed or damaged or changed; with so much effort, with a final sense of obligation, they kept their outlines intact.

They had Uncle Craig's manuscript with them and from time to time spoke of showing it to somebody, maybe to Mr Buchanan, the history teacher at the high school, or to Mr Fouks at the *Herald-Advance*. But they didn't want to look as if they were asking a favor. And who could you trust? Some people might get hold of it and bring it out as if it was their own.

One afternoon they brought the red-and-gold tin with the picture of Queen Alexandra, filled with round oatmeal cookies put together with stewed dates, and also a large black tin box, fireproof and padlocked.

'Uncle Craig's history.'

'Nearly a thousand pages.'

'More pages than *Gone with the Wind*!'

'He typed it so beautifully, no mistakes.'

'He typed the last page the afternoon of the day he died.'

'Take it out,' they urged me. 'Look at it.' Just the way they offered cookies.

I leafed through quickly to the last page.

'Read a bit,' they said. 'You'll be interested. Didn't you always get good marks in history?'

> *During the spring, summer, and early fall of that year a large amount of building went forward in Fairmile, Morris, and Grantly townships. On the corner of Concession Five and the River Sideroad, in Fairmile, a Methodist Church was erected to serve a large and growing congregation in that area. This was known as the White Brick Church and unfortunately it was only to stand until 1924 when it was destroyed by fire of unknown origins. The drive-shed, though built of wood, was spared. On the opposite corner, Mr Alex Hedley built and opened a General Store but died within two months of the opening of a stroke and the operation was continued by his sons Edward and Thomas. There was also a blacksmith shop in operation further along the Fifth Concession, O'Donnell being the name of the people that had it. This corner was known either as Hedley's Corners or Church Corners. There is nothing in that location at the present time but the building of the store, which a family rents and lives in.*

While I was reading this they were telling me, with a nice hesitation for the surprise, that the manuscript was mine.

'And all his old files and newspapers will go to you, when we – pass on, or before, no need to wait for that! – if you're ready for them.'

'Because we hope – we hope someday that you'll be able to finish it.'

'We used to think about giving it to Owen, because he's the boy –'

'But you're the one has the knack for writing compositions.'

It would be a hard job, they said, and it was asking a lot of me, but they thought I would find it easier if I took the manuscript home with me now and kept it, reading it over from time to time, to get the feel of Uncle Craig's writing.

'He had the gift. He could get everything in and still make it read smooth.'

'Maybe you could learn to copy his way.'

They were talking to somebody who believed that the only duty of a writer is to produce a masterpiece.

When I left I carried the box with me, awkwardly under my arm. Aunt Elspeth and Auntie Grace stood in their doorway, ceremoniously, to watch me go, and I felt as if I were a ship with their hopes on it, dropping down over the horizon. I put the box under my bed at home; I was not up to discussing it with my mother. A few days later I thought that it would be a good place to keep those few poems and bits of a novel I had written; I would like to have them locked away where nobody could find them and where they would be safe in case of fire. I lifted the mattress and got them out. That was where I had kept them up to now, folded inside a large flat copy of *Wuthering Heights*.

I didn't want Uncle Craig's manuscript put back with the

things I had written. It seemed so dead to me, so heavy and dull and useless, that I thought it might deaden my things too and bring me bad luck. I took it down to the cellar and left it in a cardboard box.

The last spring I was in Jubilee, when I was studying for my final exams, the cellar was flooded to a depth of three or four inches. My mother called me to help her, and we went down and opened the back door and swept the cold water, with its swampy smell, towards an outside drain. I found the box and the manuscript in it, which I had forgotten all about. It was just a big wad of soaking paper.

I didn't look to see how it was damaged, or whether it could be saved. It seemed to me a mistake from start to finish.

I did think of Aunt Elspeth and Auntie Grace. (Auntie Grace was by this time in the Jubilee Hospital, recovering, as it was thought, from a broken hip, and Aunt Elspeth was going every day to see her and sitting beside her and saying to the nurses – who loved them both – 'Would you believe what some people will do to lie in bed and get themselves waited on?') I thought of them watching the manuscript leave their house in its padlocked box and I felt remorse, that kind of tender remorse which has on its other side a brutal, unblemished satisfaction.

PRINCESS IDA

Now my mother was selling encyclopedias. Aunt Elspeth and Auntie Grace called it 'going on the road!'

'Is your mother going on the road much these days?' they would ask me, and I would say no, oh no, she isn't going out much any more, but I knew they knew I lied. 'Not much time for ironing,' they might continue compassionately, examining the sleeve of my blouse. 'Not much time for ironing when she has to go out on the road.'

I felt the weight of my mother's eccentricities, of something absurd and embarrassing about her – the aunts would just show me a little at a time – land on my own coward's shoulders. I did want to repudiate her, crawl into favor, orphaned, abandoned, in my wrinkled sleeves. At the same time I wanted to shield her. She would never have understood how she needed shielding, from two old ladies with their mild bewildering humor, their tender proprieties. They wore dark cotton dresses with fresh, perfectly starched and ironed, white lawn collars, china flower brooches. Their house had a chiming clock, which delicately marked the quarter hours; also watered ferns, African violets, crocheted runners, fringed blinds, and over everything the clean, reproachful smell of wax and lemons.

'She was in here yesterday to pick up the scones we made for you. Were they all right, we wondered about them, were they light? She told us she had got stuck away out on the Jericho Road. All by herself, stuck on the Jericho Road! Poor Ada! But the mud on her, we had to laugh!'

'We had to scrub the hall linoleum,' said Auntie Grace, with a note of apology, as if it was a thing she did not like to tell me.

From such a vantage point, my mother did seem a wild-woman.

She drove our thirty-seven Chevy over all of the highways and back roads of Wawanash County, drove it over gravel roads, dirt roads, cow tracks, if she thought they might lead her to customers. She carried a jack and a shovel in the trunk, and a couple of short planks for easing her way out of mud-holes. She drove all the time as if she would not be surprised to see the ground crack open ten feet in front of her wheels; she honked her horn despairingly at blind country corners; she was continually worried that the wooden bridges would not hold, and she would never let anything force her onto the treacherous crumbling shoulders of the road.

The war was still on then. Farmers were making money at last, making it out of pigs or sugar beets or corn. Possibly they did not mean to spend it on encyclopedias. They had their minds set on refrigerators, cars. But these things were not to be had, and in the meantime there was my mother, gamely lugging her case of books, gaining entry to their kitchens, their cold funeral-smelling front rooms, cautiously but optimistically opening fire on behalf of Knowledge. A chilly commodity that most people, grown up, can agree to do without. But nobody will deny that it is a fine thing for children. My mother was banking on that.

And if happiness in this world is believing in what you sell, why, then my mother was happy. Knowledge was not chilly to her, no; it was warm and lovely. Pure comfort even at this stage of her life to know the location of the Celebes Sea and the Pitti Palace, to get the wives of Henry VIII in order, and be informed about the social system of ants, the methods of sacrificial butchery used by the Aztecs, the plumbing in Knossos. She could get carried away, telling about such things; she would tell anybody. 'Your mother knows such a lot of things, my,' said Aunt Elspeth and Auntie Grace lightly, unenviously, and I saw that to some people, maybe to most people, knowledge was just oddity; it stuck out like warts.

But I shared my mother's appetite myself, I could not help it. I loved the volumes of the encyclopedia, their weight (of mystery, of beautiful information) as they fell open in my lap; I loved their sedate dark-green binding, the spidery, reticent-looking gold letters on their spines. They might open to show me a steel engraving of a battle, taking place on the moors, say, with a castle in the background, or in the harbor of Constantinople. All bloodshed, drowning, hacking off of heads, agony of horses, was depicted with a kind of operatic flourish, a superb unreality. And I had the impression that in historical times the weather was always theatrical, ominous; landscape frowned, sea glimmered in various dull or metallic shades of gray. Here was Charlotte Corday on her way to the guillotine, Mary Queen of Scots on her way to the scaffold, Archbishop Laud extending his blessing to Stafford through the bars of his prison window – nobody could doubt this was just the way they looked, robes black, lifted hands and faces white, composed, heroic. The encyclopedia did of course provide other sorts of things to look at: beetles, varieties of coal, diagrammed insides of engines, photographs of Amsterdam or Bucharest taken on smudgy dim days in the nineteen-twenties (you could tell by the little high square cars). I preferred history.

Accidentally at first and then quite deliberately I learned things from the encyclopedia. I had a freak memory. Learning a list of facts was an irresistible test to me, like trying to hop a block on one foot.

My mother got the idea that I might be useful in her work.

'My own daughter has been reading these books and I am just amazed at what she has picked up. Children's minds are just like flypaper, you know, whatever you give them will stick. Del, name the presidents of the United States from George Washington down to the present day, can you do that?' Or: name the countries and capitals of South America. The major explorers, tell where they came from and where they went. Dates too please. I would sit in a strange house rattling things off. I put on a shrewd, serious, competitive look, but that was mostly for effect. Underneath I felt a bounding complacency. I knew I knew it. And who could fail to love me, for knowing where Quito was?

Quite a few could, as a matter of fact. But where did I get the first hint in that direction? It might have been from looking up and seeing Owen, without two dates or capitals or dead presidents to string together, as far as anybody knew, tenderly, privately, wrapping a long chewed-out piece of gum around his finger. It might have been from the averted faces of country children, with their subtle, complicated embarrassment. One day I did not want to do it any more. The decision was physical; humiliation prickled my nerve ends and the lining of my stomach. I started to say, 'I don't know them –' but was too miserable, too ashamed, to tell this lie.

'George Washington, John Adams, Thomas Jefferson –'

My mother said sharply, 'Are you going to be sick?'

She was afraid I might be about to throw up. Both Owen and I were totally committed, on-the-spot throwers-up. I nodded and slid off the chair and went and hid in the car, holding my stomach. My mother when she came had figured out that it was more than that.

'You're getting self-conscious,' she said in a practical tone. 'I thought you enjoyed it.' The prickling started again. That was just it, I had enjoyed it, and it was not decent of her to say so. 'Shyness and self-consciousness,' said my mother rather grandly, 'those are the luxuries I could never afford.' She started the car. 'Though I can tell you, there are members of your father's family who would not open their mouths in public to say their house was burning down.'

Thereafter when asked – lightly asked – 'Do you want to do some questions today?' I would slump away down in the seat and shake my head and clutch my stomach, indicating the possible quick return of my malady. My mother had to resign herself, and now when I rode out with her on Saturdays I rode like Owen, free and useless cargo, no longer a sharer in her enterprises. 'You want to hide your brains under a bushel out of pure perversity but that's not my lookout,' she said. 'You just do as you please.'

I still had vague hopes of adventure, which Owen shared, at least on the more material level. We both hoped to buy bags of a certain golden-brown candy, broken in chunks like cement and melting almost immediately on the tongue, sold in one special harness-draped, horsy-smelling country store. We hoped at least to stop for gas at a place that sold cold pop. I hoped to travel as far as Porterfield or Blue River, towns which derived their magic simply from being places we did not know and were not known in, by not being Jubilee. Walking in the streets of one of these towns I felt my anonymity like a decoration, like a peacock's train. But by some time in the afternoon these hopes would ebb, or some of them would have been satisfied, which always leaves a gap. In my mother too there would be some ebbing, of those bright ruthless forces which pushed her out here in the first place. Approaching dark, and cold air coming up through a hole in the floor of the car, the tired noise of the engine, the indifference of the countryside, would reconcile us to each other and make us long for home. We drove through country we did not know we loved – not rolling or flat, but broken, no recognizable rhythm to it; low hills, hollows full of brush, swamp and bush and fields. Tall elm trees, separate, each plainly showing its shape, doomed but we did not know that either. They were shaped like slightly opened fans, sometimes like harps.

Jubilee was visible from a rise about three miles away, on the No. 4 Highway. Between us and it lay the river flats, flooded every spring, and the hidden curve of the Wawanash River, and the bridge over it, painted silver, hanging in the dusk like a cage. The No. 4 Highway was also the main street of Jubilee. We could see the towers of the post office and the Town Hall facing each other, the Town Hall with its exotic cupola hiding the legendary bell (rung for wars starting and ending, ready to ring in case of earthquake, or final flood) and the post office with its clock tower, square, useful, matter-of-fact. The town lay spread almost equidistantly on either side of the main street. Its shape, which at the time of our return would usually be defined in lights, was seen to be more or less that of a bat, one wing lifted slightly, bearing the water tower, unlighted, indistinct, on its tip.

My mother would never let this sighting go by without saying something. 'There's Jubilee,' she might say simply, or, 'Well, yonder lies the metropolis,' or she might even quote, fuzzily, a poem about going in the same door as out she went. And by these words, whether weary, ironic, or truly grateful, Jubilee seemed to me to take its being. As if without her connivance, her acceptance, these streetlights and sidewalks, the fort in the wilderness, the open and secret pattern of the town – a shelter and a mystery – would not be there.

Over all our expeditions, and homecomings, and the world at large, she exerted this mysterious, appalling authority, and nothing could be done about it, not yet.

My mother rented a house in town, and we lived there from September to June, going out to the house at the end of the Flats Road only for the summers. My father came in for supper, and stayed overnight, until the snow came; then he came in, if he could, for Saturday night and part of Sunday.

The house we rented was down at the end of River Street not far from the CNR station. It was the sort of house that looks bigger than it is; it had a high but sloping roof – the second story, wood, and the first story brick – and a bulging bay window in the dining room and verandas front and back; the front veranda had a useless and in fact inaccessible little balcony stuck into its roof. All the wooden parts of the house were painted gray, probably because gray does not need to be repainted so often as white. In the warm weather the downstairs windows had awnings, striped and very faded; then the house with its bleached gray paint and sloping verandas made me think of a beach – the sun, the tough windy grass.

Yet it was a house that belonged to a town; things about it suggested leisure and formality, of a sort that were not possible out on the Flats Road. I would sometimes think of our old house, its flat pale face, the cement slab outside the kitchen door, with a forlorn, faintly guilty, tender pain, as you might think of a simple old grandparent whose entertainments you have outgrown. I missed the nearness of the river and the swamp, also the real anarchy of winter, blizzards that shut us up tight in our house as if it were the Ark. But I loved the order, the wholeness, the intricate arrangement of town life, that only an outsider could see. Going home from school, winter afternoons, I had a sense of the whole town around me, all the streets which were named River Street, Mason Street, John Street, Victoria Street, Huron Street, and strangely, Khartoum Street; the evening dresses gauzy and pale as crocuses in Krall's Ladies' Wear window; the Baptist Mission Band in the basement of their church, singing 'There's a New Name Written Down in Glory, And it's Mine, Mine, Mine!' Canaries in their cages in the Selrite store and books in the library and mail in the post office and pictures of Olivia de Havilland and Errol Flynn in pirate and lady costumes outside the Lyceum Theatre – all these things, rituals and diversions, frail and bright, woven together – town! In town there were soldiers on leave, in their khaki uniforms which had an aura of anonymous brutality, like the smell of burning; there were beautiful, shining girls, whose names everybody knew – Margaret Bond, Dorothy Guest, Pat Mundy – and who in turn knew nobody's name, except if they chose; I watched them coming downhill from the high school, in their fur-trimmed velvet boots. They traveled in a little cluster, casting a radiance like a night lantern, blinding them to the rest of the world. Though one day one of them – Pat Mundy – had smiled at me in passing, and I made up daydreams about her – that she saved me from drowning, that she became a nurse and nursed me, risking her life rocking me in her velvet arms, when I nearly died of diphtheria.

If it was a Wednesday afternoon my mother's boarder, Fern Dogherty, would be at home, drinking tea, smoking, talking with my mother in the dining room. Fern's talk was low, she would ramble and groan and laugh against my mother's sharper, more economical commentary. They told stories about people in the town, about themselves; their talk was a river that never dried up. It was the drama, the ferment of life just beyond my reach. I would go to the deep mirror in the built-in sideboard and look at the reflection of the room – all dark wainscoting, dark beams, the brass lighting fixture like a little formal tree growing the wrong way, with five branches stiffly curved, ending in glass flowers. By getting them into a certain spot in the mirror I could make my mother and Fern Dogherty pull out like rubber bands, all wavering and hysterical, and I could make my own face droop disastrously down one side, as if I had had a stroke.

I said to my mother, 'Why didn't you bring that picture in?'

'What picture? *What picture?*'

'The one over the couch.'

Because I had been thinking – every so often I had to think – of our kitchen out on the farm, where my father and Uncle Benny were at that moment probably frying potatoes for their supper, in an unwashed pan (why wash away good grease?), with mitts and scarves steaming dry on top of the stove. Major our dog – not allowed into the house during my mother's reign – asleep on the dirty linoleum in front of the door. Newspapers spread on the table in place of a cloth, dog-haired blankets on the couch, guns and snowshoes and washtubs hung along the walls. Smelly bachelor comfort. Over the couch there was a picture actually painted by my mother, in the far-off early days – the possibly leisured, sunny, loving days – of her marriage. It showed a stony road and a river between mountains, and sheep driven along the road by a little girl in a red shawl. The mountains and the sheep looked alike, lumpy, woolly, purplish-gray. Long ago I had believed that the little girl was really my mother and that this was the desolate country of her early life. Then I learned that she had copied the scene from the *National Geographic*.

'That one? Do you want that in here?'

I didn't really. As often in our conversations I was trying to lead her on, to get the answer, or the revelation, I particularly wanted. I wanted her to say she had left it for my father. I remembered she had said once that she had painted it for him, he was the one who had liked that scene.

'I don't want it hanging where people would see,' she said. 'I'm no artist. I only painted it because I had nothing to do.'

She gave a ladies' party, to which she asked Mrs Coutts, sometimes called Mrs Lawyer Coutts, Mrs Best whose husband was the manager of the Bank of Commerce, various other ladies she only knew to speak to on the street, as well as neighbors, Fern Dogherty's co-workers from the post office, and of course Aunt Elspeth and Auntie Grace. (She asked them to make creamed-chicken tarts and lemon tarts and matrimonial cake, which they did.) The party was all planned in advance. As soon as the ladies came into the front hall they had to guess how many beans in a jar, writing their guess on a slip of paper. The evening proceeded with guessing games, quizzes made up with the help of the encyclopedia, charades which never got going properly because many ladies could not be made to understand how to play, and were too shy anyway, and a pencil and paper game where you write a man's name, fold it down, and pass it on, write a verb, fold it down, write a lady's name, and so on, and at the end all the papers are unfolded and read out. In a pink wool skirt and bolero, I joyfully passed peanuts.

Aunt Elspeth and Auntie Grace kept busy in the kitchen, smiling and affronted. My mother was wearing a red dress, semitransparent, covered with little black and blue pansies, like embroidery. 'We thought it was beetles she had on that dress,' whispered Aunt Elspeth to me. 'It gave us a start!' After that it did seem to me the party was less beautiful than I had supposed; I noticed some ladies were not playing any games, that my mother's face was feverish with excitement and her voice full of organizing fervor, that when she played the piano, and Fern Dogherty – who had studied to be a singer – sang 'What Is Life without My Lover?' ladies contained themselves, and clapped from some kind distance, as if this might be showing off.

Auntie Grace and Aunt Elspeth would in fact say to me, off and on for the next year, 'How is that lady boarder of yours? How is she finding life without her lover?' I would explain to them that it was a song from an opera, a translation, and they would cry, 'Oh, is *that* it? And we were all the time feeling so sorry for her!'

My mother had hoped that her party would encourage other ladies to give parties of this sort, but it did not, or if it did we never heard of them; they continued giving bridge parties, which my mother said were silly and snobbish. She gave up on social life, gradually. She said that Mrs Coutts was a stupid woman who in one of the quizzes had been uncertain who Julius Caesar was – she thought he was Greek – and who also made mistakes in grammar, saying things like 'he told her and I' instead of 'her and me' – a common mistake of people who thought they were being genteel.

She joined the Great Books discussion group which was meeting every second Thursday during the winter in the Council Chambers in the Town Hall. There were five other people in the group, including a retired doctor, Dr Comber, who was very frail, courteous, and as it turned out, dictatorial. He had pure white, silky hair and wore an ascot scarf. His wife had lived in Jubilee over thirty years and still knew hardly anybody's name, or where the streets were. She was Hungarian. She had a magnificent name she would serve up to people sometimes, like a fish on a platter, all its silvery, scaly syllables intact, but it was no use, nobody in Jubilee could pronounce or remember it. At first my mother was delighted with this couple, whom she had always wanted to know. She was overjoyed to be invited to their house where she looked at photographs of their honeymoon in Greece and drank red wine so as not to offend them – though she did not drink – and listened to funny and dreadful stories of things that had happened to them in Jubilee because they were atheists and intellectuals. Her admiration persisted through *Antigone*, dampened a bit in *Hamlet*, grew dimmer and dimmer through *The Republic* and *Das Kapital*. Nobody could have any opinions, it appeared, but the Combers; the Combers knew more,

they had seen Greece, they had attended lectures by
H. G. Wells, they were always right. Mrs Comber and my
mother had a disagreement and Mrs Comber brought up
the fact that my mother had not gone to university and
only to a – my mother imitated her accent – *backwoods*
high school. My mother reviewed some of the stories they
had told her and decided they had a persecution complex
('What is that?' said Fern, for such terms were just coming
into fashion at the time) and that they were even possibly
a little crazy. Also there had been an unpleasant smell in
their house which she had not mentioned to us at the time,
and the toilet, which she had to use after drinking that red
wine, was hideous, scummy yellow. What good is it if you
read Plato and never clean your toilet? asked my mother,
reverting to the values of Jubilee.

She did not go back to Great Books the second year.
She signed up for a correspondence course called 'Great
Thinkers of History,' from the University of Western
Ontario, and she wrote letters to the newspapers.

My mother had not let anything go. Inside that self we
knew, which might at times appear blurred a bit, or
sidetracked, she kept her younger selves strenuous and
hopeful; scenes from the past were liable to pop up any
time, like lantern slides, against the cluttered fabric of the
present.

In the beginning, the very beginning of everything,
there was that house. It stood at the end of a long lane,
with wire fences, sagging windowpanes of wire on either
side, in the middle of fields where the rocks – part of the
pre-Cambrian Shield – were poking through the soil like

bones through flesh. The house which I had never seen in a photograph – perhaps none had ever been taken – and which I had never heard my mother describe except in an impatient, matter-of-fact way ('It was just an old frame house – it never had been painted'), nevertheless appeared in my mind as plainly as if I had seen it in a newspaper – the barest, darkest, tallest of all old frame houses, simple and familiar yet with something terrible about it, enclosing evil, like a house where a murder has been committed.

And my mother, just a little girl then named Addie Morrison, spindly I should think, with cropped hair because her mother guarded her against vanity, would walk home from school up the long anxious lane, banging against her legs the lard pail that had held her lunch. Wasn't it always November, the ground hard, ice splintered on the puddles, dead grass floating from the wires? Yes, and the bush near and spooky, with the curious unconnected winds that lift the branches one by one. She would go into the house and find the fire out, the stove cold, the grease from the men's dinner thickened on the plates and pans.

No sign of her father, or her brothers who were older and through with school. They did not linger around the house. She would go through the front room into her parents' bedroom and there, more often than not, she would find her mother on her knees, bent down on the bed, praying. Far more clearly than her mother's face she could picture now that bent back, narrow shouldered in some gray or tan sweater over a dirty kimono or housedress, the back of the head with the thin hair pulled tight from the middle parting, the scalp unhealthily white. It was white as marble, white as soap.

'She was a religious fanatic,' says my mother of this kneeling woman, who at other times is discovered flat on her back and weeping – for reasons my mother does not go into – with a damp cloth pressed to her forehead. Once in the last demented stages of Christianity she wandered down to the barn and tried to hide a little bull calf in the hay, when the butcher's men were coming. My mother's voice, telling these things, is hard with her certainty of having been cheated, her undiminished feelings of anger and loss.

'Do you know what she did? I told you what she did? I told you about the money?' She draws a breath to steady herself. 'Yes. Well. She inherited some money. Some of her people had money, they lived in New York State. She came into two hundred and fifty dollars, not a lot of money, but more then than now and you know we were poor. You think this is poor. This is *nothing* to how we were poor. The oilcloth on our table, I remember it, it was worn through so you could see the bare boards. It was hanging in shreds. It was a rag, not an oilcloth. If I ever wore shoes I wore boys' shoes, hand-downs of my brothers. It was the kind of farm you couldn't raise chickweed on. For Christmas I got a pair of navy blue bloomers. And let me tell you, I was *glad*. I knew what it was to be cold.

'Well. My mother took her money and she ordered a great box of Bibles. They came by express. They were the most expensive kind, maps of the Holy Land and gilt-edged pages and the words of Christ were all marked in red. *Blessed are the poor in spirit*. What is so remarkable about being poor in spirit? She spent every cent.

'So then, we had to go out and give them away. She had bought them for distribution to the heathen. I think my brothers hid some in the granary. I know they did. But I was too much of a fool to think of that. I was tramping all over the country at the age of eight, in boys' shoes and not owning a pair of mittens, giving away Bibles.

'One thing, it cured me of religion for life.'

Once she ate cucumbers and drank milk because she had heard that this combination was poisonous and she wished to die. She was more curious than depressed. She lay down and hoped to wake in heaven, which she had heard so much about, but opened her eyes instead on another morning. That too had its effect on her faith. She told nobody at the time.

The older brother sometimes brought her candy, from town. He shaved at the kitchen table, a mirror propped against the lamp. He was vain, she thought, he had a moustache, and he got letters from girls which he never answered, but left lying around where anybody could read them. My mother appeared to hold this against him. 'I have no illusions about him,' she said, 'though I guess he was no different from most.' He lived in New Westminster now, and worked on a ferryboat. The other brother lived in the States. At Christmas they sent cards, and she sent cards to them. They never wrote letters, nor did she.

It was the younger brother she hated. What did he do? Her answers were not wholly satisfactory. He was evil, bloated, cruel. A cruel fat boy. He fed firecrackers to cats. He tied up a toad and chopped it to pieces. He drowned my mother's kitten, named Misty, in the cow trough, though he afterwards denied it Also he caught my mother and tied her up in the barn and tormented her. Tormented her? He *tortured* her.

What with? But my mother would never go beyond that – that word, *tortured*, which she spat out like blood. So I was left to imagine her tied up in the barn, as at a stake, while her brother, a fat Indian, yelped and pranced about her. But she had escaped, after all, unscalped, unburnt. Nothing really accounted for her darkened face at this point in the story, for her way of saying *tortured*. I had not yet learned to recognize the gloom that overcame her in the vicinity of sex.

Her mother died. She went away for an operation but she had large lumps in both breasts and she died, my mother always said, on the table. On the *operating* table. When I was younger I used to imagine her stretched out dead on an ordinary table among the teacups and ketchup and jam.

'Were you sad?' I said hopefully and my mother said yes, of course she was sad. But she did not linger round this scene. Important things were coming. Soon she was through school, she had passed her entrance exams and she wanted to go to high school, in town. But her father said no, she was to stay home and keep house until she got married. ('Who would I marry in God's name?' cried my mother angrily every time at this point in the story, 'out there at the end of the world with everybody cross-eyed from inbreeding?') After two years at home, miserable, learning some things on her own from old high-school textbooks that had belonged to her mother (a schoolteacher herself before marriage and religion overtook her), she defied her father, she walked a distance of nine miles to town, hiding in the bushes by the road every time she heard a horse coming, for fear it would be them, with the old wagon, come to take her back home.

She knocked on the door of a boarding house she knew from the egg business and asked if she could have her room and board in return for kitchen work and waiting on table. And the woman who ran the house took her in – she was a rough-talking, decent old woman that everybody called Grandma Seeley – and kept her from her father till time had passed, even gave her a plaid dress, scratchy wool, too long, which she wore to school that first morning when she stood up in front of a class all two years younger than she was and read Latin, pronouncing it just the way she had taught herself, at home. Naturally, they all laughed.

And my mother could not help, could never help, being thrilled and tender, recalling this; she was full of wonder at her old, young self. Oh, if there could be a moment out of time, a moment when we could choose to be judged, naked as can be, beleaguered, triumphant, then that would have to be the moment for her. Later on comes compromise and error, perhaps; there, she is absurd and unassailable.

Then, in the boarding house, begins a whole new chapter in life. Up in the morning dark to peel the vegetables, leave them in cold water for dinner at noon. Clean out the chamber pots, sprinkle them with talcum. No flush toilets in that town. 'I have cleaned chamber pots to get my education!' she would say, and not mind who was listening. But a nice class of people used them. Bank clerks. The CNR telegraph operator. The teacher, Miss Rush. Miss Rush taught my mother to sew, gave her some beautiful merino wool for a dress, gave her a yellow fringed scarf, ('What *became* of it?' asked my mother in exasperated grief), gave her some eau de cologne. My mother loved Miss Rush; she cleaned Miss Rush's room and saved the hair from her tray, cleanings from her comb, and when she had enough she made a little twist of hair which she looped from a string, to wear around her neck. That was how she loved her. Miss Rush taught her how to read music and play on Miss Rush's own piano, kept in Grandma Seeley's front room, those songs she could play yet, though she hardly ever did. 'Drink to Me Only with Thine Eyes' and 'The Harp that Once through Tara's Halls' and 'Bonny Mary of Argyle.'

What had happened to Miss Rush, then, with her beauty and her embroidery and her piano playing? She had married, rather late, and died having a baby. The baby died too and lay in her arm like a wax doll, in a long dress; my mother had seen it.

Stories of the past could go like this, round and round and down to death; I expected it.

Grandma Seeley, for instance, was found dead in bed one summer morning just after my mother had completed four years of high school and Grandma Seeley had promised to let her have the money to go to Normal School, a loan to be paid back when she became a teacher. There was somewhere a piece of paper with writing on it to this effect, but it was never found. Or rather, my mother believed, it was found, by Grandma Seeley's nephew and his wife, who got her house and her money; they must have destroyed it. The world is full of such people.

So my mother had to go to work; she worked in a large store in Owen Sound where she was soon in charge of dry goods and notions. She became engaged to a young man who remained a shadow – no clear-cut villain, certainly, like her brother, or Grandma Seeley's nephew, but not luminous and loved, either, not like Miss Rush. For mysterious reasons she was compelled to break her engagement. ('He did not turn out to be the sort of person I had thought he was.') Later, an indefinite time later, she met my father, who must have turned out to be the sort of person she thought he was, because she married him, though she had always sworn to herself she would never marry a farmer (he was a fox farmer, and at one time had thought he might get rich by it; was that any different?), and his family had already begun to make remarks to her that were not well-meant.

'But you fell in love with him,' I would remind her sternly, anxiously, wanting to get it settled for good. 'You fell in love.'

'Well yes of course I did.'

'Why did you fall in love?'

'Your father was always a gentleman.'

Was that all? I was troubled here by a lack of proportion, though it was hard to say what was missing, what was wrong. In the beginning of her story was dark captivity, suffering, then daring and defiance and escape. Struggle, disappointment, more struggle, godmothers and villains. Now I expected – as in all momentous satisfying stories – the burst of Glory, the Reward. Marriage to my father? I hoped this was it. I wished she would leave me in no doubt about it.

When I was younger, out at the end of the Flats Road, I would watch her walk across the yard to empty the dishwater, carrying the dishpan high, like a priestess, walking in an unhurried, stately way, and flinging the dishwater with a grand gesture over the fence. Then, I had supposed her powerful, a ruler, also content. She had power still, but not so much as perhaps she thought. And she was in no way content. Nor a priestess. She had a loudly growling stomach, whose messages she laughed at or ignored, but which embarrassed me unbearably. Her hair grew out in little wild gray-brown tufts and thickets; every permanent she got turned to frizz. Had all her stories, after all, to end up with just her, the way she was now, just my mother in Jubilee?

One day she came to the school, representing the encyclopedia company, to present a prize for the best essay on why we should buy Victory Bonds. She had to go to Porterfield, Blue River, Stirling schools and do the same thing; that week was a proud one for her. She wore a terrible mannish navy blue suit, with a single button at the waist, and a maroon-colored felt hat, her best, on which I agonizingly believed I could see a fine dust, She gave a little speech. I fixed my eyes on the sweater of the girl ahead of me – pale blue, little nubby bits of wool sticking out – as if hanging on to such indifferent straws of fact would keep me from drowning in humiliation. She was so different, that was all, so brisk and hopeful and guileless in her maroon hat, making little jokes, thinking herself a success. For two cents she would have launched into her own educational history, nine miles to town and the chamber pots. Who else had a mother like that? People gave me sly and gloating and pitying looks. Suddenly I could not bear anything about her – the tone of her voice, the reckless, hurrying way she moved, her lively absurd gestures (any minute now she might knock the ink bottle off the principal's desk), and most of all her innocence, her way of not knowing when people were laughing, of thinking she could get away with this.

I hated her selling encyclopedias and making speeches and wearing that hat. I hated her writing letters to the newspapers. Her letters about local problems or those in which she promoted education and the rights of women and opposed compulsory religious education in the school, would be published in the Jubilee *Herald-Advance* over her own name. Others appeared on a page in the city paper given over to lady correspondents, and for them she used the nom de plume *Princess Ida*, taken from a character in Tennyson whom she admired. They were full of long decorative descriptions of the countryside from which she had fled (*This morning a marvelous silver frost enraptures the eye on every twig and telephone wire and makes the world a veritable fairyland –*) and even contained references to Owen and me (*my daughter, soon-to-be-no-longer-a-child, forgets her new-found dignity to frolic in the snow*) that made the roots of my teeth ache with shame. Other people than Aunt Elspeth and Auntie Grace would say to me, 'I seen that letter of your mother's in the paper' and I would feel how contemptuous, how superior and silent and enviable they were, those people who all their lives could stay still, with no need to do or say anything remarkable.

I myself was not so different from my mother, but concealed it, knowing what dangers there were.

That second winter we lived in Jubilee we had visitors. It was a Saturday afternoon and I was shoveling our sidewalk. I saw a big car come nosing along between the snowbanks almost silently, like an impudent fish. American license plates. I thought it was somebody lost. People did drive out to the end of River Street – which nowhere bothered to have a sign warning that it was a dead end – and by the time they reached our house would have begun to wonder.

A stranger got out. He wore an overcoat, gray felt hat, silk scarf in winter. He was tall and heavy; his face was mournful, proud, sagging. He held out his arms to me alarmingly.

'Come on out here and say hello to me! I know your name but I bet you don't know mine!'

He came right up to me – standing stock-still with the shovel in my hand – and kissed me on the cheek. A sweetish-sour masculine smell; shaving lotion, uneasy stomach, clean starched shirt, and some secret hairy foulness. 'Was your momma's name Addie Morrison? Was it, eh?'

No one ever called my mother Addie any more. It made her sound different – rounder, dowdier, simpler.

'Your momma's Addie and you're Della and I'm your Uncle Bill Morrison. That's who I am. Hey, I gave you a kiss and you never gave me one. Is that what you call fair up here?'

By this time my mother with a fresh, haphazard streak of lipstick on her mouth was coming out of the house.

'Well, Bill. You don't believe in advance notice, do you? Never mind, we're happy to see you.' She said this with some severity, as if arguing a point.

It really was her brother then, the American, my blood uncle.

He turned and waved at the car. 'You can get out now. Nothing here going to bite you.'

The door opened on the other side of the car and a tall

lady got out, slowly, with difficulty over her hat. This hat went high on one side of the head and low on the other; green feathers sticking up made it even higher. She wore a three-quarter-length silver fox coat and a green dress and green high-heeled shoes, no rubbers.

'That's your Aunt Nile,' said Uncle Bill to me as if she couldn't hear, or understand English, as if she was some awesome feature of the landscape, that needed identifying. 'You never have seen her before. You have seen me but you were too young to remember. You never have seen her. I never saw her myself before last summer. I was married to your Aunt Callie when I saw you before and now I'm married to your Aunt Nile. I met her in August, I married her in September.'

The sidewalk was not shoveled clear. Aunt Nile stumbled in her high heels and moaned, feeling snow in her shoe. She moaned miserably like a child, she said to Uncle Bill, 'I nearly twisted my ankle,' as if there was nobody else around.

'Not far to go,' he said encouragingly, and took her arm, and supported her the rest of the way up the sidewalk and up the steps and across the veranda as if she was a Chinese lady (I had just been reading *The Good Earth*, from the town library) for whom walking is a rare and unnatural activity. My mother and I, who had exchanged no greetings with Nile, followed, and in the dark hall mother said, 'Well now, welcome!' and Uncle Bill helped Nile off with her coat and said to me, 'Here now, you take this and hang it up. Hang it up someplace by itself. Don't hang it up next to any barn jackets!' Touching the fur, my mother said to Nile, 'You ought to go out to our farm, you could see some of these on the hoof.' Her tone was jocose and unnatural.

'She means foxes,' Uncle Bill told Nile. 'Like your coat is made from.' He said to us, 'I don't think she even knew that fur come off a creature's back. She thought they manufactured them right in the store!' Nile meanwhile looked amazed and unhappy as someone who had never even heard of foreign countries, and who is suddenly whisked away and deposited in one, with everybody around speaking an undreamt-of language. Adaptability could not be one of her strong points. Why should it be? It would put in question her own perfection. She was perfect, and younger than I had thought at first, maybe only twenty-two or -three. Her skin was without a mark, like a pink teacup; her mouth could have been cut out of burgundy-colored velvet, and pasted on. Her smell was inhumanly sweet and her fingernails – I saw this with shock, delight, and some slight misgiving, as if she might have gone too far – were painted *green*, to match her clothes.

'It's a very handsome coat,' said my mother, with more dignity.

Uncle Bill looked at her regretfully. 'Your husband'll never make any money this end of the business, Addie, it's all controlled by Jews. Now, have you got such a thing as a cup of coffee in the house? Get me and my little wife warmed up?'

The trouble was, we didn't have such a thing. My mother and Fern Dogherty drank tea, which was cheaper, and Postum in the mornings. My mother led everybody into the dining room and Nile sat down and my mother said, 'Wouldn't you like a hot cup of tea? I am absolutely out of coffee.'

Uncle Bill took this in stride. No tea, he said, but if she was out of coffee he would get some coffee. 'Have you got any grocery stores in this town?' he said to me. 'You must have one or two grocery stores in this town. Big town like this, it's got street lights even, I saw them. You and me'll get in the car and go and buy some groceries, leave these two sister-in-laws to get acquainted.'

I floated beside him, in this big cream-and-chocolate, clean-smelling car, down River Street, down Mason Street, down the main street of Jubilee. We parked in front of the Red Front Grocery behind a team and sleigh.

'This a grocery store?'

I did not commit myself. Suppose I said it was, and then it had none of the things he wanted?

'Your momma shop here?'

'Sometimes.'

'Then I guess it has to be good enough for us.'

From that car I saw the team and sleigh, with sacks of feed on it, and the Red Front Grocery, and the whole street, differently. Jubilee seemed not unique and permanent as I had thought, but almost makeshift, and shabby; it would barely do.

The store had just been turned into a self-serve, the first in town. The aisles were too narrow for carts but there were baskets you carried over your arm. Uncle Bill wanted a cart. He asked if there were any other stores in town where carts were available, and was told there were none. When this was settled he went up and down the aisles calling out the names of things. He behaved as if nobody else was in the store at all, as if they only came to life when he called to ask them something, as if the store itself was not real but had been thrown together the moment he said he needed one.

He bought coffee and canned fruit and vegetables and cheese and dates and figs and pudding mixes and macaroni dinners and hot-chocolate powders and tinned oysters and sardines. 'Do you like this?' he kept saying. 'Do you like these here? You like raisins? You like cornflakes? You like ice cream? Where do they keep the ice cream? What flavor do you like? Chocolate? You like chocolate the best?' Finally I was afraid to look at anything, or he would buy it.

He stopped in front of the Selrite window where there were bins of bulk candy. 'You like candy, I bet. What do you want? Licorice? Fruit jellies? Candy peanuts? Let's get a mixture, let's get all three. That going to make you thirsty, all those candy peanuts? We better find some pop.'

That was not all. 'Have you got a bakeshop in this town?' he said, and I took him to McArter's Bakery where he bought two dozen butter tarts and two dozen buns with glazed sugar and nuts on top, and a coconut cake half a foot high. This was exactly like a childish story I had at home in which a little girl manages to get her wishes granted, one a day for a week and they all turn out, of course, to make her miserable. One wish was to have everything she had ever wanted to eat. I used to get that out and read the description of the food over again for pure pleasure, ignoring the punishments which soon followed, inflicted by supernatural powers always on the lookout for greed. But I saw now that too much really might be too much. Even Owen might in the end have been depressed by this idiot largesse, which threw the whole known system of rewards and delights out of kilter.

'You're like a fairy godfather,' I said to Uncle Bill. I meant this to sound unchildish, slightly ironic; also in this exaggerated way I meant to express the gratitude I was afraid I did not sufficiently feel. But he took it as the simplest childishness, repeating it to my mother when we got home.

'She says I'm a fairy godfather, but I had to pay cash!'

'Well I don't know what I'm supposed to do with all this, Bill. You'll have to take some home.'

'We never drove up here from Ohio to buy our groceries. You put them away. We don't need them. As long as I got my chocolate ice cream for dessert I don't care what else I've got or haven't got. My sweet tooth has never gone sour on me. But I lost some weight, you know. I lost thirty pounds since last summer.'

'You are not a case for war relief yet.'

My mother removed the tablecloth with its day-old tea and ketchup stains, and spread a fresh one, the one she called the Madeira cloth, her wedding-present best.

'You know I was a runt at one time. I was a skinny baby. When I was two years old I nearly died of pneumonia. Momma pulled me through and she started feeding me. I never got any exercise for a long time and I got fat.

'Momma,' he said with a gloomy kind of luxuriance. 'Wasn't she some sort of a saint on earth? I tell Nile she ought to have known her.'

My mother gave Nile a startled look (had these two sisters-in-law been getting acquainted?) but did not say whether she thought this would have been a good idea.

I said to Nile, 'Do you want a plate with birds on it or the one with flowers?' I just wanted to make her speak.

'I don't care,' she said faintly, looking down at her green nails as if they were talismans to keep her in this place.

My mother cared. 'Put plates on the table that match, we're not so impoverished that we don't own a set of dishes!'

'Do you wear Nile green because your name is Nile?' I said, still prodding. 'Is that color Nile green?' I thought she was an idiot, and yet I frantically admired her, was grateful for every little colorless pebble of a word she dropped. She reached some extreme of feminine decorativeness, perfect artificiality, that I had not even known existed; seeing her, I understood that I would never be beautiful.

'It's just a coincidence my name is Nile.' (She might even have said cocinidence.) 'It was my favorite color long before I even heard there was a color Nile green.'

'I didn't know you could get green nail polish.'

'You have to order it in.'

'Momma hoped we would stay on the farm the way we were raised,' said Uncle Bill, following his own thoughts.

'I wouldn't wish it on anybody to live on a farm like that. You couldn't raise chickweed on it.'

'The financial aspect isn't always the only thing, Addie. There's the being closer to Nature. Without all this – you know, running around, doing what isn't good for you, living high. Forgetting about Christianity. Momma felt it was a good life.'

'What is so good about Nature? Nature is just one thing preying on another all the way down the line. Nature is just a lot of waste and cruelty, maybe not from Nature's point of view but from a human point of view. Cruelty is the law of Nature.'

'Well I don't mean like that, Addie. I don't mean wild animals and all like that. I mean like our life we had at home, where we didn't have too many of the comforts, I'll grant you that, but we had a simple life and hard work and fresh air and a good spiritual example in our momma. She died young, Addie. She died in pain.'

'Under anesthetic,' my mother said. 'So strictly speaking I hope she did not die in pain.'

During supper she told Uncle Bill about her encyclopedia selling.

'I sold three sets last fall,' was what she said, though actually she had sold one and was still working on two fairly promising cases. 'There is money in the country now, you know. It is due to the war.'

'You won't make no money peddling to farmers,' said Uncle Bill, hanging low over his plate and eating steadily, as old people do. He looked old. 'What did you say you're selling?'

'Encyclopedias. Books. They are a very fine set. I would have given my right arm to have had a set of books like these around the house when I was a child.' This was perhaps the fiftieth time I had heard her make that statement.

'You got your education. I did without. That didn't stop me. You won't sell books to farmers. They got too much sense. They are tight with their money. Money is not in things like that. It is in property. Money is in property and investments if you know what you are doing.' He began a long story, with complicated backtracking and correcting himself on details, about buying and selling houses. Buying, selling, buying, building, rumors, threats, perils, safety. Nile did not listen at all but pushed the canned corn around on her plate, spearing the kernels one at a time with her fork – a childish game not even Owen could have got away with. Owen himself said not one word but ate with his gum on his thumbnail; my mother had not noticed. Fern Dogherty was not there; she had gone to see her mother in the County Hospital. My mother listened to her brother with a look that was a mixture of disapproval and participatory cunning.

Her brother! This was the thing, the indigestible fact. This Uncle Bill was my mother's brother, the terrible fat boy, so gifted in cruelty, so cunning, quick, fiendish, so much to be feared. I kept looking at him, trying to pull that boy out of the yellowish man. But I could not find him there. He was gone, smothered, like a little spotted snake, once venomous and sportive, buried in a bag of meal.

'Remember the caterpillars, how they used to get on the milkweed?'

'Caterpillars?' said my mother disbelievingly. She got up and brought a little brass-handled brush and pan, also a wedding present. She began to sweep the crumbs from the cloth.

'They come on the milkweed in the fall. They're after the milk, you know – the juice in it. They drink it all up and get fat and sleepy and go into their cocoon. Well, she found one was on the milkweed and she brought it into the house –'

'Who did?'

'*Momma* did, Addie. Who else would take the trouble? It was away before your time. She found this one and brought it in and she set it up above the door where I couldn't get at it. I wouldn't have meant any harm but I was like boys are. It went into its cocoon and it stayed in all winter. I forgot about it was there. Then we were all sitting after our dinner on Easter Sunday – Easter Sunday but it was a blizzard out – and Momma says, "Look!" *Look*, she says, so we looked and up above the door was that thing beginning to stir. Just thinning out the cocoon, just pulling and working it from the inside, getting tired and letting up and going to work again. It took it half an hour, forty minutes maybe, and we never quit watching. Then we saw the butterfly come out. It was like the cocoon just finally weakened, fell off like an old rag. It was a yellow butterfly, little spotty thing. Its wings all waxed down. It had to work some to get them loosed up. Works away on one, works away, flutters it up. Works away on the other. Gets that up, takes a little fly. Momma says, "Look at that. Never forget. That's what you saw on Easter." Never forget. I never did, either.'

'What became of it?' said my mother neutrally.

'I don't remember that. Wouldn't last long, weather like it was. It was a funny thing to see, though – works away on one wing, works away on the other. Takes a little fly. First time it ever used its wings.' He laughed, with a note of apology, the first and last we were to hear from him. But then he appeared tired, vaguely disappointed, and folded his hands over his stomach from which came dignified, necessary digestive noises.

That was in the same house. The same house where my

mother used to find the fire out and her mother at prayer and where she took milk and cucumbers in the hope of getting to heaven.

Uncle Bill and Nile stayed all night, sleeping on the front-room couch which could be pulled out and made into a bed. Those long, perfumed, enameled limbs of Nile's lay down so close to my uncle's dragging flesh, his smell. I did not imagine anything more they might have to do, because I thought the itchy hot play of sex belonged to childhood, and was outgrown by decent adults, who made their unlikely connection only for the purpose of creating a child.

Sunday morning, as soon as they had eaten breakfast, they went away, and we never saw either of them again.

Some days later my mother burst out to me, 'Your Uncle Bill is a dying man.'

It was nearly suppertime; she was cooking sausages. Fern was not home from work yet. Owen had just come in from hockey practice and was dumping his skates and stick in the back hall. My mother cooked sausages until they were hard and shiny and very dark on the outside; I had never eaten them any other way.

'He is a dying man. He was sitting here Sunday morning when I came down to put the kettle on and he told me. He has a cancer.'

She continued rolling the sausages around with a fork and she had the crossword puzzle from the newspaper torn out, half done, on the counter beside the stove. I thought of Uncle Bill going downtown and buying butter tarts and chocolate ice cream and cake, and coming home and eating. How could he do it?

'He always had a big appetite,' said my mother, as if her thoughts ran along the same lines, 'and the prospect of death doesn't seem to have diminished it. Who knows? Maybe with less eating he would have lived to be old.'

'Does Nile know?'

'What does it matter what she knows. She only married him for a meal ticket. She'll be well off.'

'Do you still hate him?'

'Of course I don't hate him,' said my mother quickly and with reserve. I looked at the chair where he had sat. I had a fear of contamination, not of cancer but of death itself.

'He told me he had left me three hundred dollars in his will.'

After that, what was there to do but get down to realities?

'What are you going to spend it on?'

'No doubt something will occur to me when the time comes.'

The front door opened, Fern coming in.

'I could always send away for a box of Bibles.'

Just before Fern came in one door and Owen came in the other, there was something in the room like the downflash of a wing or knife, a sense of hurt so strong, but quick and isolated, vanishing.

'There is an Egyptian god with four letters,' said my mother, frowning at the crossword, 'that I know I know, and I cannot think of it to save my soul.'

'Isis.'

'Isis is a goddess, I'm surprised at *you*.'

Soon after this the snow began to melt; the Wawanash River overflowed its banks, and carried away road signs and fence posts and henhouses, and receded; the roads became more or less navigable, and my mother was out again in the afternoons. One of my father's aunts – it never matters which – said, 'Now she will miss her writing to the newspapers.'

AGE OF FAITH

When we lived in that house at the end of the Flats Road, and before my mother knew how to drive a car, she and I used to walk to town; town being Jubilee, a mile away. While she locked the door I had to run to the gate and look up and down the road and make sure there was nobody coming. Who could there ever be, on that road, besides the mailman and Uncle Benny? When I shook my head no she would hide the key under the second post of the veranda, where the wood had rotted and made a little hole. She believed in burglars.

Turning our backs on the Grenoch Swamp, the Wawanash River, and some faraway hills, both bare and wooded, which though not ignorant of the facts of geography I did sometimes believe to be the end of the world, we followed the Flats Road which was not much more, at this end, than two wheel tracks, with a vigorous growth of plantain and chickweed down the middle. My mind would be on burglars. I saw them black and white, with melancholy dedicated faces, professional clothes. I imagined them waiting somewhere not too far away, say in those ferny boggy fields along the edge of the swamp, waiting and holding in their minds the most exact knowledge of our house and everything in it. They knew about the cups with butterfly handles, painted gold; my coral necklace which I thought ugly and scratchy but had been taught to consider valuable, since it had been sent from Australia by my father's Aunt Helen on her trip around the world; a silver bracelet bought by my father for my mother before they were married; a black bowl with Japanese figures painted on it, very peaceful to look at, a wedding present; and my mother's greenish white Laocoön inkwell awarded for highest marks and general proficiency when she graduated from high school – the serpent so cunningly draped around the three male figures that I could never discover whether there were or were not marble genitals underneath. Burglars coveted these things, I understood, but would not move unless we gave them cause, by our carelessness. Their knowledge, their covetousness, made each thing seem confirmed in its value and uniqueness. Our world was steadfastly reflected in burglar minds.

Later on of course I began to doubt the existence of burglars or at least to doubt that they could operate in this manner. Much more likely, I saw, that their methods were haphazard and their knowledge hazy, their covetousness unfocused, their relationship to us next thing to accidental.

I could go more easily up the river to the swamp when my belief in them had faded, but I missed them, I missed the thought of them, for quite a while.

I had never had a picture of God so clear and uncomplicated as my picture of the burglars. My mother was not so ready to refer to Him. We belonged – at least my father and my father's family belonged – to the United Church in Jubilee, and my brother Owen and I had both been baptized there when we were babies, which showed a surprising weakness or generosity on my mother's part; perhaps childbirth mellowed and confused her.

The United Church was the most modern, the largest, the most prosperous church in Jubilee. It had taken in all the former Methodists and Congregationalists and a good chunk of Presbyterians (that was what my father's family had been) at the time of Church Union. There were four other churches in town but they were all small, all relatively poor, and all, by United Church standards, went to extremes. The Catholic church was the most extreme. White and wooden, with a plain mission cross, it stood on a hill at the north end of town and dispensed peculiar services to Catholics, who seemed bizarre and secretive as Hindus, with their idols and confessions and black spots on Ash Wednesday. At school the Catholics were a small but unintimidated tribe, mostly Irish, who did not stay in the classroom for Religious Education but were allowed to go down to the basement, where they banged on the pipes. It was hard to connect their simple rowdiness with their exotic dangerous faith. My father's aunts, my great-aunts, lived across from the Catholic church and used to make jokes about 'nipping in for a bit of a confession' but they knew, they could tell you, all there was beyond jokes, babies' skeletons, and strangled nuns under the convent floors, yes, fat priests and fancy women and the black old popes. It was all true, they had books about it. All true. Like the Irish at school, the church building seemed inadequate; too bare and plain and straightforward-looking to be connected with such voluptuousness and scandal.

The Baptists were extreme as well, but in a completely unsinister, slightly comic way. No person of any importance or social standing went to the Baptist Church, and so somebody like Pork Childs, who delivered coal and collected garbage for the town, could get to be a leading figure, an elder, in it. Baptists could not dance or go to movies; Baptist ladies could not wear lipstick. But their hymns were loud, rollicking, and optimistic, and in spite of the austerity of their lives their religion had more vulgar cheerfulness about it than anybody else's. Their church was not far from the house we later rented on River Street; it was modest, but modern and hideous, being built of gray cement blocks, with pebbled glass windows.

As for the Presbyterians, they were leftovers, people who had refused to become United. They were mostly elderly, and campaigned against hockey practice on Sundays, and sang psalms.

The fourth church was the Anglican, and nobody knew or spoke much about it. It did not have, in Jubilee, any of the prestige or money which attached to it in towns where there was a remnant of the old Family Compact, or some sort of military or social establishment to keep it going. The people who settled Wawanash County and built up Jubilee were Scotch Presbyterians, Congregationalists,

Methodists from the north of England. To be Anglican was therefore not fashionable as it was in some places, and it was not so interesting as being Catholic or Baptist, not even proof of stubborn conviction like being Presbyterian. However the church had a bell, the only church bell in town, and that seemed to me a lovely thing for a church to have.

In the United Church the pews, of glossy golden oak, were placed in a democratic fan-shaped sort of arrangement, with the pulpit and choir at the heart of the fan. There was no altar, only a powerful display of organ pipes. The stained-glass windows showed Christ performing useful miracles (though not the water into wine) or else they illustrated parables. On Communion Sunday the wine went round on trays, in little, thick, glass cups; it was like everybody having refreshments. And it was not even wine, but grape juice. This was the church the Legion attended, uniformed, on a certain Sunday; also the Lions Club, carrying their purple-tasseled hats. Doctors, lawyers, merchants passed the plate.

My parents went to church seldom. My father in his unaccustomed suit seemed deferential but self-contained. During the prayer he would put his elbow on his knee, rest his forehead on his hand, close his eyes, with an air of courtesy and forebearance. My mother, on the other hand, never closed her eyes a minute and barely inclined her head. She would sit looking all around, cautious but unabashed, like an anthropologist taking note of the behavior of a primitive tribe. She listened to the sermon bolt upright, bright-eyed, skeptically chewing at her lipstick; I was afraid that at any moment she might jump up and challenge something. The hymns she ostentatiously did not sing.

After we rented the house in town we had a boarder, Fern Dogherty, who sang in the United Church choir. I would go to church with her and sit by myself, the only member of our family present. My father's aunts lived at the other end of town and did not take this long walk often; the service was broadcast, anyway, over the Jubilee radio station.

Why did I do this? At first, it was probably to bother my mother, though she made no outright objection to it, and to make myself interesting. I could imagine people looking at me, saying afterwards, 'Do you see that little Jordan girl there, all by herself, Sunday after Sunday?' I hoped that people would be intrigued and touched by my devoutness and persistence, knowing my mother's beliefs or nonbeliefs, as they did. Sometimes I thought of the population of Jubilee as nothing but a large audience, for me; and so in a way it was; for every person who lived there, the rest of the town was an audience.

But the second winter we lived in town – the winter I was twelve years old – my reasons had changed, or solidified. I wanted to settle the question of God. I had been reading books about the Middle Ages; I was attracted more and more to the idea of faith. God had always been a possibility for me; now I was prey to a positive longing for Him. He was a necessity. But I wanted reassurance, proof that He actually was there. That was what I came to church for, but could not mention to anybody.

On wet windy Sundays, snowy Sundays, sore-throat Sundays, I came and sat in the United Church full of this unspeakable hope; that God would display Himself, to me at least, like a dome of light, a bubble radiant and indisputable above the modern pews; that He would flower suddenly as a bank of day lilies below the organ pipes. I felt I must rigidly contain this hope; to reveal it, in fervor of tone or word or gesture, would have been inappropriate as farting. What was chiefly noticeable in people's faces during the earlier, more God-directed parts of the service (the sermon tended to take off into topical areas) was a kind of cohesive tact, the very thing my mother offended against, with that cross inquiring look, as if she was going to pull up shortly and demand that everything make sense.

The question of whether God existed or not never came up in Church. It was only a matter of what He approved of, or usually of what He did not approve of. After the benediction there would be a stir, a comfortable release in the church as if everybody had yawned, though of course no one had, and people rose and greeted each other in a pleased, relieved, congratulatory way. I felt at such times itchy, hot, heavy, despondent.

I did not think of taking my problem to any believer, even to Mr McLaughlin the minister. It would have been unthinkably embarrassing. Also, I was afraid. I was afraid the believer might falter in defending his beliefs, or defining them, and this would be a setback for me. If Mr McLaughlin, for instance, turned out to have no firmer a grasp on God than I did, it would be a huge though not absolute discouragement. I preferred to believe his grasp was good, and not try it out.

However I did think of taking it to another church, to the Anglican church. It was because of the bell, and because I was curious to see what another church was like inside

and how they went about things, and the Anglican was the
only one it was possible to try. I did not tell anybody what
I was doing, naturally, but walked with Fern Dogherty to
the steps of the United Church, where we parted, she to
go round to the vestry to get into her choir gown. When
she was out of sight I turned and doubled back across
town, and came to the Anglican church, in answer to the
invitation of that bell. I hoped nobody saw me. I went in.

There was a storm porch set up outside the main door,
to keep the wind out. Then a little cold entry with a strip
of brown matting, hymn books piled on the window-
ledge. I entered the church itself.

They had no furnace, evidently, just a space heater by
the door, making its steady domestic noise. A strip of the
same brown matting went across the back and up the aisle;
otherwise there was just the wooden floor, not varnished
or painted, rather wide boards occasionally springy
underfoot. Seven or eight pews on either side, no more. A
couple of choir benches at right angles to the pews, a pump
organ at one side and the pulpit – I didn't know at first that
was what it was – stuck up like a hen roost at the other
side. Beyond that a railing, a step up, a tiny chancel. The
floor of the chancel had an old parlor carpet. Then there
was a table, with a pair of silver candlesticks, a baize-lined
collection plate, and a cross which looked as if it might be
cardboard covered with silver paper, like a stage crown.
Above the table was a reproduction of the Holman Hunt
painting of Christ knocking at the door. I had not seen this
picture before. The Christ in it differed in some small but
important way from the Christ performing miracles in the
United Church window. He looked more regal and more

tragic, and the background against which he appeared was gloomier and richer, more pagan somehow, or at least Mediterranean. I was used to seeing him limp and shepherdly in Sunday-school pastels.

Altogether there were about a dozen people in the church. There was Dutch Monk, the butcher, and his wife and his daughter Gloria, who was in Grade Five at school. She and I were the only people under the age of forty. There were some old women.

I was barely in time. The bell had stopped ringing and the organ began to play a hymn, and the minister entered from the side door which must have led to the vestry, at the head of the choir, which was three ladies and two men. He was a round-headed, cheerful-looking young man I had never seen before. I knew that the Anglican Church could not afford a minister all its own and shared one with Porterfield and Blue River; he must have lived in one of those places. He had snowboots on under his robes.

He had an English accent. *Dearly beloved brethren, the scripture moveth us in sundry places to acknowledge and confess our manifold sins and wickedness. . . .*

There was a board in front of each bench, to kneel on. Everybody slid forward, rustling open prayer books, and when the minister finished his part, everybody else began saying something back. I looked through the prayer book I had found on the shelf in front of me but I could not find the place, so I gave up and listened to what they were saying. Across the aisle from us, and one pew ahead, was a tall, bony old lady in a black-velvet turban. She had not opened her prayer book, she did not need it. Kneeling erectly, lifting her chalky wolfish profile skyward – it reminded me of the profile of a Crusader's effigy, in the encyclopedia at home – she led all the other voices in the congregation, indeed dominated them so that they were no more than a fuzzy edge of hers, which was loud, damp, melodic, mournfully exultant.

> . . . *left undone those things which we ought to have done, And we have done those things which we ought not to have done; And there is no health in us. But thou, O Lord, have mercy upon us, miserable offenders. Spare thou them, O God, which confess their faults. Restore thou them that are penitent; According to thy promises declared unto mankind in Christ Jesu our Lord.* . . .

And further along this line, and the minister took it up in his fine, harmonizing, though perhaps more restrained, English voice, and this dialogue continued, steadily paced, rising and falling, always with confidence, with lively emotion safely contained in the most elegant channels of language, and coming together, finally, in perfect quiet and reconciliation.

> Lord, have mercy upon us.
> *Christ, have mercy upon us.*
> Lord, have mercy upon us.

So here was what I had not known, but must always have suspected, existed, what all those Methodists and Congregationalists and Presbyterians had fearfully abolished – the theatrical in religion. From the very first

I was strongly delighted. Many things pleased me – the kneeling down on the hard board, getting up and kneeling down again and bobbing the head at the altar at the mention of Jesus' name, the recitation of the Creed which I loved for its litany of strange splendid things in which to believe. I liked the idea of calling Jesus *Jesu* sometimes; it made Him sound more kingly and magical, like a wizard or an Indian god; I liked the IHS on the pulpit banner, rich, ancient, threadbare design. The poverty, smallness, shabbiness, and bareness of the church pleased me, that smell of mold or mice, frail singing of the choir, isolation of the worshippers. *If they are here,* I felt, *then it is probably all true.* Ritual which in other circumstances might have seemed wholly artificial, lifeless, had here a kind of last-ditch dignity. The richness of the words against the poverty of the place. If I could not quite get a scent of God then at least I could get the scent of His old times of power, real power, not what He enjoyed in the United Church today; I could remember His dim fabled hierarchy, His lovely moldered calendar of feasts and saints. There they were in the prayer book, I opened on them by accident – saints' days. Did anybody keep them? Saints' days made me think of something so different from Jubilee – open mows and half-timbered farmhouses and the Angelus and candles, a procession of nuns in the snow, cloister walks, all quiet, a world of tapestry, secure in faith. Safety. If God could be discovered, or recalled, everything would be safe. Then you would see things that I saw – just the dull grain of wood in the floor boards, the windows of plain glass filled with thin branches and snowy sky – and the strange, anxious pain that just seeing things could create would be gone. It seemed plain to me that this was the only way the world could be borne, *the only way it could be borne* – if all those atoms, galaxies of atoms, were safe all the time, whirling away in God's mind. How could people rest, how could they even go on breathing and existing, until they were sure of this? They did go on, so they must be sure.

How about my mother? Being my mother, she did not quite count. But even she, when cornered, would say yes, oh yes, there must be something – some *design*. But it was no use wasting time thinking about it, she warned, because we could never understand it anyway; there was quite enough to think about if we started trying to improve life in the here and now for a change; when we were dead we would find out about the rest of it, if there was any rest of it.

Not even she was prepared to say *Nothing*, and see herself and every stick and stone and feather in the world floating loose on that howling hopeless dark. No.

The idea of God did not connect for me with any idea of being good, which is perhaps odd, considering all about sins and wickedness that I did listen to. I believed in being saved by faith alone, by some great grab of the soul. But did I really, *did I really want it to happen to me*? Yes and no. I wanted it to happen, but I saw it would have to be a secret. How could I go on living with my mother and father and Fern Dogherty and my friend Naomi and everybody else in Jubilee otherwise?

The minister spoke to me at the door in a breezy way.

'Nice to see the good-looking young ladies out this nippy morning.'

I shook his hand with difficulty. I had a stolen prayer book under my coat, held in place by my crooked arm.

'Couldn't see where you were in church,' Fern said. The Anglican service was shorter than ours, economizing on sermon, so I had had time to get back to the United Church steps to meet her when she came out.

'I was behind a post.'

My mother wanted to know what the sermon had been about.

'Peace,' said Fern. 'And the United Nations. Et cetera, et cetera.'

'Peace,' said my mother enjoyably. 'Well, is he for it or against it?'

'He's all in favor of the United Nations.'

'I guess God is too then. What a relief. Only a short time ago He and Mr McLaughlin were all for the war. They are a changeable pair.'

Next week when I was with my mother in the Walker store the tall old lady in the black turban walked by, and spoke to her, and I was afraid she would say she had seen me in the Anglican Church, but she did not.

My mother said to Fern Dogherty, 'I saw old Mrs Sherriff in the Walker store today. She still has the same hat. It makes me think of an English bobby's.'

'She comes in the post office all the time and creates a scene if her paper isn't there by three o'clock,' Fern said. 'She's a tartar.'

Then from a conversation between Fern and my mother during which my mother tried unsuccessfully to send me out of the room – she would do this as a kind of formality, I think, for once she had told me to go she did not bother much about whether I went – I learned that Mrs Sherriff had had bizarre troubles in her family which either resulted from, or had resulted in, a certain amount of eccentricity and craziness in herself. Her oldest son had died of drink, her second son was in and out of the asylum (this was what the mental hospital was always called, in Jubilee), and her daughter had committed suicide, drowning herself in fact, in the Wawanash River. Her husband? He owned a dry-goods store and was a pillar of the community, said my mother dryly. Maybe he had syphilis, suggested Fern, and passed it on, it attacks the brains in the second generation, they were all hypocrites, those old boys with the stiff collars. My mother said that Mrs Sherriff for many years wore her dead daughter's clothes, around the house and to do the gardening in, until she got them worn out.

Another story: once the Red Front Grocery had forgotten to put a pound of butter in her order, and she had come after the grocery boy with a hatchet.

Christ, have mercy upon us.

Also that week I did a vulgar thing. I asked God to prove himself by answering a prayer. The prayer had to do with something called 'Household Science,' which we had at school once a week, on Thursday afternoons. In Household Science we learned to knit and crochet and embroider and run a sewing machine, and everything we did was more impossible than the last thing; my hands would be slimy with sweat and the Household Science room itself with its three ancient sewing machines and its cutting tables and battered dummies looked to me like an arena of torture. And so it was. Mrs Forbes the teacher was a fat little woman with the painted face of a celluloid doll and with most girls she was jolly. But my stupidity, my stubby blundering hands crumpling up the grimy handkerchief I was supposed to be hemming, or the miserable crocheting, put her into a dancing rage.

'Look at the filthy work, filthy work! I've heard about you, you think you're so clever with your memory work (I was famous for memorizing poems fast) and here you take stitches any six-year-old would be ashamed of!'

Now she had me trying to learn to thread the sewing machine. And I could not learn. We were making aprons, with appliquéd tulips. Some girls were already finishing the tulips or doing the hem and I had not even sewn the waistband on yet, because I could not get the sewing machine threaded, and Mrs Forbes said she was not going to show me again. It did not do any good when she showed me anyhow; her quick hands in front of me astonished and blinded and paralyzed me, with their close flashes of contempt.

So I prayed: please let me not have to thread the sewing machine on Thursday afternoon. I said this over several times in my head, quickly, seriously, unemotionally, as if trying out a spell. I did not use any special pleading or bargaining. I did not ask for anything extraordinary, like a fire in the Household Science room or Mrs Forbes slipping on the street and breaking a leg; nothing but a little unspecific intervention.

Nothing happened. She had not forgotten about me. At the beginning of the class I was sent to the machine. I sat there trying to figure out where to put the thread – I did not have any hope of putting it in the right place but had to put it some place, to show her I was trying – and she came and stood behind me, breathing disgustedly; as usual my legs began to shake, and shook so badly I moved the pedal and the machine began to run, weakly, with no thread in it.

'All right, Del,' said Mrs Forbes. I was surprised at her voice, which was not kind, certainly, but not angry, only worn out.

'I said all right. You can get up.'

She picked up the pieces of the apron that I had desperately basted together, crumpled them up, and threw them in the wastebasket.

'You cannot learn to sew,' she said, 'any more than a person who is tone deaf can learn to sing. I have tried and I am beaten. Come with me.'

She handed me a broom. 'If you know how to sweep I want you to sweep this room and throw the scraps in the wastebasket, and be responsible for keeping the floor clean, and when you are not doing that you can sit at the table back here and – memorize poetry, for all I care.'

I was weak with relief and joy, in spite of public shame, which I was used to. I swept the floor conscientiously and then got my library book about Mary Queen of Scots and read, disgraced, but unburdened, alone at the back of the room. I thought at first that what had happened was plainly miraculous, an answer to my prayer. But presently I began to wonder; suppose I hadn't prayed, suppose it was going to happen anyway? I had no way of knowing; there was no control for my experiment. Minute by minute I turned more niggardly, ungrateful. How could I be sure? And surely too it was rather petty, rather obvious of God to concern Himself so quickly with such a trivial request?

It was almost as if He were showing off. I wanted Him to move in a more mysterious way.

I wanted to tell somebody but I could not tell Naomi. I had asked her if she believed in God and she had said promptly and scornfully, 'Well of course I do, I'm not like your old lady. Do you think I want to go to Hell?' I never discussed it with her again.

I picked on my brother Owen to tell. He was three years younger than I was. At one time he had been impressionable and trusting. Once out on the farm we had a shelter of old boards that we played house in, and he sat on the end of a board and I served him mountain-ash berries, telling him they were his cornflakes. He ate them all. While he was still eating it occurred to me they might be poisonous, but I did not tell him, for reasons of my own prestige and the importance of the game, and afterwards I prudently decided not to tell anyone else. Now he had learned to skate, and went to hockey practice, and leaned over the bannisters and spat on my head, an ordinary boy.

But there were angles, still, from which he looked frail and young, pursuits of his that seemed to me lost and hopeless. He entered contests. This was my mother's nature showing in him, her boundless readiness to take up the challenges and promises of the outside world. He believed in prizes; telescopes he could see the craters of the moon through, magicians' kits with which he could make things disappear, chemistry sets that would enable him to manufacture explosives. He would have been an alchemist, if he had known about it. However, he was not religious.

He sat on the floor of his room cutting out tiny cardboard

figures of hockey players, which he would then arrange in teams and play games with; such godlike games he played with trembling absorption, and then seemed to me to inhabit a world so far from my own (the real one), a world so irrelevant, heartbreakingly flimsy in its deceptions.

I sat on the bed behind him.

'Owen.'

He didn't answer; when he was playing his games he never wanted anyone around.

'What do you think happens to someone when they die?'

'*I* don't know,' said Owen mutinously.

'Do you believe God keeps your soul alive? Do you know what your soul is? Do you believe in God?'

Owen turned his head and gave me a trapped look. He had nothing to hide, nothing to show but his pure-hearted indifference.

'You better believe in God,' I said. 'Listen.' I told him about my prayer, and Household Science. He listened unhappily. The need I felt was not in him. It made me angry to discover this; he seemed dazed, defenseless but resilient, a hard rubber ball. He would listen, if I insisted, agree with me, if I insisted on that, but in his heart, I thought, he was not paying any attention. Stupidity.

I would often hector him like this from now on, when I could get him alone. *Don't tell Mother*, I said. He was all I had to try my faith out on; I had to have somebody. His deep lack of interest, the satisfaction he seemed to take in a world without God were what I really could not bear, and kept hammering at; also I felt that because he was younger, and had been in my power so long, he had an obligation to follow me; for him not to acknowledge it was a sign of insurrection.

In my room, with the door shut, I read from the Book of Common Prayer.

Sometimes walking along the street I would shut my eyes (the way Owen and I used to do, playing blind) and say to myself – frowning, praying – 'God. God. *God.*' Then I would imagine for a few precarious seconds a dense bright cloud descending on Jubilee, wrapping itself around my skull. But my eyes flew open in alarm; I was not able to let that in, or me out. Also I was afraid of bumping into something, being seen, making a fool of myself.

Good Friday came. I was going out. My mother came into the hall and said, 'What have you got your beret on for?'

It was time to take a stand. 'I'm going to church.'

'There is no church.'

'I'm going to the Anglican Church. They have church on Good Friday.'

My mother had to sit down on the steps. She gave me as searching, pale, exasperated a look as she had examined me with a year before when she found a drawing Naomi and I had done in my scribbler, of a fat naked lady with balloon breasts and a huge, inky, sprouting nest of pubic hair.

'Do you know what Good Friday is in memory of?'

'Crucifixion,' I said tersely.

'That's the day Christ died for our sins. That's what they tell us. Now. Do you believe that?'

'Yes.'

'Christ died for our sins,' said my mother, jumping up.

In the hall mirror she peered aggressively at her own dim face. 'Well, well, *well*. Redeemed by the blood. That is a lovely notion. You might as well take the Aztecs cutting out live hearts because they thought the sun wouldn't rise and set if they didn't. Christianity is no better. What do you think of a God that asks for blood? Blood, blood, blood. Listen to their hymns, that's all they're ever about. What about a God who isn't satisfied until he has got somebody hanging on a cross for six hours, nine hours, whatever it was? If I was God I wouldn't be so bloodthirsty. Ordinary people wouldn't be so bloodthirsty. I don't count Hitler. At one time maybe they would be but not now. Do you know what I'm saying, do you know what I'm leading up to?'

'No,' I said honestly.

'God was made by man! Not the other way around! God was made by *man*. Man at a lower and bloodthirstier stage of his development than he is at now, we hope. Man made God in his own image. I've argued that with ministers. I'll argue it with anybody. I've never met anybody who could argue against it and make sense.'

'Can I go?'

'I'm not stopping you,' said my mother, though she had actually moved in front of the door. 'Go and get your fill of it. You'll see I'm right. Maybe you take after my mother.' She looked hard in my face for traces of the religious fanatic. 'If you do, I suppose it's out of my hands.'

I was not discouraged by my mother's arguments, not so much as I would have been if they had come from someone else. Nevertheless, crossing town, I looked for proof of the opposite point of view. I took simple comfort from the fact that the stores were locked, the blinds down in all their windows. That proved something, didn't it? If I knocked on the doors of all the houses along my route and asked a question – *Did Christ die for our sins?* – the answer, no doubt startled and embarrassed, would be yes.

I realized that I did not care a great deal, myself, about Christ dying for our sins. I only wanted God. But if Christ dying for our sins was the avenue to God, I would work on it.

Good Friday was, unsuitably, a mild sunny sort of day, with icicles dripping and crashing, roofs steaming, little streams running down the streets. Sunlight poured through the ordinary glass windows of the church. I was late, because of my mother. The minister was already up in front. I slid into the back pew and the lady in the velvet turban, Mrs Sherriff, gave me a white angry look; perhaps not angry, just magnificently startled; it was as if I had sat down beside an eagle on its perch.

I was heartened to see her, though. I was glad to see them all – the six or eight or ten people, real people, who had put on their hats and left their houses and walked through the streets crossing rivulets of melted snow and presented themselves here; they would not do that without a reason.

I wanted to find a believer, a true believer, on whom I could rest my doubts. I wanted to watch and take heart from such a person, not talk to them. At first I had thought it might be Mrs Sherriff, but she would not do; her craziness disqualified her. My believer must be luminously sane.

> O Lord, arise, help us, and deliver us for thy
> Name's sake.
> O Lord, arise, help us, and deliver us for thine

honor.
*Behold the Lamb of God which taketh away
the sin of the world.*

I set myself to think of Christ's sufferings. I held my
hands together in such a way that I could press a single
fingernail with all possible force into each palm. I dug
and twisted but could not even get blood; I felt abashed,
knowing this did not make me a participant in suffering.
God, if He had any taste, would despise such foolishness
(but had He? Look at the things that saints had done,
and got approval for). He would know what I was really
thinking, and trying to beat down in my mind. It was: *Were
Christ's sufferings really that bad?*

Were they that bad, when you knew, and He knew, and
everybody knew, that He would rise up whole and bright
and everlasting and sitteth on the right hand of God the
Father Almighty from whence He shall come to judge the
quick and the dead? Many people – not all, perhaps, or
even most people, but quite a few – would submit their
flesh to similar pains if they could be sure of getting what
He got, afterwards. Many had, in fact; saints and martyrs.

All right, but there was a difference. He was God; it was
more of a comedown, more of a submission, for Him. Was
He God, or God's earthly son only, at that time? I could not
get it straight. Did He understand how the whole thing
was being done on purpose, and it would all be all right in
the end, or was His God-ness temporarily blacked out, so
that He saw only this collapse? *My God, my God, why hast
thou forsaken me?*

After the long psalm with the prophecies in it about the

raiment, and casting lots, the minister went up into the pulpit and said he would preach a short sermon on the last words of Christ on the cross. The very thing I had been thinking of. But it turned out there were more last words than the ones I knew about. He started off with *I thirst*, which showed, he said, that Christ suffered in body just as much as we would in the same situation, not a bit less, and He was not ashamed to admit it, and ask for help, and give the poor soldiers a chance of obtaining grace, with the sponge soaked in vinegar. *Woman, behold thy son . . . son, behold thy mother*, showed that his last or almost his last thoughts were for others, arranging for them to be a comfort to each other when He was gone (though never really gone). Even in the hour of His agony and passion He did not forget human relationships, how beautiful and important they were. *Today thou shalt be with me in Paradise* showed of course his continuing concern for the sinner, the wrongdoer cast out by society and hanging there on the companion cross. *O Lord who hatest nothing that thou hast made and . . . desirest not the death of a sinner but rather that he may turn from his wickedness and live –*

But why – I could not stop this thinking though I knew it could bring me no happiness – why should God hate anything that He had made? If He was going to hate it, why make it? And if He had made everything the way He wanted it then nothing was to blame for being the way it was, and this more or less threw out, didn't it, the whole idea of sin? So why should Christ have to die for our sins? The sermon was having a bad effect on me; it made me bewildered and argumentative. It even made me feel, though I could not admit it, a distaste for Christ Himself, because of the way His perfections were being continually pointed out. *My God, my God, why hast thou forsaken me?* Briefly, the minister said, oh very briefly, Jesus had lost touch with God. Yes, it had happened, even to Him. He had lost the connection, and then in the darkness He had cried out in despair. But this too was part of the plan, it was necessary. It was so we should know in our own blackest moments that our doubts, our misery had been shared by Christ Himself, and then, knowing this, our doubts would all the more quickly pass.

But why? Why should they all the more quickly pass? Suppose that was the last true cry of Christ, the last true thing ever heard of Him? We had to at least suppose that, didn't we? We had to consider it. Suppose He cried that, and died, and never did rise again, never did discover it was all God's difficult drama? There was suffering. Yes; think of Him suddenly realizing: *it was not true. None of it was true.* Pain of torn hands and feet was nothing to that. To look through the slats of the world, having come all that way, and say what He had said, and then see – nothing. *Talk about that!* I cried inwardly to the minister. Oh, talk about that, drag it into the open, and then – defeat it!

But we do what we can, and the minister could not do any more.

I met Mrs Sherriff on the street a few days later. I was by myself this time.

'I know you. What are you doing all the time at the Anglican Church? I thought you were United.'

When most of the snow had melted and the river had gone down, Owen and I went out the Flats Road, separately, on

Saturdays, to the farm. The house, where Uncle Benny had been living all winter and my father had been living most of the time, except for those weekends when he came in to stay with us, was so dirty that it no longer had to be a house at all; it was like some sheltered extension of the out-of-doors. The pattern of the kitchen linoleum was lost; dirt itself made a pattern. Uncle Benny said to me, 'Now here's the cleaning lady, just the thing we need,' but I did not think so. The whole place smelled of fox. There would be no fire in the stove till evening and the door stood open. Outside were crows cawing over the muddy fields, the river high and silver, the pattern of the horizon exactly, magically the same as remembered and forgotten and remembered. The foxes were nervous, yelping, because it was the time of year the females had their pups. Owen and I were not allowed to go near the pens.

Owen was swinging on the rope under the ash tree, where our swing had been last summer.

'Major killed a sheep!'

Major was our dog, now thought of as Owen's dog, though he did not pay any particular attention to Owen; Owen paid it to him. He was a big golden-brown mongrel collie, who had grown too lazy last summer even to chase cars, but napped in the shade; awake or asleep, he had a slow senatorial sort of dignity. And now he was chasing sheep; he had taken up criminality in his old age, just as a proud and hitherto careful old senator might publicly take up vice. Owen and I went to have a look at him, Owen telling on the way that the sheep belonged to the Potters, whose land adjoined ours, and that the Potter boys had seen Major, from their truck, and had stopped and jumped over fences and yelled, but Major had separated his sheep from the others and kept right on after it and killed it.

Killed it. I imagined it all bloody, torn apart; Major had never hunted or killed a thing in his life. 'Did he want it to *eat*?' I asked in bewilderment and repugnance, and Owen was obliged to explain that the killing had been, in a way, incidental. It seemed that sheep could be run to death, frightened to death, they were so weak and fat and panicky; though Major had taken, as a trophy, a mouthful of warm wool from the neck, had pounced on that and worried it a bit, for form's sake. Then he had to streak for home (if he could streak, Major!) because the Potter boys were coming.

He was tied up inside the barn, the door open to give him some light and air. Owen jumped astride his back to wake him up – Major always woke so quickly and gravely, without fuss, that it was hard to know whether he was really asleep, or shamming – and then rolled over on the floor with him, trying to make him play. 'Old sheep killer, old sheep killer,' said Owen, punching him proudly. Major put up with this, but was no more playful than usual; he did not seem to have regained his youth in any but the one astounding way. He licked the top of Owen's head in a patronizing manner, and settled down to sleep again when Owen let go.

'He has to be tied up so he won't go after sheep again, old sheep killer. Potters said they'd shoot him if they ever caught him again.'

This was true. Major was indeed in the limelight. My father and Uncle Benny came to look at him, in his sham dignity and innocence on the barn floor. Uncle Benny saw him as doomed. In his opinion no dog who took up chasing sheep had any hope of getting over it. 'Once he's got the taste,' Uncle Benny said, fondling Major's head, 'he's got the taste. You can't let him live, a sheep killer.'

'You mean shoot him?' I cried not exactly out of love for Major but because it seemed such a brutal ending to what everybody was considering a rather comic story. It was like leading the white-haired senator out to public execution for his embarrassing pranks.

'Can't keep a sheep killer. He'd have you poor, paying for all the sheep he killed. Anyways somebody else'd put an end to him, if you didn't.'

My father, appealed to, said that perhaps Major would not chase any more sheep. He was tied up, anyway. He could stay tied up the rest of his life, if necessary, or at least until he got over his second childhood and became too feeble for chasing anything; that should not be too long now.

But my father was wrong. Uncle Benny with his grinning pessimism, his mournful satisfied predictions, was right. Major broke out of captivity, during the early morning hours. The barn door was shut but he tore some wire netting from a window that had no glass in it, and jumped out, and raced to Potter's to take up again his lately discovered pleasures. He was home by breakfast, but the broken rope and window and the dead sheep in Potter's pasture were there to tell the story.

We were at breakfast. My father had spent the night in town. Uncle Benny phoned him and told him, and my father when he came back to the table said, 'Owen. We have to get rid of Major.'

Owen began to quiver but he did not say a word. My father in a few words told about the breakout and the dead sheep.

'Well he's an old dog,' said my mother with false heartiness. 'He's an old dog and he's had a good life and who knows what's going to happen to him now anyway, all the diseases and miseries of old age.'

'He could come and live here,' said Owen weakly. 'Then he wouldn't know where a sheep was.'

'A dog like that can't live in town. And no guarantee he wouldn't get back at it anyway.'

'Think of him tied up in town, Owen,' said my mother reproachfully.

Owen got up and left the table without saying anything else. My mother did not call him back to say *excuse me.*

I was used to things being killed. Uncle Benny went hunting, and trapping muskrats, and every fall my father killed foxes and sold the pelts for our livelihood. Throughout the year he killed old and crippled or simply useless horses for the foxes' food. I had had two bad dreams about this, both some time ago, that I still remembered. Once I dreamed that I went down to my father's meat house, a screened shed beyond the barn where in summer he kept parts of skinned and butchered horses hanging on hooks. The shed was in the shade of a crab-apple tree; the screens would be black with flies. I dreamed that I looked inside and found, not unexpectedly, that what he really had hanging there were skinned and dismembered human bodies. The other dream owed something to English history, which I had been reading about in the encyclopedia. I dreamed my father had set up an ordinary, humble block of wood on the grass outside the kitchen door, and was lining us up – Owen and my mother and me – to cut off our heads. *It won't hurt,* he told us, as if that was all we had to be afraid of, *it'll all be over in a minute.* He was kind and calm, reasonable, tiredly persuasive, explaining that it was all somehow for our own good. Thoughts of escape struggled in my mind like birds caught in oil, their wings out, helpless. I was paralyzed by this reasonableness, the arrangements so simple and familiar and taken for granted, the reassuring face of insanity.

In the daytime I was not so frightened as these dreams would suggest. It never bothered me to go past the meat house, or to hear the gun go off. But when I thought of Major being shot, when I pictured my father loading the gun unhurriedly, ritualistically as he always did, and calling Major who would not suspect anything, being used to men with guns, and the two of them walking past the barn, my father looking for a good spot – I did see again the outline of that reasonable, blasphemous face. It was the deliberateness I dwelt on, deliberate choice to send the bullet into the brain to stop the systems working – in this choice and act, no matter how necessary and reasonable, was the assent to anything. Death was made possible. And not because it could not be prevented but because it was what was wanted – *wanted*, by all those adults, and managers, and executioners, with their kind implacable faces.

And by me? I did not want it to happen, I did not want Major to be shot, but I was full of a tense excitement as well as regret. That scene of execution which I imagined, and which gave me such a flash of darkness – was that altogether unwelcome? No. I dwelt on Major's trustfulness, his affection for my father – whom he did like, in his self-possessed way, as much as he could like anybody – his half-blind cheerful eyes. I went upstairs to see how Owen was taking it.

He was sitting on the bedroom floor fooling with some jacks. He was not crying. I had vague hopes that he might be persuaded to make trouble, not because I thought it would do any good, but because I felt the occasion demanded it.

'If you prayed for Major not to get shot would he not get shot?' said Owen in a demanding voice.

The thought of praying had never crossed my mind.

'You prayed you wouldn't have to thread the sewing machine any more and you didn't.'

I saw with dismay the unavoidable collision coming, of religion and life.

He got up and stood in front of me and said tensely, '*Pray.* How do you do it? Start now!'

'You can't pray,' I said, 'about a thing like that.'

'Why not?'

Why not? Because, I could have said to him, we do not pray for things to happen or not happen, but for the strength and grace to bear what does. A fine way out, that smells abominably of defeat. But I did not think of it. I simply thought, and knew, that praying was not going to stop my father going out and getting his gun and calling, 'Major! Here, Major –' Praying would not alter that.

God would not alter it. If God was on the side of goodness and mercy and compassion, then why had he made these things so difficult to get at? Never mind saying, *so they will be worth the trouble*; never mind all that. Praying for an act of execution not to take place was useless simply because God was not interested in such objections; they were not His.

Could there be God not contained in the churches' net at all, not made manageable by any spells and crosses, God real, and really in the world, and alien and unacceptable as death? Could there be God amazing, indifferent, beyond faith?

'How do you do it?' said Owen stubbornly. 'Do you have to get down on your knees?'

'It doesn't matter.'

But he had already knelt down, and clenched his hands at his sides. Then not bowing his head he screwed up his face with strong effort.

'Get up, Owen!' I said roughly. 'It's not going to do any good. It won't work, it doesn't work, Owen get up, be a good boy, darling.'

He swiped at me with his clenched fists, not taking time out to open his eyes. With the making of his prayer his face went through several desperate, private grimaces, each of which seemed to me a reproach and an exposure, hard to look at as skinned flesh. Seeing somebody have faith, close up, is no easier than seeing someone chop a finger off.

Do missionaries ever have these times, of astonishment and shame?

CHANGES AND CEREMONIES

Boys' hate was dangerous, it was keen and bright, a miraculous birthright, like Arthur's sword snatched out of the stone, in the Grade Seven Reader. Girls' hate, in comparison, seemed muddled and tearful, sourly defensive. Boys would bear down on you on their bicycles and cleave the air where you had been, magnificently, with no remorse, as if they wished there were knives on the wheels. And they would say anything.

They would say softly, 'Hello hooers.'

They would say, 'Hey where's your fuckhole?' in tones of cheerful disgust.

The things they said stripped away freedom to be what you wanted, reduced you to what it was they saw, and that, plainly, was enough to make them gag. My friend Naomi and I told each other, 'Don't let on you heard,' since we were too proud to cross streets to avoid them. Sometimes we would yell back, 'Go and wash out your mouth in the cow trough, clean water's too good for you!'

After school Naomi and I did not want to go home. We looked at advertisements for the movie that was showing at the Lyceum Theatre and the brides in the photographer's window and then we went to the library, which was a room in the Town Hall. On the windows on one side of the main door of the Town Hall were letters that read LAD ES REST RO M. On the other side they read PUBL C RE DING ROOM. The missing letters were never replaced. Everybody had learned to read the words without them.

There was a rope beside the door; it hung down from the bell under the cupola, and the browned sign beside it said: penalty for improper use $100. Farmers' wives sat in the windows of the ladies' rest room, in their kerchiefs and galoshes, waiting for their husbands to come and get them. There was seldom anybody in the library except the librarian, Bella Phippen, deaf as a stone and lame in one leg from polio. The Council let her be librarian because she could never have managed a proper job. She stayed most of the time in a sort of nest she had made behind the desk, with cushions, afghans, biscuit tins, a hot plate, a teapot, tangles of pretty ribbon. Her hobby was making pincushions. They were all the same: a Kewpie doll on top dressed in this ribbon, which made a hoop skirt over the actual pincushion. She gave one to every girl who got married in Jubilee.

Once I asked her where to find something and she crawled around the desk and limped heavily along the shelves and came back with a book. She handed it to me, saying in the loud lonely voice of the deaf, 'There is a lovely book.'

It was *The Winning of Barbara Worth*.

The library was full of books like that. They were old, dull blue and green and brown books with slightly softened, slightly loosened, covers. They would often have a frontispiece showing a pale watercolored lady in some sort of Gainsborough costume, and underneath some such words as these: *Lady Dorothy sought seclusion in the rose garden, the better to ponder the import of this mysterious communication. (p. 112)*

Jeffrey Farnol. Marie Corelli. *The Prince of the House of David*. Lovely, wistful, shabby old friends. I had read them, didn't read them any more. Other books I knew so well by their spines, knew the curve of every letter in their titles, but had never touched them, never pulled them out. *Forty Years a Country Preacher. The Queen's Own in Peace and War.* They were like people you saw on the street day after day, year after year, but never knew more than their faces; this could happen even in Jubilee.

I was happy in the library. Walls of printed pages, evidence of so many created worlds – this was a comfort to me. It was the opposite with Naomi; so many books weighed on her, making her feel oppressed and suspicious. She used to read – girls' mystery books – but had outgrown the habit. This was the normal thing in Jubilee; reading books was something like chewing gum, a habit to be abandoned when the seriousness and satisfactions of adult life took over. It persisted mostly in unmarried ladies, would have been shameful in a man.

So to keep Naomi quiet, while I looked at books, I

would find her something to read that she would never have believed could be in a book at all. She sat on the little stepladder Bella Phippen never used and I brought her the fat green *Kristin Lavransdatter*. I found the place where Kristin has her first baby, hour after hour, page after page, blood and agony, squatting on the straw. I felt a slight sadness, handing this over. I was always betraying someone or somebody; it seemed the only way to get along. This book was not a curiosity to me. No; when I had wanted to live in the eleventh century, even to have a baby in the straw, like Kristin – provided I lived of course – and particularly to have a lover like Erlund, just such a flawed and dark and lonely horseback rider.

After Naomi had read it she came to find me and ask, 'Did she have to get married?'

'Yes.'

'I thought so. Because if a girl has to get married, she either dies having it, or she nearly dies, or else there is something the matter with it. Either a harelip or clubfoot or it isn't right in the head. My mother has seen it.'

I didn't argue, though I didn't believe it, either. Naomi's mother was a practical nurse. On her authority – or what Naomi claimed was her authority – I had heard that babies born with cauls will turn out to be criminals, that men had copulated with sheep and produced little shriveled woolly creatures with human faces and sheep's tails, which died and were preserved in bottles somewhere, and that crazy women had injured themselves in obscene ways with coat hangers. I believed or did not believe these things according to the buoyancy or fearfulness of the mood I was in. I did not like Naomi's mother; she had a brassy hectoring voice and pale protruding eyes – like Naomi's – and she had asked me whether my periods had started yet. But anybody who will go into birth and death, who will undertake to see and deal with whatever is there – a hemorrhage, the meaty afterbirth, awful dissolution – anybody who does that will have to be listened to, no matter what news they bring.

'Is there a part in the book where they do it?'

Anxious to justify literature in Naomi's eyes – like a minister trying hard to show how religion can be practical, and fun – I hunted around and found the part where Kristin and Erlund took shelter in the barn. But it did not satisfy her.

'Is that supposed to be telling that they do it?'

I pointed out Kristin's thought. *Was this ill thing the thing that was sung of in all the songs?*

It was getting dark when we came out and farmers' sleighs were heading out of town. Naomi and I caught a ride on one going out Victoria Street. The farmer was wrapped up in a muffler and a great fur cap. He looked like a helmeted Norseman. He turned and swore at us to get off, but we hung on, bloated with cheerful defiance like criminals born with cauls; we hung on with the rim of the sleigh cutting into our stomachs and our feet spraying snow, until we reached the corner of Mason Street, and there we flung off into a snowbank. When we collected our books and got our breath back we shouted at each other.

'Get off you bugger!'

'Get off you bugger!'

We both hoped and feared that somebody would hear our language in the street.

Naomi lived on Mason Street, I lived on River Street; that was the basis for our friendship. When I first moved to town Naomi would wait for me in the mornings, in front of her house, which was on my way. 'Why do you walk like that?' she would say, and I would say, 'Like what?' She would walk along in a strange weaving way, oblivious, chin in her collar. Offended, I laughed. But her criticisms were proprietary; I was alarmed and elated to discover that she considered we were friends. I had not had a friend before. It interfered with freedom and made me deceitful in some ways, but it also extended and gave resonance to life. This shrieking and swearing and flinging into snowbanks was not something you could do alone.

And we knew too much about each other to ever stop being friends, now.

Naomi and I put our names down together to be board monitors, which meant we stayed after school and cleaned the blackboards, and took the red, white, and blue brushes outside and banged them against the brick wall of the school, making fan patterns of chalk. Coming in, we heard unfamiliar music coming from the teachers' room, Miss Farris singing, and we remembered. The operetta. That would be it.

Every year, in March, the school put on an operetta, which brought different forces into play, and changed everything, for a while. In charge of the operetta were Miss Farris, who during the rest of the year did nothing special, only taught Grade Three, and played 'The Turkish March' on the piano every morning, to march us to our classrooms, and Mr Boyce, who was the United Church organist, and came to the school two days a week to teach music.

Mr Boyce attracted attention and disrespect because of the ways in which he was unlike an ordinary teacher. He was short, with a soft moustache, eyes round and wet-looking, like sucked caramels. Also he was English, he had come over at the beginning of the war, surviving the sinking of the *Athenia*. Imagine Mr Boyce in a lifeboat, in the North Atlantic! Even the run from his car to the school, in the Jubilee winter, left him gasping and outraged. He would bring a record player into the classroom and play something like the *1812 Overture*, and ask us what the music made us think of, how it made us feel. Used only to factual, proper questions, we looked at the floor boards and giggled and quivered faintly, as at an indecency. He looked at us with dislike and said, 'I suppose it doesn't make you think of anything, but that you'd rather not listen to it,' and shrugged his shoulders in a gesture too delicate, too – personal, for a teacher.

Miss Farris was a native of Jubilee. She had gone to this school, she had marched up these long stairs hollowed out in two places by the daily procession of feet, while somebody else played 'The Turkish March' (because that must have been played since the beginning of time). Her first name was well known – it was Elinor. She lived in her own little house close up to the sidewalk on Mason Street, near where Naomi lived, and she went to the United Church. She also went skating, once a week, in the evening, throughout the winter, and she wore a dark blue velvet costume she had made herself, for she could never have bought it. It was trimmed with white fur, and she had a matching white fur hat and muff. The skirt was short and full, lined with pale blue taffeta, and she wore white dancer's tights. Such a costume gives a good deal away, and in more ways than one.

Miss Farris was not young, either. She hennaed her hair, which was bobbed in the style of the nineteen-twenties; she always put on two spots of rouge and a rash, smiling line of lipstick. She skated in circles, letting her sky-lined skirt fly out. Nevertheless she seemed dry and wooden and innocent, her skating, after all, more of a schoolteacherish display of skill, than of herself.

She made all her own clothes. She wore high necks and long chaste sleeves, or peasant drawstrings and rickrack, or a foam of white lacy frills under the chin and at the wrists, or bold bright buttons set with little mirrors. People did laugh at her, though not so much as if she had not been born in Jubilee. Fern Dogherty, my mother's boarder, said, 'Poor thing, she's only trying to catch a man. Everybody's got a right to do it their own way, I say.'

If that was her way, it did not work. Every year there was a hypothetical romance, or scandal, built up between her and Mr Boyce. This was while the preparations for the operetta were going on. People would report that they had been seen squeezing up together on the piano bench, his foot had nudged hers on the pedal, he had been heard to call her Elinor. But all baroque concoctions of rumor crumbled, when you looked into her face, her little sharp-boned face, self-consciously rouged and animated, with flickering commas at the corners of her mouth, bright startled eyes. Whatever she was after, it could not be Mr Boyce. Fern Dogherty notwithstanding, it could hardly even be men.

The operetta was her passion. She burned with it

discreetly at first, when she and Mr Boyce came into the classroom about two o'clock on a blurry, snowy afternoon, when we were half-asleep, copying from the board, and everything was so quiet you could hear the water pipes gurgling, deep down in the insides of the building. Almost in a whisper she requested everybody to stand and sing, when Mr Boyce gave the note.

> *D'ye ken John Peel with his coat so gay*
> *D'ye ken John Peel at the break of day*
> *D'ye ken John Peel when he's far far away,*
> *With his hounds and his horse in the morning?*

Mr McKenna our teacher, the principal of the school, showed what he thought of this by continuing to write on the board. *The Nile Valley was protected from invasion by three surrounding deserts, the Libyan, the Nubian, the Arabian.* It didn't matter what he did, in the end he would be helpless. The operetta would keep growing and growing, it would push down all his rules, his divisions of time, like so many matchstick fences. How tactful Miss Farris and Mr Boyce were now, tiptoeing ceremoniously around the room, heads bent to catch the individual voices. It would not last. The whole operetta, at present, was contained in their two selves, but when the time came they would let it loose, it would belly out like a circus balloon, and we would all just have to hold on.

They motioned gently for some to sit down. I had to sit, and so, I was glad to see, did Naomi. They made others sing again, and beckoned for the people they wanted to step out of line.

Casting of the operetta was an unpredictable thing. With everything else, from carrying the wreath of poppies up to the cenotaph on Armistice Day to putting on the Junior Red Cross program, down to carrying notes from one teacher to another through the strangely emptied halls, you could tell in advance who would be chosen most of the time, who would be chosen some of the time, and who would never under any circumstances be chosen at all. At the top of the list were Marjory Coutts, whose father was a lawyer and a member of the Provincial Legislature, and Gwen Mundy, whose father was an undertaker and proprietor of a furniture store. Nobody objected to their position. Indeed, given a free election for the officers of the Junior Red Cross, we unhesitatingly and with a graceful sense of what was fitting, elected them ourselves. Years of good will around them, in the town and at school, had in fact made them the best people to be chosen – confident and diplomatic, discreet and kind. The people not to be trusted, who would turn dictatorial in office or trip on the way to the cenotaph or read the teachers' notes in the hall, in the hope of having something to tell, were the occasionally chosen, the ambitious and unsure – like Alma Cody, a specialist in sex information, like Naomi, like me.

Secure as Marjory and Gwen, in another way, were the never chosen – a great fat girl named Beulah Bowes, whose bum overlapped her seat – boys stuck pen nibs into it – and the Italian girl who never spoke, and was often absent with kidney disease, and a very frail, weepy albino boy whose father had a little grocery store, and who bought his survival, all through school, with bags of gumdrops and chicken bones and licorice whips. Such people sat at the back of the room, were not asked to read aloud, were not sent to put arithmetic questions on the blackboard, received two valentines on Valentine's Day. (These would be from Gwen and Marjory who without fear of contamination could send cards to everybody.) They passed from year to year, grade to grade, in dreamy inviolate loneliness. The Italian girl would be the first of us all to die, when we were still in high school; then we would remember with consternation, belated pride.

'But she was in our *class.*'

A good singing voice may be found anywhere. It was not found in Beulah Bowes, or in the Italian girl, or in the albino boy, but it might have been; it came that close. For who should be borne away, between Miss Farris and Mr Boyce, like some sort of trophy, but the boy who sat behind me, a boy I would have put near the very bottom of the list of the sometimes chosen: Frank Wales.

I should not have been surprised. I could hear him behind me every morning, in 'God Save the King,' and once a week, during Mr Boyce's visits, in 'John Peel!' and 'Flow Gently Sweet Afton' and 'As Pants the Hart [for a long time I thought it was *heart*] for Healing Streams, When Heated in the Chase.' His voice was a still-unbroken soprano, unself-conscious, in fact hardly human, serene and isolated as flute music. (The recorder, which he later learned to play for his part in the operetta, seemed like an extension of this voice.) He himself was so indifferent to the possession of such a voice, unaware of it, that when he stopped singing it was completely gone and you did not think of it in connection with him.

All I knew about Frank Wales, really, was that he was a terrible speller. He had to pass his spelling up to me to be marked. Later he would go to the board, docile but unperturbed, to write the words out three times each. It did not seem to do him much good. It was hard to believe such spelling was not perversity, a furious stubborn joke, but nothing else about him showed how this could be true. Apart from spelling he was neither smart nor dumb. He would know where the Mediterranean was, most likely, but not the Sargasso Sea.

When he got back I wrote on my ruler, 'What part did you get?' and passed it back as if to lend it to him. The classroom was a truce area, where neutral, but hidden, communication between boys and girls was possible.

He wrote on the other side of the ruler: *Pide Pieper.*

So I knew the operetta we would be doing: *The Pied Piper.* I was disappointed, thinking there would be no court scenes, no ladies in waiting, no beautiful clothes. Just the same I wanted badly to get a part. Miss Farris came to choose the dancers for the 'Peasants' Wedding Dance.'

'I want four girls who can hold their heads up and have rhythm in their feet. Marjory Coutts, Gwen Mundy, who else?' Her eyes went up and down the rows, pausing on several, and on me too where I sat with my head up, my shoulders straight, my expression bright but noncommittal for pride's sake, my fingers violently twisted together, under the desk, in my private sign for luck. 'Alma Cody and – June Gannett. Now four boys who can dance without making the curtain fall down –'

I was in pain then. Suppose I only got to be a member of the crowd, pushed to the back of the stage? Suppose I never got on the stage at all? Some members of the class would not; they would have to sit on tiered benches below the stage, on either side of the piano that Mr Boyce played, with those from the lower grades picked for the chorus, all uniformed in dark skirts and white blouses, white shirts and dark trousers. There I had sat for three years, through *The Gypsy Princess*, *The Kerry Dancers*, and *The Stolen Crown*. There the Italian girl, the fat girl, the albino boy would sit, expectedly, through *The Pied Piper*. But not me! *Not me!* I could not believe in injustice so terrible as to keep me off that stage.

Naomi had not got a part either. We did not talk about this on the way home, but made fun of everything connected with the operetta.

'You be Miss Farris, I'll be Mr Boyce. Ah, my true love, my little hummingbird, this music of the Pied Piper is making me mad with passion, when will I clasp you in my arms until your spine cracks because you are so painfully skinny?'

'I am not painfully skinny I am incredibly beautiful and your moustache is giving me a rash. What are we going to do about Mrs Boyce? O my love?'

'Do not distress yourself my sweetest angel I will lock her up in a dark closet infested with cockroaches.'

'But I am afraid she will get loose.'

'In that case I will make her swallow arsenic and saw her up in little tiny pieces and flush them down the toilet. No I will dissolve them with lye in the bathtub. I will melt the gold fillings out of her teeth and make us a lovely wedding ring.'

'O you are so romantic, O my beloved.'

Then Naomi got picked to be a mother who has to say, 'Ah, my lovely little Marta, how you would dance about in the mornings when I would try to braid your hair! And I would scold you so! Ah, if only I could see you dance now!' And in the last scene she says, 'Now I am so thankful, never will I tell a tale on my neighbors or be a gossiping stingy woman again!' I believed she had been picked because of her short, rather chunky figure, which could easily be made to look matronly. I had to walk home alone; people with speaking parts stayed to practice, after school. My mother said, 'How goes the operetta?' meaning, did I have a part?

'They're not doing anything yet. They haven't picked the parts yet.'

After supper I went down to Mason Street and walked past Miss Farris' house. I had no idea what I meant to do. I walked up and down, not making any noise on the packed snow. Miss Farris did not pull her blinds; it would not have been like her. Her house was small, almost like a playhouse; white with blue shutters, a peaked roof, a tiny gable, scalloped boards over the door and windows. She had had it built for herself, with the money she got when her parents died. And though in the movies one often saw houses like this – that is, houses which set out to be charming, whimsical, which looked as if they were designed for play, not life – they were not seen yet in Jubilee. Compared to the other houses in town, hers appeared to have no secrets, no contradictions. What people said was,

'It's such a pretty house, doesn't look real.' They could not explain more than that, what there was not to trust about it.

There was nothing I could do, of course, and after a while I went home.

But the next day Miss Farris came into the classroom with June Gannett in tow, marched her straight to my desk, said, 'Up on your feet, Del,' as if I should have known to do that without being told – she was getting more of her operetta manner – and made us stand back to back. I understood that June was the wrong height but did not know if she was too short or too tall, so I could not stretch or shrink accordingly. Miss Farris put her hands on our heads, moved them off heavily. She stood so close I could smell peppery sweat, and her hands trembled slightly; a tiny, dangerous hum of excitement ran through her.

'You're half an inch too tall, June dear. We'll see what we can do about making you a mother.'

Naomi and I, and others, exchanged studiously bland looks; Mr McKenna swept a sharp frown around the room.

'Who did you get for partners?' whispered Naomi later, in the cloakroom, when we were scrambling for our boots. We had to march out, by rows, and get our outdoor clothes and bring them in again, put them on at our seats, in the interest of order.

'Jerry Storey,' I admitted. I was not very happy about the allocation of partners. It seemed meant to be apt. Gwen Mundy and Marjory Coutts got Murray Heal and George Klein, who were more or less their male counterparts in the class, being bright, athletic and, where it counted, decently behaved. Alma Cody got Dale McLaughlin, the

United Church minister's son, who was tall, loose limbed, idiotically audacious, with heavy glasses and one rolling misdirected eye. He had already had sexual intercourse, more or less, with Violet Toombs in the bicycle shed behind the school. And I got Jerry Storey, his head covered with childish curls, his eyes popping with unabashed high-voltage braininess. He would put up his hand in science period and in a boring nasal voice describe experiments he had done with his chemistry set. He knew the names of everything – elements, plants, rivers, and deserts on the map. He would know where the Sargasso Sea was. All the time we practiced this dance he never looked in my face. His hand sweated. So did mine.

'I pity you,' said Naomi. 'Now everybody is going to think you like him.'

Never mind. The operetta was the only thing at school, now. Just as during the war you could not imagine what people thought about, worried about, what the news was about, before there was a war, so now it was impossible to remember what school had been like before the excitement, the disruption and tension, of the operetta. We practiced the dance after school, and also during school hours, in the Teachers' Room. I had never been in the Teachers' Room before, and it was odd to see the little cupboard with its cretonne curtains, the teacups, hot plate, bottle of aspirin, the lumpy leather couch. Teachers were not thought of in connection with such ordinary, even shabby, domesticity.

Unlikely sights continued to present themselves. There was a manhole in the ceiling of the Teachers' Room, and one day when we came in to practice we discovered Mr McKenna, of all people, Mr McKenna, wriggling his dusty brown-trousered legs and bottom out of the manhole, trying to find the stepladder. He brought down cardboard boxes, which Miss Farris relieved him of, crying, 'Yes, that one, that one! Ah, what have we got, let's see if we've got riches here!'

She broke the string with a strong jerk, and spilled out red and blue dyed cheesecloth, trimmed with loops of the same gold and silver tinseled rope you hang on Christmas trees. Then crowns, covered with gold and silver foil. Rust-colored velvet breeches, a fringed yellow paisley shawl, some court gowns of dusty, papery taffeta. Mr McKenna could only stand by unthanked, slapping dust off his trousers.

'No dancing today! Boys out, out and play hockey.' (It was one of her fictions that whenever boys were not in school they were playing hockey.) 'Girls, stay, help me sort out. What have we got here that will do for a village in the Middle Ages, in Germany? I don't know, I don't know. These dresses are too grand. They'd fall to pieces on stage anyway. They saw their best days in *The Stolen Crown*. Would the breeches fit the mayor? That reminds me, *that reminds me* – I have to make a mayor's chain! I have to make Frank Wales' costume, too, the last Pied Piper we had was twice as big around. Who was it? I even forget who it was. It was a fat boy. We picked him solely for the voice.'

'How many different operettas are there?' That was Gwen Mundy, comfortable with teachers, taking her polite, kind, tone.

'Six,' said Miss Farris fatalistically. '*The Pied Piper. The Gypsy Princess. The Stolen Crown. The Arabian Knight. The Kerry Dancers. The Woodcutter's Daughter*. By the time we work round to the same one again we have an entire new crop of performers to pick from and the audience we trust to heaven has forgotten the last time.' She picked up a black velvet cloak, lined with red, shook it out, put it around her own shoulders. 'This is what Pierce Murray wore, you remember, when he played the captain in *The Gypsy Princess*. No of course you don't remember, it was 1937. Then he was killed, in the air force.' But she said this rather absently; after he played the captain in *The Gypsy Princess*, did it matter so much what else happened to him? 'Every time he put it on he would swing – like *this* – and make the lining show.' She herself made a swashbuckling swing. All her stage directions, dancing directions, were willfully, splendidly exaggerated, as if she thought to amaze us into self-forgetfulness. She insulted us, she told us we danced like fifty-year-old arthritics, she said she would put firecrackers in our shoes, but all the time she was hovering around us as if we contained possibilities of lovely, fiery dancing, as if she could pull out of us what nobody else, and not we ourselves, could guess was there.

In came Mr Boyce to get the recorder he was teaching Frank Wales to play. He saw the swing.

'*Con brio,*' he said with his self-possessed English *surprise*. '*Con brio,* Miss Farris!'

Miss Farris, continuing the spirit of the swing, bowed gallantly, and we allowed her this, and even understood, for that moment, that the blush absorbing her rouge like sunrise had not a thing to do with Mr Boyce, only with the pleasure of her action. We got hold of *con brio*, we planned to tell. We did not know or care what it meant, only that it

was absurd – all foreign words were in themselves absurd
– and dramatically explosive. Its aptness was recognized.
Long after the operetta was over Miss Farris could not
walk down the hall at school, could not pass us on her way
up John Street hill, singing lightly and encouragingly to
herself as her habit was (*'The Minstrel Boy* – Good morning
girls! – *to the War has gone –'*), without this phrase floating
slyly somewhere in her vicinity. *Con brio, Miss Farris.* We
felt it was the final touch to her; it wound her up.

We started going to the Town Hall for our practicing.
The Town Hall auditorium was large and draughty, as
remembered, the stage curtains ancient dark blue velvet,
gold-fringed, royal, as remembered. The lights were on,
these winter-dimmed days, but not all the way to the back
of the hall, where Miss Farris would sometimes disappear,
crying, 'I can't hear a word back here! I can't hear a word!
What are you all afraid of? Do you want the people at the
back of the hall to be calling out for their money back?'

She was approaching her peak of despair. She always
had some sewing in her hands. She beckoned me over
one day, and gave me a scrap of gold braid which she was
sewing onto the mayor's velvet hat. She told me to run to
the Walker store and get a quarter of a yard to match. She
did quiver; the hum in her had got more noticeable. 'Don't
delay,' she told me, as if she was sending me for some vital
medicine, or with a message that would save an army. So
I flew out in my unbuttoned coat and there was Jubilee
under fresh snow, its silent, woolly white streets; the Town
Hall stage behind me seemed bright as a bonfire, lit by such
fanatical devotion. Devotion to the manufacture of what
was not true, not plainly necessary, but more important,

once belief had been granted to it, than anything else we had.

Freed by the operetta from the routine of our lives, remembering the classroom where Mr McKenna kept busy with spelling bees and mental arithmetic those not chosen, as someplace sad and dim, left behind, we were all Miss Farris' allies now. We were putting our separate parts of the operetta together, seeing it as a whole. I was moved by the story, and still am. I thought how separate, and powerful, and helpless and tragic a character the Pied Piper was. No treachery could really surprise him; battered by the world's use of him, he kept, like Humphrey Bogart, his weary honor. Even his revenge (spoiled of course by the changed ending) seemed not spiteful, but almost tender, terrible tender revenge in the interests of larger justice. I thought Frank Wales, that unteachable speller, grew into the part easily, naturally, with no attempt at acting. He carried his everyday reserve and indifference onto the stage, and this was right. I saw for the first time what he was like, what he looked like – his long narrow head, hair dark and cut short like a wiry doormat, a melancholy face that might have turned out to be a comedian's though in this case it did not, the scars of old boils and a fresh one starting, on the back of his neck. His body was narrow like his face, his height was average for a boy in our class – meaning he would be a fraction of an inch shorter than I was – and he had a quick and easy way of walking, the walk of someone who does not need either to efface or call attention to himself. Every day he wore a blue-gray sweater, darned at the elbow, and this smoky color, so ordinary, reticent, and mysterious, seemed to me his color, the color of his self.

I loved him. I loved the Pied Piper. I loved Frank Wales.

I had to speak about him to somebody so I spoke to my mother, pretending objectivity and criticism.

'He has a good voice but he is not tall enough. I don't think he'll stand out on the stage.'

'What is his name? Wales? Is he the son of that corset lady? I used to get my corsets from Mrs Wales – she had the Slender-eze line, she doesn't have it any more. She lived out on Beggs Street, past the creamery.'

'It must be his mother.' I was strangely elated to think there had been this point of contact between Frank Wales' family and mine, his life and mine. 'Did you go to her house, did she come here?'

'I went to her, you had to go to her.'

I wanted to ask what the house was like, were there pictures in the front room, what did his mother talk about, did she mention her children? Too much to hope that they would have become friends, that they would talk about their families, that Mrs Wales would say that night at supper, 'Today there was such a nice lady here to get her corsets fitted and she says she has a daughter in the same class at school as you –' What good would that do? My name mentioned in his hearing, my image brought before his eyes.

The atmosphere of the Town Hall, these days, put more than me in this condition. Ritualized hostility between boys and girls was cracking in a hundred places. It could not be kept up or, where it was kept up, it would be in a joking way, with confused undercurrents of friendliness.

Naomi and I, walking home, ate five-cent toffee bars

which were extremely hard to bite in the cold, and then almost as hard to chew. We talked with cautious full mouths.

'Who would you like to be your partner if it didn't have to be Jerry Storey?'

'I don't know.'

'Murray? George? *Dale?*'

I shook my head securely, noisily sucking back toffee-flavored saliva.

'Frank Wales,' said Naomi diabolically.

'Tell me yes or no,' she said. 'Come on. I'll tell you who I would like if it was me.'

'I wouldn't mind him,' I said in a careful, subdued voice. 'Frank Wales.'

'Well I wouldn't mind Dale McLaughlin,' said Naomi defiantly and quite surprisingly, for she had kept her secret hidden better than I had mine. She hung her head over a snowbank, dribbling, and gnawed at her toffee bar. 'I know I must be crazy,' she said finally. 'I really like him.'

'I really like Frank Wales,' I said in full admission. 'I must be crazy too.'

After this we talked all the time about these two boys. We called them F.A.'s. It stood for Fatal Attraction.

'There goes your F.A. Try not to faint.'

'Why don't you get your F.A. some Noxema for his boils, ugh?'

'I think your F.A. was looking at you but it's hard to tell with his cross-eyes.'

We developed a code system of raised eyebrows, fingers fluttered on the chest, mouthed words such as *Pang, oh, Pang* (for when we stood near them on the stage), *Fury, double Fury* (for when Dale McLaughlin talked to Alma Cody and snapped his fingers against her neck) and *Rapture* (for when he tickled Naomi under the arm and said, 'Out of my way, butterball!').

Naomi wanted to talk about the incident in the bicycle shed. The girl Dale McLaughlin had done it to, asthmatic Violet Toombs, had moved away from town.

'Good thing she moved. She disgraced herself here.'

'It wasn't all her fault.'

'Yes it was. It's the girl's fault.'

'How could it be her fault if he held her down?'

'He couldn't have held her down,' said Naomi sternly, 'because he couldn't hold her down and – get his thing in – at the same time. How could he?'

'Why don't you ask him? I'll tell him you want to know.'

'My mother says it's the girl's fault,' said Naomi, ignoring me. 'It's the girl who is responsible because our sex organs are on the inside and theirs are on the outside and we can control our urges better than they can. A boy can't help himself,' she instructed me, in a foreboding, yet oddly permissive, tone of voice, which acknowledged the anarchy, the mysterious brutality prevalent in that adjacent world.

Talk along these lines was irresistible, and yet, walking on down River Street, I often wished I had kept my secret to myself, as we all do wish we had kept our secrets to ourselves. 'Frank Wales can't get hard-ons yet because his voice hasn't changed,' Naomi told me – no doubt relaying another piece of information from her mother – and I was interested but disturbed, as if I had got my feelings about him wrongly labeled, directed into an entirely unexpected channel. What I wanted from Frank Wales I did not really know. I had a daydream about him, often repeated. I imagined he walked home with me after a performance of the operetta. (It was becoming known that boys – some boys – would walk home with girls – some girls – on that night, but Naomi and I did not even discuss this possibility; we were chary of voicing real hopes.) We walked through the absolutely silent streets of Jubilee, walked under the street lights with our shadows whirling and sinking on the snow, and there in the beautiful, dark, depopulated town Frank would surround me, either with real, implausible, but cool and tender, singing, or, in the more realistic versions of the dream, simply with the unheard music of his presence. He would be wearing the pointed cap, almost a fool's cap, and the cloak patched with various colors, predominantly blue, that Miss Farris had made for him. I would often invent this dream for myself at the edge of sleep, and then it was strange how content it would make me, how it would make peace and consolation flow, and I would close my eyes and float on it into my real dreams which were never so kind, but full of gritty small problems, lost socks, not being able to find the Grade Eight classroom, or terrors, such as dancing on the hall stage and finding I had forgotten to put my headdress on.

At the dress rehearsal Miss Farris cried for all to hear, 'I might as well leap off the Town Hall! I might as well leap now! Are you all prepared to take the responsibility?' She pulled her spread fingers down her cheeks so hard it looked as if they might leave furrows. 'Back-back-back, forget the last fifteen minutes! Forget the last half hour!

Begin again from the beginning!' Mr Boyce smiled quite comfortably and struck the notes of the opening chorus.

Then the night itself. The time come, the audience packed in, all that shuffling, coughing, dressed-up expectancy where we were used to having darkness and echoes. The stage was so much brighter and so much more crowded, with cardboard house fronts and a cardboard fountain, than we had ever known it to be. Everything happened too quickly, and then it was over, gone; it did not matter how it was done, it had to do, could not be retrieved. Nothing could be retrieved. After all the practicing it was almost unbelievable that the operetta was really happening. Mr Boyce wore tails, which people would say looked ridiculous.

The Council Chambers directly below the stage – and connected to it by a back staircase – were divided into dressing rooms with sheets hung on cords, and Miss Farris with an apron over her new, peplumed, cerise pink dress was painting eyebrows and mouths, putting red dots at the corners of eyes, dabbing ocher on earlobes, dousing hair with cornstarch. There was a terrible uproar. Vital parts of costumes were lost; somebody had stepped on the hem of the mayor's wife's dress, ripping it out at the waist. Alma Cody claimed she had taken four aspirins for her nerves and now was dizzy and in a cold sweat, sitting on the floor, saying she was going to faint. Some of the sheets fell down. Girls were seen in their underwear by boys, and vice versa. Members of the chorus, who were not supposed to enter the Council Chambers at all, got in and lined up boldly in their dark skirts and white blouses, and Miss Farris, past noticing, went ahead and painted their faces too.

She was past noticing much. We expected her to be wild, as she had been all week. Nothing of the sort. 'I wonder if she's drunk,' said Naomi, apple-cheeked in her motherly kirtle. 'I smelled a smell on her.' I had not smelled a thing but Wild Roses Toilet Water and a whiff of that peppery sweat. However she glittered – sequins outlining the jacket of her dress in circus-military style – and she glided, unlike herself, speaking softly, moving through all this turmoil with bountiful acceptance.

'Pin up your skirt, Louise,' she said to the mayor's wife, 'there isn't a thing you can do about it now. From the audience it won't be noticed.'

Won't be noticed! She who had been so hard to suit about the smallest details, had forced mothers to rip things out and do them three times over!

'A big strong healthy girl like you could take six aspirins and never blink an eye,' she said to Alma Cody. 'Up on your feet, my lady!'

The dancers were dressed in bright cotton skirts, red, yellow, green, blue, and white embroidered drawstring blouses. Alma had loosened the drawstring of her blouse to show the impudent beginnings of her bust. Even that, Miss Farris just smiled at, and floated by. Anything that wanted to, it seemed, might happen now.

Near the beginning of the dance my headdress, a tall medieval cone of cardboard wrapped in yellow net, with a bit of limp veil, began to slide slightly, disastrously to the side of my head. I had to tilt my head as if I had a wry neck, and go all through the dance like that, teeth clenched, glassily smiling.

After 'God Save the King,' after the last curtain, we ran

up the street to the photographer's, all in our costumes still, without coats, to have our pictures taken. We were all crushed together, waiting, among the sepia waterfalls and Italian gardens of his discarded backdrops. Dale McLaughlin found a chair, the kind in which fathers of families used to sit for their pictures, wife and children clustered round them. He sat down, and Alma Cody sat boldly on his knee. She flopped against his neck.

'I'm so weak. I'm a wreck. Did you know I took four aspirins?'

I was standing in front of them. 'Sit down, sit down,' said Dale jovially, and pulled me down on top of Alma, who screamed. He opened his long legs and dumped both of us on the floor. Everybody was laughing. My hat and veil had fallen right off, and Dale picked it up and set it on my head backwards so the veil fell over my face.

'You look gorgeous like that. Can't see a thing.'

I tried to dust it off and get it on the right way. Frank Wales appeared suddenly between the curtains, after having his picture taken, alone, in his lordly, beggarly costume.

'Dancers! Next!' called the photographer's wife angrily, sticking her head through the curtains. I was the last to go in, because I was still trying to get my headdress on properly. 'Look in my glasses,' Dale said, so I did, though it was distracting seeing his lonely, crossed eye behind my reflection. He was making leering faces.

'You ought to walk her home,' he said to Frank Wales.

Frank Wales said, 'Who?'

'Her,' said Dale, nodding at me. My head bobbed in his glasses. 'Don't you know her? She sits in front of you.'

I was afraid it would turn out to be a joke. I felt sweat start out of my armpits, always the first sign of fear of humiliation. My face swam in Dale's foolish eyes. It was too much, too dangerous, to be flung like this into the very text of my dream.

However, Frank Wales said consideringly, and as gallantly as anybody could, 'I would too. If she didn't live such a long ways out.'

He was thinking of when I lived out on the Flats Road, and was famous in the class for my long walk to school. Didn't he know I lived in town now? No time to tell him; no way, either, and there was still the smallest risk, that I would never take, of having him laugh at me, his quiet, reflectively snorting laugh, and say he was only kidding.

'All dancers!' cried the photographer's wife, and I turned blindly and followed her through the curtains. My disappointment was after a moment drowned in gratitude. The words he had said kept repeating themselves in my mind, as if they were words of praise and pardon, the intonation so mild, matter-of-fact, acknowledging, and lovely. A feeling of rare peacefulness like that of my daydream settled on me during the picture taking and carried me back through the cold to the Council Chambers and stayed with me while we changed, even with Naomi saying, 'Everybody was killing themselves laughing, the way you held your head when you were dancing. You looked like a puppet with its neck broken. You couldn't help it, though.' She was in a bad, and worsening, mood. She whispered in my ear, 'You know all that stuff I told you about Dale McLaughlin? That was all a lie. That was all an act I put on to get your secrets out of you, ha ha.'

Miss Farris was automatically picking up and folding costumes. She had cornstarch spilled down the front of her cerise pink dress, and her chest actually looked concave, as if something had collapsed inside it. She hardly bothered to notice us, except to say, 'Leave the rosettes off your shoes, girls, leave those too. Everything will have its use another day.'

I walked around to the front of the hall and there was my mother waiting with Fern Dogherty, and my brother Owen in his flag-drill outfit (the younger grades had got to do inconsequential things, like flag drill, rhythm-band numbers, before the curtain went up on the operetta), poking his flag, which he had been allowed to keep, into a snowdrift.

'Whatever kept you so long?' my mother said. 'It was lovely, did you have a crick in your neck? That Wales boy was the only one on the entire stage who forgot to take his cap off for "God Save the King."' My mother had these various odd little pockets of conventionality.

What happened, after the operetta? In one week it had sunk from sight. Seeing some part of a costume, meant to be returned, hanging in the cloakroom was like seeing the Christmas tree, leaning against the back porch in January, browning, bits of tinsel stuck to it, reminder of a time whose hectic expectations, and effort, seem now to have been somewhat misplaced. Mr McKenna's solid ground was reassuring under our feet. Every day we did eighteen arithmetic problems, to catch up, and listened securely to such statements as 'And now because of the time we have lost we are all going to have to put our noses to the grindstone.' *Noses to the grindstone, shoulders to the wheel, feet on the pedals* – all these favorite expressions of Mr McKenna's, their triteness and predictability, seemed now oddly satisfying. We carried home large piles of books, and spent our time drawing maps of Ontario and the Great Lakes – the hardest map in the world to draw – and learning 'The Vision of Sir Launfall.'

Everybody's seat was moved; the house cleaning of desks and change of neighbors turned out to be stimulating. Frank Wales now sat across the room. And one day the janitor came with his long ladder and removed an object which had been visible in one of the hanging lights since Halloween. We had all believed this to be a French safe, and Dale McLaughlin's name had been connected with it; less scandalously, though just as mysteriously, it was discovered to be old sock. It seemed to be a time for dispelling illusions. *Getting down to brass tacks*, Mr McKenna would have said.

My love did not of course melt away altogether as the season changed. My daydreams continued, but were derived from the past. They had nothing new to feed on. And the change of season did make a difference. It seemed to me that winter was the time for love, not spring. In winter the habitable world was so much contracted; out of that little shut-in space we lived in, fantastic hopes might bloom. But spring revealed the ordinary geography of the place; the long brown roads, the old cracked sidewalks underfoot, all the tree branches, broken off in winter storms, that had to be cleared out of the yards. Spring revealed distances, exactly as they were.

Frank Wales did not go on to high school as most of the others in the class did, but got a job working for

Jubilee Dry Cleaners. At this time the dry cleaners did not have a truck. Most people picked up their clothes but a few things were delivered. It was Frank Wales' job to carry them through town, and we would meet him sometimes doing this when we were coming from school. He would say hello in the quick, serious, courteous way of a businessman or workingman speaking to those who have not yet entered the responsible world. He always held the clothes shoulder-high, with a dutifully crooked elbow; when he started working he had not yet reached his full height.

For a while – about six months, I think – I would go into Jubilee Dry Cleaners with a vestigial flutter of excitement, a hope of seeing him, but he was never in the front shop; it was always the man who owned the place, or his wife – both small, exhausted, bluish-looking people, who looked as if dry-cleaning fluids had stained them, or got into their blood.

Miss Farris was drowned in the Wawanash River. This happened when I was in high school, so it was only three or four years since *The Pied Piper*, yet when I heard the news I felt as if Miss Farris existed away back in time, and on a level of the most naive and primitive feelings, and mistaken perceptions. I thought her imprisoned in that time, and was amazed that she had broken out to commit this act. If it was an act.

It was possible, though not at all likely, that Miss Farris would have gone walking along the riverbank north of town, near the cement bridge, and that she might have slipped and fallen into the water and not been able to save herself. Neither was it impossible, the Jubilee *Herald-Advance* pointed out, that she had been taken from her house by person or persons unknown, and forced into the river. She had left her house in the evening, without locking the door, and all the lights were on. Some people who were excited by the thought of marvelous silent crimes happening in the night always believed it was murder. Others out of kindness or fearfulness held it to be an accident. These were the two possibilities that were argued and discussed. Those who believed that it was suicide, and most people, finally, did, were not so anxious to talk about it, and why should they be? Because there was nothing to say. It was a mystery presented without explanation and without hope of explanation, in all insolence, like a clear blue sky. No revelation here.

Miss Farris in her velvet skating costume, her jaunty fur hat bobbing among the skaters, always marking her out, Miss Farris *con brio*, Miss Farris painting faces in the Council Chambers, Miss Farris floating face down, unprotesting, in the Wawanash River, six days before she was found. Though there is no plausible way of hanging those pictures together – if the last one is true then must it not alter the others? – they are going to have to stay together now.

The Pied Piper; The Gypsy Princess; The Stolen Crown; The Arabian Knight; The Kerry Dancers; The Woodcutter's Daughter.

She sent those operettas up like bubbles, shaped with quivering, exhausting effort, then almost casually set free, to fade and fade but hold trapped forever our transformed childish selves, her undefeated, unrequited love.

As for Mr Boyce, he had already left Jubilee, where, as

people said, he never did seem to feel at home, and got a job playing a church organ and teaching music in London – which is not the real London, I feel obliged to explain, but a medium-sized city in western Ontario. Word filtered back that he managed to get along quite well there, where there were some people like himself.

LIVES OF GIRLS AND WOMEN

The snowbanks along the main street got to be so high that an archway was cut in one of them, between the street and the sidewalk, in front of the post office. A picture was taken of this and published in the Jubilee *Herald-Advance*, so that people could cut it out and send it to relatives and acquaintances living in less heroic climates, in England or Australia or Toronto. The red-brick clocktower of the post office was sticking up above the snow and two women were standing in the archway, to show it was no trick. Both these women worked in the post office, had put their coats on without buttoning them. One was Fern Dogherty, my mother's boarder.

My mother cut this picture out, because it had Fern in it, and because she said I should keep it, to show to my children.

'They will never see a thing like that,' she said. 'By then the snow will all be collected in machines and – dissipated. Or people will be living under transparent domes, with a controlled temperature. There will be no such thing as seasons anymore.'

How did she collect all her unsettling information about the future? She looked forward to a time when towns like Jubilee would be replaced by domes and mushrooms of concrete, with moving skyways to carry you from one to the other, when the countryside would be bound and tamed forever under broad sweeping ribbons of pavement. Nothing would be the same as we knew it today, no frying pans or bobby pins or printed pages or fountain pens would remain. My mother would not miss a thing.

Her speaking of my children amazed me too, for I never meant to have any. It was glory I was after, walking the streets of Jubilee like an exile or a spy, not sure from which direction fame would strike, or when, only convinced from my bones out that it had to. In this conviction my mother had shared, she had been my ally, but now I would no longer discuss it with her; she was indiscreet, and her expectations took too blatant a form.

Fern Dogherty. There she was in the paper, both hands coquettishly holding up the full collar of her good winter coat, which through pure luck she had worn to work that day. 'I look the size of a watermelon,' she said. 'In that coat.'

Mr Chamberlain, looking with her, pinched her arm above the bracelet wrinkle of the wrist.

'Tough rind, tough old watermelon.'

'Don't get vicious,' said Fern. 'I mean it.' Her voice was

small for such a big woman, plaintive, put-upon, but in the end good-humored, yielding. All those qualities my mother had developed for her assault on life – sharpness, smartness, determination, selectiveness – seemed to have their opposites in Fern, with her diffuse complaints, lazy movements, indifferent agreeableness. She had a dark skin, not olive but dusty looking, dim, with brown-pigmented spots as large as coins; it was like the dappled ground under a tree on a sunny day. Her teeth were square, white, slightly protruding, with little spaces between them. These two characteristics, neither of which sounds particularly attractive in itself, did give her a roguish, sensual look.

She had a ruby-colored satin dressing gown, a gorgeous garment, fruitily molding, when she sat down, the bulges of her stomach and thighs. She wore it Sunday mornings, when she sat in our dining room smoking, drinking tea, until it was time to get ready for church. It parted at the knees to show some pale clinging rayon – a nightgown. Nightgowns were garments I could not bear, because of the way they twisted around and worked up on you while you slept and also because they left you uncovered between the legs. Naomi and I when we were younger used to draw pictures of men and women with startling gross genitals, the women's fat, bristling with needly hair, like a porcupine's back. Wearing a nightgown one could not help being aware of this vile bundle, which pajamas could decently shroud and contain. My mother at the same Sunday breakfast table wore large striped pajamas, a faded rust-colored kimono with a tasseled tie, the sort of slippers that are woolly socks, with a sole sewn in.

Fern Dogherty and my mother were friends in spite of

differences. My mother valued in people experience of the world, contact with any life of learning or culture, and finally any suggestion of being dubiously received in Jubilee. And Fern had not always worked for the post office. No; at one time she had studied singing, she had studied at the Royal Conservatory of Music. Now she sang in the United Church choir, sang 'I Know that My Redeemer Liveth' on Easter Sunday, and at weddings she sang 'Because' and 'O Promise Me' and 'The Voice that Breathed O'er Eden.' On Saturday afternoons, the post office being closed, she and my mother would listen to the broadcasts of the Metropolitan Opera. My mother had a book of operas. She would get it out and follow the story, identifying the arias, for which translations were provided. She had questions for Fern, but Fern did not know as much about operas as you would think she might; she would even get mixed up about which one it was they were listening to. But sometimes she would lean forward with her elbows on the table, not now relaxed, but alertly supported, and sing, scorning the foreign words. 'Do – daa – do, da, *do*, da do-do –' The force, the seriousness of her singing voice always came as a surprise. It didn't embarrass her, letting loose those grand, inflated emotions she paid no attention to in life.

'Did you plan to be an opera singer?' I asked.

'No. I just planned to be the lady working in the post office. Well, I did and I didn't. The work, the *training*. I just didn't have the ambition for it, I guess that was my trouble. I always preferred having a good time.' She wore slacks on Saturday afternoons, and sandals that showed her pudgy, painted toes. She was dropping ashes on her stomach, which, ungirdled, popped out in a pregnant curve. 'Smoking is ruining my voice,' she said meditatively.

Fern's style of singing, though admired, was regarded in Jubilee as being just a hair's breadth from showing off, and sometimes children did screech or warble after her, in the street. My mother could take this for persecution. She would construct such cases out of the flimsiest evidence, seeking out the Jewish couple who ran the Army Surplus store, or the shrunken silent Chinese in the laundry, with bewildering compassion, loud slow-spoken overtures of friendship. They did not know what to make of her. Fern was not persecuted, that I could see. Though my old aunts, my father's aunts, would say her name in a peculiar way, as if it had a stone in it, that they would have to suck, and spit out. And Naomi did tell me, 'That Fern Dogherty had a baby.'

'She never did,' I said, automatically defensive.

'She did so. She had it when she was nineteen years old. That's why she got kicked out of the Conservatory.'

'How do you know?'

'My mother knows.'

Naomi's mother had spies everywhere, old childbed cases, deathbed companions, keeping her informed. In her nursing job, going from one house to another, she was able to operate like an underwater vacuum tube, sucking up what nobody else could get at. I felt I had to argue with Naomi about it because Fern was our boarder, and Naomi was always saying things about people in our house. ('Your mother's an atheist,' she would say with black relish, and I would say, 'No she isn't, she's an agnostic,' and all through my reasoned hopeful explanation Naomi would chant *same difference, same difference*.) I was not able to retaliate, either out of delicacy or cowardice, though Naomi's own father belonged to some odd and discredited religious sect, and wandered all over town talking prophecies without putting his false teeth in.

I took to noticing pictures of babies in the paper, or in magazines, when Fern was around, saying, 'Aw, isn't it *cute*?' and then watching her closely for a flicker of remorse, maternal longing, as if someday she might actually be persuaded to burst into tears, fling out her empty arms, struck to the heart by an ad for talcum powder or strained meat.

Furthermore, Naomi said Fern did everything with Mr Chamberlain, just the same as if they were married.

It was Mr Chamberlain who got Fern boarding with us in the first place. We rented the house from his mother, now in her third year, blind and bedridden, in the Wawanash County Hospital. Fern's mother was in the same place; it was there, in fact, on a visiting day, that they had met. She was working in the Blue River Post office at that time. Mr Chamberlain worked at the Jubilee radio station and lived in a small apartment in the same building, not wanting the trouble of a house. My mother spoke of him as 'Fern's friend,' in a clarifying tone of voice, as if to insist that the word friend in this case meant no more than it was supposed to mean.

'They enjoy each other's company,' she said. 'They don't bother about any nonsense.'

Nonsense meant romance; it meant vulgarity; it meant sex.

I tried out on my mother what Naomi said.

'Fern and Mr Chamberlain might just as well be married.'

'What? What do you mean? Who said that?'

'Everybody knows it.'

'I don't. Everybody does not. Nobody ever said such a thing in my hearing. It's that Naomi said it, isn't it?'

Naomi was not popular in my house, nor I in hers. Each of us was suspected of carrying the seeds of contamination – in my case, of atheism, in Naomi's, of sexual preoccupation.

'It's dirty mindedness that is just rampant in this town, and will never let people alone.'

'If Fern Dogherty was not a good woman,' my mother concluded, with a spacious air of logic, 'do you think I would have her living in my house?'

This year, our first year in high school, Naomi and I held almost daily discussions on the subject of sex, but took one tone, so that there were degrees of candor we could never reach. This tone was ribald, scornful, fanatically curious. A year ago we had liked to imagine ourselves victims of passion; now we were established as onlookers, or at most cold and gleeful experimenters. We had a book Naomi had found in her mother's old hope chest, under the mothballed best blankets.

Care should be taken during the initial connection, we read aloud, *particularly if the male organ is of an unusual size. Vaseline may prove a helpful lubricant.*

'I prefer butter myself. Tastier.'

Intercourse between the thighs is often resorted to in the final stages of pregnancy.

'You mean they still do it *then?*'

The rear-entry position is sometimes indicated in cases where the female is considerably obese.

'Fern,' Naomi said. 'That's how he does it to Fern. She's considerably obese.'

'Aggh! This book makes me sick.'

The male sexual organ in erection, we read, had been known to reach a length of fourteen inches. Naomi spat out her chewing gum and rolled it between her palms, stretching it longer and longer, then picked it up by one end and dangled it in the air.

'Mr Chamberlain, the record breaker!'

Thereafter whenever she came to my place, and Mr Chamberlain was there, one of us, or both, if we were chewing gum, would take it out and roll it this way and dangle it innocently, till even the adults noticed and Mr Chamberlain said, 'That's quite a game you got there,' and my mother said, 'Stop that, it's filthy.' (She meant the gum.) We watched Mr Chamberlain and Fern for signs of passion, wantonness, lustful looks, or hands up the skirt. We were not rewarded, my defense of them turning out to be truer than I wished it to be. For I as much as Naomi liked to entertain myself with thoughts of their grunting indecencies, their wallowing in jingly beds (in tourist cabins, Naomi said, every time they drove to Tupperton *to have a look at the lake*). Disgust did not rule out enjoyment, in my thoughts; indeed they were inseparable.

Mr Chamberlain, Art Chamberlain, read the news on the Jubilee radio. He also did all the more serious and careful announcing. He had a fine professional voice, welcome as dark chocolate flowing in and out of the organ music on the Sunday afternoon program *In Memoriam*, sponsored by a local funeral parlor. He sometimes got Fern singing on this program, sacred songs – 'I Wonder as I Wander' – and

nonsacred but mournful songs – 'The End of a Perfect Day.'
It was not hard to get on the Jubilee radio; I myself had
recited a comic poem, on the *Saturday Morning Young Folks
Party*, and Naomi had played 'The Bells of St. Mary's' on the
piano. Every time you turned it on there was a good chance
of hearing someone you knew, or at least of hearing the
names of people you knew mentioned in the dedications.
('We are going to play this piece also for Mr and Mrs Carl
Otis on the occasion of their twenty-eighth wedding
anniversary, requested by their son George and wife Etta,
and their three grandchildren, Lorraine, Mark, and Lois,
also by Mrs Otis' sister Mrs Bill Townley of the Porterfield
Road.') I had phoned up myself and dedicated a song to
Uncle Benny on his fortieth birthday; my mother would
not have her name mentioned. She preferred listening to
the Toronto station, which brought us the Metropolitan
Opera, and news with no commercials, and a quiz program
in which she competed with four gentlemen who, to judge
from their voices, would all have little, pointed beards.

Mr Chamberlain had to read commercials too, and
he did it with ripe concern, recommending Vick's Nose
Drops from Cross' Drugstore, and Sunday dinner at the
Brunswick Hotel, and Lee Wickert and Sons for dead-
livestock removal. 'How's the dead livestock, soldier?' Fern
would greet him, and he might slap her lightly on the rump.
'I'll tell them you need their services!' 'Looks to me more
like you do,' said Fern without much malice, and he would
drop into a chair and smile at my mother for pouring him
tea. His light blue-green eyes had no expression, just that
color, so pretty you would want to make a dress out of it.
He was always tired.

Mr Chamberlain's white hands, his nails cut straight across, his graying, thinning, nicely-combed hair, his body that did not in any way disturb his clothes but seemed to be made of the same material as they were, so that he might have been shirt and tie and suit all the way through, were strange to me in a man. Even Uncle Benny, so skinny and narrow-chested, with his damaged bronchial tubes, had some look or way of moving that predicted chance or intended violence, something that would make disorder; my father had this too, though he was so moderate in his ways. Yet it was Mr Chamberlain, tapping his ready-made cigarette in the ashtray, Mr Chamberlain who had been in the war, he had been in the Tank Corps. If my father was there when he came to see us – to see Fern, really, but he did not quickly make that apparent – my father would ask him questions about the war. But it was clear that they saw the war in different ways. My father saw it as an overall design, marked off in campaigns, which had a purpose, which failed or succeeded. Mr Chamberlain saw it as a conglomeration of stories, leading nowhere in particular. He made his stories to be laughed at.

For instance he told us about the first time he went into action, what confusion there was. Some tanks had gone into a wood, got turned around, were coming out the wrong way, where they expected the Germans to come from. So the first shots they fired were at one of their own tanks.

'Blew it up!' said Mr Chamberlain blithely, unapologetically.

'Were there soldiers in that tank?'

He looked at me in mocking surprise as he always did

when I said anything; you would think I had just stood on my head for him. 'Well, I wouldn't be too surprised if there were!'

'Were they – killed, then?'

'Something happened to them. I certainly never saw them around again. Poof!'

'Shot by their own side, what a terrible thing,' said my mother, scandalized but less than ordinarily sure of herself.

'Things like that happen in a war,' said my father quietly but with some severity, as if to object to any of this showed a certain female naiveté. Mr Chamberlain just laughed. He went on to tell about what they did on the last day of the war. They blew up the cookhouse, turned all the guns on it in the last jolly blaze they would get.

'Sounds like a bunch of kids,' said Fern. 'Sounds like you weren't grown-up enough to fight a *war*. It just sounds like you had one big, idiotic, good time.'

'What I always try to have, isn't it? A good time.'

Once it came out that he had been in Florence, which was not surprising, since he had fought the war in Italy. But my mother sat up, she jumped a little in her chair, she quivered with attention.

'Were *you* in Florence?'

'Yes, ma'am,' said Mr Chamberlain without enthusiasm.

'In Florence, you were in Florence,' repeated my mother, confused and joyful. I had an inkling of what she felt, but hoped she would not reveal too much. 'I never thought,' she said. 'Well, of course I knew it was Italy but it seems so strange –' She meant that this Italy we had been talking about, where the war was fought, was the same place history happened, in the very place, where the old

Popes were, and the Medici, and Leonardo. The Cenci. The cypresses. Dante Alighieri.

Rather oddly, in view of her enthusiasm for the future, she was excited by the past. She hurried into the front room and came back with the art-and-architecture supplement to the encyclopedia, full of statues, paintings, buildings, mostly photographed in a cloudy, cool, museum-gray light.

'There!' she opened it up on the table in front of him. 'There's your Florence. Michelangelo's statue of David. Did you see that?'

A naked man. His marble thing hanging on him for everybody to look at; like a drooping lily petal. Who but my mother in her staunch and dreadful innocence would show a man, would show us all, a picture like that? Fern's mouth was swollen, with the effort to contain her smile.

'I never got to see it, no. That place is full of statues. Famous this and famous that. You can't turn around for them.'

I could see he was not a person to talk to, about things like this. But my mother kept on.

'Well surely you saw the bronze doors? The magnificent bronze doors? It took the artist his whole life to do them. Look at them, they're here. What was his name – Ghiberti. Ghiberti. His whole life.'

Some things Mr Chamberlain admitted he had seen, some he had not. He looked at the book with a reasonable amount of patience, then said he had not cared for Italy.

'Well, Italy, maybe that was all right. It was the Italians.'

'Did you think they were decadent?' said my mother regretfully.

'Decadent, I don't know. I don't know what they were. They don't care. On the streets in Italy I've had a man come up to me and offer to sell me his own daughter. It happened all the time.'

'What would they want to sell a girl for?' I said, adopting as I easily could my bold and simple façade of innocence. 'For a slave?'

'In a manner of speaking,' said my mother, and she shut the book, relinquishing Michelangelo and the bronze doors.

'No older than Del here,' said Mr Chamberlain, with a disgust that in him seemed faintly fraudulent. 'Not so old, some of them.'

'They mature earlier,' Fern said. 'Those hot climates.'

'Del. You take this book, put it away.' Alarm in my mother's voice was like the flap of rising wings.

Well, I had heard. I did not come back to the dining room but went upstairs and undressed. I put on my mother's black rayon dressing gown, splattered with bunches of pink and white flowers. Impractical gift she never wore. In her room I stared, goose-pimpled and challenging, into the three-way mirror. I pulled the material off my shoulders and bunched it over my breasts, which were just about big enough to fit those wide, shallow cones of paper laid in sundae dishes. I had turned on the light beside the dressing table; it came meekly, warmly through a bracket of butterscotch glass, and laid a kind of glow on my skin. I looked at my high round forehead, pink freckled skin, my face as innocent as an egg, and my eyes managed to alter what was there, to make me sly and creamy, to change my hair, which was light brown, fine as a crackling bush, into rich waves more gold than muddy. Mr Chamberlain's voice in my mind, saying *no older than Del here*, acted on me like the touch of rayon silk on my skin, surrounded me, made me feel endangered and desired. I thought of girls in Florence, girls in Rome, girls my age that a man could buy. Black Italian hair under their arms. Black down at the corners of their mouths. *They mature earlier in those hot climates*. Roman Catholics. A man paid you to let him do it. What did he say? Did he take your clothes off or did he expect you to do that yourself? Did he take down his pants or did he simply unzip himself and point his thing at you? It was the stage of transition, bridge between what was possible, known and normal behavior, and the magical, bestial act, that I could not imagine. Nothing about that was in Naomi's mother's book.

There was a house in Jubilee with three prostitutes in it. That is, three if you counted Mrs McQuade who ran it; she was at least sixty years old. The house was at the north end of the main street, in a yard all run to hollyhocks and dandelions, beside the B.A. service station. On sunny days the two younger women would sometimes come out and sit in canvas chairs. Naomi and I had made several trips past and had once seen them. They wore print dresses and slippers; their white legs were bare. One of them was reading the *Star Weekly*. Naomi said that this one's name was Peggy, and that one night in the men's toilet at the Gay-la dance hall she had been persuaded to serve a line-up, standing up. Was such a thing possible? (I heard this story another time, only now it was Mrs McQuade herself who performed or endured this feat, and it was not at the Gay-la dance hall but against the back wall of the Blue Owl Cafe.) I wished I had seen more of this Peggy than the soft, mouse-brown nest of curls above the paper; I wished I had seen her face. I did expect something – a foul shimmer of corruption, some emanation, like marsh gas. I was surprised, in a way, that she would read a paper, that the words in it would mean the same things to her, presumably, as they did to the rest of us, that she ate and drank, was human still. I thought of her as having gone right beyond human functioning into a condition of perfect depravity, at the opposite pole from sainthood but similarly isolated, unknowable. What appeared to be ordinariness here – the *Star Weekly*, dotted curtains looped back, geraniums growing hopefully out of tin cans in the whorehouse window, seemed to me deliberate and tantalizing deception – the skin of every-day appearances stretched over such shamelessness, such consuming explosions of lust.

I rubbed my hipbones through the cool rayon. If I had been born in Italy my flesh would already be used, bruised, knowing. It would not be my fault. The thought of whoredom, not my fault, bore me outward for a moment; a restful, alluring thought, because it was so final, and did away with ambition and anxiety.

After this I constructed in several halting imperfect installments a daydream. I imagined that Mr Chamberlain saw me in my mother's black flowered dressing gown, pulled down off the shoulders, as I had seen myself in the mirror. Then I proposed to have the dressing gown come off, let him see me with nothing on at all. How could it happen? Other people who would ordinarily be in the

house with us would have to be got rid of. My mother I
sent out to sell encyclopedias; my brother I banished to the
farm. It would have to be in the summer holidays, when I
was home from school. Fern would not yet be home from
the post office. I would come downstairs in the heat of
the late afternoon, a sulphurous still day, wearing only this
dressing gown. I would get a drink of water at the sink,
not seeing Mr Chamberlain sitting quietly in the room,
and then – what? A strange dog, introduced into our
house for this occasion only, might jump on me, pulling
the dressing gown off. I might turn and somehow catch
the material on the nail of a chair, and the whole thing
would just slither to my feet. The thing was that it had to
be an accident; no effort on my part, and certainly none on
Mr Chamberlain's. Beyond the moment of revelation my
dream did not go. In fact it often did not get that far, but
lingered among the preliminary details, solidifying them.
The moment of being seen naked could not be solidified,
it was a stab of light. I never pictured Mr Chamberlain's
reaction, I never very clearly pictured him. His presence
was essential but blurred; in the corner of my daydream he
was featureless but powerful, humming away electrically
like a blue fluorescent light.

Naomi's father caught us, as we raced past his door on our
way downstairs.

'You young ladies come in and visit me a minute, make
yourselves comfortable.'

It was spring by this time, windy yellow evening.
Nevertheless he was burning garbage in a round tin
stove in his room, it was hot and smelly. He had washed

his socks and underwear and hung them on strings along the wall. Naomi and her mother treated him unceremoniously. When her mother was away, as now, Naomi would open a can of spaghetti and dump it on a plate, for his dinner. I would say, 'Aren't you going to heat it?' and she would say, 'Why bother? He wouldn't know the difference anyway.'

In his room, on the floor, he had stacks of newsprint pamphlets which I supposed had to do with the religion he believed in. Naomi sometimes had to bring them from the post office. Taking her cue from her mother, she had great contempt for his beliefs. 'It's all prophecies and prophecies,' she said. 'They have prophesied the end of the world three times now.'

We sat on the edge of the bed, which had no spread on it, only a rough, rather dirty blanket, and he sat in his rocker opposite us. He was an old man. Naomi's mother had nursed him before she married him. Between his words there were usually large gaps, during which he would not forget about you, however, but fix his pale eyes on your forehead as if he expected to find the rest of his thought written out there.

'Reading from the Bible,' he said genially and unnecessarily, and rather in the manner of one who chooses not to see objections he knows are there. He opened a large-print Bible with the place already marked and began to read in a piercing elderly voice, with some odd stops, and difficulties of phrasing.

> *Then shall the kingdom of heaven be likened*
> *unto ten virgins, which took their lamps, and*

went forth to meet the bridegroom.

And five of them were wise, and five were foolish.

They that were foolish took their lamps, and took no oil with them:

But the wise took oil in their vessels with their lamps.

While the bridegroom tarried, they all slumbered and slept.

And at midnight there was a cry made, Behold, the bridegroom cometh; go ye out to meet him.

Then all those virgins arose, and trimmed their lamps.

And the foolish said unto the wise, Give us of your oil; for our lamps are gone out.

Then it turned out of course – now I remembered hearing all this before – that the wise virgins would not give up any of their oil for fear they would not have enough, and the foolish virgins had to go out and buy some, and so missed the bridegroom coming and were shut out. I had always supposed this parable, which I did not like, had to do with prudence, preparedness, something like that. But I could see that Naomi's father believed it to be about sex. I looked sideways at Naomi to catch that slight sucking in of the corners of the mouth, the facial drollery with which she always recognized this subject, but she was looking obstinate and miserable, disgusted by the very thing that was my secret pleasure – poetic flow of words, archaic expressions. *Said unto; tarried; Behold the bridegroom cometh.* She was so offended by all this that she could not even enjoy the word *virgins.*

His toothless mouth shut. Sly and proper as a baby's.

'No more for now. Think about it when the time comes. There's a lesson for young girls.'

'Stupid old bugger,' said Naomi, on the stairs.

'I feel – sorry for him.'

She jabbed me in the kidney.

'Hurry up, let's get out of here. He's liable to find something else. Reads the Bible till his eyes fall out. Serve him right.'

We ran out outside, up Mason Street. These long light evenings we visited every part of town. We loitered past the Lyceum Theatre, the Blue Owl Cafe, the poolroom. We sat on the benches by the cenotaph, and if any car honked at us we waved. Dismayed by our greenness, our leggy foolishness, they drove on by; they laughed out their windows. We went into the ladies' toilet in the Town Hall – wet floor, sweating cement walls, harsh ammoniac smell – and there on the toilet door where only bad brainless girls wrote up their names, we wrote the names of the two reigning queens of our class – Marjory Coutts, Gwen Mundy. We wrote in lipstick and drew tiny obscene figures underneath. Why did we do this? Did we hate those girls, to whom we were unfailingly obsequiously pleasant? No. Yes. We hated their immunity, well-bred lack of curiosity, whatever kept them floating, charitable and pleased, on the surface of life in Jubilee, and would float them on to sororities, engagements, marriages to doctors or lawyers in more prosperous places far away. We hated them just because they could never be imagined entering the Town Hall toilets.

Having done this, we ran away, not sure whether or not we had committed a criminal act.

We dared each other. Walking under street lights still as pale as flowers cut out of tissue paper, walking past unlighted windows from which we hoped the world watched, we did dares.

'Be like you have cerebral palsy. *Dare.*'

At once I came unjointed, lolled my head, rolled my eyes, began to talk incomprehensibly, in a cross insistent babble.

'Do it for a block. Never mind who we meet. Don't stop. *Dare.*'

We met old Dr Comber, spindly and stately, beautifully dressed. He stopped, and tapped his stick, and objected.

'What is this performance?'

'A fit, sir,' said Naomi plaintively. 'She's always having these fits.'

Making fun of poor, helpless, afflicted people. The bad taste, the heartlessness, the joy of it.

We went to the park, which was neglected, deserted, a triangle of land made too gloomy, by its big cedar trees, for children's play, and not attracting people who went for walks. Why should anybody in Jubilee walk to see more grass and dirt and trees, the same thing that pushed in on the town from every side? They would walk downtown, to look at stores, meet on the double sidewalks, feel the hope of activity. Naomi and I all by ourselves climbed the big cedar trees, scraped our knees on the bark, screamed as we never needed to when we were younger, seeing the branches part, revealing the tilted earth. We hung from the branches by our locked hands, by our ankles; we pretended to be baboons, prattling and gibbering. We felt the whole town lying beneath us, gaping, ready to be astounded.

There were noises peculiar to the season. Children on the sidewalks, skipping and singing in their clear, devout voices.

> *On the mountain stands a lady*
> *Who she is I do not know.*
> *All she wears is gold and silver.*
> *All she needs is a new pair of shoes!*

And the peacocks crying. We dropped from the trees and set off to look at them, down past the park, down a poor unnamed street running to the river. The peacocks belonged to a man named Pork Childs who drove the town garbage truck. The street had no sidewalks. We walked around puddles, gleaming in the soft mud. Pork Childs had a barn behind his house for his fowl. Neither barn nor house was painted.

There were the peacocks, walking around under the bare oak trees. How could we forget them, from one spring to the next?

The hens were easily forgotten, the sullen colors of their yard. But the males were never disappointing. Their astonishing, essential color, blue of breasts and throats and necks, darker feathers showing there like ink blots, or soft vegetation under tropical water. One had his tail spread, to show the blind eyes, painted satin. The little kingly, idiotic heads. Glory in the cold spring, a wonder of Jubilee.

The noise beginning again did not come from any of them. It pulled eyes up to what it was hard to believe we had not seen immediately – the one white peacock up in a tree, his tail full out, falling down through the branches like water over rock. Pure white, pure blessing, And hidden up above, his head gave out these frantic and upbraiding and disorderly cries.

'It's sex makes them scream,' said Naomi.

'Cats scream,' I said, remembering something from the farm. 'They will scream like anything when a tomcat is doing it to them.'

'Wouldn't you?' said Naomi.

Then we had to go, because Pork Childs appeared among his peacocks, walking quickly, rocking forward. All his toes had been amputated, we knew, after being frozen when he lay in a ditch long ago, too drunk to get home, before he joined the Baptist Church. 'Good evening, boys!' he hollered at us, his old greeting, his old joke. *Hello, boys! Hello, girls!* yelled from the cab of the garbage truck, yelled down all streets bleak or summery, never getting any answer. We ran.

Mr Chamberlain's car was parked in front of our house.

'Let's go in,' said Naomi. 'I want to see what he's doing to old Fern.'

Nothing. In the dining room Fern was trying on the flowered chiffon dress my mother was helping her to make for Donna Carling's wedding, at which she would be the soloist. My mother was sitting sideways on the chair in front of the sewing machine, while Fern revolved, like a big half-opened parasol, in front of her.

Mr Chamberlain was drinking a real drink, whisky and water. He drove to Porterfield to buy his whisky, Jubilee being dry. I was both proud and ashamed to have Naomi see the bottle on the sideboard, a thing that would never appear in her house. My mother excused his drinking, because he had been through the war.

'Here come these two lovely young ladies,' said Mr Chamberlain with great insincerity. 'Full of springtime and grace. All fresh from the out-of-doors.'

'Give us a drink,' I said, showing off in front of Naomi. But he laughed and put a hand over his glass.

'Not until you tell us where you've been.'

'We went down to Pork Childs' to look at the peacocks.'

'Down to see the pea-cocks. To see the pretty pea-cocks,' sang Mr Chamberlain.

'Give us a drink.'

'Del, behave yourself,' said my mother with a mouth full of pins.

'All I want is to find out what it tastes like.'

'Well I can't give you a drink for nothing. I don't see you doing any tricks for me. I don't see you sitting up and begging like a good doggie.'

'I can be a seal. Do you want to see me be a seal?'

This was one thing I loved to do. I never felt worried that it might not be perfect, that I might not be able to manage it; I was never afraid that anybody would think me a fool. I had even done it at school, for the Junior Red Cross amateur hour, and everyone laughed; this marveling laughter was so comforting, so absolving that I could have gone on being a seal forever.

I went down on my knees and held my elbows at my sides and worked my hands like flippers, meanwhile barking, my wonderful braying bark. I had copied from an old Mary Martin movie where Mary Martin sings a song beside a turquoise pool and the seals bark in a chorus.

Mr Chamberlain gradually lowered his glass and brought it close to my lips, withdrawing it, however, every time I stopped barking. I was kneeling by his chair. Fern had her back to me, her arms raised; my mother's head was hidden, as she pinned the material at Fern's waist. Naomi who had seen the seal often enough before and had an interest in dressmaking was looking at Fern and my mother. Mr Chamberlain at last allowed my lips to touch the rim of the glass which he held in one hand. Then with the other hand he did something nobody could see. He rubbed against the damp underarm of my blouse and then inside the loose armhole of the jumper I was wearing. He rubbed quick, hard against the cotton over my breast. So hard he pushed the yielding flesh up, flattened it. And at once withdrew. It was like a slap, to leave me stung.

'Well, what does it taste like?' Naomi asked me afterwards.

'Like piss.'

'You never tasted piss.' She gave me a shrewd baffled look; she could always sense secrets.

I meant to tell her, but I did not, I held it back. If I told her, it would have to be re-enacted.

'How? How did he have his hand when he started? How did he get it under your jumper? Did he rub or squeeze, or both? With his fingers or his palm? Like *this*?'

There was a dentist in town, Dr Phippen, brother of the deaf librarian, who was supposed to have put his hand up a girl's leg while looking at her back teeth. Naomi and I passing under his window would say loudly, 'Don't you wish you had an appointment with Dr Phippen? Dr Feely Phippen. He's a thorough man!' It would be like that with

Mr Chamberlain; we would turn it into a joke, and hope
for scandal, and make up schemes to entrap him, and that
was not what I wanted.

'It was beautiful,' said Naomi, sounding tired.

'What?'

'That peacock. In the tree.'

I was surprised, and a little annoyed, to hear her use
the word *beautiful*, about something like that, and to have
her remember it, because I was used to have her act in
a certain way, be aware of certain things, nothing else. I
had already thought, running home, that I would write
a poem about the peacock. To have her thinking about it
too was almost like trespassing; I never let her or anyone
in that part of my mind.

I did start writing my poem when I went upstairs to bed.

> *What in the trees is crying these veiled nights?*
> *The peacocks crying or the winter's ghost?*

That was the best part of it.

I also thought about Mr Chamberlain, his hand which
was different from anything he had previously shown
about himself, in his eyes, his voice, his laugh, his stories.
It was like a signal, given where it will be understood.
Impertinent violation, so perfectly sure of itself, so
authoritative, clean of sentiment.

Next time he came I made it easy for him to do something
again, standing near him while he was getting his rubbers
on in the dark hall. Every time, then, I waited for the signal,
and got it. He did not bother with a pinch on the arm or a
pat on the arm or a hug around the shoulders, fatherly or

comradely. He went straight for the breasts, the buttocks, the upper thighs, brutal as lightning. And this was what I expected sexual communication to be – a flash of insanity, a dreamlike, ruthless, contemptuous breakthrough in a world of decent appearances. I had discarded those ideas of love, consolation, and tenderness, nourished by my feelings for Frank Wales; all that now seemed pale and extraordinarily childish. In the secret violence of sex would be recognition, going away beyond kindness, beyond good will or persons.

Not that I was planning on sex. One stroke of lightning does not have to lead anywhere, but to the next stroke of lightning.

Nevertheless my knees weakened, when Mr Chamberlain honked the horn at me. He was waiting half a block from the school. Naomi was not with me; she had tonsillitis.

'Where's your girl friend?'

'She's sick.'

'That's a shame. Want a lift home?'

In the car I trembled. My tongue was dry, my whole mouth was dry so I could hardly speak. Was this what desire was? Wish to know, fear to know, amounting to anguish? Being alone with him, no protection of people or circumstances, made a difference. What could he want to do here, in broad daylight, on the seat of his car?

He did not make a move towards me. But he did not head for River Street; he drove sedately along various side streets, avoiding winter-made potholes.

'You think you're the girl to do me a favor, if I asked you?'

'All right.'

'What do you think it might be?'

'I don't know.'

He parked the car behind the creamery, under the chestnut trees with the leaves just out, bitter yellowy green. Here?

'You get into Fern's room? You could get into her room when everybody was out of the house?'

I brought my mind back, slowly, from expectations of rape.

'You could get in her room and do a little investigation for me on what she's got there. Something that might interest me. What do you think it would be, eh? What do you think interests me?'

'What?'

'Letters,' said Mr Chamberlain with a sudden drop in tone, becoming matter-of-fact, depressed by some reality he could look into and I couldn't. 'See if she has got any old letters. They might be in her drawers. Might be in her closet. Probably keeps them in an old box of some kind. Tied up in bundles, that's what women do.'

'Letters from who?'

'From me. Who do you think? You don't need to read them, just look at the signature. Written some time ago, the paper might be showing age. I don't know. Written in pen I recall so they're probably still legible. Here. I'll give you a sample of my handwriting, that'll help you out.' He took an envelope out of the glove compartment and wrote on it: *Del is a bad girl*.

I put it in my Latin book.

'Don't let Fern see that, she'd recognize the writing. And not your Mama. She might wonder about what I wrote. Be a surprise to her, wouldn't it?'

He drove me home. I wanted to get out at the corner of River Street but he said no. 'That just looks as if we've got something to hide. Now, how are you going to let me know? How about Sunday night, when I come around for supper, I'll ask you whether you've got your homework done! If you've found them, you'll say yes. If you've looked and you haven't found them, you'll say no. If for some reason you never got a chance to take a look, you say you forget whether you had any.'

He made me repeat, 'Yes means found them, no means didn't find them, forget means didn't get a chance to look.' This drill insulted me; I was famous for my memory.

'All right. Cheers.' Below the level that anybody could see, looking at the car, he bounced his fist off my leg, hard enough to hurt. I hauled myself and my books out, and once I was alone, my thigh still tingling, I took out the envelope and read what he had written. *Del is a bad girl.* Mr Chamberlain assumed without any trouble at all that there was treachery in me, as well as criminal sensuality, waiting to be used. He had known I would not cry out when he flattened my breast, he had known I would not mention it to my mother; he knew now I would not report this conversation to Fern, but would spy on her as he had asked. Could he have hit upon my true self? It was true that in the dullness of school I had worked with my protractor and compass, I had written out Latin sentences [*having pitched camp and slaughtered the horses of the enemy by means of stealth, Vercingetorix prepared to give battle on the following day*] and all the time been conscious of my depravity vigorous as spring wheat, my body flowering with invisible bruises in those places where it had been touched. Wearing blue rompers, washing with soap that would nearly take your skin off, after a volleyball game, I had looked in the mirror of the girls' washroom and smiled secretly at my ruddy face, to think what lewdness I had been invited to, what deceits I was capable of.

I got into Fern's room on Saturday morning, when my mother had gone out to do some cleaning at the farm. I looked around at leisure, at the koala bear sitting on her pillow, powder spilled on the dresser, jars with a little bit of dried-up deodorant, salve, night cream, old lipstick, and nail polish with the top stuck on. A picture of a lady in a dress of many dripping layers, like an arrangement of scarves, probably Fern's mother, holding a fat woollied baby, probably Fern. Fern for sure in soft focus with butterfly sleeves, holding a sheaf of roses, curls laid in layers on her head. And snapshots stuck around the mirror, their edges curling. Mr Chamberlain in a sharp straw hat, white pants, looking at the camera as if he knew more than it did. Fern not so plump as now, but plump, wearing shorts, sitting on a log in some vacationtime woods. Mr Chamberlain and Fern dressed up – she with a corsage – snapped by a street photographer in a strange city, walking under the marquee of a movie house where *Anchors Aweigh!* was showing. The post office employees' picnic in the park at Tupperton, a cloudy day, and Fern, jolly in slacks, holding a baseball bat.

I did not find any letters. I looked through her drawers, on her closet shelves, under her bed, even inside her suitcases. I did find three separate saved bundles of paper, with elastic bands around them.

One bundle contained a chain letter and a great many

copies of the same verse, in pencil or ink, different hand-writings, some typewritten or mimeographed.

> *This prayer has already been around the world six times. It was originated in the Isle of Wight by a clairvoyant seer who saw it in a dream. Copy this letter out six times and mail it to six friends, then copy the attached prayer out and mail it to six names at the top of the attached list. Six days from the time you receive this letter you will begin to get copies of this prayer from all corners of the earth and they will bring you blessings and good luck* IF YOU DO NOT BREAK THE CHAIN. *If you break the chain you may expect something sad and unpleasant to happen to you six months to the day from the day when you receive this letter.* DO NOT BREAK THE CHAIN. DO NOT OMIT THE SECRET WORD AT THE END. BY MEANS OF THIS PRAYER HAPPINESS AND GOOD LUCK ARE BEING SPREAD THROUGHOUT THE WORLD.
>
> *Peace and love, O Lord I pray*
> *Shower on this friend today.*
> *Heal his(her) troubles, bless his(her) heart,*
> *From the source of strength and love may he (she) never have to part.* KARKAHMD

Another bundle was made up of several sheets of smudgy printing broken by blurred gray illustrations of what I thought at first were enema bags with tangled tubes, but which on reading the text I discovered to be cross sections of the male and female anatomy, with such

things as pessaries, tampons, condoms (these proper terms
were all new to me) being inserted or fitted on. I could
not look at these illustrations without feeling alarm and a
strong local discomfort, so I started reading. I read about
a poor farmer's wife in North Carolina throwing herself
under a wagon when she discovered she was going to have
her ninth child, about women dying in tenements from
complications of pregnancy or childbirth or terrible failed
abortions which they performed with hatpins, knitting
needles, bubbles of air. I read, or skipped, statistics about
the increase in population, laws which had been passed in
various countries for and against birth control, women
who had gone to jail for advocating it. Then there were the
instructions on using different devices. Naomi's mother's
book had had a chapter about this too, but we never got
around to reading it, being bogged down in 'Case Histories
and Varieties of Intercourse.' All I read now about foam
and jelly, even the use of the word 'vagina,' made the whole
business seem laborious and domesticated, somehow
connected with ointments and bandages and hospitals,
and it gave me the same feeling of disgusted, ridiculous
helplessness I had when it was necessary to undress at the
doctor's.

In the third bundle were typewritten verses. Some had
titles. 'Homemade Lemon Squeeze.' 'The Lament of the
Truck Driver's Wife.'

> Husband, dear husband, what am I to do?
> I'm wanting some hard satisfaction from you.
> You're never at home or you're never awake.
> (A big cock in my pussy is all it would take!)

I was surprised that any adult would know, or still remember, these words. The greedy progression of verses, the short chunky words set in shameless type, fired up lust at a great rate, like squirts of kerosene on bonfires. But they were repetitive, elaborate; after awhile the mechanical effort needed to contrive them began to be felt, and made them heavy going; they grew bewilderingly dull. But the words themselves still gave off flashes of power, particularly *fuck*, which I had never been able to really look at on fences or sidewalks. I had never been able to contemplate before its thrust of brutality, hypnotic swagger.

I said no to Mr Chamberlain, when he asked me if I had got my homework done. He did not touch me all evening. But when I came out of school on Monday, he was there.

'Girl friend still sick? That's too bad. Nice though. Isn't it nice?'

'What?'

'Birds are nice. Trees are nice. Nice you can come for a drive with me, do my little investigations for me.' He said this in an infantile voice. Evil would never be grand, with him. His voice suggested that it would be possible to do anything, anything at all, and pass it off as a joke, a joke on all the solemn and guilty, all the moral and emotional people in the world, the people who 'took themselves seriously.' That was what he could not stand in people. His little smile was repulsive; self-satisfaction stretched over quite an abyss of irresponsibility, or worse. This did not give me second thoughts about going with him, and doing whatever it was he had in mind to do. His moral character was of no importance to me there; perhaps it was even necessary that it should be black.

Excitement owing something to Fern's dirty verses had got the upper hand of me, entirely.

'Did you get a good look?' he said in a normal voice.

'Yes.'

'Didn't find a thing? Did you look in all her drawers? I mean her *dresser* drawers. Hatboxes, suitcases? Went through her closet?'

'I looked and looked everywhere,' I said demurely.

'She must have got rid of them.'

'I guess she isn't sentimental.'

'Sennamenal? I don't know what dose big words mean, little dirl.'

We were driving out of town. We drove south on the No. 4 Highway and turned down the first side road. 'Beautiful morning,' said Mr Chamberlain. 'Pardon me – beautiful afternoon, beautiful day.' I looked out the window; the countryside I knew was altered by his presence, his voice, overpowering foreknowledge of the errand we were going on together. For a year or two I had been looking at trees, fields, landscape with a secret, strong exaltation. In some moods, some days, I could feel for a clump of grass, a rail fence, a stone pile, such pure unbounded emotion as I used to hope for, and have inklings of, in connection with God. I could not do it when I was with anybody, of course, and now with Mr Chamberlain I saw that the whole of nature became debased, maddeningly erotic. It was just now the richest, greenest time of year; ditches sprouted coarse daisies, toadflax, buttercups, hollows were full of nameless faintly golden bushes and the gleam of high creeks. I saw all this as a vast arrangement of hiding places, ploughed fields beyond rearing up like shameless mattresses. Little paths, opening in the bushes, crushed places in the grass, where no doubt a cow had lain, seemed to me specifically, urgently inviting as certain words or pressures.

'Hope we don't meet your mama, driving along here.'

I did not think it possible. My mother inhabited a different layer of reality from the one I had got into now.

Mr Chamberlain drove off the road, following a track that ended soon, in a field half gone to brush. The stopping of the car, cessation of that warm flow of sound and motion in which I had been suspended, jarred me a little. Events were becoming real.

'Let's take a little walk down to the creek.'

He got out on his side, I got out on mine. I followed him, down a slope between some hawthorn trees, in bloom, yeasty smelling. This was a traveled route, with cigarette packages, a beer bottle, a Chicklet box lying on the grass. Little trees, bushes closed around us.

'Why don't we call a halt here?' said Mr Chamberlain in a practical way. 'It gets soggy down by the water.'

Here in the half-shade above the creek I was cold, and so violently anxious to know what would be done to me that all the heat and dancing itch between my legs had gone dead, numb as if a piece of ice had been laid to it. Mr Chamberlain opened his jacket and loosened his belt, then unzipped himself. He reached in to part some inner curtains, and 'Boo!' he said.

Not at all like marble David's, it was sticking straight out in front of him, which I knew from my reading was what they did. It had a sort of head on it, like a mushroom, and its color was reddish purple. It looked blunt and stupid, compared, say, to fingers and toes with their intelligent expressiveness, or even to an elbow or a knee. It did not seem frightening to me, though I thought this might have been what Mr Chamberlain intended, standing there with his tightly watching look, his hands holding his pants apart to display it. Raw and blunt, ugly-colored as a wound, it looked to me vulnerable, playful and naive, like some strong-snouted animal whose grotesque simple looks are some sort of guarantee of good will. (The opposite of what beauty usually is.) It did not bring back any of my excitement, though. It did not seem to have anything to do with me.

Still watching me, and smiling, Mr Chamberlain placed his hand around this thing and began to pump up and down, not too hard, in a controlled efficient rhythm. His face softened; his eyes, still fixed on me, grew glassy. Gradually, almost experimentally, he increased the speed of his hand; the rhythm became less smooth. He crouched over, his smile opened out and drew the lips back from his teeth and his eyes rolled slightly upward. His breathing became loud and shaky, now he worked furiously with his hand, moaned, almost doubled over in spasmodic agony. The face he thrust out at me, from his crouch, was blind and wobbling like a mask on a stick, and those sounds coming out of his mouth, involuntary, last-ditch human noises, were at the same time theatrical, unlikely. In fact the whole performance, surrounded by calm flowering branches, seemed imposed, fantastically and predictably exaggerated, like an Indian dance. I had read about the body being in extremities of pleasure, possessed, but these expressions did not seem equal to the terrible benighted effort, deliberate frenzy, of what was going on here. If he did not soon get to where he wanted to be, I thought he would die. But then he let out a new kind of moan, the most desperate and the loudest yet; it quavered as if somebody was hitting him on the voice box. This died, miraculously, into a peaceful grateful whimper, as stuff shot out of him, the real whitish stuff, the seed, and caught the hem of my skirt. He straightened up, shaky, out of breath, and tucked himself quickly back inside his trousers. He got out a handkerchief and wiped first his hands then my skirt.

'Lucky for you? Eh?' He laughed at me, though he still had not altogether got his breath back.

After such a convulsion, such a revelation, how could a man just put his handkerchief in his pocket, check his fly, and start walking back – still somewhat flushed and bloodshot – the way we had come?

The only thing he said was in the car, when he sat for a moment composing himself before he turned the key.

'Quite a sight, eh?' was what he said.

The landscape was postcoital, distant and meaningless. Mr Chamberlain may have felt some gloom too, or apprehension, for he made me get down on the floor of the car as we re-entered town, and then he drove around and let me out in a lonely place, where the road dipped down near the CNR station. He felt enough like himself, however, to tap me in the crotch with his fist, as if testing a coconut for soundness.

That was a valedictory appearance for Mr Chamberlain, as I ought to have guessed it might be. I came home at noon to find Fern sitting at the dining-room table, which was set for dinner, listening to my mother calling from the kitchen over the noise of the potato masher.

'Doesn't matter what anybody says. You weren't married. You weren't engaged. It's nobody's business. Your life is your own.'

'Want to see my little love letter?' said Fern, and fluttered it under my nose.

> Dear Fern, Owing to circumstances beyond my control, I am taking off this evening in my trusty Pontiac and heading for points west. There is a lot of the world I haven't seen yet and no sense getting fenced in. I may send you a postcard from California or Alaska, who knows? Be a good girl as you always were and keep licking those stamps and steaming open the mail, you may find a hundred-dollar-bill yet. When Mama dies I will probably come home, but not for long. Cheers, Art.

The same hand that had written: *Del is a bad girl*.

'Tampering with the mails is a Federal offense,' said my mother, coming in. 'I don't think that is very witty, what he says.'

She distributed canned carrots, mashed potatoes, meat loaf. No matter what the season, we ate a heavy meal in the middle of the day.

'Looks like it hasn't put me off my food, anyway,' said Fern, sighing. She poured ketchup. 'I could have had him. Long ago, if I'd wanted. He even wrote me letters mentioning marriage. I should have kept them, I could have breach-of-promised him.'

'A good thing you didn't,' said my mother spiritedly, 'or where would you be today?'

'Didn't what? Breach-of-promised him or married him?'

'Married him. Breach-of-promise is a degradation to women.'

'Oh, I wasn't in danger of marriage.'

'You had your singing. You had your interest in life.'

'I was just usually having too good a time. I knew enough about marriage to know that's when your good times stop.'

When Fern talked about having a good time she meant going to dances at the Lakeshore Pavilion, going to the Regency Hotel in Tupperton for drinks and dinner, being driven from one roadhouse to another on Saturday night. My mother did try to understand such pleasures, but she could not, any more than she could understand why people go on rides at a fair, and will get off and throw up, then go on rides again.

Fern was not one to grieve, in spite of her acquaintance with opera. Her expressed feeling was that men always went, and better they did before you got sick of them. But she grew very talkative; she was never silent.

'As bad as Art was,' she said to Owen, eating supper. 'He wouldn't touch any yellow vegetable. His mother should have taken the paddle to him when he was little. That's what I used to tell him.'

'You're built the opposite from Art,' she told my father. 'The trouble with getting his suits fitted was he was so long in the body, short in the leg. Ransom's in Tupperton was the only place that could fit him.'

'Only one time I saw him lose his temper. At the Pavilion

when we went to a dance there, and a fellow asked me to dance, and I got up with him because what can you do, and he put his face down, right away down on my neck. Guzzling me up like I was chocolate icing! Art said to him, if you have to slobber don't do it on my girl friend, I might want her myself! And he yanked him off. He did so!'

I would come into a room where she was talking to my mother and there would be an unnatural, waiting silence. My mother would be listening with a trapped, determinedly compassionate, miserable face. What could she do? Fern was her good, perhaps her only, friend. But there were things she never thought she would have to hear. She may have missed Mr Chamberlain.

'He treated you shabbily,' she said to Fern, against Fern's shrugs and ambiguous laugh. 'He did. He did. My estimation of a person has never gone down so fast. But nevertheless I miss him when I hear them trying to read the radio news.'

For the Juibilee station had not found anybody else who could read the news the way it was now, full of Russian names, without panicking, and they had let somebody call Bach *Batch* on *In Memoriam*, when they played 'Jesu Joy of Man's Desiring.' It made my mother wild.

I had meant to tell Naomi all about Mr Chamberlain, now it was over. But Naomi came out of her illness fifteen pounds lighter, with a whole new outlook on life. Her forthrightness was gone with her chunky figure. Her language was purified. Her daring had collapsed. She had a new delicate regard for herself. She sat under a tree with her skirt spread around her, watching the rest of us play volleyball, and kept feeling her forehead to see if she was feverish. She was not even interested in the fact that Mr Chamberlain had gone, so preoccupied was she with herself and her illness. Her temperature had risen to over a hundred and five degrees. All the grosser aspects of sex had disappeared from her conversation and apparently from her mind although she talked a good deal about Dr Wallis, and how he had sponged her legs himself, and she had been quite helplessly exposed to him, when she was sick.

So I had not the relief of making what Mr Chamberlain had done into a funny, though horrifying, story. I did not know what to do with it. I could not get him back to his old role, I could not make him play the single-minded, simple-minded, vigorous, obliging lecher of my daydreams. My faith in simple depravity had weakened. Perhaps nowhere but in daydreams did the trap door open so sweetly and easily, plunging bodies altogether free of thought, free of personality, into self-indulgence, mad bad license. Instead of that, Mr Chamberlain had shown me, people take along a good deal – flesh that is not overcome but has to be thumped into ecstasy, all the stubborn puzzle and dark turns of themselves.

In June there was the annual strawberry supper on the lawns behind the United Church. Fern went down to sing at it, wearing the flowered chiffon dress my mother had helped her make. It was now very tight at the waist. Since Mr Chamberlain had gone Fern had put on weight, so that she was not now soft and bulgy but really fat, swollen up like a boiled pudding, her splotched skin not shady any more but stretched and shiny.

She patted herself around the midriff. 'Anyway they

won't be able to say I'm pining, will they? It'll be a scandal if I split the seams.'

We heard her high heels going down the sidewalk. On leafy, cloudy, quiet evenings under the trees, sounds carried a long way. Sociable noise of the United Church affair washed as far as our steps. Did my mother wish she had a hat and a summer sheer dress on, and was going? Her agnosticism and sociability were often in conflict in Jubilee, where social and religious life were apt to be one and the same. Fern had told her to come ahead. 'You're a member. Didn't you tell me you joined when you got married?'

'My ideas weren't formed then. Now I'd be a hypocrite. I'm not a believer.'

'Think all of them are?'

I was on the veranda reading *Arch of Triumph*, a book I had got out of the library. The library had been left some money and had bought a supply of new books, mostly on the recommendation of Mrs Wallis, the doctor's wife, who had a college degree but not perhaps the tastes the Council had been counting on. There had been complaints, people had said it should have been left up to Bella Phippen, but only one book – *The Hucksters* – had actually been removed from the shelves. I had read it first. My mother had picked it up and read a few pages and been saddened.

'I never expected to see such a use made of the printed word.'

'It's about the advertising business, how corrupt it is.'

'That's not the only thing is corrupt, I'm afraid. Next day they will be telling about how they go to the toilet, why do they leave that out? There isn't any of that in *Silas*

Marner. There isn't in the classic writers. They were good writers, they didn't need it.'

I had turned away from my old favorites, *Kristin Lavransdatter*, historical novels. I read modern books now. Somerset Maugham. Nancy Mitford. I read about rich and titled people who despised the very sort of people who in Jubilee were at the top of society – druggists, dentists, storekeepers. I learned names like Balenciaga, Schiaparelli. I knew about drinks. Whisky and soda. Gin and tonic. Cinzano, Benedictine, Grand Marnier. I knew the names of hotels, streets, restaurants, in London, Paris, Singapore. In these books people did go to bed together, they did it all the time, but the descriptions of what they were up to there were not thorough, in spite of what my mother thought. One book compared having sexual intercourse to going through a train tunnel (presumably if you were the whole train) and blasting out into a mountain meadow so high, so blest and beautiful, you felt as if you were in the sky. Books always compared it to something else, never told about it by itself.

'You can't read there,' my mother said. 'You can't read in that light. Come down on the steps.'

So I came, but she did not want me to read at all. She wanted company.

'See, the lilacs are turning. Soon we'll be going out to the farm.'

Along the front of our yard, by the sidewalk, were purple lilacs gone pale as soft, delicate scrub rags, rusty specked. Beyond them the road, already dusty, and banks of wild blackberry bushes growing in front of the boarded-up factory, on which we could still read the big, faded, vainglorious letters: MUNDY PIANOS.

'I'm sorry for Fern,' my mother said. 'I'm sorry for her life.'

Her sad confidential tone warned me off.

'Maybe she'll find a new boy friend tonight.'

'What do you mean? She's not after a new boy friend. She's had enough of all that. She's going to sing "Where'er You Walk." She's got a lovely voice, still.'

'She's getting fat.'

My mother spoke to me in her grave, hopeful, lecturing voice.

'There is a change coming I think in the lives of girls and women. Yes. But it is up to us to make it come. All women have had up till now has been their connection with men. All we have had. No more lives of our own, really, than domestic animals. *He shall hold thee, when his passion shall have spent its novel force, a little closer than his dog, a little dearer than his horse.* Tennyson wrote that. It's true. *Was* true. You will want to have children, though.'

That was how much she knew me.

'But I hope you will – use your brains. Use your brains. Don't be distracted. Once you make that mistake, of being – distracted, over a man, your life will never be your own. You will get the burden, a woman always does.'

'There is birth control nowadays,' I reminded her, and she looked at me startled, though it was she herself who had publicly embarrassed our family, writing to the Jubilee *Herald-Advance* that 'prophylactic devices should be distributed to all women on public relief in Wawanash County, to help them prevent any further increase in their families.' Boys at school had yelled at me, 'Hey, when is your momma giving out the proplastic devices?'

'That is not enough, though of course it is a great boon and religion is the enemy of it as it is of everything that might ease the pangs of life on earth. It is self-respect I am really speaking of. Self-respect.'

I did not quite get the point of this, or if I did get the point I was set up to resist it. I would have had to resist anything she told me with such earnestness, such stubborn hopefulness. Her concern about my life, which I needed and took for granted, I could not bear to have expressed. Also I felt that it was not so different from all the other advice handed out to women, to girls, advice that assumed being female made you damageable, that a certain amount of carefulness and solemn fuss and self-protection were called for, whereas men were supposed to be able to go out and take on all kinds of experiences and shuck off what they didn't want and come back proud. Without even thinking about it, I had decided to do the same.

BAPTIZING

In our third year at high school Naomi switched to Commercial; suddenly freed from Latin, physics, algebra, she mounted to the third floor of the school where under the sloping roof typewriters clacked all day and the walls were hung with framed maxims preparing one for life in the business world. *Time and Energy are my Capital; if I Squander them, I shall get no Other.* The effect, after the downstairs classrooms with their blackboards covered with foreign words and abstract formulae, their murky pictures of battles and shipwrecks and heady but decent mythological adventures, was that of coming into cool ordinary light, the real and busy world. A relief to most. Naomi liked it.

In March of that year she got a job in the office of the creamery. She was through with school. She told me to come and see her after four o'clock. I did, without much idea of what I was getting into. I thought Naomi would make a face at me from behind the counter. I was going to put on my quavery old-lady voice and say to her, 'What is the meaning of this? Yesterday I bought a dozen eggs here and they was every one rotten!'

The office was in a low stucco addition, built on to the front of the old creamery. There were fluorescent lights and new metal filing cabinets and desks – the sort of surroundings in which I felt instinctively out of place – and an efficient noise of typewriters and an adding machine. Two girls besides Naomi were working there; I found out later their names were Molly and Carla. Naomi's nails were coral; she had done her hair quite successfully; she was wearing a pink and green plaid skirt and pink sweater. New. She smiled at me and waggled her fingers above the typewriter in minimal greeting, then went on typing at a great rate and conducting a gay, disjointed, incomprehensible conversation with her co-workers. After several minutes of this she called to me that she would be through at five o'clock. I said I had to go home. I felt that Molly and Carla were looking at me, at the ink on my bare red hands, my slipping woolen kerchief, wild hair, schoolgirlish pile of books.

Well-groomed girls frightened me to death. I didn't like to even go near them, for fear I would be smelly. I felt there was a radical difference, between them and me, as if we were made of different substances. Their cool hands did not mottle or sweat, their hair kept its calculated shape, their underarms were never wet – they did not know what it was to have to keep their elbows pinned to their sides to hide the dark, disgraceful half-moon stains on their dresses – and never, never would they feel that little extra gush of blood, little bonus that no Kotex is going to hold, that will trickle horrifyingly down the inside of the thighs. No indeed; their periods would be discreet; nature served and did not betray them. Nor would my coarseness ever be translated into their fineness; it was too late, the difference lay too deep for that. But what about Naomi? She had been like me; once she had had an epidemic of warts on her fingers; she had suffered from athlete's foot; we had hidden in the girls' toilet together when we had the curse at the same time and were afraid to do tumbling – one at a time, in front of the rest of the class – afraid of some slipping or bleeding, and too embarrassed to ask to be excused. What was this masquerade she was going in for now, with her nail polish, her pastel sweater?

She was soon great friends with Molly and Carla. Her conversation, when she came over to my house or summoned me to hers, was full of their diets, skin-care routines, hair-shampooing methods, clothes, diaphragms (Molly had been married for a year and Carla was to be married in June). Sometimes Carla came to Naomi's house when I was there; she and Naomi always talked about washing, either washing their sweaters or washing their underclothes or washing their hair. They would say, 'I washed my cardigan!' '*Did* you? Did you wash it cold or lukewarm?' 'Lukewarm but I think it's all right.' 'What did you do about the neck?' I would sit there thinking how grubby my sweater was and that my hair was greasy and my brassiere discolored, one strap held on with a safety pin. I would have to get away, but when I got home I would not sew my brassiere strap on or wash my sweater. Sweaters I washed always shrank, anyway, or the neckline sagged; I knew I did not take enough trouble with them but I had a fatalistic feeling that they would shrink or sag whatever I did. Sometimes I did wash my hair, and did it up on horrible steel curlers that prevented me from sleeping; in fact I could spend hours, now and then, in front of a mirror, painfully plucking my eyebrows, looking at my profile, shading my face with dark and light powder, to emphasize its good points and minimize the bad, as recommended in the magazines. It was sustained attention I was not capable of, though everything from advertisements to F. Scott Fitzgerald to a frightening song on the radio – *the girl that I marry will have to be, as soft and pink as a nursery* – was telling me I would have to, *have to*, learn. Love is not for the undepilated.

As for hair washing: about this time I started to read an article in a magazine, on the subject of the basic difference between the male and female habits of thought, relating chiefly to their experience of sex (the title of the article made you think it would tell a great deal more about sex than it actually did). The author was a famous New York psychiatrist, a disciple of Freud. He said that the difference between the male and female modes of thought were easily illustrated by the thoughts of a boy and girl, sitting on a park bench, looking at the full moon. The boy thinks of the universe, its immensity and mystery; the girl thinks, 'I must wash my hair.' When I read this I was frantically upset; I had to put the magazine down. It was clear to me at once that I was not thinking as the girl thought; the full moon would never as long as I lived remind me to wash my hair. I knew if I showed it to my mother she would say, 'Oh, it is just that maddening male nonsense, women have no brains.' That would not convince me; surely a New York psychiatrist must *know.* And women like my mother were in the minority, I could see that. Moreover I did not want to be like my mother, with her virginal brusqueness, her innocence. I wanted men to love me, *and* I wanted to think of the universe when I looked at the moon. I felt trapped, stranded; it seemed there had to be a choice where there couldn't be a choice. I didn't want to read any more of the article but was drawn back to it as I would be drawn back when I was younger to a certain picture of a dark sea, a towering whale, in a book of fairy stories; my eyes nervously jumped across the page, starting at such assertions as: *For a woman, everything is personal; no idea is of any interest to her by itself, but must be translated into her own experience; in works of art she always sees her own life, or her daydreams.* Finally I took the magazine out to the garbage pail, ripped it in half, stuffed it inside, tried to forget it. Afterwards when I would see an article in a magazine called 'Femininity – It's Making a Comeback!' or a quiz for teenagers with the heading 'Is Your Problem that You're Trying To Be a Boy?' I would turn the page quickly as if something was trying to bite me. Yet it had never occurred to me to want to be a boy.

Through Molly and Carla, and through her new position as a working girl, Naomi was becoming part of a circle in Jubilee that neither she nor I had really known existed. This circle took in the girls who worked in stores and in offices and the two banks, as well as some girls, married, who had recently left their jobs. If they were not married and did not have boy friends they went to dances together. They went bowling together in Tupperton. They gave showers for each other, for getting married and having babies (this latter was a new custom, offending some older ladies in town). Their relations with each other, though full of scandalous confidences, were yet hedged about with all kinds of subtle formalities, courtesies, proprieties. It was not like school; no savagery, meanness, no crude language, but always a complicated network of feuds obliquely referred to, always some crisis – a pregnancy, an abortion, a jilting – which they all knew about and talked about but guarded as their secret, keeping it away from the rest of the town. The most innocent or consoling and flattering things they said might mean something else. They were tolerant of what most people in town would think of as moral lapses in each other, but quite intolerant of departures in dress and hair style, and people not cutting the crusts off sandwiches, at showers.

As soon as she started getting paychecks Naomi began to do what it seemed all these girls did, until they got married. She went around to various stores and had them put things away for her, which she would pay for at so much a month. In the hardware store she had a whole set of pots and pans put away, in the jewelry store a case of silverware, in the Walker store a blanket and set of towels and a pair of linen sheets. This was all for when she would get married and start housekeeping; it was the first I knew that she planned on anything so definite. 'You have to get started sometime,' she said irritably. 'What are you going to get married with, two plates and an old dishrag?'

On Saturday afternoons she wanted me to go round

to the stores with her while she made her payments and
looked at her future possessions, and talked about why, like
Molly, she was going to go in for waterless cooking and
how you could tell the quality of sheets by the number of
threads to the square inch. I was amazed and intimidated
by her as her boring and preoccupied new self. It seemed
as if she had got miles ahead of me. Where she was going I
did not want to go, but it looked as if *she* wanted to; things
were progressing for her. Could the same be said for me?

What I really wanted to do on Saturday afternoons was
stay home and listen to the Metropolitan Opera. This
habit dated from the time when we had Fern Dogherty
boarding with us, and she and my mother used to listen.
Fern Dogherty had left Jubilee, she had gone to work in
Windsor, and she wrote us vague, infrequent, cheerful
letters, about going across to Detroit to a night club, going
to the races, singing with the Light Opera Society, having
a good time. Naomi said of her, 'That Fern Dogherty
was just a joke.' She was speaking from her new vantage
point. She and all these other girls were firmly set towards
marriage; older women who had not married, whether
they were perfect old maids or discreet adventuresses,
like Fern, could not expect any sympathy from them.
How was she a joke? I wanted to know, troublesomely,
but Naomi opened her pale, bright, protruding eyes at me
and repeated, 'A joke, she was just a *joke!*' like someone
dispensing, in the face of fumbling heresies, self-evident
handsome pieces of dogma.

My mother did not pay much attention to the opera
any more. She knew the characters and the plot and could
recognize the famous arias; there was nothing more to

learn. Sometimes she was out; she still kept going on her encyclopedia rounds; people who had already bought a set had to be talked into buying the yearly supplements. But she was not well. At first she had been plagued by a whole series of uncommon ailments – a plantar's wart, an eye infection, swollen glands, ringing in the ears, nosebleeds, a mysterious scaly rash. She kept going to the doctor. Things would clear up but something else would start. What was really happening was a failure of energy, a falling back, that nobody would have looked for. It was not steady. She would still sometimes write a letter to the paper; she was trying to teach herself astronomy. But sometimes she would go and lie on her bed and call me to put a quilt over her. I would always do it too carelessly; she would call me back and make me tuck it in at the knees, around the feet. Then she would say, in a petulant, put-on, childish voice, 'Kiss Mother.' I would drop one dry, stingy kiss on her temple. Her hair was getting quite thin. The exposed white skin of the temple had an unhealthy suffering look that I disliked.

I preferred to be by myself, anyway, when I listened to *Lucia di Lammermoor*, *Carmen*, *La Traviata*. Certain passages in the music excited me so that I could not sit still but would have to get up and walk round and round the dining room, singing in my head with the voices on the radio, hugging myself and squeezing my elbows. My eyes filled with tears. Swiftly formed fantasies boiled up in me, I pictured a lover, stormy circumstances, doomed throbbing glory of our passion. (It never occurred to me that I was doing what the article said women did, with works of art.) Voluptuous surrender. Not to a man but to fate, really, to darkness, to death. Yet I loved most of all *Carmen*, at the end. *Et laissez moi passer!* I hissed it between my teeth; I was shaken, imagining the other surrender, more tempting, more gorgeous even than the surrender to sex – the hero's, the patriot's, Carmen's surrender to the final importance of gesture, image, self-created self.

Opera made me hungry. When it was over I went into the kitchen and made fried-egg sandwiches, stacks of soda crackers held together with honey and peanut butter, and a rich, secret, sickening mixture of cocoa, corn syrup, brown sugar, coconut, and chopped walnuts, which had to be eaten with a spoon. Greedy eating first appeased then made me gloomy, like masturbating. (*Masturbating*. Naomi and I used to read in her mother's books how peasants in Eastern Europe did it with carrots and ladies in Japan used weighted spheres, and you could tell habitual masturbators by the dull look in their eyes and liverish cast of their skin, and we went around Jubilee looking for symptoms, thinking the whole thing so outlandish, so funny, so revolting – everything we found out about sex making it seem more and more like a carnival for us to laugh or get sick at, or as we used to say, *laugh ourselves sick*. And now we would never talk about this at all.) Sometimes after eating a lot I would fast for a day or two and drink a large dose of Epsom salts in warm water, thinking the calories wouldn't take hold if I could rush everything through in a hurry. I didn't get really fat, just large enough, solid enough, that I loved to read books where the heroine's generous proportions were tenderly, erotically described, and was worried by books where desirable women were always slim; for comfort, I would say to myself the line from the poem about 'mistresses with great, smooth, marbly, limbs.' I liked that; I liked the word *mistress*, a full-skirted word, with some ceremony about it; a mistress should not be too slim. I liked looking at the reproduction of Cézanne's *Bathers* in the art supplement of the encyclopedia, then at myself naked in the glass. But the insides of my thighs quivered; cottage cheese in a transparent sack.

Meanwhile, Naomi looked around, to see what possibilities there were.

A man named Bert Matthews, unmarried, twenty-eight or -nine years old, with a worried, jovial face and hair like a fur cap pushed back on his wrinkled scalp, came regularly into the office of the creamery. He was a poultry inspector. Naomi told me, with disgust, the things he would say to Molly and Carla. He was always asking Molly if she was pregnant yet, sneaking around to get a look at her stomach in profile, and giving Carla advice about her forthcoming honeymoon. He called Naomi 'butter tart.' He would honk the horn of his car at her on the street, and slow down, and she would turn away, saying, 'Oh, Good Lord, save me from that idiot!' She would frown dreamily at her reflection in store windows.

Bert Matthews bet her ten dollars she would not be allowed to meet him at the Gay-la Dance Hall. Naomi meant to go. She said it was for the ten dollars, and to show him. It was true her mother would not have allowed her to go there, but her mother was out of town, on a nursing case, and she did not have to worry about her father. '*Him*,' she always said, 'he's senile.' She seemed to enjoy the clinical sound of that word. He spent his time in his own room with the Bible and his religious literature, sorting out prophecies.

Naomi wanted me to go with her, and stay at her house all night, telling my mother we were going to the Lyceum Theatre. I felt I had no choice but to do this, not particularly because it was something Naomi wanted me to do, but because I truly hated and feared the Gay-la Dance Hall.

The Gay-la Dance Hall was half a mile north of town, on the highway. It was covered with chocolate-colored imitation logs and the windows had no glass, just board shutters closed tight in the daytime, propped open for a dance. When I used to drive that way with my mother she would say, 'Well, take a look at Sodom and Gomorrah!' She was referring to a sermon that had been preached in the Presbyterian Church comparing the Gay-la Dance Hall to those places and predicting a similar fate. My mother had pointed out at the time that the comparison was not valid, because what Sodom and Gomorrah went in for were *un*natural practices. (Fern Dogherty, to whom she explained this, said comfortably and mysteriously, 'Well, natural or *un*natural, doesn't that depend?') My mother was in an uneasy position; on principle she had to ridicule the stand of the Presbyterian Church, and yet the very sight of the Gay-la Dance Hall touched her, as I could tell, with the same cold blight felt by Presbyterians. And I saw it the same way she did – with its blind windows, in its scabby littered field, all a black and rumored place.

In the pine woods behind, French safes were scattered like old snakeskins, everybody said.

We walked out the highway on a Friday night, in our flowered, full-skirted dresses. I had done my best; I had washed, shaved, deodorized, done up my hair. I wore a crinoline, harsh and scratchy on the thighs, and a long-line brassiere that was supposed to compress my waist but which actually pinched my midriff and left a little bulge beneath that I had to tighten my plastic belt over. I had the belt pulled in to twenty-five inches, and was sweating underneath it. I had slapped beige make-up like paint over my throat and face; my mouth was as red, and nearly as thickly painted, as an icing flower on a cake. I wore sandals, which collected the gravel of the roadside. Naomi was in high heels. It was June by this time, the air warm, soft, whining and trembling with bugs, the sky like a peach skin behind the black pines, the world rewarding enough, if only it had not been necessary to go to dances.

Naomi went ahead of me across the unpaved haphazard parking lot, up the steps lit by a single yellow bulb. If she was afraid, like me, she did not show it. I kept my eyes on her disdainful high heels, her biscuit-pale, muscular, purposeful bare legs. Men and boys hung around the steps. I could not see their faces, and did not look. I just saw their cigarettes or belt buckles or bottles glinting in the dark. To get past the soft and easy, surely contemptuous, strangely dreaded things they were saying I tried to stop my hearing, the way you can hold your breath. What had happened to my old confidence – false confidence of the early days of buffoonery and superiority? It was every bit gone; I would think with nostalgia and disbelief of how bold I had been, for instance with Mr Chamberlain.

A fat old woman stamped our hands with purple ink.

Naomi found her way at once to Bert Matthews who was standing near the dancing platform. 'Well I never expected to see you here,' she said. 'Did your momma let you out?'

Bert Matthews took her up to dance. The dancing went on on a wooden platform about two feet high, the railing strung with colored lights, which also climbed the four posts at the corners and hung on two crossing diagonal strings above the dancers, making the platform something like a lighted ship floating above the earth and sawdust floor. Except for these lights and the light from a window open on a sort of kitchen, from which they sold hot dogs, hamburgers, soft drinks, and coffee, the place was dark. People stood around in dim huddles, the sawdust underfoot was wet and smelly with spilled drinks. A man stood in front of me, holding out a paper cup. I thought he had mistaken me for somebody else, and shook my head. Then I wished I had taken it. He might have stayed beside me and asked me to dance.

After two dances Naomi came back, bringing with her Bert Matthews and another man, thin, foxy, red faced and red haired. He stood with his head thrust forward, his long body curved like a comma. This man did not ask me to dance but took my hand when the music started and pulled me on to the platform. To my alarm he turned out to be a fancy, inventive dancer, continually throwing me away from him and snatching me back, flipping himself around, snapping his fingers, doing all this without a smile, indeed with a dead-serious, hostile expression. As well as trying to follow his dancing I had to try somehow to follow his conversation, for he talked too, during those brief unpredictable parts of the dance when we were close enough to each other. He was talking with a Dutch accent, which was not real. At this time Dutch immigrants had taken up a few farms around Jubilee, and their accent, its warm and innocent sound, was to be heard in certain local jokes and catch phrases. 'Dance me loose,' he said, using one of these phrases, and rolling his eyes at me imploringly. I did not know what he meant; surely I was dancing him, or he was dancing himself, as loose as anybody could do? Everything he said was like this; I heard the words but could not figure out the meaning; he might have been joking, but his face remained so steadily unsmiling. But he rolled his eyes, this grotesque way, and called me 'baby' in a cold languishing voice, as if I were somebody altogether different from myself; all I could think of to do was get some idea of this person he thought he was dancing with and pretend to be her – somebody small, snappy, bright, flirtatious. But everything I did, every movement and expression with which I tried to meet him, seemed to be too late; he would have gone on to something else.

We danced until the band took a break. I was glad it was over and glad he had stayed with me; I had been afraid he might recognize how inadequate I was and just whirl on to somebody else. He pulled me off the platform and over to the kitchen window where we were pushed about in the crowd until he could buy two paper cups of ginger ale.

'Drink some,' he ordered, abandoning his Dutch accent and sounding tired and practical. I drank some of mine. 'Of both,' he told me. 'I never drink ginger ale.' We were moving across the floor. I could make out faces now and I saw people I knew and smiled at them, tentatively proud of being here, proud that a man had me in tow. We reached Bert and Naomi, and Bert took out a flask of whisky and said, 'Well, corporal, what can I do for you?' He poured some into both cups. Naomi smiled at me glassily like a swimmer just come out of the water. I was warm and thirsty. I drank down my rye and ginger ale in three or four large gulps.

'Good Christ,' said Bert Matthews.

'She drinks like a fish,' said Naomi, pleased with me.

'Then she don't need the ginger ale,' said Bert, and poured rye into my cup. I drank it down, wanting to increase my new prestige, and not actually minding the taste so much. Bert began to complain that he didn't want to dance any more. He said he had a lame back. The man I was with – whose name, then or later, I learned to be Clive – let out a startling, rattling, machine-gun laugh and feinted with his fist at Bert's belt buckle.

'Howdja get a lame back, eh, howdja get a lame back?'

'Well I was just layin' there, officer,' said Bert in a high whiny voice, 'and she come up and sat down on me, what could I do about that?'

'Don't be filthy,' said Naomi happily.

'What's filthy? What did I say? You want to rub my back, honey? N'omi, rub my back?'

'I don't care about your stupid back, go out and buy some liniment.'

'Will you rub it on me, h'm –' sniffing in Naomi's hair, '– rub it on me good?'

The colored lights had gone blurry, they were moving up and down like stretched elastic bands. People's faces had undergone a slight, obscene enlargement across the cheeks; it was as if I was looking at faces reflected on a curved polished surface. Also the heads seemed large, out of proportion to the bodies; I imagined them – though I did not really see them – detached from bodies, floating smoothly on invisible trays. This was the height of my drunkenness, as far as alteration of perceptions went. While I was experiencing it Clive went to buy hot dogs, wrapped in paper napkins, and a case of ginger ale, and we all left the dance hall and I got into the back seat of a car with Clive. He put his arm around me and rather roughly tickled my armored midriff. We drove along the highway at what seemed to be great speed, Bert and Clive singing, with falsetto harmonies, 'I don't care if the sun don' shine, I git my lovin' in the evenin' ti-ime.' The windows were all down, the wind and stars rushed by. I felt happy. I was no longer responsible for anything. *I am drunk*, I thought. We entered Jubilee; I saw the buildings along the main street and it seemed they had a message for me, something concerning the temporary, and playful, and joyously improbable nature of the world. I had forgotten about Clive. He bent over and pressed his face against mine and stuffed his tongue, which seemed enormous, wet, cold, crumpled, like a dishrag, into my mouth.

We had stopped behind the Brunswick Hotel.

'This is where I live,' said Bert. 'This is my happy home.'

'We can't get in,' said Naomi. 'They won't let you take girls in your room.'

'Wait and see.'

We went in a back door, up some stairs, down a corridor at the end of which shone a bubble-shaped container of red liquid, utterly beautiful to me in my present state. We entered a bedroom and sat down, in sudden hot light, apart from each other. Bert sat, and later lay, on the bed.

Naomi sat on the chair and I on a ripped hassock, our skirts properly spread. Clive sat on the cold radiator but got up at once to fit a screen in the window, then pour us all more whisky, mixing it with the ginger ale he had bought. We ate the hot dogs. I knew it had been a mistake stopping the car, coming inside. My happiness was leaking away and, though I drank more and hoped it would come back, I only felt bloated, thick in the body, particularly in the fingers and toes.

Clive said to me sharply, 'You believe in equal rights for women?'

'Yes.' I tried to get my wits together, encouraged, and feeling some sense of obligation, at the prospect of a discussion.

'You believe in capital punishment for women, too?'

'I don't believe in capital – punishment at all. But if you are going to have it – yes, for women.'

Quick as a bullet Clive said, 'You believe women should be hung like men?'

I laughed hard, unhappily. Responsibility was coming back.

That started Bert and Clive telling jokes. Every joke would start off seriously, and would continue so for quite a time, like a reflective or instructive anecdote, so that you had to be always on guard, not to be left stupidly gaping when the time came to laugh. I was afraid that if I did not laugh at once I would give the impression of being too naive to understand the joke, or of being offended by it. In many of these jokes as in the first one it was necessary for Naomi or me to supply the straight lines, and the way to do this, so as not to feel foolish as I had that time was to answer in a reluctant, exasperated, but still faintly tolerant way, to follow the joke with narrowed eyes and a slight smile as if you knew what was coming. Between jokes Bert said to Naomi, 'Come on the bed with me.'

'No thanks. I'm happy where I am.' She refused to have any more to drink, and flicked cigarette ashes in the hotel glass.

'What have you got against beds? That's where you get more bounce to the ounce.'

'Go ahead and bounce, then.'

Clive was never still. He had to jump around the room, shadow-boxing, illustrating his jokes, lunging at Bert on the bed, until finally Bert jumped up too and they pretended to be fighting, taking little close-in punches at each other, bouncing up from their knees, laughing. Naomi and I had to pull our feet back.

'Pair of morons,' Naomi said.

Bert and Clive finished up by putting their arms around each other's shoulders and facing us formally, as from a stage.

'I can see by your outfit you must be a cowboy –' Bert said, and Clive sang back, 'I can see by your outfit that you're a cowboy too –'

'You can see by our outfits that we are both cowboys –'

'Hey Rastus,' said Bert spookily.

'Yas?'

'Is yo' fo' years old or is yo' five?'

'Ah don' know. Ah don' know if Ah is fo' years old or five.'

'Hey Rastus? Yo' know 'bout women?'

'No-o.'

'Yo' is *fo'*.'

We laughed but Naomi said, 'That was in the Kinsmen's Minstrel Show at Tupperton, I heard that before.'

'I have to go to the bathroom,' I said, and got up. I must have been still drunk, after all. Ordinarily I would never have said that in front of men.

'You have my permission,' said Bert magnanimously. 'You go right ahead. You have my permission to leave the room. Go right down the hall and go in the door where it says –' He peered at me closely and then stuck his face almost into my chest – 'Ah, I can see *now* – *Ladies.*'

I found the bathroom and used it without closing the door, later remembering. On my way back to the room I saw the bubble of red liquid, and a light beyond it, at the end of the corridor. I walked toward it past the door of Bert's room. Past the light there was a door, open because of the warm night, onto the fire escape. We were on the third, or top, floor of the hotel. I stepped outside, tripped and nearly fell over the railing, then recovered, bent down and with great difficulty removed my sandals, which I blamed for making me trip. I walked down the steps, all the way. There was a drop of about six feet at the bottom. I threw my shoes down first, feeling clever to have thought of that, then sat on the bottom step, let myself down as far as I could and jumped, landing on hard dirt, in the alley between the hotel and the radio station. Putting my shoes on, I was bewildered; I had really meant to go back to the room. I could not think where to go now. I had forgotten all about our house on River Street and thought we were living out on the Flats Road. At last I remembered Naomi's house; with careful planning I thought I could get to it.

I walked along the wall of the Brunswick Hotel bumping up against the brick, came out at the back of it, and walked along the Diagonal Road – first starting in the wrong direction, and having to turn around – and crossed the main street not looking either way, but it was late, there were no cars anywhere. I could not see the time on the blurry moon of the post-office clock. Once off the main street I decided to walk on the grass, on people's front yards, because the sidewalk was hard. I took off my shoes again. I thought I must tell everybody about this discovery, that the sidewalk hurt and the grass was soft. Why had nobody ever thought of this before? I came to Naomi's house on Mason Street, and forgetting that we had left the back door unlocked went up the front steps, tried to open the front door, failed, and knocked, politely at first, then harder and louder. I thought Naomi must be inside, and would hear me and come to let me in.

No lights went on, but the door did open. Naomi's father in a nightshirt, with his bare legs and white hair, glowed in the dark of the hall like a risen corpse. I said, 'Naomi –' and then I remembered. I turned and stumbled down the steps and headed towards River Street, which I had also remembered at the same time. There I was more prudent. I lay down in the veranda swing and fell asleep, in deep engulfing swirls of light and darkness, helplessness, belched smell of hot dogs.

Naomi's father did not go back to bed. He sat in the kitchen in the dark until Naomi came home and then he got his belt and beat her on the arms, legs, hands, wherever he could hit. He made her get down on her knees on the kitchen floor and pray to God that she would never taste liquor again.

As for me, I woke chilled, sick, aching in the early dawn, got off the veranda in time and vomited in a patch of burdocks at the side of the house. The back door had been open all the time. I ducked my head and hair in the kitchen sink, trying to get rid of the smell of whisky, and climbed safely up to bed. I told my mother, when she woke up, that I had got sick at Naomi's house and come home in the night. All day I lay in bed with a pounding headache, rocking stomach, great weakness, a sense of failure and relief. I felt redeemed by childish things – my old Scarlett O'Hara lamp, the blue-and-white metal flowers that held back my limp dotted curtains. I read *The Life of Charlotte Brontë*.

Through my window I could see low weedy meadows beyond the CNR tracks, purply with June grass. I could see a bit of the Wawanash River, still fairly high, and the silvery willow trees. I dreamed a nineteenth-century sort of life, walks and studying, rectitude, courtesy, maidenhood, peacefulness.

Naomi came up to my room and said in a harsh whisper, 'Christ, I could just about kill you for walking out on everybody.'

'I got sick.'

'Sick my bally old foot. Who do you think you are? Clive is not an idiot you know. He has a good job. He's an *insurance* adjustor. Who do you want to go out with? *High-school boys?*'

Then she showed me her welts and told me about her father.

'If you had've come home with me he probably would've been ashamed to do that. How the hell did he know I was out, anyway?'

I never said. Neither did he. Perhaps he had got it muddled up or thought I was some sort of apparition. Naomi was going out with Bert Matthews again next week end. She did not care.

'He can beat me till he's blue in the face. I have to have a normal life.'

What was a normal life? It was the life of the girls in the creamery office, it was showers, linen and pots and pans and silverware, that complicated feminine order; then, turning it over, it was the life of the Gay-la Dance Hall, driving drunk at night along the black roads, listening to men's jokes, putting up with and warily fighting with men and getting hold of them, getting hold – one side of that life could not exist without the other, and by undertaking and getting used to them both a girl was putting herself on the road to marriage. There was no other way. And I was not going to be able to do it. No. Better Charlotte Brontë.

'Get up and get dressed and come downtown with me. It'll do you good.'

'I feel too sick.'

'You are a big baby. What do you want to do, crawl in a hole the rest of your life?'

Our friendship faded from that day. We became strangers to each other's houses. We would meet on the street next winter, she in her new fur-trimmed coat and I with my great pile of schoolbooks, and she would bring me up-to-date on her life. Usually she was going out with someone I had never heard of, someone from Porterfield or Blue

River or Tupperton. Bert Matthews she had quickly left behind. His role, it turned out, was to take young girls out for the first time; he was only after young inexperienced girls, though he never really bothered them, or got them in trouble, for all his talk. Clive had been in a car accident, she told me, and had to have one leg amputated below the knee. 'No wonder, they all drink like fish and drive like fools,' she said. She spoke with a maternal sort of resignation, pride even, as if to drink like a fish and drive like a fool was somehow the proper thing, deplorable but necessary. After a while she stopped giving me these progress reports. We met in Jubilee and all we said to each other was hello. I felt that she had moved as far beyond me, in what I vaguely and worriedly supposed to be the real world, as I in all sorts of remote and useless and special knowledge, taught in schools, had moved beyond her.

I got A's at school. I never had enough of them. No sooner had I hauled one lot of them home with me than I had to start thinking of the next. They did seem to me tangible, and heavy as iron. I had them stacked around me like barricades, and if I missed one I could feel a dangerous gap.

In the main hall of the high school, around the honor roll of those former students killed in action in 1914–18, and 1939–45, were hung wooden shields, one for each grade; inserted in these shields were little silver name tags bearing the names of those who had come first in marks each year, until they faded into jobs and motherhood. My name was there, though not for every year. Sometimes I was beaten by Jerry Storey. His I.Q. was the highest ever seen in Jubilee High School or in any high school in Wawanash County. The only reason I ever got ahead of him at all was that his preoccupation with science made him impatient and sometimes completely forgetful of those subjects he referred to as 'memory work' (French and history), and English literature, which he seemed to regard fretfully as some kind of personal insult.

Jerry Storey and I drifted together. We talked in the halls. We developed, gradually, a banter, vocabulary, range of subject matter that was not shared with anybody else. Our names appeared together in the tiny, mimeographed, nearly illegible school paper. Everyone seemed to think that we were perfectly suited to each other; we were called 'The Brains Trust' or 'The Quiz Kids' with a certain amount of semitolerant contempt, which Jerry knew how to bear better than I. We were depressed at being paired off like the only members of some outlandish species in a zoo, and we resented people thinking we were alike, for we did not think so. I thought that Jerry was a thousand times more freakish, less attractive than I was, and it was plain that he thought putting my brains and his in the same category showed no appreciation of categories; It was like saying Toscanini and the local bandmaster were both talented. What I possessed, he told me frankly when we discussed the future, was a first-rate memory, a not unusual feminine gift for language, fairly weak reasoning powers, and almost no capacity for abstract thought. That I was immeasurably smarter than most people in Jubilee should not blind me, he said, to the fact that I would soon reach my limits in the intellectually competitive world outside ('The same goes for myself,' he added severely.

'I always try to keep a perspective. I look pretty good at Jubilee High School. How would I look at M.I.T.?' In talking of his future he was full of grand ambitions, but was careful to express them sarcastically, and fence them round with sober self-admonitions.)

I took his judgment like a soldier, because I did not believe it. That is, I knew it was all true, but I still felt powerful enough, in areas that I thought he could not see, where his ways of judging could not reach. The gymnastics of his mind I did not admire, for people only admire abilities similar to, though greater than, their own. His mind to me was like a circus tent full of dim apparatus on which, when I was not there, he performed stunts which were spectacular and boring. I was careful not to let him see I thought this. He was truthful in telling me what he thought about me, apparently; I had no intention of being so with him. Why not? Because I felt in him what women feel in men, something so tender, swollen, tyrannical, absurd; I would never take the consequences of interfering with it: I had an indifference, a contempt almost, that I concealed from him. I thought that I was tactful, even kind; I never thought that I was proud.

We went to movies together. We went to school dances, and danced badly, self-consciously, irritated with each other, humiliated by the disguise of high-school sweethearts which we had somehow felt it necessary to adopt, until we found that the way to survive the situation was to make fun of it. Parody, self-mockery were our salvation. At our best we were cheerful, comfortable, sometimes cruel, comrades, rather like a couple who have been married for eighteen years. He called me *Eggplant*, in honor of a dreadful dress I had, a purply-wine-colored taffeta, made over from one Fern Dogherty had left behind. (We were suddenly poorer than usual, due to the collapse of the silver-fox business after the war.) I had hoped, while my mother was altering it, that the dress would turn out to be all right, would even show a voluptuous sheen on my rather wide hips, like the Rita Hayworth dress in the ads for *Gilda*; when I put it on I tried to tell myself that this was so, but as soon as Jerry made a face and gulped exaggeratedly and said in a squeaky, delighted voice, 'Eggplant!' I knew the truth. Immediately I tried to find it as funny as he did, and nearly succeeded. On the street we improvised further.

'Attending last evening's gala midwinter dance at the Jubilee Armory were Mr Jerry Storey, the Third, scion of the fabulous fertilizer family, and the exquisite Miss Del Jordan, heiress to the silver-fox empire, a couple who dazzle all beholders with the unique and indescribable style of their dancing –'

Many of the movies we went to were about the war, which had ended a year before we started high school. Afterwards we would go to Haines' Restaurant, preferring it to the Blue Owl where nearly everybody else from the high school went, to play the jukebox and the pinball machines. We drank coffee and smoked menthol cigarettes. Between the booths there were high, dark wooden partitions, topped by fanlights of dark-gold glass. Creasing a paper napkin into geometrical designs, wrapping it around a spoon, tearing it into fluttering strips, Jerry talked about the war. He gave me a description of the Bataan Death March, methods of torture in Japanese prison camps, the fire-bombing of Tokyo, the destruction of Dresden; he bombarded me with unbeatable atrocities, annihilating statistics. All without a flicker of protest, but with a controlled excitement, a curious insistent relish. Then he would tell me about the weapons now being developed by the Americans and the Russians; he made their destructive powers seem inevitable, magnificent, useless to combat as the forces of the universe itself.

'Then biological warfare – they could reintroduce the bubonic plague – they're making diseases there are no antidotes for, storing them up. Nerve gas – how about controlling a whole population by semistupifying drugs –'

He was certain there would be another war, we would all be wiped out. Cheerful, implacable behind his brainy boy's glasses, he looked ahead to prodigious catastrophe. Soon, too. I responded with conventional horror, tentative female reasonableness, which would excite him into greater opposition, make it necessary to horrify me further, argue my reasonableness down. This was not hard to do. He was in touch with the real world, he knew how they had split the atom. The only world I was in touch with was the one I had made, with the aid of some books, to be peculiar and nourishing to myself. Yet I hung on; I grew bored and cross and said all right, suppose this is true, why do you get up in the morning and go to school? If it's all true, why do you plan on being a great scientist?

'If the world is finished, if there is no hope, then why *do* you?'

'There is still time for me to get the Nobel Prize,' he said blasphemously, to make me laugh.

'Ten years?'

'Give it twenty. Most great breakthroughs are made by men under thirty-five.'

After he had said something like this he would always mutter, 'You know I'm kidding.' He meant about the Nobel Prize, not the war. We could not get away from the Jubilee belief that there are great, supernatural dangers attached to boasting, or having high hopes of yourself. Yet what really drew and kept us together were these hopes, both denied and admitted, both ridiculed and respected in each other.

On Sunday afternoons we liked to go for long walks, along the railway tracks, starting behind my house. We would walk out to the trestle over the big bend in the Wawanash River, then back. We talked about euthanasia, genetic control of populations, whether there is such a thing as a soul, whether or not the universe is ultimately knowable. We agreed on nothing. At first we were walking in the fall, then in the winter. We would walk in snowstorms, arguing with our heads down, hands in our pockets, the fine bitter snow in our faces. Worn out with arguing, we would take our hands out of our pockets and spread our arms out for balance and try to walk the rails. Jerry had long frail legs, a small head, curly hair, round bright eyes. He wore a plaid cap with fleece-lined ear-flaps, which I remembered him wearing ever since the Sixth Grade.

I remembered that I used to laugh at him, as everybody else did. I was still sometimes ashamed to be seen with him, by somebody like Naomi. But I thought now there was something admirable, an odd, harsh grace about the way he conformed to type, accepting his role in Jubilee, his necessary and gratifying absurdity, with a fatalism, even gallantry, which I would never have been able to muster myself. This was the spirit in which he appeared at dances, steered me spastically over the treacherous miles of floor, in which he swung uselessly at the ball in the yearly, obligatory baseball game, and marched with the Cadets. He offered up himself, not pretending to be an ordinary boy, but doing the things an ordinary boy would do, knowing that his performance could never be acceptable, people would always laugh. He could not do otherwise; he was what he seemed. I, whose natural boundaries were so much more ambiguous, who soaked up protective coloration wherever it might be found, began to see that it might be restful to be like Jerry.

He came to my house for supper, against my will. I hated bringing him up against my mother. I was afraid that she would be excited, try to outdo herself in some way, because of his brainy reputation. And she did; she tried to get him to explain relativity to her – nodding, encouraging, fairly leaping at him with facile cries of understanding. For once, his explanations were incoherent. I was critical of the meal, as I always was before company; the meat seemed overdone, the potatoes slightly hard, the canned beans too cool. My father and Owen had come in from the Flats Road, because it was Sunday. Owen lived out on the Flats Road all the time now, and cultivated churlishness. While Jerry talked, Owen chewed noisily and directed at my father looks of simple, ignorant, masculine contempt. My father did not answer these looks but talked little, perhaps embarrassed by my mother's enthusiasm, which he might have thought enough for them both. I was angry at everybody. I knew that to Owen, and to my father too

– though he would not show it, he would know it was only one way of looking at things – Jerry was a freak, shut out of the world of men; it did not matter what he knew. They were too stupid, it seemed to me, to see that he had power. And to him my family were part of the great mass of people to whom it is not even worthwhile to explain things; he did not see that they had power. Insufficient respect was being shown all round.

'It makes me laugh the way people think they can ask a few questions and get to understand something, without knowing any of the groundwork.'

'Laugh then,' I said sourly. 'I hope you enjoy yourself.'

But my mother had taken a liking to him, and from then on lay in wait for him, to know his opinions about laboratory-created life, or machines taking over man. I could understand how her hectic flow of questions baffled and depressed him. Wasn't this how I had felt when he himself grabbed *Look Homeward, Angel* off the top of my pile of books – I was taking it back to the library – and opened it and read in flat-voiced puzzlement, '*A stone, a leaf, a door – O lost, and by the wind grieved, ghost –*' I snatched it back from him, as if it was in danger. 'Well what does that *mean*?' he said reasonably. 'To me it just sounds stupid. Explain it to me. I'm willing to listen.'

'He is extremely shy,' my mother said. 'He is a brilliant boy but he must learn to put himself across better.'

It was easier having supper at his place. His mother was the widow of a teacher. He was her only child. She worked as the high-school secretary, so I knew her already. They lived in half of a double house out on the Diagonal Road. The dish-towels were folded and ironed like the finest linen handkerchiefs and kept in a lemon-scented drawer. For dessert we had molded Jello pudding in three colors, rather like a mosque, full of canned fruit. After supper Jerry went into the front room to work on the weekly chess problem he received through the mail (an example of what I mean about his pure, impressive conforming to type) and shut the glass doors so our talking would not distract him. I dried the dishes. Jerry's mother talked to me about his I.Q. She spoke as if it were some rare object – an archaeological find, maybe, something immensely valuable and rather scary, which she kept wrapped up in a drawer.

'You have a very nice I.Q. yourself,' she said reassuringly (all records were open to her, in fact were kept by her, at the school) 'but you know Jerry's I.Q. puts him in the top *quarter* of the top one percent of the population. Isn't it amazing to think of that? And here I am his mother, what a responsibility!'

I agreed it was.

'He will be years and years at university. He will have to get his Ph.D. Then they even go on after that, postdoctoral, I don't *know* what all. Years.'

I thought by her sober tone she was going to go on to talk about the expense.

'So you mustn't get into trouble, you know,' she said matter-of-factly. 'Jerry couldn't get married. I wouldn't allow it. I have seen these cases of young men forced to sacrifice their lives because some girl has got pregnant and I don't think it's right. You and I have both seen it, you know the ones I mean, in the school. Shotgun weddings. That's the style in Jubilee. I don't agree with it. I never did.

I don't agree that it's the boy's responsibility and he should have to sacrifice his career. Do you?'

'No.'

'I didn't think you would. You are too intelligent. Do you have a diaphragm?' She said that like a flash.

'No,' I said numbly.

'Well why don't you get one? I know the way it is with you young girls nowadays. Virginity is all a thing of the past. So be it. I don't say I approve or disapprove but you can't turn back the clock, can you? Your mother, she should have taken you in and got you fitted. That's what I would do, if I had a daughter.'

She was much shorter than I was, a plump but smart little woman, hair fluffy yellow, tulip color, gray roots showing. She always had earrings and brooches and necklaces in bright, matching, plastic colors. She smoked, and allowed Jerry to smoke in the house; in fact they were always squabbling in a comradely, husband-and-wifely way about whose cigarettes were whose. I had been prepared to find her very modern in her ideas, not as modern as my mother intellectually – who was? – but a great deal more modern about ordinary things. But I had not been prepared for this. I looked down at her gray roots as she said that about my mother taking me to get me fitted for a diaphragm and I thought of my mother, who would publicly campaign for birth control but would never even think she needed to talk to me, so firmly was she convinced that sex was something no woman – no *intelligent* woman – would ever submit to unless she had to. I really liked that better. It seemed more fitting, in a mother, than Jerry's mother's preposterous acceptance, indecent practicality. I thought it quite offensive for a mother to mention intimacies a girl might be having with her own son. The thought of intimacies with Jerry Storey was offensive in itself. Which did not mean that they did not, occasionally, take place.

Why offensive? It was a strange thing. Heavyheartedness prevailed, as soon as we left off talking. Our hands lay moistly together, each one of us wondering, no doubt, how long in decent courtesy they must remain. Our bodies fell against each other not unwillingly but joylessly, like sacks of wet sand. Our mouths opened into each other, as we had read and heard they might, but stayed cold, our tongues rough, mere lumps of unlucky flesh. Whenever Jerry turned his attention on me – this special sort of attention – I grew irritable and did not know why. But I was, after all, morosely submissive. Each of us was the only avenue to discovery that the other had found.

Curiosity could carry things quite a long way. One evening in the winter, in his mother's front room – she was out attending a meeting of the Eastern Star – Jerry asked me to take off all my clothes.

'Why do you want me to?'

'Wouldn't it be educational? I have never seen a real live naked woman.'

The idea was not without appeal. The words 'naked woman' were secretly pleasing to me, making me feel opulent, a dispenser of treasure. Also, I thought my body handsomer than my face, and handsomer naked than clothed; I had often wished to show it off to somebody. And I had a hope – or, more accurately, I was curious about a possibility – that at some further stage in our intimacy my feelings for Jerry would change, I would be able to welcome him. Didn't I know all about desire? I was in the old, trite, married sort of situation, trying to direct its dumb torments towards the available body.

I wouldn't do it in the front room. After some arguing and delaying he said we could go upstairs, to his room. Mounting the stairs I did feel a pricking of eagerness, as if we were seven or eight years old, and going somewhere to pull down our pants. While pulling down the blind in his room Jerry knocked the lamp off the table, and I almost turned around, then, and went back downstairs. Nothing sets things back like a stroke of awkwardness, at a time like this, unless you happen to be in love. However, I decided to remain good-humored. I helped him pick up the lamp and set the shade on it properly and did not even resent his turning it on once to see if it was damaged. Then turning my back I pulled off everything I had on – he did not help or touch me, and I was glad – and lay down on the bed.

I felt absurd and dazzling.

He stood by the bed looking down at me, making faint comical faces of astonishment. Did he feel my body as inappropriate, as unrealizable, as I did his? Did he want to turn me into some comfortable girl with lust uncomplicated by self-consciousness, a girl without sharp answers, or a large vocabulary, or any interest in the idea of order in the universe, ready to cuddle him down? We both giggled. He put a finger against one of my nipples as if he was testing a thorn.

Sometimes we talked a dialect based roughly on the comic strip *Pogo*.

'Yo' is shore a handsome figger of a woman.'

'Has I got all the appurtances on in the right places does yo' think?'

'Ah jes' has to git out my lil ole manual an' check up on that.'

'Yo' don' min' this lil ole third breast Ah hopes?'

'Ain't all the ladies got them lil ole third breasts? Ah has led a rather sheltered life.'

'Boy, yo' sho' has –'

'Shh –'

We heard his mother's voice outside, saying goodnight to somebody who had driven her home. The car door closed. Either the Eastern Star meeting was over earlier than usual, or we had spent more time than we had thought arguing, before we came upstairs.

Jerry pulled me off the bed and out of the room while I was still trying to grab my clothes. 'Closet,' I hissed at him. 'I can hide – closet – get *dressed!*'

'Shut up,' he begged me, whispering too, furious and almost tearful. 'Shut up, shut *up.*' His face was white; he was shaky but strong, for Jerry Storey. I was struggling and pulling back, protesting, still trying to convince him that I had to get my clothes, and he was pulling me forward, getting me down the back stairs. He opened the cellar door just as his mother opened the front door – I heard her cheerful cry, 'Nobody ho-ome?' – and he pushed me inside and bolted the door.

I was all by myself on the back cellar stairs, locked in, naked.

He switched the light on, to give me my bearings, then quickly switched it off again. That did no good. It made the cellar blacker than before. I sat down cautiously on the step, feeling cold splintery wood on my bare buttocks, and tried to think of any possible way I could get myself out of here. Once I got used to the dark perhaps I could find the cellar windows and try to force one of them open, but what good was that going to do me, when I was naked? Maybe I could find some old ragged curtain or piece of shelf oilcloth to wrap myself up in, but how could I ever get into my own house in that? How could I get across Jubilee, right across the main street, at not much more than ten o'clock at night?

It was possible Jerry would come and let me out, when his mother was asleep. When he did, if he did, I would kill him.

I heard them talking in the front room, then in the kitchen. Jerry and his mother. 'Wants to get her beauty sleep?' I heard his mother say, then laugh – unkindly I thought. He called his mother by her first name, which was Greta. How affected, how *unhealthy* I thought that was. I heard pots and cups clattering. Evening cup of cocoa, toasted raisin buns. While I was locked up cold and bare in that hole of a cellar. Jerry and his I.Q. His intellect and his imbecility. If his mother was so modern and knew about none of us girls being virgins nowadays why did I have to be shoved in here? I did hate them.'I thought of banging on the door. That was what he deserved. Tell his mother I wanted a shotgun wedding.

My eyes got used to the dark, a bit, and when I heard a whooshing sound, a lid closing upstairs, I looked in the right direction and saw a tin thing sticking out of the cellar ceiling. A clothes chute, and something light colored flying out of it and landing with a muffled heavy sound on the cement floor. I crept down the stairs and across the cold cement praying that this was my clothes, and not just a bundle of dirty things Jerry's mother had thrown down for the wash.

It was my blouse, sweater, skirt, pants, brassiere, and stockings, and even my jacket which had been hanging in the downstairs closet, all wrapped around my shoes to make that quiet thud. Everything except my garter belt had made the trip. Without it I couldn't put my stockings on, so I rolled them up and stuffed them in my brassiere. By this time I could see fairly well and I saw the washtubs and a window above them. It was hooked at the bottom. I climbed up on the washtub and unhooked it and crawled out, through the snow. The radio had been turned on in the kitchen, perhaps to cover my noise, perhaps only to get the ten o'clock news.

I ran home barelegged through the cold streets. I was furious now, to think of myself naked on that bed. Nobody to look at me but Jerry, giggling and scared and talking dialect. That was who I had to take my offerings. I would never get a real lover.

The next day at school Jerry came up to me carrying a brown paper bag.

'I beg yo' pardon, lady,' he said softly in his Pogo dialect, 'I think I got one of yo' personal-type possessions.'

It was my garter belt, of course. I stopped hating him. Walking down John Street hill after school we transformed the night before into a Great Comic Scene, something jerky and insane from a silent movie.

'I was yanking you down the stairs and you were yanking just as hard the other way –'

'I didn't know what you were going to do with me. I thought you were going to throw me out on the street like the woman taken in adultery –'

'You should have seen the look on your face when I pushed you down in the cellar.'

'You should have seen yours when you heard your mother's voice.'

'Most inopportune, Mamma,' said Jerry, trying out an English accent which we also used sometimes, 'but it just so happens that I have a young female person here unclothed on my bed. I was about to perform an exploratory –'

'You were about to perform nothing.'

'Well.'

So we left it, and oddly enough got on after this fiasco much better than before. We treated each other's bodies now with a mixture of wariness and familiarity, and no longer made demands. No more long hopeless embraces, no more tongues in the mouth. And we had other things to think about; we got the forms to fill out for scholarship exams, we got the calendars from several universities, we began looking forward to June, when we would write the examinations, with pleasure and dread. Nothing we had come up against in our lives equaled in importance those examinations, sent from the Department of Education, sealed; the principal of the high school would break the seal in front of our eyes. To say we studied does not half describe the training we put ourselves into; we submitted ourselves like athletes. It was not just high marks we wanted, not just to win the scholarships and get into university; it was the highest possible marks: glory, glory, the top of the pinnacled A's, security at last.

I would shut myself up in the front room, after supper. Spring was coming, the evenings were getting longer; I turned the lights on later. But I noticed nothing, only noticed, without being aware of it, the things in that room, which was my cell or chapel. The faded pattern of the rug, straw-colored at the seams, the old unworkable radio, big as a tombstone, with dials promising Rome and Amsterdam and Mexico City, the mossy ferned chesterfield and the two pictures – one of the Castle of Chillon, dark out of the pearly lake, and the other of a little girl lying on two unmatched chairs, in a rosy light, parents weeping in the shadows behind and a doctor beside her looking tranquil, but not optimistic. All this which I stared at so often, fixing verbs, dates, wars, phyla, in my mind, took on a significance, an admonitory power, as if all these ordinary shapes and patterns of things were in fact the outward form of the facts and relationships which I had mastered, and which, once I had mastered them, came to seem lovely, chaste, and obedient. From this room I would go out pale, exhausted, incapable of thought as a nun after hours of prayer or a lover, maybe, after punishing devotions, and I would wander down to the main street, to Haines' Restaurant, where Jerry and I would have agreed to meet at ten o'clock. Under the fanlights of amber glass we would drink coffee and smoke, talk a little, surfacing slowly, able to understand and approve each other's haggard, hardened looks.

My need for love had gone underground, like a canny toothache.

That spring there was to be a revival meeting in the Town Hall. Mr Buchanan, our history teacher, stood at the top of the stairs, at school, handing out buttons which said *Come to Jesus*. He was an elder of the Presbyterian Church, not the Baptist, which was in the forefront of all the arrangements for the revival; but all the churches in town, with the exception of the Catholic and possibly the Anglican – so small it couldn't matter – were giving their support. All over the country revivals were becoming respectable again.

'You wouldn't care for one of these, Del,' said Mr Buchanan, not interrogatively, in his flat mournful voice. Tall, dry, and skinny, hair parted in the middle in the style of a turn-of-the-century cyclist – which he was old enough to have been – half his stomach cut away for ulcers, he smiled at me with that faint twitching irony he usually kept for some historical personage (Parnell would be a good example) who cut a fine figure for awhile but did overreach himself, in the end. So I felt obliged, out of contrariness, to say, 'Yes, I'd like one, thank you very much.'

'Are you going to that?' Jerry said.

'Sure.'

'What for?'

'Scientific curiosity.'

'There are things there is no point in being curious about.'

The revival was held upstairs in the Town Hall, where we used to do the school operettas. This was the first week in May; the weather had suddenly turned warm. It would do this, right after the annual flood. Before eight o'clock the hall was already crowded. It was the same sort of crowd you would see at the Twelfth of July parade, or the Kinsmen's Fair – a good number of town people, but many more from the country. Mud-splashed cars were parked all along the main street and up the side streets. Some men wore hot black suits, some women wore hats. There were other men in clean overalls and women in loose print dresses, running shoes on their feet, arms bare, big and rosy as hams, holding quilt-wrapped babies. Old men and women, who had to be supported and guided into chairs. Unearthed from country kitchens, they wore clothes that seemed to have grown mold. I wondered if you could tell by looking at them what part of the country they came from. Jerry and I, watching from the science-room windows the loading of the three school buses – gaudy old rickety buses that looked as if they should be rocking over some mountain road in South America, live chickens flapping out the windows – used to play this game, talking like sociologists, in elegant prudish tones.

'From Blue River they are well dressed and quite respectable-looking. Lots of industrious Dutch out there. They have been to the dentist.'

'Almost on an urban level.'

'From St. Augustine they are run-of-the-mill. Farm folk. They have big yellow teeth. They look as if they eat a lot of oatmeal porridge.'

'From Jericho Valley they are moronic and potentially criminal. Their I.Q. never breaks a hundred. They have cross-eyes, clubfeet –'

'Cleft palates –'

'Hump shoulders –'

'It's the inbreeding that does it. Fathers sleep with daughters. Grandfathers sleep with granddaughters. Brothers sleep with sisters. Mothers sleep with fathers –'

'*Mothers sleep with fathers?*'

'Oh, it's downright terrible what they get up to out there.'

The seats were all filled. I stood at the back, behind the last row of chairs. People were still coming in, crowding down the sides of the hall, filling up the space behind me. Boys sat up on the windowsills. The windows were up as high as they would go and still it was very hot. The low sun was shining on the old cracked and stained, plastered and wainscoted walls. I had never known it was so shabby, that hall.

Mr McLaughlin from the United Church did the opening prayer. His son Dale had run away from home, long ago. Where was he now? Cutting grass on a golf course, the last anybody heard. I felt as if I had lived a lifetime in Jubilee, people going away and coming back, marrying, starting their lives, while I kept on going to school. There was Naomi with the girls from the creamery. They had all done their hair the same way, tied in two little bunches behind the ears, and they wore bows.

Four Negroes, two men and two women, walked onto the stage, and there was a craning of necks, a hush of appreciation. Many people in the hall, including me, had never seen a Negro before, any more than we had seen a giraffe or a skyscraper or an ocean liner. One man was thin and prune black, dried up, with a powerful, frightening voice; he was the bass. The tenor was fat and yellow skinned, smiling, munificent. Both women were plump and well girdled, coffee colored, splendidly dressed in emerald green, electric blue. Sweat oiled their necks and faces when they sang. During their song the revival preacher, recognizable by his face which had been plastered

on telephone poles and stuck in store windows for weeks –
but smaller, tireder, grayer than that picture would suggest
– came modestly on stage and stood behind the reading
stand, turning toward the singers with an expression of
tender enjoyment, lifting his face, in fact, as if their singing
fell on it like rain.

A young man, boy, on the other side of the hall was
looking at me steadily. I did not think I had seen him
before. He was not very tall, dark skinned; a bony face
with deep eye sockets, long slightly hollowed cheeks, a
grave, unconsciously arrogant expression. At the end of
the Negroes' singing he moved from where he had been
standing under the windows and disappeared in the crowd
at the back of the hall. I thought at once that he was coming
to stand beside me. Then I thought what nonsense; like a
recognition in an opera, or some bad, sentimental, deeply
stirring song.

Everybody rose, twitched cotton away from sweaty
backsides, began to sing the first hymn.

> *Into a tent where a gypsy boy lay*
> *Dying alone at the end of the day*
> *News of Salvation we carried; said he*
> *Nobody ever has told it to me –*

I desperately wished that he would come. I concentrated
my whole self into a kind of white prayer, willing him to
show up beside me even while I told myself *now he's going
round behind me, now he's heading for the door, he's going down
the stairs –*

A change in the level of voices behind me told me he

was there. People had drawn aside, there was a space with a body in it but no singing. I smelled the thin, hot, cotton shirt, sunburnt skin, soap, and machine oil. My shoulder was grazed by his arm (it is like fire, just as they say) and he slipped into place beside me.

We both looked straight ahead at the stage. The Baptist minister had introduced the revivalist, who began to talk in a friendly, conversational way. After a little while I rested my hand on the back of the chair in front of me. A little girl was sitting there bent forward, picking a scab off her knee. He put his hand on the back of the chair about two inches from mine. Then it seemed as if all sensation in my body, all hope, life, potential, flowed down into that one hand.

The revivalist, who had started off so mildly, behind the reading stand, gradually worked himself up, and began pacing back and forth across the stage, his tone growing more and more intense, despairing, grief stricken. Every so often he would emerge from his grief and whirl around, to roar like a lion directly into the audience. He painted a picture of a rope bridge, such as he had seen, he said, in his missionary days in South America. This bridge, frail and swaying, hung over a bottomless canyon and the canyon was filled with fire. It was the River of Fire, the River of Fire down below, in which were drowning, but never drowned, all that yelping, shrieking, blaspheming, tortured horde he now enumerated – politicians and gangsters, gamblers and drinkers and fornicators and movie stars and financiers and unbelievers. Each one of us, he said, had our own individual rope bridge, swaying over the inferno, tied up at the banks of Paradise on the other side. But Paradise was just what we could not hear or see, sometimes could not even imagine, for the roarings and writhings in the pit, and the fumes of sin it sent up all round us. What was that bridge called? It was The Lord's Grace. The Lord's Grace, and it was wonderfully strong; but every sin of ours, every word and act and thought of sin put a little nick in that rope, frayed that rope a little bit more –

And some of your ropes can't take much more! Some of your ropes are almost past the point of no return. They are frayed out with sin, they are eaten away with sin, they are nothing left but a thread! Nothing but a thread is holding you out of Hell! You all know, every single last one of you knows what condition your own bridge is in! One more nibble at the fruits of Hell, one more day and night of sin, and once that rope is broken you haven't got another! But even a thread can hold you, if you want! God didn't pass all his miracles back in the Bible days! No, I can tell you from my heart and from my own experience. He is passing them here and now, and in the midst of us. Catch ahold of him and hold right on till the Day of Judgment, and you need fear no Evil.

Ordinarily I would have been interested in listening to this and in seeing how people were taking it. For the most, calmly and pleasurably, no more disturbed than if he had been singing them a lullaby. Mr McLaughlin, sitting on the stage, kept a suave downcast face; it was not his kind of exhortation. The Baptist minister had a broad, impresario's smile. Old people in the audience would sing out, 'Amen!' and rock themselves gently. Movie stars and politicians and fornicators gone beyond rescue; it seemed, for most people, a balmy comfortable thought. The lights were on now; bugs came in at the windows, just those few early bugs. You could hear now and then a quick, apologetic slap.

But my attention was taken up with our two hands on the back of the chair. He moved his hand slightly. I moved mine. Again. Until skin touched lightly, vividly, drew away, came back, stayed together, pressed together. Now then. Our little fingers rubbing delicately against one another, his gradually overlapping mine. Hesitation; my hand spreading out a bit, his little finger touching my fourth finger, the fourth finger captured, and so on, by stages so formal and inevitable, with such reticence and certainty, his hand covering mine. When this was achieved he lifted it from the chair and held it between us. I felt angelic with gratitude, truly as if I had come out on another level of existence. I felt no further acknowledgment was needed, no further intimacy possible.

The last hymn.

> I love to tell the story,
> 'Twill be my theme in Glory,
> To tell the old, old story –

The Negroes led us, all of them except the little black man exhorting, drawing out voices upwards with their arms. Singing, people swayed together. A sharp green smell of sweat, like onions, smell of horse, pig manure, feeling of being caught, bound, borne away; tired, mournful happiness rising like a cloud. I had refused the hymn sheets which Mr Buchanan and other churchmen were handing out but I remembered the words and sang. I would have sung anything.

But when the hymn was over he dropped my hand and moved away, joining a crowd of people who were all going down to the front of the hall, responding to an invitation to make a decision for Jesus, sign a pledge or renew a pledge, put some stamp of accomplishment on the evening. It did not occur to me that he meant to do this. I thought he had gone to look for somebody. There was great confusion and I lost him in a moment. I turned and found my way out of the hall, down the stairs, looking around several times to see if I could see him (but ready to pretend I was looking for somebody else, if I saw him looking at me). I loitered up the main street, looking in windows. He did not come.

This was on a Friday evening. All week end the thought of him stayed in my mind like a circus net spread underneath whatever I had to think about at the moment. I was constantly letting go and tumbling into it. I would try to recreate the exact texture of his skin, touching my own, try to remember accurately the varying pressure of his fingers. I would spread my hand out in front of me, surprised at how little it had to tell me. It was noncommittal as those objects in museums that have been handled by kings. I would analyze that smell, sorting out its familiar and unfamiliar elements. I would picture him as I first saw him across the hall, because I never really saw him after he came to stand beside me. His dark, wary, stubborn face. His face contained for me all possibilities of fierceness and sweetness, pride and submissiveness, violence, self-containment. I never saw more in it than I had when I saw it first, because I saw everything then. The whole thing in him that I was going to love, and never catch or explain.

I did not know his name, or where he came from, or whether I would ever see him again.

Monday, after school, I walked down John Street hill with Jerry. A horn honked at us, and from an old truck, dusty with chaff, this face looked out. It was in no way changed or diminished by daylight.

'The encyclopedias,' I said to Jerry. 'He's got some money for Mother. I have to talk to him. You go on.'

Dizzy at this expected, yet unhoped-for reappearance, solid intrusion of the legendary into the real world, I got into the truck.

'I thought you would be going to school.'

'I'm almost through,' I said hastily. 'I'm in Grade Thirteen.'

'Lucky I saw you. I have to get back to the lumberyard. Why didn't you wait up for me the other night?'

'Where did you go?' I said, as if I hadn't seen him.

'I had to go down the front. There was so many people down there.'

I realized then that 'had to go down the front' meant he had gone to sign a pledge card, or be saved by the revivalist. It was typical of him that he did not say this in any more definite way. He never would explain, unless he had to. What I got out of him about himself, that first afternoon in the truck, and later, was a string of simple facts, offered usually in reply to questions. His name was Garnet French, he lived on a farm out past Jericho Valley but worked here in Jubilee, in the lumberyard. He had spent four months in jail, two years ago, for his part in a terrible fight outside the Porterfield beer parlor, in which a man had lost an eye. In jail he had been visited by a Baptist minister who had converted him. He had quit school after Grade Eight but had been allowed to start a couple of high-school courses in jail because he thought he might go to Bible college and become a Baptist minister himself. He spoke of this goal without urgency now. He was twenty-three years old.

The first thing he asked me to go to was a meeting of the Baptist Young People's Society. Or perhaps he never asked me, just said, 'All right, I'll pick you up after supper,' and drove down our street that short distance and led me, dazed and silent, into the last place in Jubilee, except possibly the whorehouse, where I ever expected to be.

This was what I was going to do every Monday night all spring and into the summer – sit in a pew halfway back in the Baptist church, never getting used to it, always amazed and lonely as somebody thrown up in a shipwreck. He never asked me if I wanted to be there, what I thought of it once I was there, anything. He did say once, 'I would probably have landed back in jail if it hadn't been for the Baptist church. That's all I know, that's good enough for me.'

'Why would you?'

'Because I got in the habit of fighting and drinking like that.'

On the back of Baptist pews were pieces of old gum, silvery black and hard as iron. The church smelled sour, like a kitchen washed down with gray scrub water, scrub rags drying out behind the stove. The Young People were not all young. There was a woman named Caddie McQuaig who worked in Monk's Butcher Shop, slapping chunks of raw meat into the grinder, hacking away with a big saw at a leg of beef, wrapped in a bloody white apron, hefty and jovial as Dutch Monk himself. Here she was in a flowered organdy dress, scrubbed hands on the pump organ, red neck bared by her shingled hair, meek and attentive. There was a pair of short, monkey-faced brothers from the country, Ivan and Orrin Walpole, who did gymnastic tricks. And a big-busted, raw-faced girl who had worked with Fern Dogherty in the post office; Fern always called her *Holy Betty*. Girls from the Chainway store, with their dusty Chainway pallor, lowest paid, lowest on the social scale of all girls who worked in stores in Jubilee. One of them, I could not remember which, was supposed to have had a baby.

Garnet was the president. Sometimes he would lead a prayer, beginning in a firm mannerly voice, 'Our Heavenly Father –' The early heat of May had disappeared, and cold spring rain washed down the windows. I had that strange and confident sensation of being in a dream from which I would presently wake up. At home on the table in the front room lay my open books and the poem, 'Andrea del Sarto,' which I had been reading before I came out, and which was still going through my head:

> *A common greyness silvers everything,*
> *All in a twilight, you and I alike –*

After what was called the worship service we would go down to the basement of the church where there was a ping-pong table. Ping-pong games would be organized, Caddie McQuaig and one of the Chainway girls would unwrap sandwiches brought from home and make cocoa on a hot plate. Garnet taught people to play ping-pong, encouraged the Chainway girls who seemed to have hardly enough strength to lift the paddle, joked with Caddie McQuaig who would become as boisterous, once she got down to the basement, as she was in the butcher shop.

'I worry about you sitting there on that little organ stool, Caddie.'

'What'd you say? What do you worry about?'

'You sitting there on that little organ stool. Looks too small for you.'

'You think it's in danger of disappearing?' Her loud, outraged, delighted voice, face red as fresh meat.

'Why, Caddie, I never thought any such thing,' said Garnet, with a regretful, downcast face.

I smiled at everybody but was jealous, appalled, waiting only for all this to end, the cocoa cups to be washed, the church lights put out, Garnet to lead me out to the truck. Then we would drive down that muddy road that led past Pork Childs' place ('I know Pork, he'll loan me a chain and get me out if I get stuck,' Garnet said, and the thought of being on these equal terms, social terms, with Pork Childs who was of course a Baptist, produced in me that quiet, now very familiar, sinking of the heart). Presently nothing mattered. The unreality, long-drawn-out embarrassment and tedium of the evening vanished in the cab of the truck, in the smell of its old split seats, and poultry feed, the sight of Garnet's rolled-up sleeves and bare forearms, of his hands, loose and alert on the wheel. Black rain on the closed windows sheltered us. Or if the rain was over we would roll down the windows and feel the rank soft air near the invisible river, smell mint crushed under the truck wheels, where we pulled off the road to park. We nosed deep into the bushes, which scratched against the hood. The truck stopped with a last little bump that seemed a signal of achievement, permission, its lights, cutting weakly into the density of night, went out, and Garnet turned to me always with the same sigh, the same veiled and serious look, and we would cross over, going into a country where there was perfect security, no move that would not bring delight; disappointment was not possible. Only when I was sick, with a fever, had I ever before had such a floating feeling, feeling of being languid and protected and at the same time possessing unlimited power. We were still in the approaches to sex, circling, backtracking, hesitating, not because we were afraid or because we had set any sort of prohibition on 'going too far' (such explicitness, in that country, and with Garnet, was next to unthinkable) but because we felt an obligation as in the game of our hands on the back of the chair, not to hurry, to make shy, formal, temporary retreats in the face of so much pleasure. That very word, *pleasure*, had changed for me; I used to think it a mild sort of word, indicating a rather low-key self-indulgence; now it seemed explosive, the two vowels in the first syllable spurting up like fireworks, ending on the plateau of the last syllable, its dreamy purr.

I would go home from these sessions by the river and not be able to sleep sometimes till dawn, not because of unrelieved tension, as might be expected, but because I had to review, could not let go of, those great gifts I had received, gorgeous bonuses – lips on the wrists, the inside of the elbow, the shoulders, the breasts, hands on the belly, the thighs, between the legs. Gifts. Various kisses, tongue touchings, suppliant and grateful noises. Audacity and revelation. The mouth closed frankly around the nipple seemed to make an avowal of innocence, defenselessness, not because it imitated a baby's but because it was not afraid of absurdity. Sex seemed to me all surrender – not the woman's to the man but the person's to the body, an act of pure faith, freedom in humility. I would lie washed in these implications, discoveries, like somebody suspended in clear and warm and irresistibly moving water, all night.

Garnet took me also to baseball games, sometimes played too soon after rain. These took place in the evening, in the fairgrounds out at the end of the Diagonal Road, and in the neighboring towns. Garnet was the first baseman on the Jubilee team. The players wore red and gray uniforms. The ball parks all had rickety bleachers, board fences painted with old soft-drink and cigarette ads. The bleachers were never more than a third full. Old men came – the same old men who were always sitting on the long bench in front of the hotel, or who played checkers, in the summer, on the painted cement checkerboard behind the cenotaph, who walked out to inspect the Wawanash River in flood every spring and stood nodding and commenting as if they had brought it up themselves. Boys ten or eleven years old sat in the grass over by the fence, smoking. The sun would often come out after a long gloomy day, and lie across the field in tranquil bars of gold. I sat with the women – a few girl friends and young wives, who would scream and bounce up and down on the bleachers. I never could scream. I was mystified by baseball as by the Baptist church, but it did not make me uncomfortable. I liked to think of this male ritual as the prelude to ours.

I still studied, other evenings. I learned things, I had not forgotten how. But I would fall into daydreams lasting half an hour. I still met Jerry at Haines' Restaurant.

'What are you going out with that Neanderthal for?'

'What do you mean Neanderthal? He's Cro-Magnon,' I said, in cheerful shameful treachery.

But Jerry did not have many thoughts to spare for me. Decisions about his future were heavy on him. 'If I go to McGill –' he said. 'On the other hand, if I go to Toronto –' The scholarships he was likely to win had to be taken into account, and he had to look ahead too; which university would give him the best chance of getting into a top American graduate school? I took an interest. I looked at the calendars, compared the alternatives with him, turning over in my mind the melting details of my last meeting with Garnet.

'You're still going to university, aren't you?'

'Why wouldn't I be?'

'You better be careful, in that case. I'm not being sarcastic. I'm not *jealous*. I'm thinking of your own good.'

My mother thought of it too. 'I know who the Frenches are. Out beyond Jericho Valley. That's the poorest Godforsaken backwoods you ever hope to see.' I didn't tell her about Baptist Young People's but she found out. 'I can't understand it,' she said. 'I think you must have softening of the brain.'

I said roughly, 'Can't I go where I like?'

'You've gone addled over a *boy*. You with your intelligence.

Do you intend to live in Jubilee all your life? Do you want to be the wife of a lumberyard worker? Do you want to join the Baptist Ladies Aid?'

'No!'

'Well I'm only trying to open your eyes. For your own good.'

When Garnet came to our house she treated him with courtesy, asked him questions about the lumber business. He called her *Ma'am*, just as Jerry and I would do in our parodies of country people. 'Well I don't really know so much about that end of it, Ma'am,' he would say, polite and self-possessed. Any attempt at this kind of general conversation, any attempt to make him think in this way, to theorize, make systems, brought a blank, very slightly offended, and superior look into his face. He hated people using big words, talking about things outside of their own lives. He hated people trying to tie things together. Since these had been great pastimes of mine, why did he not hate me? Perhaps I successfully hid from him what I was like. More likely, he rearranged me, took just what he needed, to suit himself. I did that with him. I loved the dark side, the strange side, of him, which I did not know, not the regenerate Baptist; or rather, I saw the Baptist, of which he was proud, as a mask he was playing with that he could easily discard. I tried to get him to tell me about the fight outside the Porterfield beer parlor, about being in jail. I would pay attention to the life of his instincts, never to his ideas.

I tried to make him tell me why he had come over to me that night at the revival meeting.

'I liked your looks.'

That was all the declaration I was going to get.

Nothing that could be said by us would bring us together; words were our enemies. What we knew about each other was only going to be confused by them. This was the knowledge that is spoken of as 'only sex,' or 'physical attraction.' I was surprised, when I thought about it – am surprised still – at the light, even disparaging tone that is taken, as if this was something that could be found easily, every day.

He took me out to see his family. It was a Sunday afternoon. The examinations began on Monday. I said I had meant to study, and he said, 'You can't do that. Momma has already killed two chickens.'

The person who could study was in fact already lost, locked away. I could not have made sense of any book, put one word after another, with Garnet in the room. It was all I could do to read the words on a billboard, when we were driving. It was the very opposite of going out with Jerry, and seeing the world dense and complicated but appallingly unsecretive; the world I saw with Garnet was something not far from what I thought animals must see, the world without names.

I had driven the road to Jericho Valley before, with my mother. In some places it was just wide enough for the truck. Wild roses brushed the cab. We drove for miles through thick bush. There was a field full of stumps. I remembered that, remembered my mother saying, 'One time it was all like that, all this country. They haven't progressed here much beyond the pioneer stage. Maybe they're too lazy. Or the land isn't worth it. Or a combination of both.'

Skeletons of a burned-out house and barn.

'You like our house?' Garnet said.

His real house was down in a hollow, with big trees around so close you could not get a look at it as a whole house; what you could see were the brown-shingled, faded gables and the veranda, which had been painted yellow so long ago the paint was just streaks now on the splintered wood. As we drove into the yard, and swung around, there was a great fluttery eruption of chickens, and two big dogs came yapping, leaping up at the open windows of the truck.

Two girls, about nine and ten years old, were jumping up and down on a set of bedsprings that had been sitting in the yard long enough to whiten the grass. They stopped and stared. Garnet led me past and did not introduce me to them. He did not introduce me to anybody. Members of his family would appear – I was not sure which were members of his immediate family and which were uncles, aunts, cousins – and would start talking to him, looking sideways at me. I found out their names sometimes by listening to them talk to each other, and they never called me by name at all.

There was a girl I thought I had seen at the high school. She was barefoot and brilliantly made-up and swinging moodily around one of the veranda posts. 'Look at Thelma!' Garnet said. 'When Thelma puts on lipstick, she uses up a whole tube. Any guy that kissed her, he'd get stuck. He wouldn't ever be able to haul himself away.' Thelma filled her rouged and powdered cheeks with air, let it out with a crude sound.

Out came a short, round, angry-looking woman wearing

running shoes without laces. Her ankles were swollen so that her legs looked perfectly round, like drainpipes. She was the first person to speak to me directly. 'You're the daughter of the encyclopedia lady. I know your momma. Can't you find any place to sit down?' She pushed a little boy and a cat out of a rocker and stood by it till I had seated myself. She herself sat down on the top step, and began yelling instructions and reproofs at everybody.

'Shut them chickens up in the back! Get me some lettuce and green onions and radishes out of the garden! Lila! Phyllis! Quit that jumping up and down! Can't you think of anything better to do? Boyd, get out of that truck! Get him out of that truck! He put it in gear the other day and it rolled across the yard and missed this veranda by inches.'

She took a package of tobacco and some cigarette papers out of her apron pockets.

'I'm not a Baptist lady, I enjoy a cigarette now and then. Are you a Baptist?'

'No. I go with Garnet.'

'Garnet got going to it after his trouble – you know about Garnet's trouble?'

'Yes.'

'Well he got into it after his trouble and I never said it's not a good thing for him, but has some strict ideas. We all used to be – we *are* – United, but it's quite a distance to drive and I'm at work sometimes, Sunday's not any different day in a hospital.' She told me she worked in the Porterfield Hospital, as a nurses' aide. 'Me and Garnet, we mainstay the family,' she said. 'Farms like this is no place to make a living.' She told me about accidents, a poisoned child who had been brought into the hospital recently turned as black as shoe polish, a man with a crushed hand, a boy who got a fishhook in his eye. She told me about an arm that was hanging from the elbow by a strip of skin. Garnet had disappeared. In the corner of the veranda sat a man in overalls, vast and yellow as a Buddha, but with no such peaceful expression. He kept raising his eyebrows and showing his teeth in an immediately fading grin. At first I thought this was a sardonic commentary on the stories about the hospital; later I realized it was a facial tic.

The girls had stopped jumping on the bedsprings and come to hang around their mother, supplying her with details she might miss. The boys fell into a fight in the yard, rolling over and over on the hard dirt, savage, silent, their bare backs as brown and smooth as bark is, on the inside. 'I'll go and get a kettle of boiling water!' the mother warned. 'I'll scald the hide off you!' One of the girls said, 'Would she like to see the creek?'

She meant me. They took me down to the creek, a trickle of brown water among the flat white stones. They showed me where it came to in the spring. One year it had flooded the house. They took me to the haymow to look at a family of kittens, orange and black, that did not have their eyes open yet. They took me through the empty stable and showed me how the barn was propped up with makeshift beams and poles. 'If we ever get a big windstorm this barn is going to fall down.'

They skipped through the stable making up a song: *This old barn is falling down, falling down –*

They showed me through the house. The rooms were large, high ceilinged, sparsely and strangely furnished. There was a brass bed in what seemed to be the living room, and piles of clothes and quilts in the corners, on the floor, as if the family had just moved in. Many windows were uncurtained. Sunlight came into the high rooms through the barely moving trees, so the walls were covered with leafy floating shadows. They showed me the marks the floodwater had left on the walls, and some pictures from magazines they had cut out and tacked up. These were of movie stars, and ladies in lovely ethereal dresses advertising sanitary napkins.

In the kitchen the mother was washing vegetables. 'How'd you like to live here, eh? It looks pretty plain to anybody from town, but we always get enough to eat. The air's lovely, in summer anyway, lovely and cool down by the creek. Cool in the summer, protected in the winter. It's the best situated house I know of.'

All the linoleum was black and bumpy, just islands of the old pattern left, under the table, by the windows where it didn't get so much wear. I smelled that gray smell of stewing chicken.

Garnet opened the screen door, stood dark against the glare of the back yard. He had a pair of work pants on, no shirt.

'I've got something to show you.'

We went out on the back porch, his sisters too, and he made me look up. Carved on the underside of one of the roof beams of the porch was a list of girls' names, each one with an X after it. 'Garnet's girl friends!' one of the sisters cried, and they giggled rapturously, but Garnet read out in a serious voice, 'Doris McIver! Her father owned a sawmill, up past Blue River. Still does. If I had've married her, I would've been rich!'

'If that's any way to get rich!' said his mother, who had followed as far as the screen door.

'Eulie Fatherstone. She was a Roman Catholic, worked in the coffeeshop of the Brunswick Hotel.'

'Married her you would have been poor,' said his mother significantly. 'You know what the Pope tells them to do!'

'You did okay without the Pope yourself, Momma – Margaret Fraleigh. Red hair.'

'You can't trust their kind of a temper.'

'She didn't have no more of a temper than a baby chick. Thora Willoughby. Sold the tickets at the Lyceum Theatre. She's in Brantford now.'

'What is the X for, son? That when you stopped going out with them?'

'No, ma'am, it's not.'

'Well what is it *for*?'

'Military secret!' Garnet jumped up on the porch railing – his mother warning, 'That'll never take your weight!' – and began carving something at the bottom of this list. It was my name. When he finished the name he did a border of stars around it and drew a line underneath. 'I think I've come to the end,' he said.

He snapped his knife shut, jumped down. 'Kiss her!' the sisters said, giggling wildly, and he put his arms around me. 'He's kissing her on the mouth, look at Garnet, kissing her on the mouth!' They crowded up close and Garnet batted them away with one hand, still kissing. Then he began tickling me, and we had a tremendous tickling fight in which the sisters took my side, and we tried to pin Garnet down on the porch floor, but he got away, finally, and raced towards the barn. I went inside and proudly asked his mother what I could do to help get supper. 'You'll spoil your dress,' she said, but gave in and let me slice radishes.

For supper we had stewed chicken, not too tough, and good gravy to soften it, light dumplings, potatoes ('Too bad it's not time for the new!'), flat, round, floury biscuits, home-canned beans and tomatoes, several kinds of pickles, and bowls of green onions and radishes and leaf lettuce, in vinegar, a heavy molasses-flavored cake, blackberry preserves. There were twelve people around the table; Phyllis counted. Along one side everybody sat on planks laid over two sawhorses, to make a bench. I sat on a varnished chair brought from the front room. The big yellow man was brought from the veranda and sat at the head of the table; he was the father. From the barn, with Garnet, came an older but sprier man who talked about how he hadn't slept all the previous night, with toothache. 'You better not try any chicken,' Garnet told him, mock solicitously. 'We better just give you some warmed-up milk and roll you off to bed!' The old man ate heartily, describing how he had tried warm oil of cloves. 'And something stronger than that, I'll bet you my wedding ring!' Garnet's mother said. I sat between Lila and Phyllis, who were working up a play fight, refusing to pass each other things, hiding the butter under a saucer. Garnet and the old man told a story about a Dutch farmer on the next concession who had shot a raccoon, believing it to be a dangerous forest animal. We drank tea. Phyllis quietly took the top off the saltcellar and poured salt into the sugar bowl and passed it to the old man. Her mother grabbed it just in time. 'I'll skin you alive someday!' she promised.

There is no denying I was happy in that house.

I thought of saying to Garnet, on the way home, 'I like your family,' but I realized how strange it would sound to him, because he had never thought of my not liking them, becoming part of them. To pass judgments of this sort would seem self-conscious, pretentious, with him.

The truck broke down just after we turned off the main street, in Jubilee. Garnet got out and looked under the hood and said he thought so, it was the transmission. I said he could sleep in our front room, but I could tell he did not want to, because of my mother; he said he would go and stay with a friend of his who worked at the lumberyard.

Since our arrival at my house had not been signaled by the noise of the truck we were able to go around to the side and crush up against the wall, kissing and loving. I had always thought that our eventual union would have some sort of special pause before it, a ceremonial beginning, like a curtain going up on the last act of a play. But there was nothing of the kind. By the time I realized he was really going ahead with it I wanted to lie down on the ground, I wanted to get rid of my panties which were wound around my feet, I wanted to take off the belt of my dress because he was pressing the buckle painfully into my stomach. However there was no time. I pushed my legs as far apart as I could with those pants tangling my feet and heaved myself up against the house wall trying to keep my balance. Unlike our previous intimacies, this required effort and attention. It also hurt me, though his fingers had stretched me before this time. With everything else, I had to hold his pants up, afraid that the white gleam of his buttocks might give us away, to anybody passing on the street. I developed

an unbearable pain in the arches of my feet. Just when
I thought I would have to ask him to stop, wait, at least
till I put my heels to the ground for a second, he groaned
and pushed violently and collapsed against me, his heart
pounding. I was not balanced to receive his weight and we
both crashed down, coming unstuck somehow, into the
peony border. I put my hand to my wet leg and it came
away dark. Blood. When I saw the blood the glory of the
whole episode became clear to me.

In the morning I went around to look at the broken
peonies, and a little patch of blood, yes, dried blood on
the ground. I had to mention it to somebody. I said to my
mother, 'There's blood on the ground at the side of the
house.'

'Blood?'

'I saw a cat there yesterday tearing a bird apart. It was a
big striped tom, I don't know where it came from.'

'Vicious beasts.'

'You should come and look at it.'

'What? I've got better things to do.'

That day we began to write the examinations. Jerry and
I were writing and Murray Heal and George Klein, who
were going to be a dentist and an engineer, respectively,
and June Gannett whose father was making her get her
Senior Matric before he would let her marry a hollow-
chested, dissipated-looking boy who worked in the Bank
of Commerce. There were also two girls from the country,
Beatrice and Marie, who planned to go to Normal School.

The principal broke the seal before our eyes, and we
signed an oath that it had never been broken before. We

were alone in the high school, all the lower grades dismissed for the summer. Our voices, our footsteps, sounded huge in the halls. The building was hot, and smelled of paint. The janitors had taken all the desks out of one classroom and stacked them in the corridor; they were varnishing the floor.

I felt far away from all this. The first examination was on English literature. I began to write about 'L'Allegro' and 'Il Penseroso.' I could understand perfectly well what the question meant, and yet somehow I could not credit that it really meant that, it seemed nonsensical, oblique, baleful as some sentence in a dream. I wrote slowly. Every once in a while I would stop, screw up my forehead, flex my fingers, trying to get a sense of urgency, but it was no use, I could not go any faster. I did get to the end, but I had no time, or energy, or even desire, to check my paper over. I suspected that I had left out part of one question; I deliberately did not look at the question paper to see if that was true.

I had a radiant sense of importance, physical grandeur. I moved languidly, exaggerating a slight discomfort. I remembered now, over and over again, Garnet's face, both in extreme effort and in the instant of triumph, before we crashed. That I could be the occasion to anyone of such pain and release made me marvel at myself.

Beatrice, one of the girls from the country, had brought her family's car, because the school buses were no longer running. She asked me to have a Coke with her at the drive-in that had been opened – in a refitted, repainted blacksmith shop – at the south end of town. She asked me because she wanted to find out what my answers had been. She was a big hard-working girl who wore broadcloth dresses buttoned down the front. Naomi and I used to giggle at her because she came to school in winter with white horsehairs on her coat.

'What did you do for this?' she said, and read out slowly: *Englishmen in the eighteenth century valued formal elegance and social stability. Discuss, with reference to one eighteenth-century poem.*

I was thinking that if I got out of the car and walked to the back of the graveled lot where we were parked, I would be on the street that ran up behind the lumberyard. The men who worked in the lumberyard parked their cars on this street. If I walked over there and stood in the middle of the street I would be able to see the back fence, the entrance, the roof of the long open shed and the top of some piles of lumber. In the town were certain marked, glowing places – the lumberyard, the Baptist Church, the service station where Garnet bought gas, the barbershop where he got his hair cut, the houses of his friends – and strung between these places, the streets where he habitually drove appeared in my mind like bright wires.

Now was the end of all our early sweet gropings, rainy games in the truck. From now on we made love in earnest. We made love on the truck seat with the door open, and under bushes, and in the night grass. Much was changed. At first I was numb, overwhelmed by the importance, the name and thought of what we were doing. Then I had an orgasm. I knew that was what it was called, from Naomi's mother's book, and I knew what it was like, having discovered such seizures by myself, some time ago, with many impatient, indeed ravenous, imaginary lovers. But I was amazed to undergo it in company, so to speak; it did seem almost too private, even lonely a thing, to find at the heart of love. So quickly it came to be what had to be achieved – I could not imagine how we had once stopped short. We had come out on another level – more solid, less miraculous, where cause and effect must be acknowledged, and love begins to flow in a deliberate pattern.

We never spoke a word, to each other, about any of this.

This was the first summer my mother and I had stayed in Jubilee, instead of going out on the Flats Road. My mother said she was not equal to it and anyway they were happy as they were, my father and Owen and Uncle Benny. Sometimes I walked out to see them. They drank beer at the kitchen table and cleaned eggs with steel wool. The fox-farming business was finished, because the price of pelts had fallen so low after the war. The foxes were gone, the pens were pulled down, my father was switching over to poultry. I sat and tried to clean eggs too. Owen had half a bottle of beer. When I asked for some my father said, 'No, your mother wouldn't like it.' Uncle Benny said, 'No good ever come of any girl that drunk beer.'

That was what I had heard Garnet say, the same words.

I would scrub the floor and clean the windows and throw out moldy food and line the cupboards with fresh paper, working with an aggrieved and driven air. Owen grunted at me, to show he was a man, and stretched out his feet in a lordly way and moved them fractionally when I said, 'Move! I want to scrub here. *Move.*' Sometimes I would kick him or he would trip me and we would fall into kicking, pounding fights. Uncle Benny would laugh at us, his old gulping, shamefaced way, but my father would make Owen stop fighting a girl, make him go outside. My father treated me politely, he praised my house cleaning, but he never joked with me as he would with girls who lived on the Flats Road, with the Potter girl, for instance, who had quit school at the end of Grade Eight and gone to work in the glove factory in Porterfield. He approved of me and he was in some way offended by me. Did he think my ambitiousness showed a want of pride?

My father slept on the kitchen couch, not upstairs where he used to sleep. On the shelf above it, by the radio and the ink bottle were three books – H. G. Wells' *Outline of History*, *Robinson Crusoe*, and a collection of pieces by James Thurber. He read the same books over and over again, putting himself to sleep. He never talked about what he read.

I walked back to town in the early evening, when the sun, though still an hour or more away from setting, would throw a long shadow out on the gravel road in front of me. I watched this strange elongated figure with the faraway, small round head (one afternoon, with nothing to do, I had cut off my hair), and it seemed to me the shadow of a stately, unfamiliar African girl. I never looked at the Flats Road houses, I never looked at the cars that met me, raising dust, I saw nothing but my own shadow floating over the gravel.

I came in late at night sore in unexpected places – I always had an ache across the top of my chest, and in my shoulders – and damp and frightened of my own smell, and there would be my mother sitting up in bed, the light shining right through her hair to her tender scalp, her cup of tea gone cold on the table beside the bed, along with the other cups of tea abandoned earlier in the day or the day before – sometimes they sat there till the milk in them soured – and she would read to me out of the university catalogues which she had sent away for.

'Tell you what I would take –' She was not afraid of Garnet any more, he was fading in the clear light of my future. 'I would take astronomy, arid Greek. Greek, I have always had a secret desire to learn Greek.' Astronomy, Greek, Slavonic languages, Philosophy of the Enlightenment – she bounced them at me as I stood in the doorway. Such words would not stay in my head. I had to think, instead, of the dark, not very heavy, hairs on Garnet's forearms, lying so sleekly parallel that it looked to me as if they had been combed, the knobs of his narrow wrists, the calm frown with which he drove the truck, a particular expression, combining urgency and practicality, with which he led me into the bush or along the riverbank, looking for a place to lie down. Sometimes we would not even wait until it was really dark. I did not fear discovery, as I did not fear pregnancy. Everything we did seemed to take place out of range of other people, or ordinary consequences.

I talked to myself about myself, saying *she. She is in love. She has just come in from being with her lover. She has given herself to her lover. Seed runs down her legs.* I often felt in the middle of the day as if I would have to close my eyes and drop where I was and go to sleep.

As soon as the examinations were over Jerry Storey and his mother had left on a car trip through the United States. Irregularly throughout the summer I would get a postcard with a view of Washington, D.C., Richmond, Virginia, the Mississippi River, Yellowstone Park, with a brief message written on the back in cheerful block letters: PROGRESSING ACROSS LAND OF THE FREE BEING GYPPED BY MOTEL OWNERS, GARAGES, ETC. LIVING ON HAMBURGERS AND ROTTEN U.S. BEER, ALWAYS READ DAS KAPITAL IN RESTAURANTS TO ASTONISH NATIVES. NATIVES DON'T RESPOND.

Naomi was going to get married. She phoned me up and told me, and asked me to come over to her house. Mason Street was just the same, except that Miss Farris' house was occupied by a newly-wed couple who had painted it robin's-egg blue.

'Hello, stranger,' said Naomi accusingly, as if the break in our friendship had been all my idea. 'You're going out with Garnet French, aren't you?'

'How did you know?'

'You think you were keeping it secret? Are you a Baptist yet? He's an improvement on Jerry Storey anyway.'

'Who are you getting married to?'

'You wouldn't know him,' said Naomi dejectedly. 'He's from Tupperton. Well, no, he's from Barrie originally but now he works out of Tupperton.'

'What does he do?' I asked, just meaning to be polite, and show an interest, but Naomi scowled.

'Well he's not a great genius or anything. He didn't go to *university*. He works for the Bell Telephone. He's a lineman. His name is Scott Geoghagen.'

'Scott what?'

'Geoghagen.' She spelled it. 'I'd better just get used to it, it's going to be my name. Naomi Geoghagen. Four months ago that was a name I never even heard. I was going out with an altogether different guy when I met him. Stuart

Claymore. He has got a new Plymouth, now that I quit going out with him. Come on up and I'll show you my stuff.'

We went up the stairs, past her father's door.

'How is he?'

'Who, him? There's so many holes in his head the birds are laying their eggs in it.'

Her mother appeared at the top of the back stairs and accompanied us into Naomi's room.

'We decided we'd just have a quiet wedding,' she said. 'What is a great big wedding anyway? It's just for the show.'

'You have to be my bridesmaid,' said Naomi. 'After all you are my oldest friend.'

'When is it going to be?'

'A week from this coming Saturday,' her mother said. 'We're going to have it in the garden under a trellis if the weather holds out. We're getting a loan of the United Church chairs and the W.A. is going to cater, not that we'll need much. You'll have to get a dress, dear. Naomi's is powder blue. Show her your dress, Naomi. Coral color would be a nice choice for you.'

Naomi showed me her dress and her going-away outfit and her underwear and her bridal nightgown. She cheered up some, doing this. Then she opened her hope chest and another chest and several drawers and took boxes out of the closet and showed me all those things she had acquired for furnishing and maintaining a home. I was thinking unhappily that being the bridesmaid I would have to give a shower for her, and decorate a chair with streamers of pink crepe paper and cut the crusts off sandwiches and make radish roses and carrot curls. She had bought plain pillowcases and embroidered every one of them, with garlands of flowers and baskets of fruit and little poke-bonneted girls with watering cans. 'Bella Phippen will be giving you a pincushion,' I said, with a feeling of sadness for our old days in the library after school.

Naomi was pleased at the idea. 'I hope it's green or yellow or orange, because those are the colors I'm using for my decorating scheme.' She showed me doilies she had crocheted in those colors. Some she had stiffened with a solution of sugar and water, so they would stand up around the edges, like baskets.

Her mother had gone downstairs. Naomi folded every-thing and closed the drawers and boxes and said to me, 'Well, what have you heard about me?'

'What?'

'I know. There are a lot of people in this town have got damn big mouths.'

She sat down heavily on her bed, her bum making a big hollow. I remembered that mattress, how when I stayed all night we would always roll into the middle and wake up kicking and butting each other.

'I'm pregnant you know. Don't look at me with that stupid look. Everybody does it. Its just everybody isn't unlucky enough to get pregnant. Everybody *does* it. It's getting to be just like saying hello.' With her feet on the floor she lay back on the bed, put her hands behind her head and squinted at the light. 'That lamp is full of bugs.'

'I know. I've done it too,' I said.

She sat up. '*You* have? Who with? *Jerry Storey.* He wouldn't know how. Garnet?'

'Yes.'

She flopped back. 'Well, how did you like it?' She sounded suspicious.

'Fine.'

'It gets better as it goes along. The first time it hurt me so bad. That wasn't Scott, either. He had a thing on, you know. *Hurt!* We should have had some Vaseline. Where are you going to get Vaseline, out in the bush in the middle of the night? Where did it happen to you the first time?'

I told her about the peonies, the blood on the ground, the cat killing a bird. We lay on our stomachs across the bed and told everything, scandalous details. I even told Naomi, all this time later, about Mr Chamberlain, and how that was the first one I had ever seen, and what he did with it. I was rewarded with her pounding the bed with her fist, laughing and saying, 'Jesus, I never yet saw anybody do that!' After some time, though, she grew gloomy again, and raised herself on the bed to look down at her stomach.

'You're lucky yet. You better start using something. You better be careful. Nothing is sure, anyway. Those rotten old safes split sometimes. When I first knew I was pregnant I took quinine. I took slippery elm and damn laxative and jujubes and I sat in a mustard bath till I thought I was going to turn into a hot dog. Nothing works.'

'Didn't you ask your mother?'

'That was her idea, the mustard bath. She doesn't know as much as she lets on.'

'You don't have to get married. You could go to Toronto –'

'Sure, stick me in a Salvation Army home. Praise Jesus!' she quavered, and added somewhat inconsistently in view of the mustard and quinine, 'Anyway I wouldn't think it was right to give my baby up to strangers.'

'All right, but if you don't want to get married –'

'Oh, who says I don't want to? I've collected all this stuff, I might as well get married. You always get depressed when you're first pregnant, it's hormones. I've got the most God-awful constipation as well.'

She walked me out to the sidewalk. She stood there looking up and down the streets, hands on her hips, stomach pushing out of her old plaid skirt. I could see her married, a bossy, harassed, satisfied young mother out looking for her children, to call them in to bed or braid their hair or otherwise interfere with them. 'Good-bye nonvirgin,' she said affectionately.

When I was halfway up the block, under the street light, she yelled, 'Hey, Del!' and came running clumsily after me, panting and laughing, and when she got close she put her hands up on either side of her mouth and said in a shouting whisper, 'Don't trust withdrawal either!'

'I won't!'

'The bastards never get it out in time!'

Then we each walked in our own directions, turning around and waving two or three times, with mocking exaggeration, as we used to.

Garnet and I went to Third Bridge to swim, after supper. We made love first, in the long grass, after scouting around for a while to find a place free of thistles, then walked awkwardly holding on to each other down a path meant for one person, stopping and kissing along the way. The quality of kisses changed a good deal, from before to after;

at least Garnet's did, going from passionate to consolatory, pleading to indulgent. How quickly he came back, after crying out the way he did, and turning his eyes up and throbbing all over and sinking into me like a shot gull! Sometimes when he had barely got his breath back I would ask him what he was thinking and he would say, 'I was just figuring out how I could fix that muffler –' But this time he said, 'About when would we get married.'

Naomi was married now, living in Tupperton. We were past the peak of summer. Mountain-ash berries were out. The river had gone down, after weeks with little rain, revealing lush peninsulas of waterweeds that looked as if they would be solid enough to walk on.

We walked into the water, sinking in mud until we reached the pebbly, sandy bottom. The results of the examinations had become known that week. I had passed. I had not won my scholarship. I had not received a single first-class mark.

'Would you like to have a baby?'

'Yes,' I said. The water which was almost as warm as the air touched my sore prickled buttocks. I was weak from making love, I felt myself warm and lazy, like a big cabbage spreading, as my back my arms my chest went down into the water, like big cabbage leaves loosening and spreading on the ground.

Where would such a lie come from? It was not a lie.

'You have to join the church first,' he said shyly. 'You have to get baptized.'

I fell on the water, arms spread. Bluebottles made their quivering, directly horizontal flights on a level with my eyes.

'You know how they do it in our church? Baptizing?'

'How?'

'Dunk you right under the water. They got a tank behind the pulpit, covered up. That's where they do it. But it's better to do it in a river, several at one time.'

He threw himself into the water and swam after me, trying to catch hold of one foot.

'When are you going to get it done? Could be this month.'

I turned on my back and floated, kicking water in his face.

'You have to get saved sometime.'

The river was still as a pond; you couldn't tell to look at it which way the current was going. It held the reflection of the opposite banks, Fairmile Township, dark with pine and spruce and cedar bush.

'Why do I have to?'

'You know why.'

'Why?'

He caught up to me and grabbed me by the shoulders, pushed me gently up and down in the water. 'I ought to baptize you now and get the job over with. I ought to baptize you now.'

I laughed.

'I don't want to be baptized. It's no good if I don't want to be baptized.' Though it would have been so easy, just a joke, to give in, I was not able to do it. He kept saying, 'Baptize you!' and bobbing me up and down, with less and less gentleness, and I kept refusing, laughing, shaking my head at him. Gradually, with the struggle, laughing stopped, and the wide, determined, painful grins on our faces hardened.

'You think you're too good for it,' he said softly.

'I don't!'

'You think you're too good for anything. Any of *us*.'

'I don't!'

'Well get baptized then!' He pushed me right under the water, taking me by surprise. I came up spluttering and blowing my nose.

'Next time you won't get out so easy! I'm going to keep you down till you say you'll do it! Say you'll get baptized or I'll baptize you anyway –'

He pushed me down again but this time I was expecting it. I held my breath and fought him. I fought strongly and naturally, as anybody does, held down in the water, and without thinking much about who was holding me. But when he let me come up just long enough to hear him say, 'Now say you'll do it,' I saw his face streaming with water I had splashed over him and I felt amazement, not that I was fighting with Garnet but that anybody could have made such a mistake, to think he had real power over me. I was too amazed to be angry, I forgot to be frightened, it seemed to me impossible that he should not understand that all the powers I granted him were in play, that he himself was – in play, that I meant to keep him sewed up in his golden lover's skin forever, even if five minutes before I had talked about marrying him. This was clear as day to me, and I opened my mouth to say whatever would make it clear to him, and I saw that he knew it all already; this was what he knew, that I had somehow met his good offerings with my deceitful offerings, whether I knew it or not, matching my complexity and play-acting to his true intent.

You think you're too good for it.

'Say you'll do it then!' His dark amiable but secretive face broken by rage, a helpless sense of insult. I was ashamed of this insult but had to cling to it, because it was only my differences, my reservations, my life. I thought of him kicking and kicking that man in front of the Porterfield beer parlor. I had thought I wanted to know about him but I hadn't really, I had never really wanted his secrets or his violence or himself taken out of the context of that peculiar and magical and, it seemed now, possibly fatal game.

Suppose in a dream you jumped willingly into a hole and laughed while people threw soft tickling grass on you, then understood when your mouth and eyes were covered up that it was no game at all, or if it was, it was a game that required you to be buried alive. I fought underwater exactly as you would fight in such a dream, with a feeling of desperation that was not quite immediate, that had to work upward through layers of incredulity. Yet I thought that he might drown me. I really thought that. I thought that I was fighting for my life.

When he let me come up again he tried the conventional baptizing position, bending me backwards from the waist, and this was a mistake. I was able to kick him low in the belly – not in the genitals though I would not have cared, I did not know or care where I kicked – and these kicks were strong enough to make him lose his hold and stagger a bit and I got away. As soon as there was a yard of water between us the absurdity and horror of our fight became plain and it could not be resumed. He did not come towards me. I walked slowly safely out of the water which at this time of year was not much more than armpit-deep, anywhere. I was shaking, gasping, drinking air.

I dressed at once in the shelter of the truck, with difficulty making my legs go through the legs of my shorts, trying to hold my breath to steady myself, so I could do up the buttons of my blouse.

Garnet called me.

'I'll give you a ride home.'

'I want to walk.'

'I'll come and pick you up Monday night.'

I didn't answer. I guessed this was said for courtesy. He would not come. If we had been older we would certainly have hung on, haggled over the price of reconciliation, explained and justified and perhaps forgiven, and carried this into the future with us, but as it was we were close enough to childhood to believe in the absolute seriousness and finality of some fights, unforgivability of some blows. We had seen in each other what we could not bear, and we had no idea that people do see that, and go on, and hate and fight and try to kill each other, various ways, then love some more.

I started walking along the track that led to the road and after awhile walking calmed me down and strengthened me; my legs were not so terribly weak. I walked down the Third Concession, which came out at the Cemetery Road. I had about three and a half miles to walk altogether.

I cut through the cemetery. It was getting dark. August was as far away from midsummer as April, a fact always hard to remember. I saw a boy and girl – I could not make out who they were – lying on the clipped grass over by the Mundy mausoleum, on whose dark cement walls Naomi and I had once written an epitaph that we had made up, and thought wicked and hilarious, and that I could no longer fully remember:

> Here lies the bodies of lots of Mundys
> Who died from peeing in their soup on
>   Sundays –

I looked at these lovers lying on the graveyard grass without envy or curiosity. As I walked on into Jubilee I repossessed the world. Trees, houses, fences, streets, came back to me, in their own sober and familiar shapes. Unconnected to the life of love, uncolored by love, the world resumes its own, its natural and callous importance. This is first a blow, then an odd consolation. And already I felt my old self – my old devious, ironic, isolated self – beginning to breathe again and stretch and settle, though all around it my body clung cracked and bewildered, in the stupid pain of loss.

My mother was already in bed. When I had failed to win the scholarship, something she had never questioned – her hopes of the future, through her children – had collapsed. She was faced with the possibility that Owen and I would do nothing and become nothing after all, that we were mediocre, or infected with the dreaded, proud, scared perversity of my father's family. There was Owen, living out on the Flats Road, saying 'turrible' and 'drownded' and using Uncle Benny's grammar, saying he wanted to quit school. There was I going out with Garnet French and refusing to talk about it, and not getting the scholarship.

'You will have to do what you want,' she said bitterly.

But was that so easy to know? I went out to the kitchen, turned on the light, and made myself a big mixture of fried potatoes and onions and tomatoes and eggs, which I ate greedily and somberly out of the pan, standing up. I was free and I was not free. I was relieved and I was desolate. Suppose, then, I had never wakened up? Suppose I had let myself lie down and be baptized in the Wawanash River?

I entertained this possibility off and on, as if it still existed – along with the leafy shade and waterstains in his house, and the bounty of my lover's body – for many years.

He did not come on Monday. I waited to see if he would. I combed my hair and waited, classically, behind the curtains in our front room. I did not know what I would do if he came; the ache of wanting to see his truck, his face, swallowed up everything else. I thought of walking past the Baptist Church, to see if the truck was there. If I had done that, if it had been there, I might have walked on inside, rigid as a sleepwalker. I did get as far as our veranda. I was crying, I noticed, whimpering in a monotonous rhythm the way children do to celebrate a hurt. I turned around, went back into the hall to look in the dim mirror at my twisted wet face. Without diminishment of pain I observed myself; I was amazed to think that the person suffering was me, for it was not me at all; I was watching. I was watching, I was suffering. I said into the mirror a line from Tennyson, from my mother's *Complete Tennyson* that was a present from her old teacher, Miss Rush. I said it with absolute sincerity, absolute irony. *He cometh not, she said.*

From 'Mariana,' one of the silliest poems I had ever read. It made my tears flow harder. Watching myself still, I went back to the kitchen and made a cup of coffee and brought it into the dining room where the city paper was still lying on the table. My mother had torn the crossword out and taken it up to bed. I opened it up at the want ads, and got a pencil, so I could circle any job that seemed possible. I made myself understand what I was reading, and after some time I felt a mild, sensible gratitude for these printed words, these strange possibilities. Cities existed; telephone operators were wanted; the future could be furnished without love or scholarships. Now at last without fantasies or self-deception, cut off from the mistakes and confusion of the past, grave and simple, carrying a small suitcase, getting on a bus, like girls in movies leaving home, convents, lovers, I supposed I would get started on my real life.

Garnet French, Garnet French, Garnet French.
Real Life.

EPILOGUE: THE PHOTOGRAPHER

'This town is rife with suicides,' was one of the things my mother would say, and for a long time I carried this mysterious, dogmatic statement around with me, believing it to be true – that is, believing that Jubilee had many more suicides than other places, just as Porterfield had fights and drunks, that its suicides distinguished the town like the cupola on the Town Hall. Later on my attitude towards everything my mother said became one of skepticism and disdain, and I argued that there were, in fact, very few suicides in Jubilee, that certainly their number could not exceed the statistical average, and I would challenge my mother to name them. She would go methodically along the various streets of the town in her mind, saying, '– hanged himself, while his wife and family were at church – went out of the room after breakfast and shot himself in the head –' but there were not really so many; I was probably closer to the truth than she was.

There were two suicides by drowning, if you counted Miss Farris my old teacher. The other one was Marion Sherriff, on whose family my mother, and others, would linger with a touch of pride, saying, 'Well, there is a family that has had its share of Tragedy!' One brother had died an alcoholic, one was in the asylum at Tupperton, and Marion had walked into the Wawanash River. People always said she *walked into* it, though in the case of Miss Farris they said she *threw herself into* it. Since nobody had seen either of them do it, the difference must have come from the difference in the women themselves, Miss Farris being impulsive and dramatic in all she did, and Marion Sherriff deliberate and take-your-time.

At least that was how she looked in her picture, which was hanging in the main hall of the high school, above the case containing the Marion A. Sherriff Girls Athletic Trophy, a silver cup taken out each year and presented to the best girl athlete in the school, then put back in, after having that girl's name engraved on it. In the picture Marion Sherriff was holding a tennis racket and wearing a white pleated skirt and a white sweater with two dark stripes around the V of the neck. She had her hair parted in the middle, pinned unbecomingly back from the temples; she was stocky and unsmiling.

'Pregnant, naturally,' Fern Dogherty used to say, and Naomi said, everybody said, except my mother.

'That was never established. Why blacken her name?'

'Some fellow got her in trouble and walked out on her,'

said Fern positively. 'Otherwise why drown herself, a girl seventeen?'

A time came when all the books in the library in the Town Hall were not enough for me, I had to have my own. I saw that the only thing to do with my life was to write a novel. I picked on the Sherriff family to write it about; what had happened to them isolated them, splendidly, doomed them to fiction. I changed the family name from Sherriff to Halloway, and the dead father from a storekeeper to a judge. I knew from my reading that in the families of judges, as of great landowners, degeneracy and madness were things to be counted on. The mother I could keep just as she was, just as I used to see her in the days when I went to the Anglican Church, and she was always there, gaunt and superb, with her grand trumpeting supplications. I moved them out of their house, though, transported them from the mustard-colored stucco bungalow behind the *Herald-Advance* building, where they had always lived and where even now Mrs Sherriff kept a tidy lawn and picked-clean flower beds, and into a house of my own invention, a towered brick house with long narrow windows and a *porte cochère* and a great deal of surrounding shrubbery perversely cut to look like roosters, dogs, and foxes.

Nobody knew about this novel. I had no need to tell anybody. I wrote out a few bits of it and put them away, but soon I saw that it was a mistake to try to write anything down; what I wrote down might flaw the beauty and wholeness of the novel in my mind.

I carried it – the idea of it – everywhere with me, as if it were one of those magic boxes a favored character gets

hold of in a fairy story: touch it and his troubles disappear.
I carried it along when Jerry Storey and I walked out on
the railway tracks and he told me that some day, if the
world lasted, newborn babies could be stimulated with
waves of electricity and would be able to compose music
like Beethoven's, or like Verdi's, whatever was wanted. He
explained how people could have their intelligence and
their talents and preferences and desires built into them, in
judicious amounts; why not?

'Like *Brave New World*?' I asked him, and he said, what
was that?

I told him, and he answered chastely, 'I don't know, I
never read fiction.'

I just kept hold of the idea of the novel, and felt better;
it seemed to make what he said unimportant even if true.
He began to sing sentimental songs with a German accent
and tried goose-stepping along the rails, falling off as I
knew he would.

'Be-*lieff* me if all those en-dearing jung tcharms –'

In my novel I had got rid of the older brother, the
alcoholic; three tragic destinies were too much even for a
book, and certainly more than I could handle. The younger
brother I saw as gentle and loving, with an offensive
innocence about him; pink freckled face, defenseless
fattish body. Bullied at school, unable to learn arithmetic
or geography, he would be happy once a year, when he was
allowed to ride round and round on the merry-go-round at
the Kinsmen's Fair, beatifically smiling. (I got this of course
from Frankie Hall, that grown idiot who used to live out
on the Flats Road, and was dead by now; he was always
let ride free, all day long, and would wave at people with a

royal negligence, though he never acknowledged anybody at any other time.) Boys would taunt him about his sister, about – *Caroline!* Her name was Caroline. She came ready-made into my mind, taunting and secretive, blotting out altogether that pudgy Marion, the tennis player. Was she a witch? Was she a nymphomaniac? Nothing so simple!

She was wayward and light as a leaf, and she slipped along the streets of Jubilee as if she was trying to get through a crack in an invisible wall, sideways. She had long black hair. She bestowed her gifts capriciously on men – not on good-looking young men who thought they had a right to her, not on sullen high-school heroes, athletes, with habits of conquest written on their warm-blooded faces, but on middle-aged weary husbands, defeated salesmen passing through town, even, occasionally, on the deformed and mildly deranged. But her generosity mocked them, her *bittersweet flesh, the color of peeled almonds*, burned men down quickly and left a taste of death. She was the sacrifice, spread for sex on moldy uncomfortable tombstones, pushed against the cruel bark of trees, her frail body squashed into the mud and hen dirt of barnyards, supporting the killing weight of men, but it was she, more than they, who survived.

One day a man came to take photographs at the high school. She saw him first shrouded in his photographer's black cloth, a hump of gray-black, shabby cloth behind the tripod, the big eye, the black accordion pleating of the old-fashioned camera. When he came out, what did he look like? Black hair parted in the middle, combed back in two *wings*, dandruff, rather narrow chest and shoulders, and a pasty, flaky skin – and in spite of his look of scruffiness and ill health, a wicked fluid energy about him, a bright unpitying smile.

He had no name in the book. He was always called *The Photographer*. He drove around the country in a high square car whose top was of flapping black cloth. The pictures he took turned out to be unusual, even frightening. People saw that in his pictures they had aged twenty or thirty years. Middle-aged people saw in their own features the terrible, growing, inescapable likeness of their dead parents; young fresh girls and men showed what gaunt or dulled or stupid faces they would have when they were fifty. Brides looked pregnant, children adenoidal. So he was not a popular photographer, though cheap. However no one liked to refuse him business; everybody was afraid of him. Children dropped into the ditches when his car was coming along the road. But Caroline ran after him, she tramped the hot roads looking for him, she waited and waylaid him and offered herself to him without the tender contempt, indifferent readiness she showed to other men, but with straining eagerness and hope and cries. And one day (when she could already feel her womb swollen *like a hard yellow gourd in her belly*), she found the car overturned beside a bridge, overturned in a ditch beside a dry creek. It was empty. He was gone. That night she walked into the Wawanash River.

That was all. Except that after she died her poor brother, looking at the picture The Photographer had taken of his sister's high-school class, saw that in this picture *Caroline's eyes were white.*

I had not worked out all the implications of this myself, but felt they were varied and powerful.

For this novel I had changed Jubilee, too, or picked out some features of it and ignored others. It became an older, darker, more decaying town, full of unpainted board fences covered with tattered posters advertising circuses, fall fairs, elections that had long since come and gone. People in it were very thin, like Caroline, or fat as bubbles. Their speech was subtle and evasive and bizarrely stupid; their platitudes crackled with madness. The season was always the height of summer – white, brutal heat, dogs lying as if dead on the sidewalks, waves of air shuddering, jellylike, over the empty highway. (But how, then – for niggling considerations of fact would pop up, occasionally, to worry me – how then was there going to be enough water in the Wawanash River? Instead of moving, head bowed, moonlight-naked, acquiescent, into its depths, Caroline would have to lie down on her face as if she was drowning herself in the bathtub.)

All pictures. The reasons for things happening I seemed vaguely to know, but could not explain; I expected all that would come clear later. The main thing was that it seemed true to me, not real but true, as if I had discovered, not made up, such people and such a story, as if that town was lying close behind the one I walked through every day.

I did not pay much attention to the real Sherriffs, once I had transformed them for fictional purposes. Bobby Sherriff, the son who had been in the asylum, came home for a while – it seemed this was something that had happened before – and was to be seen walking around Jubilee chatting with people. I had been close enough to him to hear his soft, deferential, leisurely voice, I had observed that he always looked freshly barbered, talcumed, wore clothes of good quality, was short, stout, and walked with that carefree air of enjoyment affected by those who have nothing to do. I hardly connected him with my mad Halloway brother.

Jerry Storey and I coming back from our walks could see Jubilee so plainly, now the leaves were off the trees; it lay before us in a not very complicated pattern of streets named after battles and ladies and monarchs and pioneers. Once as we walked over the trestle a car full of people from our class at school passed underneath, hooting at us, and I did have a vision, as if from outside, of how strange this was – Jerry contemplating and welcoming a future that would annihilate Jubilee and life in it, and I myself planning secretly to turn it into black fable and tie it up in my novel, and the town, the people who really were the town, just hooting car horns – to mock anybody walking, not riding, on a Sunday afternoon – and never knowing what danger they were in from us.

Every morning, starting about the middle of July, the last summer I was in Jubilee, I would walk downtown between nine and ten o'clock. I would walk as far as the *Herald-Advance* building, look in their front window, and walk home. I was waiting for the results of the departmental examinations which I had written in June. The results would come to us in the mail but they always came to the paper a day or so in advance, and were taped up in the front window. If they had not come in the morning mail, they would not come that day. Every morning when I saw that there was no sheet of paper in the window, nothing but the potato shaped like a pigeon that Pork Childs had dug up in his garden, and which sat on the windowsill waiting for the double squash and deformed carrot and enormous pumpkin which would surely join it later, I felt reprieved. I could be at peace for one more day. I knew I had done badly in those exams. I had been sabotaged by love, and it was not likely I would get the scholarship which for years I and everybody else had been counting on, to carry me away from Jubilee.

One morning after I had gone down to the *Herald-Advance* I walked past the Sherriffs' house instead of going back up the main street as I usually did, and Bobby Sherriff surprised me, standing by the gate, saying, 'Good morning.'

'Good morning.'

'Could I persuade you to step into my yard and try a piece of cake? Said the spider to the fly, eh?' His good manners were humble and, I thought, ironic. 'Mother went to Toronto on the six o'clock train so I thought well, I'm up anyway, why don't I try and bake a cake?'

He held the gate open. I did not know how to get out of it. I followed him up the steps.

'It's nice and cool on the porch here. Sit over here. Would you like a glass of lemonade? I'm an expert at making lemonade.'

So I sat on the porch of the Sherriffs' house, rather hoping that nobody would go by and see me, and Bobby Sherriff brought me a piece of cake on a small plate, with a proper cake fork, and an embroidered napkin. He went back inside and brought me a glass of lemonade with ice cubes, mint leaves, and a maraschino cherry. He apologized for not bringing both the cake and the lemonade at once, on a tray; he explained to me where the trays were in the cupboard, under a great pile of plates, so that it was difficult to get one out, and he would rather be sitting here with me, he said, than down on his knees poking around in some dark old cupboard. Then he apologized for the cake, saying he was not a great baker, it was just that he liked to try some recipe once in a while, and he did feel he shouldn't offer me a cake without icing, but he had never mastered the art of making icing, he relied on his mother for that, so here it was. He said he hoped I liked mint leaves in my lemonade – as if most people were very fussy about this, and you never could tell whether they would take it into their heads to throw the mint leaves out. He behaved as if it was a great act of courtesy, of unlooked-for graciousness on my part, to sit here, to eat and drink at all.

There was a strip of carpet on the porch floorboards, which were wide, had cracks between, and were painted gray. It looked like an old hall carpet, too worn for inside. There were two brown wicker chairs, with faded, lumpy cretonne cushions, which we were sitting on, and a round wicker table. On the table was something like a china mug, or vase, with no flowers in it, but a tiny red ensign, and a Union Jack. It was one of those souvenirs that had been sold when the king and queen visited Canada in 1939; there were their youthful, royal faces, shedding kind light, as at the front of the Grade Eight classroom in the public school. Such an object on the table did not mean that the Sherriffs were particularly patriotic. These souvenirs could be found in plenty of houses in Jubilee. That was just it. The ordinariness of everything brought me up short, made me remember. *This was the Sherriffs' house.* I could see a little bit of the hallway, brown and pink wallpaper, through the screen door. That was the doorway through which Marion had walked. Going to school. Going to play tennis. Going to the Wawanash River. Marion was Caroline. She was all I had had, to start with; her act and her secrecy. I had not even thought of that when I first entered the Sherriffs' yard, or while I sat waiting on the porch for Bobby to bring me my cake. I had not thought of my novel. I hardly ever did think of it, any more. I never said to myself that I had lost it, I believed that it was carefully stored away, to be brought out some time in the future. The truth was that some damage had been done to it that I knew could not be put right. Damage had been done; Caroline and the other Halloways and their town had lost authority; I had lost faith. But I did not want to think about that, and did not.

But now I remembered with surprise how I had made it, the whole mysterious and, as it turned out, unreliable structure rising from this house, the Sherriffs, a few poor facts, and everything that was not told.

'I know you,' said Bobby Sherriff shyly. 'Didn't you think I knew who you were? You're the girl who's going to university, on scholarships.'

'I haven't got them yet.'

'You're a clever girl.'

And what happened, I asked myself, to Marion? Not to Caroline. *What happened to Marion?* What happened to Bobby Sherriff when he had to stop baking cakes and go back to the asylum? Such questions persist, in spite of novels. It is a shock, when you have dealt so cunningly, powerfully, with reality, to come back and find it still there. Would Bobby Sherriff give me a clue now, to madness?

Would he say, in his courteous conversational voice, 'Napoleon was my father'? Would he spit through a crack in the floorboards and say, 'I'm sending rain over the Gobi Desert'? Was that the sort of thing they did?

'You know I went to college. The University of Toronto. Trinity College. Yes.

'I didn't win any scholarships,' he went on in a minute, as if I had asked. 'I was an average student. Mother thought they might make a lawyer out of me. It was a sacrifice to send me. The Depression, you know how nobody had any money in the Depression. Now they seem to. Oh, yes. Since the war. They're all buying. Fergus Colby, you know, down at Colby Motors, he was showing me the list he's got, people putting their names down to get the new Oldsmobiles, new Chevrolets.

'When you go to college you must look after your diet. That is very important. Anybody at college tends to eat a lot of starchy food, because it is filling and cheap. I knew a girl who used to cook in her room, she lived on macaroni and bread. Macaroni and bread! I blame my own breakdown on the food I was eating. There was no nourishment for the brain. You have to nourish the brain if you want to use the brain. What's good for that are the B vitamins. Vitamin B_1, vitamin B_2, vitamin B_{12}. You've heard of those, haven't you? You get them in unpolished rice, unrefined flour – am I boring you now?'

'No,' I said guiltily. 'No, no.'

'I must beg your pardon if I do. I get carried away on this subject, I know it. Because I think my own problems – all my own problems since my young days – are related to undernourishment. From studying so hard and not replenishing the brain. Of course I did not have a first-rate brain to begin with, I never claimed that.'

I kept watching him attentively so he would not ask me again if he was boring me. He wore a soft, well-pressed yellow sport shirt, open at the neck. His skin was pink. He did resemble, distantly, Caroline's brother that I had made him into. I could smell his shaving lotion. Odd to think that he shaved, that he had hair on his face like other men, and a penis in his pants. I imagined it curled up on itself, damp and tender. He smiled at me sweetly, reasonably talking; could he read what I was thinking? There must be some secret to madness, some *gift* about it, something I didn't know.

He was telling me how rats, even, refused to eat white flour, because of the bleach, the chemicals that were in it. I nodded, and past his head saw Mr Fouks come out the back door of the *Herald-Advance* building, empty a wastebasket into an incinerator, and plod back in. That back wall had no windows in it; it had certain stains, chipped bricks, a long crack running down diagonally, starting a bit before the middle and ending up at the bottom corner next to the Chainway store.

At ten o'clock the banks would open, the Canadian Bank of Commerce and the Dominion Bank across the street. At twelve-thirty, a bus would go through the town, southbound from Owen Sound to London. If anybody wanted to get on it there would be a flag out in front of Haines' Restaurant.

Bobby Sherriff talked about rats and white flour. His sister's photographed face hung in the hall of the high school, close to the persistent hiss of the drinking fountain.

Her face was stubborn, unrevealing, lowered so that shadows had settled in her eyes. People's lives, in Jubilee as elsewhere, were dull, simple, amazing, and unfathomable – deep caves paved with kitchen linoleum.

It did not occur to me then that one day I would be so greedy for Jubilee. Voracious and misguided as Uncle Craig out at Jenkin's Bend, writing his history, I would want to write things down.

I would try to make lists. A list of all the stores and businesses going up and down the main street and who owned them, a list of family names, names on the tombstones in the cemetery and any inscriptions underneath. A list of the titles of movies that played at the Lyceum Theatre from 1938 to 1950, roughly speaking. Names on the cenotaph (more for the First World War than for the Second). Names of the streets and the pattern they lay in.

The hope of accuracy we bring to such tasks is crazy, heartbreaking.

And no list could hold what I wanted, for what I wanted was every last thing, every layer of speech and thought, stroke of light on bark or walls, every smell, pothole, pain, crack, delusion, held still and held together – radiant, everlasting.

At present I did not look much at this town.

Bobby Sherriff spoke to me wistfully, relieving me of my fork, napkin, and empty plate.

'Believe me,' he said, 'I wish you luck in your life.'

Then he did the only special thing he ever did for me. With those things in his hands, he rose on his toes like a dancer, like a plump ballerina. This action, accompanied by his delicate smile, appeared to be a joke not shared with me so much as displayed for me, and it seemed also to have a concise meaning, a stylized meaning – to be a letter, or a whole word, in an alphabet I did not know.

People's wishes, and their other offerings, were what I took then naturally, a bit distractedly, as if they were never anything more than my due.

'Yes,' I said, instead of thank you.

Also available from Vintage

Alice Munro

The Progress of Love

'Whatever it is that makes some writing come alive in every phrase and sentence, Alice Munro has it... I wouldn't willingly miss one of her stories'
Sunday Times

These dazzling and utterly satisfying stories explore varieties and degrees of love – filial, platonic, sexual, parental and imagined – in the lives of apparently ordinary folk. In fact, Munro's characters pulse with idiosyncratic life. Under the polished surface of these unsentimental dispatches from the small-town and rural front lies a strong undertow of violence and sexuality, repressed until something snaps, with extraordinary force in some of the stories, sadly and strangely in others.

'A writer of great sensitivity and delicacy'
Guardian

VINTAGE BOOKS
London

Alice Munro

Friend of My Youth

'The particular brilliance of Alice Munro is that in range and
depth her short stories are almost novels'
Daily Telegraph

A woman haunted by dreams of her dead mother. An adulterous
couple stepping over the line where the initial excitement ends
and the pain begins. A widow visiting a Scottish village in search
of her husband's past – and instead discovering unsettling truths
about a total stranger. The ten stories in this collection not only
astonish and delight but also convey the unspoken mysteries at
the heart of all human experience.

'Alice Munro's stories in *Friend of My Youth* are wonderful:
intricate, deep, full of absorbing and funny detail'
Independent on Sunday

VINTAGE BOOKS
London

Also available from Vintage

Alice Munro

Something I've Been Meaning to Tell You

'No one else can – or should be allowed to – write like
the great Alice Munro'
Julian Barnes

A remarkable early collection of stories by one of the greatest
fiction writers of our time.

'Read not more than one of her stories a day, and allow
them to work their spell: they are made to last'
Observer

VINTAGE BOOKS
London

www.vintage-books.co.uk